Reviewers Love Melissa Brayden

"Melissa Brayden has become one of the most popular novelists of the genre, writing hit after hit of funny, relatable, and very sexy stories for women who love women."—*Afterellen.com*

Strawberry Summer

"The characters were a joy to read and get to know. Maggie's family is loving, supportive, and charming. They're the family we all wish we had, through good times and bad."—*C-Spot Reviews*

"The tragedy is real, the angst well done without being over the top, and the character development palpable in both the main characters and their friends."—*Lesbian Reading Room*

First Position

"Brayden aptly develops the growing relationship between Ana and Natalie, making the emotional payoff that much sweeter. This ably plotted, moving offering will earn its place deep in readers' hearts."—*Publishers Weekly*

"*First Position* is romance at its finest with an opposites attract theme that kept me engaged the whole way through."—*The Lesbian Review*

How Sweet It Is

"'Sweet' is definitely the keyword for this well-written, character-driven lesbian romance novel. It is ultimately a love letter to small town America, and the lesson to remain open to whatever opportunities and happiness comes into your life."—Bob Lind, *Echo Magazine*

T0098843

"Oh boy! The events were perfectly plausible, but the collection and the threading of all the stories, main and sub plots, were just fantastic. I completely and wholeheartedly recommend this book. So touching, so heartwarming and all-out beautiful."
—*Rainbow Book Reviews*

Heart Block

"The story is enchanting with conflicts and issues to be overcome that will keep the reader turning the pages. The relationship between Sarah and Emory is achingly beautiful and skillfully portrayed. This second offering by Melissa Brayden is a perfect package of love—and life to be lived to the fullest. So grab a beverage and snuggle up with a comfy throw to read this classic story of overcoming obstacles and finding enduring love."—*Lambda Literary Review*

"Although this book doesn't beat you over the head with wit, the interactions are almost always humorous, making both characters really quite loveable. Overall a very enjoyable read."
—*C-Spot Reviews*

Waiting in the Wings

"This was an engaging book with believable characters and story development. It's always a pleasure to read a book set in a world like theater/film that gets it right...a thoroughly enjoyable read."
—*Lez Books*

"This is Brayden's first novel, but we wouldn't notice if she hadn't told us. The book is well put together and more complex than most authors' second or third books. The characters have chemistry; you want them to get together in the end. The book is light, frothy, and fun to read. And the sex is hot without being too explicit—not an easy trick to pull off."—*Liberty Press*

"Sexy, funny, and all-around enjoyable."—*Afterellen.com*

Praise for the Soho Loft Series

"The trilogy was enjoyable and definitely worth a read if you're looking for solid romance or interconnected stories about a group of friends."—*The Lesbrary*

Kiss the Girl

"There are romances and there are romances...Melissa Brayden can be relied on to write consistently very sweet, pure romances and delivers again with her newest book *Kiss the Girl*...There are scenes suffused with the sweetest love, some with great sadness or even anger—a whole gamut of emotions that take readers on a gentle roller coaster with a consistent upbeat tone. And at the heart of this book is a hymn to true friendship and human decency."—*C-Spot Reviews*

"An adorable romance in which two flawed but well-written characters defy the odds and fall into the arms of the other."
—*She Read*

Just Three Words

"A beautiful and downright hilarious tale about two very relatable women looking for love."—*Sharing Is Caring Book Reviews*

Ready or Not

"The third book was the best of the series. Melissa Brayden has some work cut out for her when writing a book after this one."—*Fantastic Book Reviews*

By the Author

Waiting in the Wings

Heart Block

How Sweet It Is

First Position

Strawberry Summer

Soho Loft Romances:

Kiss the Girl

Just Three Words

Ready or Not

Seven Shores:

Eyes Like Those

Visit us at www.boldstrokesbooks.com

EYES LIKE THOSE

by

Melissa Brayden

2017

EYES LIKE THOSE

© 2017 By Melissa Brayden. All Rights Reserved.

ISBN 13: 978-1-63555-012-2

This Trade Paperback Original Is Published By
Bold Strokes Books, Inc.
P.O. Box 249
Valley Falls, NY 12185

First Edition: October 2017

THIS IS A WORK OF FICTION. NAMES, CHARACTERS, PLACES, AND INCIDENTS ARE THE PRODUCT OF THE AUTHOR'S IMAGINATION OR ARE USED FICTITIOUSLY. ANY RESEMBLANCE TO ACTUAL PERSONS, LIVING OR DEAD, BUSINESS ESTABLISHMENTS, EVENTS, OR LOCALES IS ENTIRELY COINCIDENTAL.

THIS BOOK, OR PARTS THEREOF, MAY NOT BE REPRODUCED IN ANY FORM WITHOUT PERMISSION.

CREDITS
Editor: Lynda Sandoval
Production Design: Stacia Seaman
Cover Design by Jeanine Henning

Acknowledgments

When I stumbled upon the idea for Seven Shores, I was excited to get back to the celebration of not just romance, but female friendships. I knew from the beginning that there would be four books in this series, and as I write them, I have a fantastic time learning more about the characters, television, surfing, fashion, and coffee. I hope you, the reader, enjoy this first slice of California life designed as a flirty beach read.

Many thanks, as always, to everyone at Bold Strokes Books, my ever-supportive and fun-loving family, my publishing friends Rachel, Georgia, Carsen, and so many more for inspiration and commiseration. Appreciation goes, as well, to Nikki Little for always letting me bounce ideas off her, for work or life.

My editor, Lynda Sandoval, is a fantastic supplier of patience, humor, and focused advice, and without her I'd walk around in proverbial circles. I count the blessings of our storytelling partnership daily.

Lastly, unending thanks to Alan, who is always there to steady the ship, remind me of the bigger picture, and graciously give up the remote control.

For the Sunseekers

EYES LIKE THOSE

Chapter One

Isabel Chase sang quietly to herself as she climbed the stairs. Angry singing would be the most accurate way to describe it, born from the soul-sucking night she'd just experienced at the hands of the food service industry in America. She clutched tightly to that Bon Jovi anthem, the effects of which were half security blanket, half soothing cocktail. She sang the song quietly to herself as she climbed the final flight to her third-floor walkup. She sang a little louder once she landed outside her door, her outrage over the night's happening bubbling to the surface with each step closer to home. She was pissed off, and though it was close to midnight, angry, aggressive singing helped.

Today had been yet another sucky day among many as she slogged through the dim, dark drudgery of her current existence. Her calves pulled from the climb, coupled with the lengthy night on her feet. At long last she opened the door and stared blankly into her studio apartment. "So, I got fired," she said matter-of-factly, and tossed her bag onto the floor of her cluttered makeshift living room. "Again." She slammed the door, causing pages of her most recent screenplay to flutter and scatter in a beautiful snowstorm of white. Only there was nothing beautiful about tonight. Nothing at all. She blew a strand of dark hair off her face only to have it flutter back and cover her right eye. Well, wasn't that just par for the golf course of defeat?

Isabel's black-and-white cat, Fat Tony, blinked back at her in utter disappointment. Of *course* he was disappointed. They needed that job for food. His disapproval seemed endless lately, and today it had surely hit a new low. Because who loses five jobs over two years? Okay, so she'd quit three of them herself and maybe, possibly, she was projecting the disappointment onto her cat, but it cut deep regardless. Fat Tony's opinion mattered. She didn't have very many people she could count on in her life, but Tony was a constant.

"You don't understand, Tony, or you wouldn't look at me that way." She walked past him into the room, grappling for the right words to properly express her outrage, to articulate the injustice of this particular job dismissal. "That waiter captain guy is an ass who's been gunning for me for six months now, ever since I came on at that restaurant. He's been waiting for any opportunity to take me down, and tonight he found one. I'm pretty sure he's banging the hostess, too, if that matters to you."

Fat Tony blinked.

"So I didn't know the precise seasoning on the special. Is it the end of the free world? The dish is seasoned, right?" She held out a hand to punctuate and then repeated the gesture for extra emphasis. "We know that much. So just order the sixty-five-dollar special and I will happily bring it to you with a smile."

Fat Tony stared back at her evenly.

"You come to a five-star restaurant to have seasonings listed back to you? No. No one does that! Fennel is a stupid seasoning anyway. I think we can all agree. As in, who wakes up in the morning and thinks, tonight I'm going out for something with a little fennel in it? Zero people. That's who."

She was halfway to shouting at Fat Tony and felt bad about that. He, on the other hand, didn't seem to care and jumped in supreme boredom from his spot on the entryway table to underneath the flap of the shabby and threadbare armchair, leaving her to commiserate on her own. "Fine. You'll be back when I pop the can on your dinner. Why? Because you and I need each other, Buster. Just don't expect me to list the ingredients."

Annoyed that she still wore her all-black server's attire, she unbuttoned the shirt as she walked to her portable closet and exchanged it for a comfy off-the-shoulder sweatshirt that felt like a magnificent exhale. Oh, yeah. That was nice. A beer would also alleviate some of the tension, and there was a stout in the fridge with her name on it.

Isabel popped it and sat at her very simple wooden desk, the one she loved with her whole heart. She'd found it at a secondhand store right there in Keene and stored away extra cash until she could bust it free. They'd been inseparable ever since. The small town in New Hampshire where she'd lived most of her life carried very little in the way of excitement, except for the brilliance that came each autumn when the leaves changed and the landscape streaked with bright purples, yellows, oranges, and all hues of red. She loved it when the seasons shifted, dazzling the eye. That didn't mean she wasn't ready to get the hell out of there, first chance she got. Leaves and colors only went so far.

Her eyes fell to the small framed photo of her and her dad when he'd lifted her onto his shoulders following a softball game when she was nine. She'd only played one season and was easily the worst on the team, but he had wanted her to play so badly. She adjusted the frame in its spot and made a mental note to call him the next day. See if he wanted to grab a beer. Make sure he was eating. Check in on any possibility he might go on a date and end his long streak of "lonely but okay with it."

Isabel opened her laptop to her latest project, a short she'd been tweaking for submission to the Vital Reel Film Festival in New Mexico. With any luck, they could start shooting in a couple of months once the budget and logistics were somehow squared away. Just thinking about it made her feel better about the fennel. She'd always found success on the festival circuit and waited for the moment it would turn into more. Any day now, right? Until then, she schlepped from one annoying day job to the next, living for the moment she could return to her laptop and lose herself in another crazy, awesome, or human story. There weren't a million things Isabel was good at in life, but writing was one of them. She just hadn't been able to convince the wider world of that thus far. So she pressed on. It's what she did.

Bzzz. Bzzz.

She flicked a gaze to her vibrating phone across the room.

Bzzz. Bzzz.

She could stare at it until it stopped or make the short journey to answer it. Uh-uh. No thanks. People sucked lately, and sometimes, she just needed a few hours away. Plus, her feet hurt. When the notification ceased, she pulled in a breath and refocused on the project. This one was grittier than her last. She'd already killed two characters. Perhaps a result of her own soul-murdering struggles of late. But really, who knew?

Bzzz. Bzzz.

"This day is not finished with me." She stalked the length of the room and answered the phone without bothering to check the readout. "Isabel Chase, glutton for punishment."

A pause. "Izzy, is that you?"

Celeste. Isabel smiled at the sound of her good friend's voice and sank into the armchair. They'd gone to Boston University together, bonded in a creative writing course, and had never looked back. She and Celeste could go months without speaking only to fall right back into their unique friendship groove whenever they did. Not too many people *got* Isabel. Celeste did.

"Yes!" She tried to backpedal. "Oh, man. Sorry about the asshole greeting. Rough night."

"I think it's about to get better."

Isabel smiled curiously into the phone. "Why? Whatcha got?"

"I'm taking off next week for London. One of their indie networks is gonna shoot my pilot. The one about the bipolar funeral director looking for love."

Isabel shot up from the chair. "Get out. I love that script."

"If you mean get out of the country, then yes. That part is already happening. I'm packing as we speak. It's been a whirlwind."

"You're getting a TV show in England?" Isabel asked slowly. She tapped her lips, attempting to process. "Are you magical or just way better at your job than me?"

"Neither. But there's more."

"You're a very generous infomercial. What else could there possibly be?" Isabel squinted at the wall as she tried to fathom what it must be like to be Celeste. To be successful doing what she'd always wanted to do. To be out there writing for a living wage and not living project to project with a side of waitress. "But you should also know that the awful part of me is nothing but envious right now and wishing you overwhelming failure as soon as your plane lands. It's not pretty in my head and I'm not willing to apologize."

Celeste chuckled. "Yeah, well, you wouldn't be Izzy without the sarcasm-laced death threats every now and then. I've come to expect them."

"I'm not that bad, am I?" Isabel asked.

"No. It's endearing generally. I just wish you believed in yourself as much as I do."

Isabel kicked the end table softly. "Working on it. So, tell me the more." Fat Tony peeked out from beneath the chair and swiped at her feet. She dodged him and the game continued. Unfortunately, he was better at it than she was.

"Now that I'm heading to London," Celeste said, "there's a staff writer job open on *Thicker Than Water*."

Isabel went still, her game with Tony forgotten as his claws latched onto her sock. *Thicker Than Water* was the family drama Celeste wrote for. The *hit* family drama that lived at the top of the ratings. Everyone and their mother watched that show. It warmed hearts and tugged at heartstrings. That's what it was known for. The romances weren't half bad either. Steamy, if predictable. "Oh yeah?"

"It's possible I was able to slide the spec script you wrote over to Taylor Andrews. It's also possible she wants to meet with you Monday morning on my recommendation."

Isabel didn't say anything. She couldn't. There were no words. She'd written that spec script for an episode of *Thicker Than Water* on the off chance Celeste would see a moment to present it without damaging any of her professional relationships on the show. And now it had happened. And it had *worked*. Taylor Andrews was the showrunner on *Water* and executive producer at only thirty-two years of age. She was the It Girl in TV these days, as pretty much anything she touched turned to solid gold in the ratings. She offered the occasional master class online, which Isabel had hoped to be able to afford one day. "So, what you're saying is—"

"That there's a very good chance you're the next staff writer on *Thicker Than Water*, so don't blow it. And make sure you bring a copy of your short, the one that won at South by Southwest. Totally her style. She'll eat it up."

Isabel moved to her desk and began scribbling notes as she listened, little goose bumps popping up on her arms as a powerful bolt of energy hit. She felt the dreaded prickling on the back of her neck and gripped the phone hard, fighting off the irrational fear. Nope. She would not do this now. "Got it. What else? What can I do? Any tips? This is too major to screw up, and sometimes I babble when I'm nervous."

"Well then, don't be nervous. Be yourself, but maybe not…too much."

Isabel laughed as her symptoms receded. "Got it. Keep my snarky opinions under lock and key."

"At least for now." Celeste rattled off the important details of the meeting and let Isabel know that the gate guard at Paramount would have her name. God, she would need a plane ticket. A hotel room. A Valium.

"I owe you big-time, Celeste. I'm serious. I'm not even going to wish bad things for you in England anymore. No poisonous smog.

Chapter Two

The iconic Bronson Gate at Paramount Pictures loomed large in front of Isabel's rental car. She swallowed, but her mouth was dry. This gate, though a replica of the original, was historic. The arch was recognizable in most any social circle, and looking at it now made this whole thing a little more real. And terrifying. Must not forget the dash of that.

She gave her name to Jesse the gate guard (it said so on his name tag). He took her license into his booth to call the *Thicker Than Water* production offices to announce her arrival. Isabel took a moment to ruminate on the people throughout Hollywood history who'd passed through this very entrance. Cecil B. DeMille, Orson Welles, Gloria Swanson, Gene Kelley. Don't even get her started on the Brady Bunch. Jan Brady was more than just an idol. She was a way of life. Imagining herself creating a character that would resonate with someone similarly had Isabel chomping at the bit to get to that meeting and prove herself. If only underneath that passion wasn't an ocean of crippling self-doubt and anxiety. Story of her complicated life.

Isabel wasn't new to the writing game. In fact, she couldn't remember a time when she wasn't crafting stories. As a kid, she'd have her Transformers act them out, doing all the voices for the different characters. Nowadays, she collaborated with her director friends and found nothing as rewarding as seeing her work brought to life with skilled precision, even if on a small budget. She'd received awards, local write-ups, and film festival glory. None of that had amounted to a full-time career. No one had come banging on her door as a result.

But all of it *had* led up to this meeting.

The one that could be the break she needed to put away her server shoes forever. She'd pretty much auction off her soul for the chance. Cheap too. She'd Craigslist the sucker.

"Ma'am, Ms. Andrews's assistant will meet you in Bronson Parking Lot E to your right once you're through the gate. Put this on your windshield."

She accepted the visitor's pass and smiled. "Will do. Thanks." The guard saluted her with a grin, which seemed both excessive and exciting. Seconds later, she was off, her heart thudding away with nervous, pent-up energy. Cue a reprisal of the goose bumps as they trotted back onto the stage of her life.

She drove slowly, nodding to the steady beat of the song on the radio, doing her best to take in as much of the studio's property as she could on the short drive. Who knew when she'd be back? She passed the wrought iron *original* Bronson Gate just inside and wondered how she could get her photo next to it. Next, she zoomed past the Paramount Theatre, where all the fancy screenings and premieres took place on the lot. She'd read all about it.

Golf carts crisscrossed the narrow street, and stressed-out-looking people spoke into headsets as they passed. She'd nearly taken out an entire tour group because she'd been watching the numbers on the large warehouses that served as soundstages, looking for a glimpse of Stage 9. She hadn't been able to spot it. Though she did locate a bookish-looking twentysomething waving from the entrance to a small parking lot. Isabel rolled down her window and stuck her head out.

"Isabel Chase?" the woman asked. She carried a file folder and sported those large, black intellectual glasses that were so popular lately. She should probably look into getting a pair for herself if she had any hope of looking intellectual, or popular, for that matter.

"Right. I'm Isabel. Chase." The woman had already said that part. Fuck. She should work on her listening skills. And her language.

"Great. You can park here. I'll wait." Once she exited the car, she joined the woman who, while friendly, seemed in a hurry. "I'm Scarlett Mann, Taylor's assistant. If you'll follow me, we can head to the writers' room and see if we can snatch her up for your chat."

"Awesome. I'll follow you." Were her palms itching? Yes. She flexed them, hateful hands that they were. Deep breaths. Shoulder rolls. Anything to get her through this day without looking like she didn't know what she was doing. Why was she so horrible at this kind of thing?

Isabel followed Scarlett past several soundstages, dodging

equipment trucks and cables along the way. "Do you watch the show?" Scarlett asked.

Of course she did. Sometimes. The content was tame for a nighttime drama, but the characters were solid and had huge followings. She knew, however, what the correct answer to the question was. "I watch, yes. It's a fantastic show."

Scarlett smiled at her. "Well played."

They entered a small, nondescript one-story building across from Stage 9. It was beige on the outside and the opposite of glamorous. She glanced up at the soundstage across the street briefly as they made their way inside and saw the plaque on the outside that read *Thicker Than Water*. On the other side of those walls was where it all came together. Surreal.

Down a short hallway, and past what looked to be several offices and an open space dotted with cubicles, Scarlett paused in front of a closed door and knocked. They waited in silence, the sounds of overlapping voices floating out until, impatiently, Scarlett finally opened the door herself.

And there it was, the writers' room.

A long wooden table sat in the middle of the space, occupied by three men and two women. A box of donuts sat in the center of the table, close to empty, and the room smelled of strong, and maybe a little stale, coffee. A large flat-screen monitor took up almost an entire wall to their right. In front of them at a white board stood Taylor Andrews herself. She held a dry erase marker and used it to point at one of the men. Isabel tried not to stare but easily lost the battle. Taylor Andrews was standing just feet from her, and she had to cue herself to breathe.

"The problem is if we leave those two onscreen for too long, their lack of chemistry really starts to show and then the episode shrivels up and dies a slow death. Why did we cast that guy again? He has as much presence as a hibernating turtle."

The man with a patchy brown beard shook his head. "Because that pushy casting agent swore by him."

"Yeah, well, lesson learned," Taylor said. "We need to be more aggressive at those auditions. Make a note."

"Can we kill him off?" the young brunette woman asked. "Worked last season for what's-his-name."

"Not yet," Taylor said. "We might need him to wrap up the whole embezzlement storyline, which definitely needs fleshing out. Kathleen, can you see what you can come up with on that front, and make it specific. Candace, maybe you can help her? We're playing it way too broad in the planning stages and we're going to screw ourselves later."

The second woman, who looked to be in her fifties, was apparently Kathleen. She nodded and started tapping away on her laptop. "Already on it. I have an idea, but let me play around with it first. Candace, maybe we can chat this afternoon?"

Candace nodded. "Done."

"Great," Taylor said. "Let's address it on Thursday. Is that doable?"

"Thursday is perfect," Kathleen said.

Scarlett stepped into the room and raised one finger. "Taylor, don't mean to interrupt, but I have Isabel Chase for you. She's your ten a.m."

Taylor turned to them, drew a breath, and smiled as if another giant boulder had just been strapped to her already heavy load.

Isabel winced internally and felt the self-doubt slither up her spine. She was not an imposter. She was not an imposter.

"Right. I'll be right there."

That smile sideswiped Isabel, and she faltered. She knew Taylor Andrews was attractive, but the photos she'd seen hadn't done her justice. She now realized they'd been startlingly conservative because the woman looking back at her was stunning. Perfectly layered blond hair that fell just past her shoulders and perhaps the most piercing green eyes she'd encountered in her twenty-nine years of life. But then, eyes like those wouldn't transfer to a photo in a magazine, the color too unique. Taylor wore designer-looking jeans, black heels, and a blue top underneath a slim white jacket. She held the room easily, and there was no question who the showrunner was. That, right there, was a woman with presence.

"I'll get her set up in your office," Scarlett said and led the way out.

"Thank you, Scar," she heard Taylor say before jumping right back into the story meeting. Isabel wanted desperately to stay and listen, be a fly on the wall of the brainstorming session. She'd collaborated with other writers on more than one occasion, but never on such a high-profile project, or on a long-term narrative. *Thicker Than Water* was entering its fifth season, and though the ratings had slipped from the rare heights of seasons one and two, it was still the show people talked about around the water cooler each week.

Opposite the writers' room on the other end of the hallway, they arrived at Taylor's office. In between, the open space made up of a series of cubicles was likely for Scarlett and the writing staff.

"Have a seat," Scarlett said. "Can I get you some coffee while you wait? It shouldn't be long."

"I would do hard labor for some. Thank you."

Scarlett smiled. "Careful what you promise around here. Cream and sugar?"

"Just black."

Scarlett nodded, and the sides of her mouth turned down. "You're hard-core. Black coffee coming right up."

Left alone in the quiet office, Isabel peered across the desk at the various documents. Scripts, notes, schedules, and red tape paperwork, no doubt requiring a signature. Taylor Andrews would have a busy life, but she was actually *doing* everything Isabel only dreamt about. She could learn a lot from this woman if only she was given the chance. She took a steadying breath and tried to relax, reminding herself that she was a real writer and not some phony hack. She'd written hundreds of decent scripts, some of them quite excellent, or she wouldn't be sitting here. In Hollywood. On the Paramount lot. This was happening. It was real and she better just—

"Sorry to keep you waiting," a rich voice said from behind. She turned to see Taylor breeze past her to her desk, leaving an aroma of something fruity and awesome. "It's nice to meet you. Taylor Andrews."

Isabel stood and accepted Taylor's outstretched hand. Her grip was firm, her eye contact direct. Unfortunately, she was even more attractive up close. Man. She shook it off because *don't be stupid.* "Isabel Chase." She took a seat as her nerves clenched and the back of her neck prickled. She was a good writer. She was a good writer. She was a good writer. She just needed to be a good writer who projected an aura of confidence. "I hope I didn't pull you from a valuable session. You guys seemed to be in the middle of a, uh, complicated story meeting."

Taylor inclined her head to the side. "We always are, but I'm hoping in the end, the interruption will have been worth it. So, let's get to it." She leaned back in her chair, letting go of some of the formality she'd started with. "Celeste speaks highly of you, and her opinion goes a long way with me. Most of my writers have come from the recommendation of people I trust, and that formula has never failed me. Well, thus far."

"Celeste is good people."

"Tell me how you know each other."

"We were classmates, and worked on a few projects together after graduation. We had a great synergy, which is hard to find."

"Any of those projects include an ongoing narrative?"

"No." Dammit. "I have to be honest, I've never worked on a series before, though I've written a million spec scripts. Just hard to get them in the right hands." She nodded a few dozen times and hated herself for it. "As you just alluded to, it's about who you know."

"True." Taylor met Isabel's eyes and studied her. "Why don't you tell me about them."

"Them?" Isabel blinked in an attempt to clear her head. She had to chase away the extra energy and stop herself from staring. Taylor was striking in the rarest sense, which was an entirely insulting thought. This woman was accomplished and respected in the world of television and deserved more than an ogling from a nobody like Isabel. She thought instead about Fat Tony hacking up furballs. A handy distraction.

"The projects. What was one of your favorites?"

"Oh! Right." She reached into her bag and located the DVD that contained her reel. "These are a few of the shorts I'm most proud of, interspersed with clips from some longer-form projects." She lifted her bag. "I also have a thumb drive, if that's easier. Or there's my website."

Taylor accepted the disc and set it on her desk. "This is fine. Right now, I'd rather hear about your work from you."

"Okay." Isabel clenched and unclenched her fists before diving in. She smiled because she really was passionate about her writing. "My last project was a twenty-seven-minute grunge piece about a bass guitarist in a metal band who fantasized about playing in the New York Philharmonic Orchestra. It was a commentary on clean and dirty, of grit and gloss."

Taylor leaned forward and pointed. "It was at South by Southwest last year."

Isabel smiled, caught off guard by the fact that her work was known. "It was."

"You wrote and directed and won your division."

Hold the phone. Taylor Andrews had looked her up. "Yeah, well, the audience was really receptive. I was lucky."

"Don't sell yourself short. That festival comes with a discerning audience. I should know. I'm there every year and remember your short."

"Wow. I didn't realize you'd seen it. That's—"

"It was brilliant, and I don't mind saying so, one of the standouts of the festival. But there's a big difference between that and this. Huge. *Thicker Than Water* is every bit as artistic. The distinction comes in the structure. Pacing."

"Of course." Isabel sat back. "Five acts and a teaser. I've studied the show a lot. I'm not just a writer, I'm a fan. I hope that doesn't make me seem less focused."

Taylor smiled. "I'm happy you've done your homework. I love my show and what I do. I want my staff to share my passion."

"I do. I will." Isabel didn't know how to articulate how hungry she was for this opportunity, how very hard she was willing to work to prove herself. She decided to lay it all out there for Taylor. "My mom walked out on my dad and me when I was a baby. He raised me on his own, but he worked a lot. I used to watch *Full House* reruns, *The Brady Bunch*, even the older stuff like *The Patty Duke Show*, which my friends made fun of me for." She brushed a strand of hair from her eye, feeling somehow vulnerable during this confession. "Those characters kept me company those nights on my own. They were, in a way, my family when my dad couldn't be. I get how important television can be, an escape from the world and its awful complications. Television kept me from being lonely. It was my first love."

"And that is something I can work with," Taylor said quietly. She took a moment and studied Isabel, clearly processing. "Let's talk about your spec script." She reached behind her and found Isabel's script, recognizable by the bright yellow cover.

"Great. I'd love to."

Taylor leafed through the pages. "It's good, I'll admit, and it's why you're sitting here. You have a knack for capturing individual dialogue, a hard skill to teach."

"Thank you."

"You've worked your way into the characters' heads nicely. However, I am concerned about your lack of experience writing a series. This script shows what you can do on a one and done, but can you map out a season? Can you track characters over time through growth and change? There are big differences from the world of features, and shorts too, for that matter."

Isabel nodded because Taylor was right. "No, I get it. But it's actually the ongoing narrative that attracts me to the work, the chance to write a character for an extended amount of time. To really explore their internal lives in a way a two-hour film doesn't allow for."

Taylor nodded. "It's not easy, though, to tell a story so rich that it has enough staying power to extend over several years. In some cases, over a decade."

Isabel took a breath. "Ms. Andrews, if I could—"

"Taylor is fine. We drop most pretense around here."

"Taylor, then." She took a deep breath and ran her fingers across the gravelly surface of the coffee mug. "I feel more than ready for this challenge. No one works harder. I feel like everything I've done has led me to this moment, and I'm not about to let anyone down. Myself included."

"As a staff writer, you won't be writing your own scripts," Taylor said, sitting forward. "You should know that up front."

"I'll do whatever you need."

A long pause hit and circled the room. A chill moved across Isabel's skin and she braced herself for whatever Taylor would say next.

"Fine then. Can you start next Monday?" Taylor asked. "We're into August and you've missed weeks of season planning already. If you're not there for this week's meetings, you'll have even more catch-up."

And just like that, she was in. Wait. She was *in*? Tiny leprechauns danced a jig in her head in some random celebration both perplexing and enjoyable. She didn't even like leprechauns.

Hired.

She refrained from leaping out of her chair and leading a parade across the Paramount lot, and took the more professional approach. "Sure. I just need to head home and pack. Figure out where I'm going to live."

"If you want more time, we can hold off. I'm anxious for the help, though. Losing Celeste has been a blow that has us all pulling more hours."

"No, no. I'll be there on Monday. I'd like to jump in as soon as possible."

Taylor stood. "I have to run to a production meeting, but I'm looking forward to having you on the team, Isabel."

"Me too," she said, smiling, like she could help it if she tried. "Not looking forward to having myself. To being on the team, I mean. That's more what I was going for."

Taylor had the decency to chuckle. "I understand. If you'll wait here, Scarlett will get you set up with new-hire paperwork and you'll need to check in with security for your studio credentials. See you on Monday."

"Monday it is." She leaned forward to set her mug on the desk only to overreach and send it tumbling onto its side, opening the floodgates of rushing coffee that covered Taylor's desk, her papers, and splashed onto her crisp white jacket.

Oh no.

That did not just happen. Satan on a Triscuit. That *did* just happen. She glanced up at Taylor and winced, leaping into action, looking around the room for some way to rectify the situation, to save this awfulness from spiraling further. Taylor's only reaction was a step back from the coffee and the rescue of a nearby file folder from the attack.

She held up a hand. "It's fine. Scarlett will take care of it." She shrugged out of her jacket and hung it on the hook behind the door. "See? Good as new."

"I'm *so* sorry." Isabel was shaking and doing anything in her power to roll back the last two minutes of her life. How quickly the pendulum had swung. Elation to mortification in the span of seconds. That could be the title of her jaded little memoir.

"No need. It was an accident."

"Right, but still." Isabel surveyed the brown, soggy mess, frustrated with herself. "I've ruined everything on your desk."

Taylor tilted her head from side to side. "All replaceable." She seemed to act on an impulse and took a seat in the chair across from her desk and next to Isabel's. "I'm getting two things from you. Tell me if I'm right."

Isabel met Taylor's eyes. For the first time that day, they didn't cause her pulse to race. In fact, staring into their depths, she found an unexpected calm, prompting her to release some of the shock and horror from the coffee catastrophe. "Okay."

"You seem like a person who probably comes with some strong opinions. You know what you want and you go after it. I'm getting that from your work."

"That's true. Sometimes to a fault." Why was she being so honest? Stop that.

"You also seem incredibly anxious."

She smiled and nodded. "Also true." She gestured around the

room. "All of this. It's what I've worked so hard for, and I guess it has me freaking out, which is the most unprofessional thing in the world to say to someone who just hired me."

Taylor took both of Isabel's hands in hers. She had nice hands, Isabel realized absently. Feminine and warm and strong. "Well, you can relax because the hard part is over. You're in. You're one of us now, and I look forward to the strong opinions."

"Be careful what you wish for," Isabel said, managing a smile. She gave Taylor's hands a squeeze. "And thank you. For the pep talk. A slap across the face might have been quicker."

"I'll file that away," Taylor said with a wink and stood to go. "Scarlett will be in about those credentials. Try not to destroy the rest of the place in the meantime." And then she was gone, leaving Isabel alone with a myriad of warring thoughts. Two words floated to the top.

Studio credentials.

They were arranging for studio credentials. She closed her eyes and swallowed, taking a moment to commemorate the occasion, pushing aside the last ten minutes to fully focus on just how many years she'd slogged away on her laptop, script after script, character after character, one festival entry followed by another to get to this very moment. Finally. Her limbs numbed. Her mind slowed down. Her spirit soared. She hadn't skipped since the fourth grade, but she was feeling a distinct pull in that direction.

Days like today didn't happen to her. They just didn't. She was a nobody who kept her head down and spent all her time putting words on the page. For the first time in years, she could breathe, and she welcomed the abundance of fresh air as it infiltrated her lungs, and what glorious air it was! Maybe she was turning into a somebody after all. Fennel oversights and server shoes might just be a thing of the past. Isabel basked in that thought before snapping into action.

So much to accomplish in a very short amount of time. Packing. Planning. Panicking.

Monday was right around the corner.

CHAPTER THREE

Taylor checked her watch. Six minutes to the production meeting, which was cutting it closer than she'd like. She swung by Scarlett's desk on her way, in need of some help.

"Coffee spill. Mayday. All over everything, including my jacket."

Scarlett's eyes went wide. "The white designer one? No."

"That's the one."

"No, no, no. I love that jacket. You said I could borrow it." Scarlett placed her hand over her heart. "This is awful. Are we going to have to have a funeral?"

"Probably, unless Bernard in wardrobe can save us. He's the only one who could."

Scarlett pointed at Taylor and pushed her glasses up on her face. "I'll send him a bottle of the 2004 Cabernet he likes. He's a sucker for it. He'll save the jacket and life will return to normal."

"This is why I never want you to leave me."

"So, do we have a verdict on our new staff writer?" Scarlett pushed right on to business. She kept Taylor on track in that way.

"She's in." Taylor relaxed her hip against Scarlett's desk. "A little on edge, but her work is killer if not, well, dark. Celeste was spot-on in her recommendation, though. Maybe we should send *her* a bottle of the Cabernet." Scarlett began to scribble a note. "I was kidding." Scarlett lifted her pen. "But can you get Ms. Chase set up with paperwork and credentials and everything you do so expertly and then take a look at what's salvageable on my desk. I rescued what I could."

Scarlett nodded. "You got it, boss. Production meeting in three."

She squinted at her friend and assistant. "It never slows down, does it? My life is like a roller coaster without an off switch."

"Good analogy." Scarlett held up her hand, and Taylor smacked it in their high-five ritual. She headed off to the meeting, getting her agenda points in order as she walked the narrow streets of the property. All the while, she couldn't help but ruminate on the meeting with the new hire. Isabel Chase showed a lot of promise, and if that hint of spunk in her work came to fruition on the show, she might just be a great addition to the staff. But there was something else about Isabel, something she couldn't quite put her finger on, that had Taylor…circling.

The production meeting flew by in a hail storm of bargaining, planning, and budget workarounds. "What this essentially comes down to is that we can't afford for it to rain in Ashbury Pass for the rest of the season?" she asked Emily Tanner, her line producer.

"Not if you want to bring in those two guest stars," Emily said matter-of-factly. "We can't afford both."

She sighed. "And I do. No rain it is, then. I'll let my staff know not to write any. Are we done for today?" She glanced around at the faces of everyone assembled. The team nodded, and no one seemed to have anything new.

"Great. I will see you at tomorrow's table read. Email me with fires to put out, but maybe give me a fifteen-minute head start to my office."

A typical Monday.

When Taylor arrived back at the writers' headquarters, she ran into Isabel Chase exiting the building just as she was entering. "All set?" she asked. Isabel looked noticeably more at ease, which was nice to see. She even smiled.

"Almost," Isabel said. She'd worn her hair in a slicked-back ponytail earlier. It was down now, medium length with the gentlest of waves. "I have to have my photo made in the admin building, which I'm told is…" She shielded what Taylor had come to realize were blue eyes with her hand to her forehead.

Taylor pointed. "Right over there. Fourth Street."

"Fourth Street," Isabel repeated. "Thanks! Have a great one, Ms. Andrews. Taylor."

"Now you're getting the hang of it."

Taylor watched Isabel walk away, noticing the modest heels, the simple black pants and pink cuffed shirt. The dark hair swung ever so slightly across her shoulder blades as she walked. She was pretty, Isabel Chase. Not that it mattered. Nor did the flush that came over Taylor as she watched. What she needed more than anything was Isabel's brain, her imagination, and her dedication.

Time would tell if she got them.

❖

At 9:33 on what had been the best day of her life, Isabel huddled in the farthest corner of the closet in her hotel room. The light was off. She'd wrapped her arms around herself and clung tightly, unable to move. Her pulse skyrocketed and she had trouble taking normal breaths, wondering distantly if this was what it felt like to drown. Beads of sweat pooled above her eyebrows though it was cold in the room.

"You're doing fine," she managed to whisper to herself. It was the sentence that had seen her through panic attacks as a child. "You're doing fine," she repeated. She wanted badly to give her face a scrub, imagining that the sensation might help jar her to a feeling of control, but her muscles coiled tight and rigid and it felt like the world was crashing in on her. The impending dread only increased as the seconds ticked by.

It had been over a year since her last attack, and honestly, Isabel should have seen it coming. She was at her most vulnerable when there was something to lose, and today she'd just been handed an opportunity that she heavily valued. She could screw it up in her first week. Find herself on a plane back to Keene, devastated and embarrassed and right back where she started.

She shoved her back against the wall, hoping that the cool and steady surface would ground her. The stability should be comforting. It wasn't. She still couldn't get air, and no matter how small the space, the world felt too big. She sat in that closet for over two hours, clenched and miserable and praying for an end. She listened as the distant sound of the television slowly moved from garish and terrifying to everyday. She blinked and took a very slow inhale, pleased to find she could control her breathing.

She'd made it.

In that tiny, dark room, she'd survived one monster of a panic attack. Still not quite ready to move, Isabel sat there listening to the sounds of her breath slowing down, underscored by the local weather. Tomorrow, she would wake up and go back to life already in progress and push this whole thing behind her.

"You did fine." She relaxed her hands until they rested in her lap and forced her fists to unclench. "You did just fine."

CHAPTER FOUR

The sun seemed to shine all the time in Los Angeles. Well, at least in August it did. Isabel added this to the list of things she was learning about the Golden State, her new home for the foreseeable future. She reminded herself to invest in a decent pair of sunglasses as she squinted against the sunlight as it slanted through her windshield. She lowered her head to better see the passing street signs and aha, there it was. She turned onto Shores Drive in Venice, looking for #7. Celeste had been nice enough to sublet her apartment to Isabel, even going so far as to float her for the first couple of months until she was on her feet enough to pay her back. She would forever search out a way to return the favor to Celeste, who'd gone above and beyond. Saint Celeste was how she should henceforth be known and hailed. Some sort of statue seemed in order, but knowing Celeste, she would demur.

Shores Drive, it turned out, was palm tree lined and a tad too cheerful, probably named for its proximity to Venice Beach, just a few blocks south. Brightly colored storefronts whizzed past and folks in flip-flops dotted the street looking relaxed and at ease. She didn't identify with them in the least, black being the most abundant color in her wardrobe. Did these people have jobs? Didn't they have somewhere to be? The ambling indicated that no, they did not. She abandoned her curiosity, realizing that she'd arrived at her destination, #7 Shores Drive. The little complex had a white stucco exterior with black trim and shutters. A sign with the words "Seven Shores" written in script hung from a post in front. The complex was relatively compact, just as Celeste had described, but surprisingly quaint. Not your cookie cutter apartment building, which came as a welcome revelation.

"You ready for this?" she asked Tony, who blinked back at her in toleration from his carrying crate. Together, they'd driven forty-one hours over five days to get here, bringing only what they could fit in the car, though her dad would be mailing a few more boxes in the coming days. Tony stared hard back at her. He was over the car, and she felt for the guy. "You're a California cat now, so you're gonna have to mellow. Eat veggies. All of it. It's the law here." He closed his eyes, much preferring to take a nap.

Leaving her belongings in the car while she investigated, Isabel made her way with Fat Tony through the black iron gate that marked the entrance to the complex. The units, on two levels, faced inward to a central courtyard. A quick scan had her estimating twelve total apartments. The courtyard was attractive, outfitted with a handful of wrought iron circular tables and chairs. Across from them sat a comfortable-looking outdoor seating area. Two couches with green patio cushions faced each other, flanked by four matching club chairs. Did people actually congregate here? How unexpectedly social. Her apartment experience had been limited to an occasional nod to that older couple who lived next door and occasionally stole her parking space. Making friends with her neighbors was a foreign, though not unwelcome, concept. After all, she knew very few people in town. Maybe she'd actually make a friend.

"Hey," a brunette said in greeting, as she crossed the courtyard. Speak of the devil, an actual neighbor. She looked to be close to Isabel's age and had come out of a second-floor unit, carrying a surfboard—which explained the jeans and bikini top.

"Hi." Isabel nodded as the woman passed.

The neighbor turned back. "You look lost. Need help?" Her thick dark hair was in a ponytail and she showed off an athletic physique and a remarkable tan. As in, a *really* good one. Beach people made her own northern skin glow white, a fact that she'd never been more aware of than in this moment.

"Oh. Yeah, actually. Looking for apartment 1F."

"Over there." The woman pointed to the black door of a first-story unit behind Isabel. "But I should tell you that Celeste is out of town. Not sure when she'll be back."

"Right. No. I'm subletting her—well, pretty much her whole life, now that I think about it. Apartment included. We're friends."

The woman brightened and leaned the surfboard against the staircase. "In that case, we're neighbors, and I should introduce myself.

Gia Malone." She extended her hand. "I live up there in 2D and my best friend, Hadley, lives next door in 2E. I'm sure you'll run into her soon enough."

"I'll look forward to that," she said, trying not to be socially awkward.

"Welcome to Seven Shores. We're a pretty casual group. Cups of sugar are never a problem."

"Nice to meet you. I'm Isabel. Izzy. Either is fine."

"Well, Izzy or Isabel, it's a pleasure. I'm sure I'll be seeing you around and whatnot. Gotta head to my office before I lose the waves. Let me know if you need anything. That cup of sugar or eats recommendations." With that, she picked up her surfboard and was on her way to her "office." Were these people real?

Isabel let herself into the apartment and was happy to find that it was decent-sized and fully furnished just as Celeste had promised. It was also decorated with a decidedly Southwestern flair. Celeste seemed to have embraced that part of the country in a big way. It wasn't necessarily Isabel's style, but she was too grateful to care. She could embrace the cow-skull-in-the-dirt photos in the turquoise frames. Well, she could *try*. The realistic-looking iguana sitting on top of the fridge might take up a life in the closet, however.

"Look, Tony. It's our new place." She set her cat on the floor and opened the door to his carrier, knowing it would take him a good fifteen minutes to get the courage to come out and explore.

She looked around. The front door opened to a moderate-sized living room combined with the kitchen and breakfast nook in one. A single bedroom branched off a small hallway to the left. She strolled through the space and nodded at the dark beige carpet, then winced at the giant photograph of a wolf peering over a cliff. It was a choice. Perhaps one she would tuck safely away with Mr. Iguana.

So, this was home for the foreseeable future. Yep. She could work with this. Relief hit, fast and wonderful, energizing her, because she'd made it. She was home.

Isabel grabbed another armful of her belongings from the car and smiled at a middle-aged gentleman with jet black hair crossing the courtyard. He wore a plaid tie, kidnapper glasses, and a permanent scowl. "Are you Isabel Chase?" he asked.

With luggage hanging off every part of her, she paused to readjust the strap hanging on her shoulder. "I am. Hi. What can I do for you?"

"Celeste told me you'd be moving in today, so I've been keeping an eye out. I'm Larry Herman. I own the complex. Just so we're clear, no loud parties." He seemed intense, too intense, which, for whatever reason, amused her.

"As in, I can't attend any? That's depressing news." Her euphoria seemed to have enabled her sarcastic side. "That's really gonna cut into my social world, Larry. I guess I'll just stay home. Eat macaroni." She smiled, which seemed to throw him completely.

"No *hosting* loud parties is the rule. No attending them on the property either. I'm not going to follow you once you leave the premises, though. Once you leave, you're on your own."

"I was just kidding about the attendance thing. We're good. No loud parties on site. You have my word."

"If there are loud parties, I'll have to evict you. No exceptions. It's a Larry Herman rule."

"I will not be breaking any Larry Herman rules." She squinted at him. "However, I'm sensing some history with loud parties on your part." She was already percolating on fifteen different scripts starring this guy. She could talk to him all day.

He shook his head emphatically. "I don't stand for them. That's all. No loud parties."

"Hmm. I'm getting from you that you don't like loud parties." She tapped her lips thoughtfully.

"That's entirely true."

"And why would you? They're awful. You can barely speak to anyone for all the...*loud*."

That seemed to make him happy, as if they'd stumbled onto some common ground. They were really bonding now. "They *are* awful," he said, leaning in as if sharing a secret. He then eyed her curiously. "Oh, and you have a lot of luggage there." She thought he was about to offer his assistance. Instead, he headed off in the direction of the parking lot. "Welcome to Seven Shores," he called. "From the second-story apartments, you can glimpse the ocean."

"I'm on the first floor," she yelled after him.

"Oh, I know," he said without looking back.

Curious fellow, Larry Herman. She was looking forward to interacting with him more in the future. It's what she did when someone enthralled her, and c'mon, people who named rules after themselves simply didn't come along every day. Once inside, she sought out her spiral notebook and jotted down a few details of their conversation for inspiration later.

Isabel spent the rest of the afternoon watching the screeners Scarlett had supplied her with of the episodes of *Thicker Than Water* that had yet to air. This way, she could catch herself up on the action leading up to where they'd pick up on Monday. She took notes as she watched, anything and everything that popped into her head. You never knew from where the next creative nugget would sprout.

Honestly, the storytelling on the show was solid, but after four seasons she couldn't help wonder about shaking things up a little. Killing a few people off. Scandalizing others. Holding on to the character-driven storytelling that put the show on the map, but sprinkling in a few bigger plot twists that the regular viewership wasn't used to. Most shows died off after a handful of seasons unless they pivoted and offered something fresh. No doubt Taylor Andrews was well aware of all of this already, and while Isabel had some ideas on possible new storylines, as the new girl, she should probably keep them to herself until called upon.

Four episodes later, the midafternoon had Isabel in desperate need of caffeine, and fast. Her brain swirled with the complex lives of Dr. Lisette James, her younger sister Karen, a prosecutor, and their older brother Dominic, who raced cars for a living. They got along too well, the three of them, and found their problems in the outside world. That needed to change. Now on a caffeine mission, she remembered spotting a coffee shop adjacent to the complex. Having instant access to a plethora of espresso drinks was the thing a writer's dreams were made of. This was a lucky break.

There was a blond woman reading on one of the outdoor couches as she crossed the courtyard on her way to the nearby shop. Okay, so people really did use those things. This would take getting used to. All the people. And the talking to them. The woman glanced up and smiled warmly, offering a quick wave to Isabel as she passed. Isabel nodded back politely and the woman went back to her book. She looked like California personified. *Sports Illustrated*, live and in person, in her very own courtyard. Perky blond hair that didn't quite make it to her shoulders and blue eyes. Isabel smothered the feelings of inadequacy that eased slowly up her spine. She refused to be intimidated by this new and glamorous world she'd stepped into.

As she walked next door to the coffee shop, she smiled at the realization that she could hear the ocean if she concentrated hard enough and filtered out the traffic noise from the street. A couple of seagulls sailed overhead and the afternoon glimmered bright. California was nothing like New Hampshire, but there seemed to be a lot of good to counteract the scary.

She glanced up at the sign above the coffee shop that read *The Cat's Pajamas*, complete with a cat clad in loud pajamas and playing the guitar. One had to smile. Cats playing guitars demanded it. Inside, the place was just as fun. The entire perimeter of the square room was outfitted with guitars, some new, some vintage. About ten chocolate brown tables dotted the main floor and off to the right, nestled among two tall shelves containing books and board games, stood a pair of worn-in sofas, all overstuffed and soft looking. She dug the vibe and could see herself spending tons of time in this space when she needed a new spot to write.

"What can I get for you?" the barista asked. She had gorgeous hair, dark red, curly and thick as it fell around her shoulders. Isabel would kill for that hair. She would wage wars. Sell insurance policies. Anything. "Did you need another minute?" the woman asked when she didn't immediately answer.

"Sorry. I was just admiring your hair, and thus wondering why I even got up in the morning." With her finger, she flicked a strand of her own, boring, brown, straight hair.

The woman laughed. "You're sweet, but it's more trouble than it's worth. The monthly budget takes a huge hit in the name of hair product."

"Totally worth it. Trust me." They smiled at each other. She liked this woman. She had fun energy and a cool, mellow voice. Plus, there was something laid back and friendly about her. "This is a great place. Great name, too."

"I'm glad you like it. Named after my childhood cat, Pajamas. We called him PJ." She grabbed a towel and wiped down the counter.

"Oh. So, you're the owner?"

"Yep. That's me. We've been here six years now and going strong. People like a good cup of coffee before hitting the beach. Luckily, you won't find any better than mine. And that's a legit challenge."

"Sold. I'll take one. Black."

"Excellent choice." She grabbed a cardboard cup with the guitar-playing cat on the side. "So, are you on vacation?"

"Nope. New to the area, actually. Just moved in next door, so you might see more of me."

The woman turned back, her interest clearly piqued. "You're at Seven Shores?"

"We just moved in today. Haven't even unpacked."

"Get out. Why didn't you say so? I'm Autumn. It just so happens that Seven Shores folks are some of my best customers. Friends, too."

"Isabel Chase. Nice to meet you. So, does that mean you live next door as well?"

"No, I live in West Hollywood, but a handful of us meet up in the courtyard to unwind, shoot the breeze, that kind of thing. Strong LGBT presence in Venice, so I linger."

Well, well, well. Her people. "This place just gets better and better."

Autumn grinned and studied her as if trying to work a puzzle. Isabel knew exactly the variety. She wasn't an easy read in the sexuality department and didn't mind that. It could go either way based on her appearance and what she wore on a given day. She liked the versatility. She could go for clear lesbian one day and confuse the world the next.

Autumn inclined her head. "You said *we* just moved in."

"Right. Me and Fat Tony. He's got an attitude. You've been forewarned. We're working on it, but honestly there hasn't been a lot of progress."

She laughed. "You call your boyfriend Fat Tony?" Clearly Isabel was pinging in the wrong direction today.

"I don't. But I call my cat Fat Tony."

A pause. "I knew I liked you." Autumn handed over her cup, steam billowing. "You'll have to tell me what you think of the coffee. Those beans were roasted this morning." She inclined her head to the left, indicating a giant silver roaster that stood impressive and imposing in the corner. This woman was serious about her coffee. She didn't just serve it, she fucking roasted it.

"I will get back to you with my review, though I have to say, my expectations are relegated to Starbucks."

"I forgive you for what you do not know, but this is your lucky day."

Isabel nodded. She was starting to feel like it was. She popped a to-go lid on her cup and held it up to Autumn. "Thanks for the nice welcome. I'm sure I'll be seeing you around."

"Take care. Oh, and say hi to that Fat Tony for me. Sounds like my kind of guy."

"If you're into judgmental assholes."

"In cat form? There's no other way."

Isabel made her way back across the courtyard to begin the process of unpacking what would be her work clothes, making sure everything essential was accessible. "Holy shit," she said after taking a sip of the coffee.

"Everything all right?" the blonde on the couch asked.

She glanced over. "Oh. Sorry. I didn't mean to—this is just really good coffee." She raised the cup in the air. "A choir of angels has taken residence on my shoulder, so I was…expressing myself. With profanity."

The blonde smiled. "Pajama coffee tends to have that effect on people."

"Right? That woman over there knows what she's doing."

"Autumn? She's the best around. A keeper." She cocked her head. "Are you new? Not that this is second grade, but are you? New." There was the friendly smile again.

Isabel nodded. "Yeah. Just minted from New Hampshire." She gestured to her door. "I'm subletting from my friend Celeste."

"Who I already miss more than Barack Obama. Well, a close second. I'm so glad she sent a replacement." She hesitated. "I don't suppose you like Barry Manilow and guacamole, by chance?"

"That's a question I've never been asked before. Huh." Isabel considered the odd combination and took a few steps toward the seating area. "I mean, I don't have anything against either, though I have questions about the decision to pair them. That's not judgment. Just a quandary."

The woman hugged herself briefly. "I could write a dissertation on the sheer perfection of that combo. If I were the type to write dissertations. It's okay, though. I'm sure you come with many fantastic qualities of your own." She gestured to Isabel's hand. "You already appreciate good coffee. Hadley, by the way. I'm so sorry. I should have started with that. I live upstairs." She indicated the apartment in the corner.

"Oh! You're Gia's friend."

Hadley beamed. "Yes, and you're one step ahead."

Isabel reflected on the LGBT vibe Autumn had assigned the place and couldn't help but wonder rudely. "So, are you two…"

"Both right-handed? Yes." She seemed pleased with herself. "But we're also just friends, if that was your larger question. No euphemism attached."

Guilt struck Isabel for leaping there, and she felt her cheeks warm.

She should really keep her thoughts in her head more. She would work on this. Implement a schedule. "I hope I didn't overstep."

"You didn't." She offered a warm smile. Isabel pegged Hadley as a kind person, the sort you just knew you could relax around. "Seven Shores is a colorful place. Your gaydar is not off, so rest assured." Aha, so she wasn't entirely off base. "And neither is mine, for that matter. Welcome to the neighborhood. And the community."

Isabel grinned. "Thank you."

"I head to work in an hour, but if there's anything I can do to help you move in, I'm willing. I'm great at carrying stuff and wouldn't mind pitching in if you need it."

See? Now that was a thoughtful offer. Now she felt guilty about the *Sports Illustrated* categorization. "I might take you up on that next week when a few more boxes arrive. For now, just me, a handful of suitcases, and a sleepy cat. What do you do for work?"

"I'm the assistant manager of a boutique in Hollywood."

"Impressive. Boutique sounds high end. Don't tell me it's on Rodeo Drive or I might get all *Pretty Woman* fangirl on you." Isabel laughed.

"No, it is," Hadley said quite seriously, "on Rodeo Drive. Silhouette is the name of the store. You should stop by. I'd be happy to show you the place."

Isabel's mouth fell open. "You *are* one of the women from the movie! I was kidding, but here you are in person. You don't kick people out of the store with their little hearts in their hand, do you?"

"I promise we're much nicer. We would let Vivian shop. I'd personally see to it."

"Thank God." Because those women in the film were vicious vipers. Isabel used to fantasize about all the ways she would get back at them. Stick up for Vivian and then get to spend time with her. Lots and lots of time. Okay, to be fair, *Pretty Woman* had been pivotal to her journey of self-discovery.

Hadley studied her. "Let me guess your job. I'm good at this."

Isabel made a sweeping gesture with her arm. "Have at it."

"Okay, so you're understated but very pretty, so I'm going to guess you're moving here to audition. You're also wearing a lot of black." She pointed at Isabel. "You're a budding actress. The serious kind, though, who cares a great deal about craft and not just the potent lure of Hollywood." She looked nervous and sincere, as if her success or failure carried true consequence. "Am I close?"

Okay, maybe she was nicer than the woman in the movie. "Thank you, but no. I write."

"Books?" She held up the novel she'd been reading and beamed. "Reading is my escape. There's nothing like it."

"No, for TV. I'm a new staff writer for *Thicker Than Water*." Hadley didn't say anything and Isabel wondered if she hated television or maybe even the show itself. "Did I lose you with that little revelation?"

Hadley shook her head slowly. "I'm just happy. You took Celeste's spot!" She held out a hand as her energy grew. "You should know that *Thicker Than Water* is only the reason I get up in the morning. Celeste was my inroad to all the good clues about what might happen next, which I thought were gone forever. But here you are."

Isabel laughed. "So, you're a fan? Me too. It's good TV, one of the more thoughtful serial dramas out there."

Hadley sat forward. "It's my favorite show. I have a cardboard cutout of Aspen Wakefield on the back of my closet door." She covered her face in embarrassment and sat back against the couch.

Isabel couldn't help but laugh along with her. Hadley seemed adorable, big hearted, and kind. "You will get nothing but commiseration from me in the TV fandom department. I get it. I'm a junkie myself. Jan Brady is everything."

"Have you met her yet? Aspen? Not Jan. Though I'm sure Jan is great." Hadley's blue eyes were wide and full of hope and wonder, like one of those people life had yet to step on in any true way. Her question had been about Aspen Wakefield, who played Dr. Lisette James on the show and was by far the most popular character among viewers. Lisette, the character, was hardworking and benevolent, and served as the show's moral compass. It didn't hurt matters that Aspen Wakefield, the actress, was an incredibly hot, voluptuous brunette. She had throngs of fans who obsessed about her every move. Tabloids couldn't snap enough photos to satisfy their readerships. Hollywood A-list all the way.

"Not yet, but I'm sure we'll cross paths. I should be in on the weekly table reads."

Hadley shook her head in wonder. "You have to report back when that happens. Celeste tended to downplay. I hope you'll dish the details."

Isabel walked to the couch and held out her hand for a fist bump. "I won't let you down."

Like a pro, Hadley bumped her fist and pulled back an explosion.

Good people, this one. "Don't get me wrong, I love Celeste's guacamole and will miss it dearly, but I'm very happy you've moved in, Isabel."

"Likewise. I'll let you get back to your book, Hadley…?"

"Cooper," she supplied.

"Happy reading, Hadley Cooper." Isabel took a sip of coffee on her way to her door. "Holy hell, this stuff is good. Fuck. Me." She turned to Hadley. "Sorry again for the swearing."

Hadley chuckled quietly from the couch.

Chapter Five

"Taylor, the network is on line three," Scarlett called from her office next door.

"Did they say what they want? I'm buried right now," she called back. Taylor's Monday morning already felt like a category four hurricane made up of petty little issues all revolving around shooting. Dealing with the network would only take it to category five, and it wasn't even noon yet. She still had a story meeting with the writers, a conference call with her gaggle of producers, and a director of an upcoming episode making too many design demands.

Scarlett popped her head into Taylor's office. She had a way of doing so that reminded Taylor of a prairie dog. The whole thing made Taylor smile because it was so quintessentially Scarlett. "It's Hagerman and he's doing that thing where he stammers a lot, which means he's unhappy about something."

"When is he ever happy? When?" Taylor asked not just Scarlett but the world at large. As one of the many vice presidents at WCN, he was forever a pebble in her shoe.

Scarlett pushed her glasses up on her nose. "I can fight him off, but you know he'll just call back in an hour. If you take his call now, you might save yourself time on the back end."

"Good point."

She lifted the receiver and forced herself to smile. "Gerald, good morning. To what do I owe the pleasure?" Scarlett mouthed the word "coffee," to which Taylor shook her head. She'd already had two cups. There would be lots of coffee in her future, but perhaps it was wiser to pace herself.

"Taylor, we, uh, we have to talk." There was the stammer. Scarlett was right.

"And we are. What's up?"

"We've, uh, taken a look at the draft of this week's episode and, uh, the sex scene between the two male characters has left us with a few questions." Ah, the cousin Bobby spreading his wings storyline.

She suppressed a sigh. "We've been through this already, Gerald. The pairing has been huge with the audience, and the sponsors are on board. Cousin Bobby is out of the closet now, and as such, he has to have a decent shot at a love life. Same-sex scenes are not new anymore. At all. So, what's the problem?"

"Don't get upset, but it's the, uh, the thrusting and the, uh, nudity. We just feel the need to proceed cautiously. We're a network that's known for our family-appropriate primetimes."

She suppressed a snort.

"How many seconds are we talking? How many of the, um, thrusts?"

"No idea." She covered her eyes because seriously? "How could I possibly answer that question until we shoot the scene? You're asking me to predict the creative collaboration of a lot of brilliant minds."

"We'll sign off on two minor thrusts and give you ten seconds after the clothes come off to, uh, cut away."

"I don't do well with limits. This is storytelling, not sixth grade behind the gym with a stopwatch."

"You're the showrunner. Make it happen. Ten seconds once clothes come off, Taylor. I could give you more if these were, you know, girls."

"I think you mean women, Gerald. Do you know how sexist and archaic that viewpoint is?"

"I do. You have ten seconds. Two thrusts."

"Fine." She agreed to his terms knowing full well if they needed more time onscreen, she could address it then. Plus, having the director of the episode chime in would reinforce her stance. Which one was it that week? She flipped through the call sheets on her desk. Simon LaRue. Perfect. Simon was a bulldog and fiercely protective of his work. She smiled into the phone. "Ten seconds it is. And, Gerald?"

"Yep."

"I'd like to throw another number at you. It's the number four. As in four Emmys," she said in reminder. "I know you're just doing your job like the rest of us, but I've won four Emmys for WCN, ten if you count the acting awards. That should buy me some breathing room, no?"

"We have nothing but the highest regard for your work, Taylor. You're our superstar, and don't you ever doubt it."

"I appreciate it. Let's have lunch next week." A little schmoozing might be in order. Best to keep the network close and off her back.

"I'll have my assistant arrange it with yours."

"See you then." She hung up and sank back into the wonderfully cushioned leather of her office chair and closed her eyes. Best damn investment of her life, this chair. She could get lost right here and not care. She allowed herself five seconds of bliss before turning to her email, of which there were fifty-two.

"Knock, knock."

She glanced up in time to see the new hire, Isabel, standing in her doorway all fresh-faced and bright. She smiled conservatively, but looked sharp in dark dress pants and a slim-fitting gray jacket. She had her hair pulled up again today and looked fantastic. Not at all the hastily thrown together (okay, in some cases, slovenly) exterior of the typical writer on her team. It was also encouraging that she cared about perception. Maybe this girl was everything Celeste had promised.

"Just wanted to say good morning before the story meeting. I brought bagels and schmear." She lifted the bag. "Northern thing. Plus, there's a coffee shop near my place, so…"

Taylor forced a smile she didn't have time for, but she wanted to make Isabel's first day a good one. "Bagels are always welcome. Glad to have you here. We'll get started in just a bit."

"Thank you. I will…see you in there." Isabel gestured behind herself to the writers' room. "Yep."

"Great."

She turned to go and then paused, gesturing between them. "I promise to get better at this."

"I'm not worried. Would you mind closing the door behind you? I want to tear through some email before we begin."

"Right. Of course. Sorry."

"No need." She offered another smile and waited as Isabel exited her office and closed the door. She liked this girl. Now it was only a matter of whether she could deliver on the page.

As she dashed off a response to the studio head about the increased cost of back lot rental, Scarlett's voice interrupted her yet again.

"Todd on line two."

"Of course he is." Her ex-husband had a way of picking the worst time to call. She grabbed the receiver and opened the line. "Hey, you. What's up? I'm in the middle of death by Monday."

A familiar baritone chuckle filled the line. "So, what else is new?"

She didn't take offense, as she'd grown to appreciate Todd and his perceptions of her fast-paced life. They got along better now than even in their most positive moments as a married couple. Some people were meant to just be friends, and Todd had turned into a decent one. She was grateful for that.

"We need to talk about Raisin."

"What about him?" They still shared custody of the six-year-old dappled miniature dachshund they'd purchased in their last few months together, a Hail Mary attempt to save the marriage. It hadn't worked. While Raisin was home-based with Taylor, Todd took him for occasional weekends, including the one that had just passed.

"I want you to consider letting him live with me full-time," Todd said delicately.

"What? No, no, no. We agreed that he and I are bonded. We cuddle every night. We tug-of-war for hours as I work on the couch. He needs me. I need him. End of story."

"I agree with all of those statements, but he's left on his own the majority of the time. Tay, you live at the studio these days. That's not a criticism, just a statement of fact. If he moves with me to Denver, then—"

"What do you mean Denver? When did Denver come into play?"

He sighed. "That's the next part. I didn't want to say anything until I was sure, but I've taken a job with the Denver office. It's a step up. I couldn't say no."

"What? I don't want you hightailing it to Denver. Who's gonna be my sounding board? Tell me when I'm being an idiot?" Outside of Scarlett, Todd was the one who kept her world in perspective.

He chuckled. "While I can do that easily from Denver, there'll still be lots of back and forth to LA."

She stood. Todd was becoming a well-known architect in the world of education, building one celebrated high school after another. It had only been a matter of time before a promotion like this one hit. "Wow. Congratulations. I'm happy for you, honestly, but you can't take my dog with you."

"Our dog."

"You can't take *our* dog with you. Todd, Raisin follows me from room to room wherever I go. You've seen it. We're best friends." The concept of life without little Raisin had her in a minor panic.

"Then make a change, or I'm going to make him *my* best friend. I'm thinking of the dog."

Taylor blew out a breath and tucked a strand of hair behind her ear in frustration. Underneath it all, Todd was right. Raisin, whom she adored, got more quality time when he was with Todd. The long hours the show required seemed to have only gotten worse over the years, but she had an idea. "I hear what you're saying. Let me see if I can work out a better arrangement. If I can't, I will drive him to Denver myself."

A pause. "If you say so."

"I do."

"Okay, well, that's all I'm asking. I'll drop him at your place in an hour."

"Wait," she said, pivoting.

"What is it?"

"Would you mind dropping him off here?"

❖

"I don't think that's the best way to go," Taylor told Scruffy, one of her writers and a full-fledged producer on the show. He'd been with her from the beginning and was someone she trusted, regardless of the moody thing he always seemed to have going on. The story meeting was in its second hour and all minds were firing. "If we send Dominic down the addiction road, we're going to have to see that storyline through responsibly. In other words, I'm not willing to half-ass an addiction arc for convenience and then magically act like it never happened later."

"Agreed," Scruffy said. "I'm not suggesting we half-ass it. It has to become a part of who he is."

They'd been at it in the writers' room for a couple of hours, tossing around ideas for a mid-season shake-up. Their first pass weeks ago hadn't yielded much fruit, prompting a revisit of the subject. The morning had been made up of heavy silences as the wheels turned and the room pondered, interspersed with lively debates as proposals were batted around and examined.

Taylor thought on the prospect. "If we go for it, that pulls the character out of the world of women, where he's most loved by the viewership, and eventually away from racing."

Scruffy shook his head in frustration. "I'm just saying that it's time the character got a meatier storyline. He's played the role of town Casanova for four seasons. We need to do something with him!"

He had a valid point, and she valued his perspective. She turned to the other five members of her team, which now included Isabel Chase, who raised her hand.

"What do you have, Isabel?" Taylor asked.

Scruffy laughed. "You don't have to raise your hand, for fuck's sake."

Isabel passed him a look and held it for a weighted moment, which told Taylor that she wasn't a doormat. "I have to agree with this guy. Patchy, is it?"

"Scruffy," he corrected in the form of a touché and ran a hand over the scruff on his face absently. Point for Isabel. "The man-whore thing was fun for a while, but it's feeling played out to me as well. Shake his world the hell up."

Cedric and Lyle nodded. Candace, who served as story editor, furrowed her brow but said nothing. Taylor turned to Kathleen, the only other producer on the writing staff and the most levelheaded of the group.

Kathleen hesitated. "It's a slippery slope. I think we should go there, but keep him engaged with the core group. A happening-right-under-their-noses kind of thing, which can lead to some shock and awe from the other characters. Lisette especially. Aspen can play the hell outta that on camera. My suggestion would be, have him fall for someone for the first time in his sad, playboy life and have her lead him down the dark road."

"I like that," Taylor said, pointing at Kathleen. "I'd like you to take the lead on the storyline and write the episode that introduces it. We should talk about a character sketch for the love interest when you get there." She consulted her notes. "Let's intro that in episode 517." Kathleen offered a quick salute and began furiously typing on her laptop, likely to capture any initial ideas before they floated away.

"Taylor," Scarlett said, poking her head into the room prairie dog style. "There was a delivery for you."

"Great. Leave it in my office?"

Scarlett paused. "Not that kind of delivery." She opened the door wider and Raisin burst into the room and did a playful lap. Oh, right. She laughed. She'd temporarily forgotten her request that he be brought to the studio, but couldn't help enjoying his exuberance. Her staff seemed into it as well. Even Scruffy smiled. He did have teeth.

Taylor pointed at her dog, who was now sniffing Lyle's shoes as if his life depended on it. "Everyone, meet Raisin, my dachshund. Raisin, meet everyone. He'll be spending more time at the office due to, well, my crazy life."

"We have a mascot?" Kathleen asked.

Taylor nodded. "That's a good way to put it. Let's embrace that moniker."

"It seems the mascot has found his chair," Scruffy said, and inclined his head toward Raisin, who now sat quite contentedly on Isabel's lap.

"I'm so sorry," Taylor said, moving to her. "He'll be fine on the floor. I'll just—"

"Oh, no. He's welcome. We're bonding newbies. New writer. New mascot." Isabel smiled up at Taylor, who was caught off guard by the unexpected radiance. Isabel had a beautiful smile that made her eyes light up and her cheeks dust with pink.

She blinked. "You sure?"

Isabel shrugged casually. "I was hoping for a first-day security blanket." Raisin seemed to like that idea as he curled into a ball and rested his chin on his paw, as if ready to listen.

"Well, I guess Raisin's squared away. Why don't we press on?" She returned to the front of the room. "We need to talk about our crown jewel. Where are we going with Lisette's character?"

Cedric scanned his notes and jumped right in. "We could give her a pregnancy scare, which in the end leaves her questioning her relationship with Jackson. She wouldn't want kids with this guy. He's shady."

"Then she can finally notice Thomas," Isabel said, eyes still on her laptop. "And lose Jackson altogether."

All eyes turned to her in question. "Thomas? No, he's more of a brother figure to Lisette," Kathleen said, almost as a correction. "He dates her sister, Karen. He proposes to her in 510."

Isabel ignored the redirect and turned her gaze to Taylor. "If you put those two together, you're going to have water cooler conversation galore happening across the country the next morning. That's where the story is for Lisette. It's all about Thomas."

The concept was off the wall. The character of Thomas had been written in as an endgame love interest for Lisette's little sister. "We specifically cast that actor for his onscreen chemistry with Karen."

"Have you seen his chemistry with *Lisette*?" Isabel asked. "It was flying off my television. I had to add ice to my drink."

"Let's table that for now," Taylor said, not buying into the concept but not wanting to totally demoralize Isabel on her first official day. Isabel nodded and focused on her laptop. She took copious notes throughout the meeting, but didn't offer any further suggestions. Taylor found herself stealing glances at her as the meeting progressed. She'd occasionally scratch Raisin behind his ears. She also had a habit of running a hand over the back of her head. Why was she collecting Isabel Chase mannerisms?

The story breaking meeting came to an end, and the writers headed to their cubicles to tackle a myriad of different assigned tasks. Isabel, however, remained in her chair, typing away, her eyes trained on her screen.

Taylor paused, grabbed a script from her bag, and placed it in front of Isabel. "Will you do a rewrite of the dialogue on 512, specifically the first two acts?"

"Sure," Isabel said and scooped up the script. Taylor walked on, only turning back at the sound of Isabel's voice. "I hope it was okay, jumping in with that suggestion."

Taylor relaxed into a smile. She was glad to clear the air on the topic and wondering at the same time why she cared. It was one suggestion from one writer in a sea of them, yet it pulled at her. "You did fine. I have to admit, it was an odd proposal. I'm not sure I'd put those two characters together, but we're open to ideas. That's what meetings like this are for. Throwing things at the wall and seeing what sticks. Nothing's out of bounds when we're brainstorming. Remember that."

And almost like she couldn't help it, Isabel jumped right back into the argument, a hint of fire in her eyes. It made Taylor's stomach tighten and dip. "Watch them the next time they're onscreen together. That's all I'm asking, because I'm telling you, there's something big there just waiting for someone to write it. It's an unspoken spark between them, and it would be scandalous for those siblings to deal with the fallout. It's the ultimate betrayal, and they need a healthy dose of betrayal in their mundane little lives."

"You think their lives are mundane?" Okay, that one got to her. Maybe Isabel had that feisty side after all.

"I do, yeah, and I think we should mess with them more, if you want my opinion." She seemed to hear herself and backpedaled. "Though I'm not sure you do."

"No. I do. I just—I do." Why was she letting this get to her?

"Just watch. That's all I'm asking."

An unspoken spark, Taylor repeated in her head. *An unspoken spark.* "I will watch," she said. "I promise. Now if you'll follow me, we'll get you set up with a workstation." She escorted Isabel out of the writers' room and into the common workspace just outside of her own office. Cubicles dotted the space from which her team worked. "Any desk without personal belongings is up for grabs. Feel free to take your pick."

"Thank you," she said, meeting Taylor's gaze. The fire behind her blue eyes hadn't dimmed, and Taylor had to admit, she liked it. It had her all tingly, and it had been a while since that had happened. "I'll get started on those rewrites."

"Let me know if you need anything. My door is always open." Her standard offer. Making herself available for her team was important to Taylor. While their respect mattered, she needed them to know that she cared about what they had to say. Part of her job was to put out the best show possible, and she couldn't do that all on her own. The onscreen pairing seemed highly implausible, but she would pay attention to any Lisette/Thomas screen time because a talented writer asked her to.

She watched Isabel walk briskly to the back of the room to select the cubicle near the window, leaving the faintest trail of perfume, a scent Taylor wasn't familiar with. Cucumber, perhaps? Clean cotton? Something refreshing. Isabel had pulled her hair down three-quarters of the way through the meeting, and the thick dark strands now fell loosely in a tumble.

Taylor didn't have time for such inconsequence, however, and she propelled herself into motion. There was work to be done, and every second counted. Still...that glorious hair held center stage in her mind, and for just a hint of a second, she imagined her hands in it, which was an idiotic thing to imagine. She gave her head a firm come-to-Jesus shake. She would need to have a conversation with her inner self about boundaries. She walked back to her office, prepared to be productive.

"Hey, Scar?"

"What can I do for you?" Scarlett asked, following her to her office.

"Is the air-conditioning on? It's warm, no?"

She disappeared briefly, before returning. "An even seventy-two, as always."

"Huh. Interesting. Just me, then." She took a seat at her desk and ruminated. *An unspoken spark.*

Chapter Six

By the time Isabel pulled up to her apartment, it was past eight. Her neck ached and her brain had taken a holiday from the intense dialogue rewrite. She was worn out and highly interested in a dark foamy beer, five of which were in the door of her fridge like welcome little soldiers. As she trekked in from the parking lot, laughter emanated from the courtyard, and her muscles relaxed as she realized she was home.

"It's the new girl," a voice said as she approached.

"Isabel, right?" another voice asked quietly.

As she rounded the corner, she saw Autumn from the coffee shop and Hadley, who liked to read, sitting on the green-cushioned couches. Without even thinking, she collapsed in a heap next to Autumn. "Isabel would be correct. Or Izzy. Or Iz. I'm real, real flexible."

"Izzy is fun," Autumn said. "You strike me as an Izzy."

Hadley grinned. "You do. Long day?"

"Longest ever. I'm getting a beer. Anybody up for one?"

"I'll join you. Yeah," Autumn said. "Had hates beer," she added, to which Hadley nodded emphatically.

Isabel frowned. "That's a shame."

"It's not. It's awful," Hadley called after her as she dashed inside for a couple of beers. When Isabel returned, Hadley hooked a thumb her way and turned to Autumn. "Izzy here is a writer for *Thicker Than Water*. Did she share that little tidbit with you?"

"That show about the family? The one Celeste wrote for?" Autumn asked. "Get out. That's impressive."

Isabel held up a hand. "You might want to table that admiration. I'm pretty low on the totem pole. As in, I'm the girl waiting in line to be on it."

Autumn shrugged. "You're what? Twenty-five. You're right on track."

"Eight," Isabel corrected. "I'm twenty-eight, and that's old lady status in Hollywood-speak. Case in point, my boss is only four years older than me and already an executive producer and showrunner of one of the most popular shows on television and has been for more than four years."

"Taylor Andrews," Hadley said. "If she writes it, I'll watch it."

Isabel reflected on Taylor, the way she'd run the meeting with such finesse. She kept the writers moving, accepting and rejecting ideas summarily and without hurting anyone's ego. She knew what she wanted and how to achieve it, which was inspiring. What's more, her team seemed to really respect her. "She's good. The real deal."

"So, you'll be writing episodes?" Autumn asked. "And if so, which one will the character inspired by me be appearing in? Small business owner with a heart of gold meets a stunning woman with a mysterious past."

Isabel grinned. "A slam dunk. But as of now, I won't be writing my own episodes. I don't have a producer title, so I'll be used for things like research, script rewrites, or brainstorming."

"Still incredible to me," Hadley said, pulling her blond hair into a ponytail and giving her head a shake. "So, are you in love?"

"With Taylor?" Isabel asked automatically.

"No." Hadley laughed. "I just meant in general, but Taylor Andrews is certainly fair game in regard to the question."

Autumn leaned in to Isabel. "I should explain that Hadley collects information on the love lives of practically everyone she meets. She's a wide-eyed romantic."

"And Autumn exaggerates," Hadley said, and drank from her Evian bottle. "I'm a naturally curious person who happens to like a good love story."

Isabel nodded. "Got it."

"So, you're gay?" Autumn asked Isabel.

Wow, just like that. "Am I wearing a sign or something?" Isabel asked.

"Not at all, but it would have made this easier." She shrugged. "You just leapt to the Taylor conclusion way too quickly, so I thought it was a possibility. I hope you don't think I'm prying. You can tell me to back the hell off and I won't be offended."

"I don't think you're prying." It honestly wasn't a big deal. "I date women, yes."

"So do I," a broad-shouldered guy with blond hair said as he passed. His hand went up for a high five and Isabel obliged.

"Who was that?" she asked once he'd passed.

"That would be Barney," Autumn said. "He's a tool, but we like him anyway."

"We do," Hadley said, nodding. "He lives next door to you. Use him for chores. He loves it. So, you're not, then?"

"Not gay? No, I am. Very, very gay."

"Not in *love*," Hadley clarified.

"Oh, definitely not in love. Unless you consider vintage video games a relationship."

"Which ones?" a voice called from behind them. They turned to see the surfer girl heading their way.

"All of them," Isabel supplied. "But Adventure ranks pretty high, as do Circus, Centipede, Ms. Pac-Man, and Burger Time. But I'd give them all up for the Cyclone pinball game. I search them out as if it were my life's work."

"Look out," Hadley said, grinning widely. "I see a Gia/Izzy bonding moment on the imminent horizon, and it makes me happy."

Gia strolled to the couches wearing trunks and a bikini top, and Isabel wondered if she was cold beneath the night air. She certainly didn't seem to be. "Ms. Pac-Man high score?"

Isabel looked skyward. "I don't want to brag or anything, but we're talking over 100,000."

Gia sat on the arm of the couch and smiled down at Isabel. "Where have you been all my life?"

Isabel laughed. "I think there's a tournament in our future."

"Name the time and place."

Autumn raised her hand. "Can I ask a question? What is the difference between Ms. Pac-Man and Pac-Man? I'm sorry if I seem daft."

"Well, she has a bow," Isabel deadpanned.

Gia jumped on. "And the ghosts move in random patterns on this one."

"Yep. Too predictable in Pac-Man." Isabel shook her head in judgment. "I mean, where's the challenge?" She pointed at Autumn. "Oh, and Clyde-the-ghost has transitioned to Sue which, in my opinion, is super progressive for the eighties."

"Gotcha," Autumn said, glazing over and exchanging a look with Hadley. "While I'm happy you two have found each other, I'm opening tomorrow and should probably head home."

"It's not even nine," Gia pointed out.

"And while you sleep in, I'll be on the road at five thirty."

Gia winced and accepted what was left of Autumn's beer. "I always forget that part. Sorry 'bout that."

Autumn stood. "I will see you all in the morning for coffee."

A chorus of "you better believe it" and "I wouldn't survive otherwise" were her answers.

Isabel looked up at Gia. "So, you're a surfer?"

"I am."

"One of the best in California," Hadley said. "She's a real-life celebrity."

"I wouldn't go that far," Gia said, waving off the categorization.

Hadley grinned proudly. "I would. Tell her your ranking."

Gia didn't say anything.

"C'mon. I want to know," Isabel said, and took a pull of her beer. "Tell me."

"I'm currently eight."

"In all of California?" Isabel asked, because this state had a million female surfers. She'd passed them in droves on her way to work.

"In the *world*," Hadley countered. "She's number eight in the Women's World Surf League."

Isabel's mouth dropped open. "Holy shit."

Hadley pushed forward. "Last month, she was seven and sometimes she's nine, but you get the general idea."

"So you're really good, then."

"I do okay," Gia said. She didn't seem to be the type to toot her own horn, which was admirable. Hadley was all too happy to do it for her, again proving her big heart.

"She's amazing." Hadley put her hair back in the ponytail. Hair shuffling seemed to be her thing. "And often on the road during certain parts of the year."

"Oh, so a tour?" Isabel asked.

"The Samsung Championship Tour," Hadley told her. "Which is as good as it gets. I'll take you to watch her practice sometime when you're free."

"If you don't mind," she said to Gia.

"Nope. Maybe we'll even get you on a board."

"For laughs? Because that's all it would be." Isabel grinned, as she was beginning to enjoy her neighbors, a first in her life. "Just tell me when. In the meantime, I have to feed my cat and myself in that order."

"Night, Izzy," Hadley said.

"Night, you guys. And you, I'm very impressed with," she said, pointing at Gia as she walked to her apartment.

"Thank you," Gia said smiling.

"And you know, you're pretty great yourself," Isabel said, pointing at Hadley. "I'm not leaving you out. We have a beach date."

"Counting on it," Hadley said sincerely. "Get some rest."

Fifteen minutes later, Fat Tony ate slowly from his dish as Isabel lay flat on her back on Celeste's couch, staring up at the ceiling with a bowl of ramen on her stomach that she was too tired to eat. Her thoughts drifted to the interplay of the story meeting, the script she'd spent the afternoon polishing for Scruffy, and last but certainly not least, the subtle sway of Taylor's hips as she'd left Isabel with her assignment.

She had no business ruminating on that last part. No business at all.

Somehow, that didn't stop her.

❖

The following Tuesday, the clock in Taylor's kitchen read 6:05 when she emerged from her bedroom, dressed and ready for work in a T-shirt, blazer, and heels. Mornings were hard for Taylor, who required a little extra time before her ambition, not to mention her lucidity, floated back down to her from her night of slumber. Perhaps she was slow to wake up because sleep was scarce these days. But then, when had it ever been bountiful? She'd been slogging away in LA for the past ten years, working extra hours to prove herself in the world of television, widely dominated by men. She'd burned the midnight oil and then some, simply trying to keep up.

She took a fortifying sip of the coffee she'd brewed purposefully strong and watched as the California sun peeked from the horizon, casting ribbons of orange, pink, and red. Her home in the Hollywood Hills was inarguably her proudest possession and had cost her a good portion of her savings. Not only did it boast jaw-dropping views that left her guests envious, but the higher elevation had her feeling as if the house was her own little escape. Plus, because it was her first purchase post-divorce, the place felt innately…hers.

"Raisin!" she called to her dog, who was last seen snuggled up in his dog bed, paws tucked beneath him. "Time for the car!" That did it. Almost instantly at the word, she heard the clicking of his little paws on the hardwood and then his sleepy little face appeared around the corner. Raisin eyed her to be sure the promise was legitimate, and when he saw her extract his blue leash from the closet, he leapt into action, racing and twirling like a lovable maniac. She had to maneuver his excited little body in creative ways just to get him into his harness.

"Who's ready to go make a TV show? This dog is." Another twirl until, not sure what to do with himself anymore, he flipped onto his back in surrender. She ruffled the fur on his soft belly as he squirmed.

Distantly, she registered the repetitive vibration of her phone where it rested on the kitchen counter, but she'd learned not to jump at the sound or she'd never stop. When you're the executive producer, a myriad of people need things from you at all hours of the day and night. Some of those people would have to wait.

With Raisin ready for the commute, she snatched her phone and bag and headed to the door. She glanced casually at the readout to see that the most recent message came from Aspen.

I'll be wearing the blue scarf today. The one you think matches my eyes.

Taylor closed her eyes, and her soul sank. She'd learned many lessons during her time in television, but none rang truer than what she'd learned from getting involved with Aspen Wakefield: Don't sleep with people you work with. Do. Not. Especially when that person is vitally important to the success of your show. The relationship between her and her lead actress had only lasted four months, but oh, had it been a fiery four months, in more ways than one. Aspen was beautiful, smart, and successful. She also required a hell of a lot of attention and came with a temper she unleashed when she didn't get enough. Aspen also didn't seem to remember that the relationship had ended when she made out with a woman in the bathroom of a restaurant during a dinner party in Malibu. And now Taylor found herself in a difficult spot. She had two goals on that front: 1. Keep Aspen happy. 2. Keep her at arm's length. If she could accomplish both, she'd keep her show on track and her sanity in check. As for the text, she'd see Aspen at the table read that morning. No need to respond and encourage her further.

Taylor was routinely fifteen minutes early to the table read, and strategically so. If that week's director had any concerns about the script, she wanted to hear it right off the bat, so she and her staff could look for fixes during the read. It also gave her a chance to say hello to the actors, as those deliberate check-ins often served to head off problems before they could start. She made her way to the soundstage and joined the small group that was already gathering around the long table the cast would read from while the creatives listened. Assistants prepped each chair with notepads and bottles of water.

"Luke, how are you?" Taylor smiled widely at the actor who played Thomas, the same character Isabel Chase thought should be paired with Lisette. While the concept sounded ludicrous at the time, she hadn't been able to stop thinking about it. Maybe Isabel saw something she'd missed.

"Taylor," he said warmly, as he took her hand. "I'm great. Excited to hear what you all have in store for us this week."

"You're about to find out. And pucker up," she said, by way of a hint.

Luke laughed. "Aha. Things are moving along with Karen, then."

"Full steam." There was, in fact, a scene in this episode where Thomas surprised Karen, Lisette's younger sister, with flowers on her front porch after a rough day in court. While the coupling had been conceived as endgame, the probably stupid notion of a Thomas/Lisette pairing hung over her like a pushy little alarm clock that she couldn't seem to snooze.

Luke stepped forward. "Hey, I know you're busy, but I'd love to bend your ear about some thoughts I had about Thomas's trajectory next season. It might be somewhat, I don't know, premature, but if you have time."

"My door is always open." It was her standard reply to the actors, whom she very much valued. She wanted them to know she welcomed their input, though it didn't mean she'd use it in the end. She had to focus on the bigger picture.

"Great. I'll stop by next week."

"I look forward to chatting."

She turned in time to see Isabel approach the craft services table and pour herself a cup of coffee. Today, she sported a low and loose ponytail, a slim-fitting plaid skirt, and a black top. Taylor had no clue why she paid attention. Except that she sadly did and hated her lecherous self. While the entire writing staff wasn't required to attend the table reads, many did, and she'd specifically wanted Isabel to sit in and learn the ropes. Taylor crossed the room and joined Isabel, pouring a second cup of the day for herself. She should buy stock in coffee the way she fiendishly blew through it.

"Surviving your second week?" Taylor asked, as she reached for the creamer.

Isabel looked over at her, and pink dusted her cheeks.

Taylor stifled the thought that it was cute.

"Yeah, it's a faster pace than I was expecting, but I'm holding my own. At least I think I am." She lowered her voice. "Do you think I am?"

Taylor smiled. "I do. And this read-through will be educational as well. Sit next to me so I can guide you through it."

"Okay, sure. That'd be really helpful. Thanks."

"No problem." Taylor believed strongly that understanding the larger mechanism of the show and how it all happened helped shape a writer's work. When they got to see it all play out, they tended to grasp that the show existed on a budget and under the thumb of the network. Taylor was a big believer in not only utilizing her writers, but developing them for the business of television. She wanted them to walk away from this job ready to conquer the next one.

"Did you happen to get a chance to look at that dialogue rewrite from last week? Just wondered if I'm on the right track. Scruffy handed me his most recent draft to tweak."

Taylor opened her mouth to answer and was halted by the hand that snaked around her waist. "Now, this is a nice look for you," Aspen said. "The jacket says power, the T-shirt says creative."

"I think I was just going for dressed and out the door." Taylor delicately stepped forward and extracted herself from Aspen's arm, feigning a search for sweetener. Not only was the contact unprofessional, it was long past its expiration date.

"I don't believe we've met before," Aspen said, eying Isabel. "Aspen Wakefield. I play Lisette."

"I know." Isabel beamed the way everyone who met Aspen did. "A pleasure to meet you. Isabel Chase. I'm the new staff writer. I'll try not to blow anything for you."

Aspen's eyes lit up. She had a way of making people feel important, which wasn't a horrible quality. "A new member of the

Water family! We're so happy to have you. Taylor is the best boss anyone could ask for. You're going to love it here."

Taylor suppressed an eye roll at Aspen's compliment, because there was always an ulterior motive. "I don't know about that," she said conservatively. "But I do have an eye for talent."

Isabel bowed her head in thanks.

"Shall we?" They adjourned to the table, and the reading commenced. Throughout, she vacillated between watching the actors as they read and listening with her eyes closed. The script they were reading that day was one she wrote personally, and this was the first opportunity she'd had to hear the actors give voice to her words. There were several clunky lines that were apparent right off the bat. She made notes in her script to rework them ASAP and silently pointed them out to Isabel, who nodded. She was wearing that perfume again, and it reminded Taylor of those fresh fruit salads her mother would make on hot summer days. There was something comforting in that.

They approached the third act of the episode in which Lisette advises Thomas to go to her sister, that she desperately needs him. Only now a new subtext rose to the surface, the selfless Lisette once again sidelining her own feelings for someone else's, this time her younger sister. Taylor had her eyes closed as she listened to the words, but they flew open as the scene progressed. She watched the actors who sat side by side, and damn it if they didn't set off a few million fireworks. How had she missed this?

She turned wide-eyed to Isabel, who nodded knowingly.

As they walked back to their building later, Taylor turned to her. "I can't believe it, but you were right. There's something there."

Isabel nodded. "And there are many different directions you can take it."

"*We* can take it," Taylor corrected. "We're all on one team."

"Right. Right. We."

"Write up some ideas and send them my way. Preferably by tomorrow morning. If I'm going to drop a few clues in this week's script, I'll need to get the rewrites done quickly."

"I'm on it." Isabel nodded and headed off to her cubicle, seemingly energized by the validation. Taylor couldn't help but smile to herself as she headed back to her office to look at this week's script with new eyes.

"You have a visitor," Scarlett said as she passed. "I told her you were booked but—"

"Aspen?"

Scarlett nodded apologetically. "She doesn't take no for an answer."

"No, she doesn't," Taylor said, knowing all too well. "Raisin?"

"Asleep on my foot."

"I'm sorry. I can take him." She moved to Scarlett's desk, until Scarlett held up a hand.

"I actually kind of like him there."

Scarlett was good people. Taylor smiled at the soft snore emanating from the floor. "If you don't see Aspen exit my office in five minutes, call my desk line with an emergency."

"Way ahead of you."

Taylor sighed, gulped in some air, and opened the door to her office, ready to play nice with Aspen for a few minutes before shipping her back to the set. But Aspen was nowhere to be seen. That's when she saw that her desk chair faced the window. The blinds had been closed. "Aspen? Scarlett said you—"

"Close the door," Aspen said. At the sound of the click, the chair swiveled around to reveal Aspen wearing the same pencil skirt from the read-through, a pair of heels, and nothing else.

Taylor blinked and quickly faced the wall. "Aspen, what the hell? C'mon now."

Taylor heard her stand and then the clack, clack, clack of her heels on the floor. "You used to love it when I surprised you in your office."

"That was different. We're business associates now. And you're naked."

"We've known each other a long time now, Taylor. You're telling me we're not friends?"

She felt Aspen's fingers run down the back of her jacket and she closed her eyes. "No, we're friends."

"Good. Nothing has changed if you think about it. Turn around." Taylor reluctantly did as she was asked, thinking through how to delicately handle what she'd just walked into. Setting Aspen off was the last thing she wanted to do. They had a day of work ahead of them, and it was in her best interest to not summon Hurricane Aspen if she could work around it. Embracing that plan, she focused on Aspen's face, on her mouth anywhere but—dammit. She hated herself for looking. Aspen's body hadn't been the problem. She was gorgeous, heaven sent. She was also selfish, manipulative, and maybe even a little crazy. Aspen smirked at Taylor's misstep, knowing her power.

"It's okay to look. You can touch if you want to, too. I remember how much you like them."

No, no, no. As Aspen moved closer, Taylor stepped around her to the chair where she retrieved the discarded blouse. "A lot has changed, Aspen. You know that. And it's important, for the sake of the show, that you and I keep our relationship in perspective." She held out the blouse and waited what seemed like a year before Aspen accepted it and slowly slipped her arms into the sleeves, leaving it unbuttoned. Perfect. Taylor couldn't help but wonder what she'd done with her bra.

"All I'm saying is that we have fun together, and you know it."

Taylor flashed to Aspen hurling glassware at a wall just two months ago. "Tons. But now we have a job to do."

Aspen flashed a smile. "If we must. This week's script is *très* juicy. I really love it when you write the words I'm going to say."

"Yeah, well, it's my job."

A knock at the door. A knock? Scarlett must have forgotten the logistics of the plan. "Come in," Aspen called.

"What? No," Taylor said, but it was too late. The door flung open and there stood Isabel, laptop in hand. She looked from Taylor to Aspen to Aspen's unbuttoned and parted blouse.

"I can come back. Apologies."

"No apology necessary," Aspen said, buttoning her blouse.

"Impressive," Isabel said, and stared at the floor.

Aspen laughed. "Why, thank you. I'm late for rehearsal. Taylor, we'll talk later." Isabel stepped back and Aspen breezed past, looking every bit satisfied with herself.

Taylor did what she did best and remained calm in the face of shame. "What can I help you with?" she asked Isabel, who must have a million wild questions racing through her brain.

"Oh. It was just...I wanted to ask..." Isabel shook her head. "I honestly don't remember, because that was...not what I expected."

"No, I'm sure it wasn't. Well, let me know if you do remember. I have a lunch with the network."

Isabel nodded several times and headed off down the hallway.

For whatever reason, Taylor couldn't let it go. She hated what Isabel had just walked in on. Not only did it look bad, it was a wildly inaccurate representation of the truth. She couldn't let it stand. "Isabel, wait." She caught up with her halfway down the hall.

"Yep?" she asked.

Taylor shook her head as she tried to settle on the appropriate words. "What you saw back there was not at all what it looked like, I can assure you."

"Got it. We can just forget all about the boobs. Really."

"I appreciate that. But it matters to me."

Isabel's features softened and Taylor felt herself relax. She took note of the interesting cause and effect. "Okay."

"Full disclosure. Aspen and I used to date. We don't anymore. She hasn't exactly moved on, and maybe I'm saying too much, but for whatever reason, I needed you to know."

Isabel nodded and held Taylor's gaze. "I appreciate you trusting me with that information. Exes can be tricky. Especially ones that get naked in your office looking the way she does. Are you sure you want it to be over, because I might be overstepping, but..."

Taylor quirked a smile. "You don't hold back, do you?"

"I really should. My mouth gets me in so much trouble."

"I had a suspicion." They smiled at each other. "Do you remember what it was you came to ask?"

Isabel shook her head. She had an amazing smile, and from what Taylor could tell, it came in a variety of forms. Who knew so much could be communicated with a smile selection? She felt her cheeks heat, prompting her to glance away, hoping that little detail went unnoticed. "Right. Well. I better head to lunch, then." She turned and headed off down the hallway on unsteady feet, leaving Isabel probably wondering why she was cursed with such a lunatic for a boss.

"Taylor!" Scarlett called out as she approached the building with Raisin in tow. "Oh my God. Raisin woke up and I took him for a potty break and completely forgot about our plan."

"I'll kill you later rather than sooner, but only because I have to get to lunch."

Scarlett threw a glance over her shoulder to be sure no one was in earshot. "Was it bad?"

"If you call a naked crazy woman in your office bad, then bad. Very bad. No more granting her access to my office when I'm out. She cannot be trusted."

Scarlett's jaw went slack as she followed Taylor to the parking lot. "Taylor, I'm so sorry. I won't let her in again. It's just that when she wants something she's just so..."

"Presumptive?"

Scarlett pushed her glasses up on her nose. "I was going to say scary. She happens to terrify me."

Taylor knew all too well. "Just make up an excuse. Tell her my office is closed for fumigation. That the Secret Service is scouring it for hidden recording devices. Literally anything."

Scarlett nodded. "I can do that."

"Oh, and Isabel walked in on the whole thing."

"You should really fire me," Scarlett explained in horror.

"I wish I could, but you know where all the bodies are buried." She bumped Scarlett's shoulder in solidarity.

A ghost of a smile appeared. "That's true. I have that to cling to."

Taylor knelt and pulled Raisin into her arms. "After lunch, you're coming with me, mister. No more cheating on me with Scarlett. I don't care if she's extra nice to you." Raisin whined softly and rested his head on Taylor's shoulder. She, in turn, became a puddle of goo on the sidewalk. "I think someone's ready for his afternoon snooze." She kissed his warm cheek and handed him over to Scarlett. "See you in an hour once the network has been officially schmoozed."

An hour later, however, Taylor felt she had done anything but. After saying a few hellos to familiar industry faces, she'd settled into a table by the window at Cecconi's in West Hollywood. She loved the restaurant with its leather-backed turquoise chairs and perfectly spaced dining area. Gerald arrived shortly, and it appeared he'd gained even more weight than the last time she'd seen him. His stomach pulled further outward and his shirt size had not been adjusted. He'd always been a stubborn bastard, but she worried for his heart. To no one's surprise, he ordered his standard bourbon and Coke and paired it with a marbled ribeye. For lunch. Knowing he hated to drink alone, she'd gone with the lighter choice of a Chardonnay and the salmon special.

"We should do this more often," she told him, once their drinks arrived.

He nodded. "Always good to see you, sweetheart. You know I have a, uh, high regard for you and your show. You're my ringer."

Things went downhill from there. After the tiniest bit of chitchat, he leveled the news.

"We're moving *Water* to Mondays at ten effective next month."

Her glass of Chardonnay went still midway to her mouth, but only temporarily. Taylor played it cool as always, sipping slowly, knowing how important it was to never show any signs of weakness. "Is that so?" Moving the show from its prime spot at nine on Thursday would prove disastrous. Not only was Monday an undesirable time slot, but the less dedicated viewers wouldn't go out of their way to seek them out when they went missing on the schedule. It was a lose-lose, and a pill she was not about to swallow.

"I'm sure you're not surprised," Gerald said. "We're into a fifth season on *Water*. It's an important show for the network, but we have to keep our eyes on the future. You, uh, understand the old TV game."

"Sending us out to pasture a tad early, don't you think, Gerald?" She said it with her most serene smile firmly in place.

He tossed back a slug of bourbon. "Have you seen the early numbers?"

"I have. It's just a blip. We have a big season ahead."

He chuckled dismissively. "Well, you'll have to have it on Mondays. It's a, uh, done deal."

The telltale stammer had yet to evaporate, which meant there was more to this whole thing. She sat back in her chair and regarded him, searching for clues. She met his stare and didn't back down. She could play ball if that's what he wanted. "Nothing's a done deal in this town and you know it, so cut the bullshit, Gerald, and put it on the table so we can tussle over it here and now. What is it you want?"

He eyed her and she knew she wasn't wrong. "*Sister Dale.*"

"The stupid nun show? What about it?"

"It's tanking."

"You're damn right it's tanking. Unless you have Sally Field and a time machine, a primetime series about a convent was never going to find a solid audience in a world of grande Frappuccinos and Twitter feuds. Who greenlit that anyway?"

"It's Ted's daughter's show."

And there it was. Theodore Larkin was the president of WCN and apparently didn't have a problem with nepotism. In an unfortunate coincidence, she knew his daughter, Lyric, from high school. She was precocious, out of touch, and entitled. She also had a mean streak of which the high school version of Taylor had been the target for years. "I see," she said conservatively. Taylor didn't hate anyone, but Lyric topped the "not a friend of mine" list.

Gerald drained his bourbon and Coke. "It needs a patch job. Someone who can step in and get the narrative back on track. Tutor the kid on how to speak with directors. Show her some things."

"You want me to swoop in and save it." She closed her eyes. The concept of dealing with Lyric Larkin was hell on a stick, but stepping away from her own show to do it was what body-slammed her. "Tell me you're kidding. Gerald, you and I both know that I've worked too hard to babysit."

He waved her off. "It's temporary. Get the show back on its feet and ride off into the sunset as the hero who saved the network."

She sat forward. "I don't care about being a hero, and the network can take care of itself. I have my own show to run."

He shrugged. "So you go back and forth. Let Scruffy take the wheel in your absence."

"Like hell." She sipped her wine slowly. She would not let him see her unravel. "No one gets along with Scruffy. It's his goal in life to taunt others. I'd come back to World War Three."

"Then the girl producer. What's her name?"

Taylor sighed. "She's a woman, Gerald, with grown children of her own, and I can't believe you're doing this to me." She pinched the bridge of her nose.

"Look at it this way. You come out smelling like roses, Taylor. Save that floundering show and you prove there's nothing you can't do. You'll be writing your own ticket."

She met his eyes calmly, all the while dying inside. "When do they need me?"

He handed his credit card to the waiter. "Yesterday."

And just like that, she watched her perfectly choreographed life flutter away like shredded tissue in the Santa Ana wind.

❖

Isabel rolled her shoulders, pumped and ready to get to work. In less than two weeks working on the show, a suggestion she'd made was taking off, and she didn't want to lose momentum. This was her shot and she was not about to blow it. She pulled her hair into a ponytail and popped on her baseball cap, a ritual that seemed to help her focus. Staring at a blank canvas (in this case, the wall of her very gray cubicle) helped her mind tumble into the land of make-believe.

She spent time exploring the ins and outs of the characters as she'd come to know them. Lisette was levelheaded and kind, which, in the scheme of things, could be boring. If she were to prey upon her sister's boyfriend, she'd face an intense internal conflict and draw ire from the other family members. Plus, forbidden love could be hot. Viewers would be outraged but wouldn't be able to look away. The smartest route was to put Thomas with the younger sister, make her the happiest she'd ever been in her entire little-sister-life, all the while back-channeling a sparks-laden relationship with Lisette behind the scenes, leaving Lisette the choice to deprive herself or break the highest code of honor there was.

She made notes throughout the afternoon—not scenes per se, as she wasn't tasked with writing those yet, but details of what potential scenes might be comprised of.

Just after eight, she leaned back in her desk chair with one hand on her aching neck and one on her keyboard. Time to call it a day. She was proud of herself and some of the proposals she'd come up with and looked forward to sharing them with Taylor…whose light was still on. Well, look at that. She glanced around as she exited Cubicle Village, which was a ghost town. Dare she knock?

She did. She dared.

"It's open," she heard in response to her double knock. She swung the door open to find Taylor shrugging into her blazer. Her makeup had faded from the long day, but her friendly smile hadn't. God, she was easy to like.

"What's up?" she asked Isabel, her tone just as friendly as the smile.

Isabel lost her train of thought, blinded once again by her over-the-top attraction to Taylor, and the way Taylor's eyes shone brightly when she really looked at you, like she was right now. She blinked to refocus, because those eyes… "I was going to see if you had a second to talk Lisette and Thomas."

She hesitated. "I always have time to talk story, but I have to get out of here. It's been one of those days where nothing really goes right."

Isabel flashed to the scene she'd interrupted between Taylor and Aspen earlier. "Don't give it another thought, boss. We can chat tomorrow."

Taylor glanced up, seemingly amused. "Did you just call me 'boss'?"

Isabel nodded. "I did, yeah. I'm sorry. Did that sound flippant? I've been told I can come off flippant when I don't mean to be."

"That's okay. Sometimes I can come off as judgmental when I don't mean to be. Like now." She eyed Isabel as if circling around an idea. "Would you be up for a drink while we talk shop? I need to get off this lot. Two birds."

"Sure. I'd love one." She pointed at Raisin, who sat in his dog bed heartily chewing on a giant rawhide bone twice the size of his face. "Would he?"

"I know it's surprising, but Raisin's not a big drinker. He is, however, excellent at sitting outside. There's a spot across the street, Bo Jangles, and it's a nice night."

Isabel grinned. "I'm in. Let's do it."

Taylor grabbed her keys. "I'll meet you there in ten."

Turned out Taylor was right. While Isabel hadn't been outdoors since early that morning, the night had shaped up to be serene with only a touch of a chill in the air. A cocktail would chase it away rather quickly.

As they waited on their drinks, Taylor turned to her. "What were you doing with yourself before accepting my offer?"

"Is this still part of the interview?"

Taylor winced. "Sorry. No. I was honestly just curious. Let me try again." She made a show of loosening her shoulders, rolling her head around. "So, what was your last gig, or whatever? No big deal."

Isabel laughed. "That was an awful impersonation of casual."

"Hey!" Taylor said, joining her in laughter. "I should at least get some points for effort."

"Fine. But maybe don't ever do that again. You just be you. Put together and smart."

"So? What was it? Your last job?" She rested the side of her head on her fist and Isabel felt the butterflies.

"I'm afraid, with all due respect, I can't tell you that."

"CIA?" Taylor deadpanned.

Isabel laughed at the unexpected leap. She wasn't aware of Taylor's humor, but then again, her scripts were laced with tons of it. Made sense that it would transfer to the real-life woman. It was charming and a nice surprise. "I wish."

"Me too. We'd have built-in research on a future storyline." She stirred her whiskey sour and Isabel couldn't help but notice her hands, slender and feminine.

"Well, now I'm filled with regret."

"Don't be," Taylor said dismissively. "We'll find a way, even if we have to enlist Scruffy on the fly."

"I don't think he's happy about my joining the staff." The words were out of her mouth before she'd carefully weighed the wisdom of such a confession. She didn't want to seem needy or weak. In fact, she wanted to project the opposite.

However, Taylor didn't balk. "Scruffy's an asshole. To everyone. It's just how he was born. He happens to be a talented asshole, so we keep him. But if you're looking for advice—"

"I am."

"Give it back to him in spades. It's what he responds to."

"Now that, I can definitely do."

"From what I've seen, you can. So now tell me."

"Tell you what?" Isabel asked.

"What you were doing before coming out to LA." There was smiling, lots of eye contact, and a playful back and forth. Were they flirting? Isabel was fairly confident they were. It felt like the best kind of drug. "You've made a secret out of it, so I can't resist. I'm like Nancy Drew with a bone when it comes to people's backstories. It's the character writer in me. So, dish."

Isabel smiled at the imagery and knew there was no way around the truth. "It's humiliating, but I'll tell you." She sighed. "While you were running television as we know it, I was waiting tables in New Hampshire until the next writing gig came around the mountain. The former ensures the latter by design."

Taylor looked intrigued yet uncertain. "You might have to explain that one to me."

"Well, if I took a job I could tolerate, I'd get complacent. Lose my drive to make it as a screenwriter and lay up with the tolerable job. Food service is hell, however, which forced me to keep the writing momentum going."

Taylor sipped her drink delicately. "That's admirable, Isabel. I envy that kind of hunger. How's the drink?"

Isabel set down her Chianti. "It's smooth."

"Mine is already working." She gestured to her glass, her eyes widened, signaling the strength of the booze. "They don't hold back here."

"Good."

Taylor laughed, and it was melodic. "Why good?"

"So, when you're slightly on the tipsy side, I can bend your ear with all of my industry questions and not feel as foolish. Plus, it also helps *me* get to know *you* better."

She studied Isabel. "You're fearless, aren't you?"

"I'm not. But I'm good at pretending." She flashed on her most recent panic attack before shoving it aggressively from her mind.

Not now. Not when she was having such a nice time. "What I am is ambitious and sitting across from someone I admire."

"You're sweet."

She shook her head. "I'm honest." Isabel decided to seize the opportunity. "What made you want to executive produce as well as write?"

"Now who's the interviewer?" Taylor rested her chin on her palm, and Isabel stopped breathing for a moment as goose bumps prickled her skin.

"It's only fair." Her thought was interrupted by Raisin, who chose that moment to yawn loudly and at a very high pitch. She and Taylor chuckled, as did the occupants of the neighboring table.

Taylor reached down and gave his head a pat. "Raisin has had quite a day."

"He did. He spent half of it asleep in my lap."

Taylor's eyes went wide. "He did?"

"Don't worry about it. He seems to like my lap. Plus, it was the most action I've seen in months."

Taylor nearly spat her drink across the table, which made Isabel laugh and hold her hand out to make sure she was okay. Taylor sputtered into a coughing fit, pounded her chest a few times, and finally sat back in her chair, wiping her eyes. "You have to warn a person."

"Sometimes they just fly out of my mouth."

"I'm learning. And you know what? I think I like that about you, Isabel Chase."

"Finally." That's when Isabel noticed something remarkable. The piercing green eyes that had captivated her over the past two weeks were now distinctly gray. How in the world had that happened? Those eyes alone had her coming apart, her skin humming pleasantly, her whole body warm.

"But, to answer your question…"

Right, there had been a question.

"The executive producer title ensures I have the last word. I don't know if you've noticed, but I'm a control freak." As the waiter passed, she signaled him for a second. "I try not to be when it comes to the writing staff, but the network is another story. I need it to be my show, my way. And if you get your own show one day, fight tooth and nail for that title. There's nothing worse than an EP who doesn't share your vision."

"Trust me when I tell you that I'm jotting notes." About so many things. Taylor had the hint of a dimple on her right cheek and a freckle just to the side of her eye.

"While we're on the topic of work, I want to apologize again for earlier. Mortified does not begin to cover the feelings that came out of that…scenario."

"We've already done the apologizing. We all have exes. Some are just more famous than others."

"That's true," Taylor said, deflating.

Isabel dipped her head. "Hey, I didn't mean that as a hit."

"Yeah, well, if you're still taking notes, that's another. Don't sleep with the people you work with. Especially if they're more powerful than they are stable." Well, that was an unfortunate revelation.

Isabel lowered her voice. "Aspen's not stable?"

"I exaggerate." Taylor's second drink arrived and she took a moment with it. "She's less than predictable. That's a better way to explain her."

Isabel had always been good at reading people, and the look on Taylor's face suggested she was backpedaling from perhaps too much honesty. "Fair enough."

"I can't believe I ordered a second. I never do that, which says something about my day."

"How long were you together? If you don't mind my asking, and I fully realize you might."

"Four months." She shook her head. "I knew it was an awful idea after two."

"I once had an ex steal my identity, if that helps. My credit has still not recovered."

Taylor covered Isabel's hand with her own. "Bless you." When she pulled her hand back, the air between them was thicker. They'd both noticed that touch, the spark, and the smiles had all but faded. Isabel was confident that alcohol had stolen the safety of inhibition, and if this were any other woman, she'd go out of her way to take this one step further. But she wasn't stupid. Taylor Andrews was out of her league and had just announced she'd sworn off work-related romance.

"We're going to be friends, aren't we?" a slightly tipsy Taylor asked with a shy smile.

Isabel nodded. "I think we are."

"This ex, did he go to jail?"

"*She* did not. She journeyed into the world to ruin the lives of many more to come."

Taylor paused as if something important had just occurred.

Another long silence ensued. Taylor sat back and Isabel smiled, reaching down to pat Raisin on the head. The street lamp to their left buzzed and the table nearby laughed. Isabel was enjoying herself. And though she wasn't positive, tonight felt significant.

CHAPTER SEVEN

Justin Timberlake accompanied Taylor on her drive through the hills that night, and the lighter traffic had her singing right along with him. The day had been full of twists and turns, much like the roads she took now. Her drink with Isabel was a definite bright spot and might have been partially responsible for her high notes.

The idea of spending time with Lyric Larkin on her silly nun show had been the opposite. Lyric was nothing but a potent reminder of a time in her life when Taylor's own self-worth was startlingly different from what it was now. She didn't think about those old high school days anymore for a reason, but alone in her car, under the veil of the night sky, she allowed her mind to travel.

Ninth-grade gym had always been the nightmare portion of Taylor's day. Except, with a nightmare, at least you could always wake up. For Taylor, her high school years had seemed never-ending. Her mother had been a casting agent and her father a props artisan, which left her growing up right in the middle of Los Angeles and everything sparkly and shiny. This included the students at Hollywood High School, who floated through the halls without touching steady ground. To say that most of them came from famous parents was not at all an overstatement. To say that nearly all of them were beautiful, and rich, and highly judgmental wasn't either.

If you weren't a ten on the looks scale, you were instantly outcast. Your only chance at redemption was a famous parent to dangle in front of the elite as payment for taking up space. Taylor, being forty pounds overweight and from two unheard of parents, wasn't even up for social consideration. In LA, it was far more acceptable to be a drug addict, liar, or common thief than it was to be overweight. She'd committed the ultimate crime and thereby existed only to entertain the students who came with names reflecting either exotic locations or sexy objects. Paris, Lyric, and Cloud, yes, Cloud, were the worst of her classmates and sought to make her life a living hell for sport. Did she report them to the administration when they'd left a live rat in her locker wearing the nametag Tubby Taylor? Of course she did. But things had only gotten worse from there. Centerfolds from *Playgirl* had been taped to her backpack when she wasn't looking with the words "The Object of Tubby's Dreams," scrawled across the male model's picture-perfect abs. Lower on the page, they'd written, "Tubby Taylor sucks on this." As horrifying as the experience was, she never did correct anyone or argue that she didn't dream about men at all—out of fear for how much worse things might get. Why give them another reason to paint her as different?

Taylor blamed those adolescent years for the extended amount of time it took her to finally admit that she was, in fact, gay. A failed marriage to a guy she actually liked and years of lying to herself were certainly influenced by her early need for acceptance. Now, she could shake her head at the lunacy of it all, because Katia Rolinski, with the dark curls and smoky eyes, should have cleared it all up for her if nothing else had. She was a grade older than Taylor in high school, and a good two notches above her on the social ladder, which still wasn't high. Katia was scholastic and opinionated, not unlike Isabel Chase, now that Taylor thought about it. She argued back against the beautiful elite and called them to the carpet when they said or did something hateful. She snuck cigarette breaks and read poetry quietly to herself. Katia had captured Taylor's attention when she'd debated their history teacher, for twenty straight minutes, on the merits of the English monarchy. She'd somehow found the nerve to mention it to Katia when she saw her reading in the corner of the library.

"I thought what you had to say in history class was spot-on."

Katia had looked up and smiled. As in, she didn't look past Taylor or offer a belittling comment. She *saw* her. "Thanks. I perhaps should not have argued, but I couldn't stop myself. You sit at the back, yes?"

Taylor nodded. "Yes. I don't say a whole lot."

"And why is that?"

"Not a ton of people care what I have to say."

Katia slid the chair next to her out with her foot, and that was the start of Taylor's first real friendship since elementary school. They'd started eating lunch together at the back of the cafeteria to avoid the Bostons and Candles of the school. Katia's exotic past was what kept the popular kids at bay and her torment level set to low. She'd been born and raised for the most part in Prague and thereby came with a certain amount of intrigue that got her a pass. She'd lecture Taylor in her thin European accent on the importance of environmental preservation, to which Taylor would nod and moon, and nod and moon, thinking Katia was the most wonderful and attractive person she'd ever met. When Katia left for college two years later, Taylor thought she'd seen the last happy day of her life. She'd emailed Taylor once just to check in on her, but that was the last she'd heard.

Taylor's naïveté hadn't been limited to her sexuality. She'd also had no concept that she'd go on to leave a decent-sized footprint on the world through the simple act of storytelling.

She remembered the moment it had all changed.

"What are you staring at, Tubs?" Lyric had asked one afternoon, perched atop her desk before trigonometry like the princess she truly believed herself to be. Her father was a television producer and her mother one of the most famous actresses in all of Hollywood.

"Did you not hear the question?" her sidekick asked.

"I'm not looking at anything," Taylor said simply, politely. "I'm just waiting for class to begin." To escape from the moment and their accusatory stares for her merely breathing the same air, she'd buried her nose in the leather-bound journal her mother had given her for Christmas and set to writing straight away, anything to look busy, anything to make them lose interest. It had worked. Lyric and Co. had moved on to discussing their very busy weekend of shoe shopping and party planning, but Taylor didn't stop writing. She also didn't employ the journal to record her thoughts, as her mother had intended. Instead, she used the pages to write a short story. And the next day, another. The more she wrote, the more invisible she became, wrapped in a world of her own creation, where she was in control and safe and sane. She wrote until she had more stories than she knew what to do with. Generally, her plotlines surrounded an underdog character who won out in the end, stories where the ugly duckling rose to power and showed all the beautiful ducks once and for all that she was worthy. While those kinds of tales were fantastically motivating, she moved beyond them as weeks turned to months and her pen kept moving. She wrote about dragons, and wizards, and stockbrokers, and teachers, and high school kids, and the elderly. No subject was off-limits or beyond the bounds of Taylor's imagination.

"The short story you submitted for class is really quite

exceptional," Mr. Delacroix told her one day when he asked her to stay after his creative writing class. She'd selected the course as an elective her senior year, hoping to score more time to write. Mr. Delacroix took off his glasses and regarded her with a candor she wasn't expecting. He seemed to truly mean it. For the second time, she felt like someone *saw* her. "I've never read that level of precise detail from a high school student, and I've been teaching a long time. I didn't want to put your story down, Ms. Andrews. It was that good. Have you considered writing as a career? You have a flair."

A *flair*. She took a moment with that. Someone thought she had a flair, and they weren't just saying so to be nice or cheer her up. Mr. Delacroix wasn't the type. "I'd like that very much," she said, attempting to hide her smile and losing the battle. He thought she could be an actual writer.

"You'll have to put in a lot of work, but I think it just might pay off. USC isn't an easy school to get into, but you have an impressive GPA. You should take a look at their dramatic writing offerings." He reached behind him and handed her a brochure. It felt like a ticket of sorts, and she ran her thumb across the bright colors and texturized paper, enjoying the weight of it in her hand. Taylor still had that brochure, tucked securely away in the jewelry box on her dresser. It was too important for the attic.

After that conversation, she'd found her stride and pushed herself that much harder.

In a remarkable turn of events, she was accepted to USC, and though she couldn't come close to paying for it, she'd taken out a gazillion dollars in school loans to attend. She'd also tentatively joined a gym and slogged away day after day until, one pound at a time, the weight crept off. She'd learned healthier eating habits and how to not use food as a method of cheering herself up when she was feeling down—the hardest of all habits to break. The thing was, Taylor had never been obese. She just hadn't fallen into the one percent, a necessity at Hollywood High.

What a strange feeling it was to receive an appreciative look as she walked down the sidewalk. The concept of people taking notice of her was foreign and odd and, well…not awful. Who knew that under the weight, she was decent looking. Maybe even, dare she say, the slightest bit pretty.

Working with Lyric in the here and now, however? A gut punch, and one she needed to wrap her brain around, and fast, before it undid years of work. No, Lyric Larkin and her crazy affinity for wacky nuns was not about to get her down again. She would fix that show, get back to her job, and find a way to stop noticing Isabel Chase.

Her to-do list was a lofty one, sure. But she'd been up against worse.

❖

The nuns, it turned out, were in complete and utter fucking shambles. It didn't take Taylor long to come to that conclusion once she arrived outside the *Sister Dale* soundstage, two weeks after her meeting with Gerald. Members of the production staff walked past on the sidewalk like victims wandering around a nightmare. She knew that look. She'd worked on shows like this one, limping along without direction. The concept that you were weeks from unemployment could be suffocating.

"Hello, Ms. Andrews."

"Ms. Andrews, hi. It's so nice to see you."

"Taylor, good morning."

"Welcome to *Sister Dale*."

The way the production staff responded to her made it clear they'd been briefed on her new role. The tiny bit of hope that crossed their downturned faces jabbed at Taylor, because she honestly felt the ship was likely to sink regardless of what she did. The world was less interested in zany nuns when they could have outer space, serial killers, and political warfare with just a flick of the remote control. It was difficult enough to keep a family drama like *Water* relevant.

"Excuse me," she asked a woman carrying a large rug on her shoulder. "Lyric Larkin's office?"

At just the mention of the showrunner's name, the woman's face fell before she remembered herself. "Through there," she grumbled and pointed at the building next door to the soundstage and continued on her way.

"Thank you for the help," Taylor called after her. She followed the woman's directions and walked to the building much like the one she worked in for *Water*. She sighed at the thought. *Water*, where she'd much rather be right now. With her staff. Shooting her show. Living her life, not someone else's.

The writers' office was noticeably quiet, lacking the normal chatter she was used to, where staff bounced ideas off each other, off her, or just shot the breeze. The environment here felt sterile, cold, and solitary.

She approached a young man at his cubicle who typed with a ferocity she had to admire. Okay, so maybe they were just working extra hard. "Can you direct me to Lyric's office?"

Upon recognizing her, he stood and ran a hand through his curly locks. The kid couldn't have been more than twenty-three. "Ms. Andrews, hello. I'm Seth, a story editor on the show." Another brush of his hair.

She admired the way it sprang back into place each time, like those Superhero punching bags from her youth. "It's a pleasure to meet you, Seth."

"Likewise. I'll take you to Ms. Larkin's office."

Ms. Larkin seemed formal, but maybe Seth was just on his best behavior for visitors. Once he delivered her to an emerald green door, he said a quick farewell and dashed back to his cubicle. Eager kid.

"Come in," Lyric called from behind the door. Taylor cringed. The voice could best be described as singsongy Kardashian and hadn't changed in years.

"Lyric, good to see you," Taylor said upon entering.

"Taylor, thank God. I mean, thank *God*! It is so wonderful to lay eyes on you." She made a high-pitched noise in celebration. "How long has it been?"

"About thirteen years and four months," she answered evenly.

"Seems like yesterday you were wobbling around the halls of our high school, and now look at you. Fantastic! You lost the weight and then got all successful."

"Just to clarify, I'm not successful because I lost weight. Those two things don't exist on the same plane."

"Oh, I don't know about that," Lyric said, and shimmied her shoulders several times in punctuation. "I believe all things are cosmically connected, don't you?" She didn't wait for a response. But you know what? Lyric had changed, too. Her medium blond hair was now garishly bleached. She wore it straight and long and it looked like she'd gone extra hard on the ol' Botox. Her lips didn't move a whole lot when she spoke, and her eyebrows looked...hard, like Taylor could maybe bounce a quarter off them. She kind of wanted to try.

Deciding to skip the rest of the small talk, Taylor jumped right in. "The studio asked me to step in, as you know, to see what I can do to help with the show's—"

"Shhhh," Lyric said, and rushed to close the door behind Taylor. "No one knows we're failing."

Taylor glanced at the door and back to Lyric, squinting. "Don't they, though? The ratings are public knowledge."

"Do you think they look at them?" Lyric asked, horrified by the concept.

Taylor hooked a thumb. "The staff? Only if they want to…eat."

That prompted Lyric to burst into tears, and not the delicate kind. This was a mascara sprinkler for the ages. Taylor vacillated between taking cover or taking action. Her mature side won out. "Oh. Oh. You're crying. Well, okay," Taylor said, taking her by the arms and steering her to the plump pink—yes, pink—couch next to a desk with a bright green chair. She would marinate on the bold color combination later. Lyric always had been a trendsetter. Maybe Taylor was just late to the pink and green party. "We can't have you crying," she said, attempting to sound soothing and rubbing her back for good measure. "You're the big boss around here."

"I'm not!" Lyric wailed. "The show's about to be canceled and I have no clue what to do. Everyone hates me. The network! My father! My father's mistress!"

Taylor forced herself to move past that last one. "Well, that's why I'm here. To help. This is actually something I'm pretty good at."

Lyric stared at her. "I had no idea you were smart back in high school."

Taylor stared at the ceiling and chose not to push back with "because you never once attempted an actual conversation with me." But Lyric was already shuffling in the highest of heels around her desk. Taylor looked on in intrigue as she began to assemble odd and crumpled sheets of paper. She then took out a tape dispenser and pulled out the longest piece of Scotch tape Taylor had ever seen. "These are the scripts for the rest of the season. They're in pieces because I got angry, but we can—"

"Is it possible you could email them to me?" Taylor asked. "Might be simpler than re-taping." She glanced around, wondering what the chances were that she was on the hidden camera show that shot regularly a few stages down.

"Email," Lyric said and took a lengthy pause. "Yes, I can figure out how to do that." She quickly went to work on her computer, humming what Taylor decided was the Honeycomb commercial from her youth. She tried it out. *Honeycomb, big, yeah, yeah, yeah. No, not small, no, no, no.* It fit. She hadn't been wrong, but the fact that Lyric had it running on repeat certainly made it hard for Taylor to concentrate on any work of her own. She also now craved cereal.

"Done!" Lyric said nearly half an hour later. She seemed to have relaxed, and a ghost of a smile settled on her barely movable face.

"Great," Taylor said, taking out her laptop. She downloaded the scripts as Lyric fixated on her phone. As she opened each file, she picked up on a startling trend. "Hey, Lyric?"

"Yes?" Her eyes still hadn't left her phone.

"Every single one of these scripts says it was written by you. Is that a typo?" No answer. "Lyric, what's so important on your phone?"

She held up one manicured finger, and after a long pause, "Hold on just a sec. Candy Crush." Unbelievable. After nearly an entire minute of silence passed, Lyric raised her gaze with a victorious smile. "Not a typo, I write everything myself. I'm a hard worker."

"Everything?"

"All of it. Every word. Penned by moi." She wrote the cursive of the word in the air and dotted an imaginary "i." It would have been cute, if the implication wasn't so tragic.

Taylor took a moment, attempting to latch on. She was starting to detect her first problem. "Well, then what about your staff? I was told you have seven writers and even some freelancers lined up for episodes later this season."

"That's true. I do. The staff is out there. At their desks." She pointed eagerly at the door as if she'd solved Taylor's problem.

She thought back to Seth typing so earnestly. "This is what I don't understand. If you're writing everything, what are *they* doing?"

Lyric took a moment. "I honestly don't know. I just figured they had things to do."

That did it. Taylor opened the door and walked to the grouping of cubicles in the space adjacent. "Can I have everyone's attention?"

A handful of surprised faces rose from the dividers like meerkats in an open field. These meerkats looked nervous. Taylor pointed at the guy at the back, the one with the beanie. "Can you tell me what you're working on?"

He stared at her as if unsure whether to speak or run. "Oh, you mean me?"

She smiled to let him know she meant no harm. "Yes. You were all very busy when I walked in, so I was curious what it is you're working on."

"Right." The guy nodded and exchanged glances with his coworkers. "We were. Busy." Clearly, he was refusing to commit.

"But doing what?" She turned. "Seth, I might need your help here."

He did the rake and bounce with his mountain of curls. "I am working on a screenplay."

"Same," said the bored-looking girl across from him.

"Spec script for *Thicker Than Water*, actually," Beanie Guy told her. He leaned her direction. "I'd give anything to work on your show, Ms. Andrews."

"Fascinating," she said, taking it all in. Was this real life? She took a minute to decide. They went around the room, and the answers all carried the same depressing theme. These writers were being paid full-time salaries to either work on their own stuff or twiddle their thumbs. She didn't blame them for their choice.

"You've all been very helpful."

Ten minutes later, she sat in front of a very angry-looking Lyric.

"I don't want them touching my scripts."

"That's what they're here for. They were vetted and hired to *help* you. They're professional writers."

"They want me to fail!" She started to shake. "I can see it in the way they eye me when I walk past them."

"Lyric, they absolutely don't want you to fail. Those are expectant looks. They're just waiting for you to give them something to work on, probably longing for it. As showrunner, it's your job."

Her hands were up and moving around her face like spiders. "I think we need to take a break. I need to speak to the network right away." Code for running to Daddy. But Taylor had a job to do, and the quicker she did it, the quicker she got back to her own show. She left Lyric in her office and headed back out to the staff.

"Meet me in the writers' room in two minutes," she said, breezing past their desks. As she waited, they shuffled in one at a time. Some looked excited, ready for whatever it was Taylor had to say. Others looked like they'd been caught with their hands in the cookie jar and dreaded the forthcoming punishment. She glanced around the room, making eye contact with as many of them as possible before beginning. They needed to know that she cared, but also that she meant business. They had no time to waste.

"As most of you know, my stay on *Sister Dale* is temporary. However, you can expect changes, and you can expect them soon. Be ready to come at me with ideas starting later today in our story breaking session. Script assignments are forthcoming. I'm afraid you'll have to say good-bye to your screenplays for a while. See you after lunch."

To their credit, the writers looked relieved, and that was an excellent sign. After a trying morning, Taylor knew she needed to step away for lunch and give herself some breathing room. She set off across the lot for the Water Tower Café and waited patiently in line for her standard green salad with chicken.

"Hey, there," a voice said behind her. She turned around to meet the eyes of Isabel Chase. Though she'd only been gone from *Water* half a day, it felt like a lifetime. She had to refrain from crushing Isabel, someone familiar, into a hug. She missed her show and the people who worked on it.

"Isabel, hi." She grinned. "And how is your day going?"

"Oh, you know, just doing some script polishing, which seems to be my usual, and then the screening this afternoon."

"Right. The screening." She felt her smile falter. She'd be missing it and would have to watch the episode on her own time rather than with her staff, which was their tradition. The line shuffled forward and Taylor grabbed a tray.

"Kathleen updated us all on *Sister Dale*. You don't have anything to worry about. She's got everything under control. You have fun with those nuns. Send them on the run. Give them guns. Write them puns."

Taylor raised an amused eyebrow. "You're on a roll."

"I need to be stopped."

"You need to be *dones*," Taylor said with a triumphant smile.

Isabel covered her face. "Oh, man. I thought I was bad." They chuckled and moved forward in line.

"I know Kathleen will be just fine filling in. She's always been levelheaded and practical." Taylor met Isabel's eyes. "You realize that with me doing double duty, there's going to be more work for you coming down the pike." She smiled at the woman in a chef's apron. "I'll take the salad with chicken."

"Kathleen's already talked with me about writing an episode."

"Oh, yeah?" Taylor nodded. It made sense to pull in the rookie writer, now that she was out of pocket more. "That's a big deal. An entire episode your first season out of the gate. That doesn't happen too often."

"I better put up or shut up, huh?" Isabel laughed. "I'll take a cheeseburger all the way."

There was something about the confident way Isabel just ordered her unhealthy lunch that Taylor had to admire. She held up her plastic salad bowl lamely. "You're making me jealous."

"Yeah, well, there's a reason I don't look like you."

"You look fantastic." She hadn't even hesitated. While a hundred percent true, it probably would have been better to have laughed off Isabel's comment.

"Thank you," Isabel said, and met her stare evenly. Yep, those were tiny little fireworks going off in the air around them, right there in the middle of the damn lunch line. Isabel accepted the cheeseburger that looked like heaven on a plate. But now Taylor's mind fixated on how fantastic Isabel *did* look. Her dark hair was tucked behind her right ear today and she wore the most interesting lace-up flats with her black jeans. She couldn't have been that much younger than Taylor, but she came with a devil-may-care exterior that Taylor found infectious, and with a more vulnerable interior that made her human.

Taylor paid the cashier and glanced over her shoulder. "Let me know if you need any consults on that episode. I'm sure Kathleen has made herself available, but I should be by the office tomorrow."

Isabel nodded. "You're on. And, Taylor?"

"Yeah?"

"Nuns in buns. You got this."

Taylor shook her head. "For all our sakes, let's hope so."

Isabel wasn't sure, but Taylor might have checked her out earlier that afternoon. Scratch that. She *had*, and it had been life altering. Isabel had knocked the thought aside until the very long workday had ended, but she pulled it back out again as she walked to her Honda Civic. She hadn't been hallucinating. Taylor's eyes had run down her body for the briefest of glances while they'd waited in line for lunch, causing a noticeable shiver to roll through her. Thinking about it now had the same effect. Shivers galore.

"'Night, Jesse," she called to the gate guard through her rolled-down window. "Don't hit up that cigar bar behind your wife's back tonight."

He waved her off. "I don't know why I tell you my damn secrets."

"Because I demand it in exchange for Hershey Bars with Almonds." In the few weeks that she'd been working on the lot, she'd made a habit out of dropping him snacks. She adored the iconic gate, so she had to adore Jesse. They went together.

"That's true," he conceded. "I forgot about that part for a short minute. See you tomorrow, Ms. Chase."

"Call me Izzy or I'm breaking up with you," she yelled, as she turned right out of the studio and into traffic. If she weren't so tired, she'd have pretended to be mega-important as she drove off the Paramount lot, one of her favorite fantasies.

But no, still just her, a very tired version longing for a microwavable bowl of ravioli and a Mike's Hard Lemon. The drink made her think of her father back home in Keene. With the three-hour time difference, he'd likely just be getting home from work as well and would be popping a Mike's the second he did. He worked hard running lines for the local cable company and spent his weekends fishing with his buddies. Isabel was his only child, and he'd raised her all on his own when her mom handed her over as a baby and never looked back. Their life together had been simple—peanut butter sandwiches in front of the TV, not a ton of conversation—but at the same time, that had been comfortable. She understood her dad, and he got her right back. Their home may not have been bubbling over with large displays of affection and laughter, but he was always there, a sturdy presence she could depend on.

"So, you're going to La-La Land?" he'd said, when she'd told him about her job offer. He'd stood on one side of the kitchen counter and Isabel on the other. He still lived in her childhood home, all nine hundred square feet of it.

"That's the plan."

"You nervous?"

She nodded.

"Nah, don't be. You're gonna eat 'em all for breakfast." He'd handed her a Mike's and popped one for himself. They'd cheered silently, and his eyes briefly filled before he sucked up the emotion. Because this also meant she'd be leaving.

"I'm gonna be back to visit all the time, Pops."

"Course you are," he said, and began shuffling through the mail. "And you'll be right there on the TV. Stuff you wrote." He ran a hand across his full beard several times. "That part is cool. My daughter, writing for the big Holly Wood."

She smiled, enjoying that he thought so. "We'll have to coordinate on Christmas."

"Well, you know my busy schedule." He glanced at her and then back at the mail. They both knew he didn't have one.

There wasn't a ton about Keene that she outright missed, but her dad was one exception. She made a mental note to give the guy a call and make sure he was eating.

When she arrived home at Seven Shores that night, she found Gia sitting on the stairs, third step from the bottom. She wore cutoffs and a sweatshirt, her dark hair in a braid that fell down her right shoulder, enviable tan still firmly in place. She glanced up from the laptop that rested on her knees when she heard Isabel approach. "What's up, Iz? You been out on the town tonight?"

Isabel sighed, as that would have been something. Having a life. "Not even close. Just wrapped up at work. Not easy being the new kid on the block. Lots of busywork."

"I'm sorry to hear that."

"So, what are you up to out here?" she asked.

Gia shook her head, and it was clear that whatever it was, it troubled her. "Part of my life I hate the most. PR. I've found that fresh air helps me concentrate, so I'm giving it a go outdoors."

Isabel tilted her head, trying to understand. "What exactly are you giving a go?"

Gia gestured to her laptop. "I have a publicist, and she's great for sponsorships, things like that. But she also sets up these interviews that I hate." She gestured to her screen. "So tonight I have these questions I'm supposed to answer for this important surfer blog, and they need them by morning." She shook her head. "It's not what I do. I don't explain things well, especially on paper."

"It is what I do, though. Move over." As tired as she was, Isabel took pity on her dejected-looking new friend and took a spot next to Gia on the stairs. "May I?"

Gia happily handed over the laptop. "Okay, but you have no idea what you're getting yourself into."

Isabel waved her off. "Please, Surf Queen. Let me do my part. Question one. In the Maui Women's Pro, you never really found your footing with only seven point rides in heats two and three." She looked to Gia. "I have no clue what that means. Is that bad?"

"It's not good." Gia shrugged. "Sometimes you have off days."

"It's rude of them to point it out."

Gia nodded emphatically. "Right? Doesn't stop 'em, though."

Isabel nodded and refocused on the laptop. "So, the question is, how do you shake off a disappointment like that and go on to steal gold in the Cascais Pro just two weeks later?" She looked to Gia, waiting for her answer.

"Oh, you want me to…right. Okay." She thought a minute. "Well, you push it out of your mind and concentrate on the wave in front of you. Nothing else. If you allow all that noise into your head, you'll miss your timing and the wave will own you instead of the other way around."

Isabel went to typing, doing a tad bit of polishing for the written version. She turned the laptop to Gia for approval. "All right, surfer chick. Survey says?"

After scanning the few lines, she beamed up at Isabel. "You're a genius, that's what it says. The problem is when I *write* my answers rather than just saying them, I come off sounding like an uptight idiot."

"Then speak the words first and tweak as needed. We can do this one together so you get the hang of it."

Gia shook her head in awe. "You're saving my life. I don't know why I hadn't considered that."

"Because it's not your job to. Hey, Hadley promised she'd take me to watch you surf this weekend. Are we still on?"

"Saturday is a practice day for me. I can surf and then we can chill."

"I'm in on the chilling, though I sound lame saying it."

Gia nodded. "You'll get better."

Isabel gestured to the laptop apologetically. "In the meantime, we have six more of these. You ready or do you need to do a few wind sprints to gear up?"

"I think I'm good." Gia nodded for her to continue, and the two of them hammered out her interview. It turned out to be a lot of fun, and Isabel learned a great deal about surfing, a topic she knew next to nothing about previously. She decided to file Gia away as a great source for surfing research, should she ever need it.

"And now I just have to attach my bio and I'm set."

Isabel held up one finger and set to typing. When she was finished, she dusted off her hands and handed the laptop back to Gia. "Wrote that for you, too."

"Gia from upstairs is the queen of surfing. She surfs better than you walk and requests a lightsaber and tiara in recognition of said accomplishment." Gia nodded several times at the screen as a grin spread slowly across her face. "Can I have this framed?"

"I'd be honored." She stood. "And that's my grand finale. Until tomorrow, Surf Queen."

"Hey, Iz?"

"Yeah."

"This would have taken me hours to get right. You saved my ass. You're gonna slay this new job."

"Either slay it or fuck it up." She lifted her hands and let them drop. "I think it could go either way."

Gia quirked her head. "I'm gonna stick with slay."

"I'm lusting after my boss," Isabel blurted. She blinked hard, shocked by the words that had flown from her lips. "Hardcore. And I also really like her as a person."

Gia stared at her. "Well, damn. Okay."

Isabel shook her head at her own lunacy and walked to her apartment door. "Ignore me. Everyone should. I should ignore myself."

Gia didn't seem fazed and, in fact, was smiling. "Well, does she lust back?"

Isabel paused and turned back. "No, not at all. Except for maybe a little. Unless it's just my overactive imagination."

Gia stood. "Maybe it's not."

"It had to be. I'm a pathetic loser," she said matter-of-factly. "My role in life is clear, and I accept it with grace."

"I don't know Grace, so I think you should stick with the boss."

Isabel pointed at her. "You're a funny one."

"My advice? Follow the lust. Always, always follow the lust. Work hard. Play hard."

"Are you speaking Nike to me?"

Gia nodded sincerely. "Nike gets life, and I'm not gonna be embarrassed for thinking that."

"Mmm-hmm. Learning more about you each day, new neighbor."

Gia pointed at her as she headed up the stairs. "Don't forget the beach this weekend. Forecast is right for killer swells."

She smiled up at Gia through the railing. "I can't wait. Swells will abound."

"And bring sunscreen for that snow white northern skin."

"I'm feeling judged," Isabel called out.

"At least you're owning it."

"'Night, Surf Queen."

"'Night, Iz."

When she snuggled into bed that night, Isabel could no longer escape it. As she ruminated on her day, her week, her struggles with Scruffy, her attraction to Taylor, she was hit with a jolt of crippling imposter syndrome. While she hadn't had another panic attack since arriving in LA, she consistently felt them looming, circling like vultures. The little voice in the back of her head seemed to gain more and more momentum as the days rolled forward.

It's only a matter of time before they realize you have no idea what you're doing. You're out of your league, and soon everyone will know.

You're not good enough.

You never will be.

Go home.

She blinked hard against the mental assault. Tears pooled and her heart felt like it might break out of her chest. Deep breaths, she reminded herself. She sucked in air, and as the ringing in her ears hit, the sense of dread descended over her like a straitjacket. She gripped the sheets and balled her fists and waited for the self-imposed prison to release her.

CHAPTER EIGHT

Taylor couldn't believe it was already late September, but the rain outside signaled that the blue skies of summer might be firmly behind them. With Raisin curled in a circle on her lap, Taylor flipped to page one of the new *Water* script, the one written by Isabel on her very first time out. This was a big deal for a new writer, and she was interested to see what Isabel had turned in.

It had been raining since late the night before, and she heard the drops pelt the windows of the *Sister Dale* offices, creating a noticeable rat-tat-tat that somehow helped ease her into reading mode. In the office across the hall, Lyric Larkin was prepping for a writers' meeting in which they'd offer feedback to Seth, who'd penned the latest episode. Until then, she had time to focus on *Water*.

The script in her hands, however, left her anything but relaxed. Isabel had not only run with the Lisette/Thomas storyline Taylor had okayed, she'd taken off with it like a rocket ship. This was not innuendo, or flirtation, or anything relying on suggestion. In other words, way beyond the scope of anything she'd talked with Isabel and the staff about.

What the hell was going on over there?

This had to have come from Isabel and Kathleen putting their heads together. She read on, shocked at the blatant direction of the storyline and irritated that they'd go this far, so soon, deviating from the slow-burn plan. Isabel had gone full steam ahead and forced the two into a secluded cabin in the woods after a flat tire stranded them. She flipped the page to find a fire roaring and Thomas unbuttoning his drenched shirt. She rolled her eyes at the cliché. This wasn't going to fly. Lisette as a blatant man-stealing whore? She'd never done anything like that in the past. Taylor needed to discuss the new direction with Kathleen, and quick. She fired off a frustrated email and copied Isabel.

She picked up the phone. "Scarlett, have you read the new *Water* script?"

There was a long pause on the line. "I have. It's awesome."

Taylor stood. "It's not awesome. It's overboard and reckless to just shove our lead into a wildly new and morally questionable relationship without laying more groundwork. The struggle, the internal battle has all been glossed over. It's flimsy."

"Or just accelerated." Another long pause. "I think," Scarlett began delicately, "that the reason I liked it so much was that I didn't see it coming and then once I did, it really just…works. It's also really hot."

"Yeah, well don't get too attached." Taylor clicked off the call and stared up at the ceiling. It had only been two weeks since she'd handed over the reins, and now all hell had broken loose. Unbelievable.

The door to her temporary office burst open and Lyric stood there with eyes resembling a heavily mascaraed owl. "The nuns are going to Vegas? They would never leave the convent for Sin City. Never! You think nuns gamble?"

Taylor held up a hand and mentally prepped herself for the battle she'd known was coming all week. "Hear me out." Lyric began to pace the length of Taylor's office as if she were trapped, and in many ways, she probably felt she was. Her show was being hijacked from beneath her by someone she'd spent most of her youth squashing like a bug. "You've established a comedic theme throughout the whole first half of the season. All of the marketing is geared to a wacky nun show. But there's only so much comedy one can find within the convent walls, ya know? Let's let these girls get their nun on."

"Sister Dale is human, though," Lyric said, referencing the show's protagonist. "She's not a cartoon character."

"Nor should she be." Taylor stood to join Lyric. "But her adventures are going to have to be a lot more fun to pull in more viewers, or the show won't see a second season." If this show was renewed, regardless of what they did, Taylor would eat her hat with mustard. Even she wasn't that good.

"No, no, no. This is not what I'd envisioned for my sweet Sister Dale. This is so very wrong. It's like a nightmare."

Taylor tried to soothe. "I know it's not what you intended, but sometimes you have to bunt."

Lyric turned to her, pausing her pacing. "Like the cake?"

She sighed. "Sure."

"And you think this is for the best."

"I know it is. And while I have you here, Lyric, I'm gonna be out tomorrow. I need to spend some time over at *Water*. There's a few fires to put out. Can you handle a script meeting with the staff?"

Lyric stared at her. "Do we have to keep Vegas?"

"We do. Seth wrote this one and the script is funny. Give it another read."

She nodded numbly and stared at the ground like the most dejected toddler not ready to go to bed. "Can I pet your dog?"

Taylor softened. "He would love that." She passed Raisin a "be sweet to her" look which must have worked, as he immediately rolled onto his back and offered up his tummy for a rub. Lyric smiled and obliged him.

Score one for Raisin, the therapy dog.

The recognizable rhythm of salsa music floated out to the courtyard when Isabel arrived home. The door to Hadley's upstairs apartment stood open and Barney, the Gia-described tool who lived across from Isabel, bopped his head from just outside their door, sipping what looked to be sangria. Autumn emerged and waved down to Isabel.

"Hey, sweet girl! You coming up?"

"Coming up to what is the question. What's going on?"

Autumn took a few steps away from the apartment and leaned over the railing. "It's Latin night!"

Isabel cocked her head. "Not computing. That's a thing?"

"Around here, yes. Hadley is all about the once-a-month theme parties for us all to get together and cut loose. It makes her happy, so we do it. It's also kinda fun. Come up and snark with me!"

Well, how could one resist such a conveniently placed Latin night? Isabel decided she could indulge in a glass of sangria. "Snark on the way!"

"Izzy's here!" Hadley said as Isabel entered the apartment, which at first glance was laid out much like her own. Only upon further inspection, it wasn't like hers at all. To begin with, where her living room ended, Hadley's opened to a second bedroom that she'd turned into what seemed to be a sewing room, complete with a creepy faceless mannequin. Secondly, the place looked like it came straight out of an interior decorating magazine.

"Wow. This place is gorgeous."

"That's Hadley for you," Gia said, ladling a glass full from the punch bowl brimming with fruit and wine. "For you." She handed the glass to Isabel.

"I'm a fan of clean lines," Hadley told her. And apparently complementary colors. A variety of beiges, creams, and a dash of recurring sage worked together to create a serene color scheme.

"Can I hire you to do my place?" Isabel asked. "I can pay in cans of Campbell's soup."

"What? Not a fan of the desert?" Hadley looped her arm through Isabel's. She wore what looked to be a flamenco dancer's costume. Scarlett red with a line of ruffles. Her blond hair was secured in a tight bun. Lucky for her, she had the looks and the body to pull it off easily.

"Would it surprise you to know that it scares me? Howling wolves and reptiles are the things my nightmares are made of."

Hadley winced. "In that case, I will be happy to waive my fee, because we're friends now, right?"

Isabel grinned. "We are. More soup for me." She gestured to the outfit. "You really go all out. I wouldn't have the guts."

"I can help with that, too. Next month we're celebrating the Irish, so search out your green ahead of time. I can lend you buckled shoes if you like." She glanced down at Isabel's feet. "I'm guessing a seven and a half."

"Next month is October," Isabel said, trying to make the connection she knew wasn't there.

"I just really like St. Patrick's Day," Hadley said, as if were the most obvious thing in the world.

Gia laughed. "It's best not to ask questions. Hadley just enjoys life. Many, many aspects of it."

That earned her Hadley's elbow in the ribs. "You get free snacks, so how about a little support?"

Gia wrapped Hadley in a sideways hug and gave her a shake. "For snacks, you have my undying support."

Autumn pointed at the action from the couch. She had her feet up and still wore her Cat's Pajamas T-shirt from work. "I second that motion and am available for menu consultation."

Isabel slid into the spot next to Autumn on the couch. "You didn't dress for Latin night."

She turned her face against the couch to Isabel, dropping her tone. "I tolerate the themes for Had. I'm here for the people. And the booze." As always, Autumn served as the voice of reason.

They clinked glasses as Barney and his muscles cha-cha-ed his way past, wearing a matador's hat. "Hey, new girl," he said, and bobbed his head. "Doin' that new girl thing?"

Isabel bobbed back. "Hey, Barney. Yep. Sure am." Whatever the hell that meant.

He continued his dance solo around the living room, and Autumn grinned. "Barney's a keeper for no other reason than he entertains the hell out of me. Watch him. He's entirely off rhythm and couldn't care less." Isabel was starting to appreciate Autumn's wry outlook. They were kindred spirits that way. "He'll also happily change a hard-to-reach lightbulb, which should be filed away."

Isabel tapped her head and pointed at Autumn in gratitude.

"What's going on in here?" a male voice said from the doorway. They glanced up.

"Larry Herman, as I live and breathe." Isabel wondered when she'd run into the guy again.

He turned to her. "Ms. Chase. Is this a party?"

"Not even close," she deadpanned. "A get-together, and a very quiet one."

He stood taller, and didn't seem sure of her answer. "I see you've met the neighbors."

"I have."

"Some sangria, Larry?" Hadley asked from the punch bowl, picking up the ladle and letting the fruity liquid trickle like a beckoning waterfall.

He seemed mesmerized by her for a moment but then held up a hand. "No. No alcohol." His lips pursed and his brow seized up. "I have a re-enactment in the morning. I have to be fresh."

Hadley grinned. "Larry is a member of a history buff club of some sort. They do little plays."

"The Preservation of Dramatic History," he said quietly, through gritted teeth. He turned to Isabel. "We don't do plays, we re-enact history with precise attention to detail."

"What's being re-enacted tomorrow, Larry?" she asked.

"The Battle of Yorktown."

Gia shook her head. "Can't say I know it. I sucked at history in school."

This seemed to ruffle Larry's feathers and he blew out his cheeks.

Isabel jumped in. "Victory of the Americans over the British. Are you playing Washington, Larry?" Her tone shifted in exaggerated awe. "Do you get to play General George Washington?"

More agitation. His eyebrows drew in. "No. It's a very long and sordid story, but I will not be playing Washington this time. I lost out to Timothy Bottoms."

Isabel stared at him evenly. "With that name, I think Timothy lost a long time ago."

He snapped out of it. "I better go home and look over my notes while I'm thinking about it. But I swear, if there is a report of a loud party, I will be back."

Hadley smiled. "I promise you, Larry, I will make sure we stay quiet."

He softened and bowed his head to Hadley as his cheeks glowed pink. He seemed to like her. "Thank you."

As Larry headed to the door, Isabel turned to Hadley. "So, we can have a loud party later though, right? We just have to wait until he's gone?"

"No!" he said loudly, whirling around. "No loud parties ever. None. That's the main rule!"

She smiled and pointed at him happily with both index fingers. "Gotcha." She would never get tired of Larry Herman and the fun she had with him.

"That's not funny," he deadpanned.

"Yes, it is," she deadpanned back.

Autumn covered her mouth in amusement. "I think you've met your match, Larry."

Larry stared Isabel down. "Ms. Chase's ability to match me has yet to be determined." He turned once again and exited the apartment.

Isabel stared after him and shook her head slowly. "He's so many things wrapped up in a tight little ball of hostile."

"He means well," Hadley said. "He does."

"Why is he so nice to you?" Isabel asked her.

Gia fielded the question instead. "I think he needs a girlfriend, and I think he wants her name to be Hadley."

"Yeah. He's gaga in love with her," Autumn said.

"He's not in love with me." Hadley joined them around the couch. "He just has a soft spot for me."

"Is it called, 'Please, softly get into bed with me'?" Isabel asked innocently.

"Let's keep this girl," Gia said, and indicated Isabel with her chin.

Autumn nodded. "I second the motion."

In spite of the ribbing, Hadley softened. "Unanimous. Now I need to introduce Gia to my friend Richie, who doesn't believe I actually know her."

"Who says you do?" Isabel heard Gia quip as they headed off across the room.

"Behave," Hadley admonished.

"Hey," Autumn said, and gestured to the very gothic, very pierced, highly tattooed woman who filled the doorway. "Iz, have you met Stephanie yet?"

"That would be a no," Isabel said. "Should I be afraid? She's glaring at the room."

"Only a little. Steph," Autumn said, signaling the sullen girl. "This is Isabel. She lives in the unit below you."

Stephanie blinked at Autumn in mild toleration. "No, Celeste lives in the unit below me," she said, in a monotone delivery. There was a large spike through Stephanie's eyebrow. Isabel swallowed and wondered absently how much effort it would take to impale someone with it.

"Not anymore," Autumn told her. "Isabel moved in last month."

"That's extraordinary," Stephanie said with the excitement level of someone who'd just been told their flight was canceled.

Isabel attempted an olive branch of a grin. "Well, it's cool to meet you. And if you ever need anything, you know, just knock and—"

"Yeah. Super *cool*," Stephanie said, looking through her. "Steer me to the food."

Autumn and Isabel pointed to the table across the room in unison. "She dislikes me," Isabel whispered once Stephanie had gone. "Intensely."

"Yeah. You're done for. Stephanie's bad side is…not where you want to be." Isabel turned but saw that Autumn was smiling. "Relax. That's just how Steph is. Brooding. Terrifying. You get used to it."

Isabel raised a half-hearted shoulder. "Yay."

"What are we celebrating? Did you score with the boss?" Gia asked.

"What boss?" Hadley stared at them, taking a seat on her coffee table across from Isabel. The music shifted to a sultry salsa beat, which felt both perfect and inappropriate for the topic at hand. Stephanie leaned against the wall and munched a taquito aggressively. Barney twirled.

Isabel focused on the question. "Her name is Taylor. But it doesn't matter. She's been out of pocket for the past couple of weeks, and it was stupid to begin with."

"Taylor Andrews," Hadley whispered. A smile blossomed on her face and she grabbed her heart. "Of course it matters. I should have seen this coming. One attractive writer falling in love with another attractive writer. Sultry glances across their laptops. Like sands through the hourglass. Oh, I'm gonna love hearing about this one developing."

"Not in love. Not in love at all." Isabel scrubbed her face, realizing that she was about to confess all, and maybe that was good. Using her friends as a sounding board might actually prove helpful. "All right. Yes, I have a crush, and how could I not? That woman comes with the kind of beauty that slams a person's throat shut. You just have to accept that kind of fucked-up punishment because that's what life demands." It was all pretty cut and dried to Isabel.

"Wow," Hadley said. "I want to slam some woman's throat shut." She turned to Gia with hope in her eyes. "How can I do that?"

"Just be you," Gia said gently. "There's only one Hadley. Plus, you don't give yourself enough credit for being hot. Girls on the beach check you out all the time. You just forget to notice because you're thinking of ways to make the world better. That makes you unique."

Hadley nodded. "Okay, I like that. I can work with that. I'm a hot do-gooder," she said quietly to herself.

"Now that," Isabel said, pointing, "is the kind of self-affirmation I need."

"I'm willing to share the moniker," Hadley said.

Isabel shook her head. "I'm more of a sardonic, jaded train wreck than a do-gooder, but I appreciate the offer."

"So, what's next with you and the boss, then?" Autumn asked Isabel. "Or will there be a next step, given the hands-off policy you're implementing at work?"

Isabel shook her head and sliced her hand through the air. "There will not be a next step. The buck stops with the crush. The torturous, all-consuming crush. Besides the obvious conflict of interest, she's way out of my league. Dates starlets and people with lengthy IMDB pages."

Autumn placed a hand on Isabel's knee and nodded. "I think that's a very mature, adult approach."

Hadley shook her head sadly. "It's also a boring approach."

Autumn held up a finger. "It's not, if you think about it. This is her livelihood we're talking about. Not to mention, she's still new at her job. This is not the time to make waves, professional or erotic ones."

Hadley wasn't done, her starry-eyed innocence in full effect. "Since when does a paycheck trump love?" While sweet, it wasn't exactly an identifiable sentiment to Isabel, who valued living in the land of hard-core realism.

"When it just doesn't make sense," Isabel answered. "And when I finally have the dream job in my eager little hands. I just need to keep my head down and my eyes off Taylor Andrews."

"So, *you* work for Taylor?"

Isabel looked up to see that Stephanie had pushed herself off the wall. "Yes. I do."

"Right on. That lady's my boyfriend's aunt. We're having dinner with her this week." And with that, Stephanie headed right out the door, leaving a very confused Isabel grappling.

"Wait. What?" Isabel asked, pointing after Death in Doc Martens as she exited the apartment. She turned back to the group. "Stephanie knows Taylor? Stephanie. Knows. Taylor. This is awful."

Gia looked confused. "That's the longest sentence I've ever heard her speak."

Isabel moved her hand in a circular motion. "And she heard everything I just said, right? I mean, we're sure about that?"

Hadley looked thoughtful. "It's hard to say with Stephanie. Sometimes I think she's checked out and other times not so much. She's a hard one to pin down."

"Hey," Autumn said, reining her in. "Just because she knows your boss doesn't mean she's going to race off and tell all. Like Had said, she's a quiet girl. I bet she stays that way."

"A quiet girl who has already made up her mind about me," Isabel said in combination of shock and dread.

Autumn nodded solemnly. "I'm thinking more sangria."

Gia and Hadley leapt up in pursuit, while Isabel contemplated how quickly one could die of mortification.

Chapter Nine

Taylor luxuriated in the feeling of being back on home turf. She'd even brought snacks for the script meeting, hot little pigs in a blanket. Okay, she'd *ordered* pastries for the meeting, but the thought was there, right? People would appreciate that. She made a point to arrive in the writers' room first and smiled and greeted each member of her staff as they filed in. Why was she nervous and obsessively grasping at the sleeve of her suit jacket? She never did that.

Kathleen and Isabel walked in with their heads together in a quiet chat. She hadn't seen Isabel since their cafeteria run-in some weeks back. She looked...amazing, and seemed more sure of herself and in control—that is, until she met Taylor's eyes and her smile faltered. She offered the briefest of nods before heading to her chair at the table, her cheeks coloring noticeably.

Conversely, Kathleen made her way to the front of the room to greet Taylor. Normally, her gray hair was pinned neatly into a bun. Today, a handful of strands fell haphazardly from the pins, as if escaping a house fire. "Am I glad to see you," she said quietly, as the other writers made small talk.

"Oh, come on. It can't have been that bad."

Kathleen frowned. "I had no idea how much you did around here. I come with a newfound respect. Over these past few weeks, I've barely had time to sleep."

"You're sweet. I'm just a phone call away if you need anything. I mean that."

"I didn't want to bother you."

Taylor smiled sweetly. "I'd much rather you bother me than be blindsided with a script I'm not on board with."

Kathleen hesitated. "I anticipated that. Give me time to convince you."

"I'm willing to listen." But she carried lingering doubt. Kathleen had returned Taylor's email the night before and had been quite receptive to the criticism. However, to her credit, she'd held her ground and they'd agreed to table the discussion until the script meeting.

"How are things on *Sister Dale*?" Kathleen asked as she took her seat next to Taylor.

She met Kathleen's gaze. "It's a shit-show, no pun intended, and it's sucking my soul into a never-ending oblivion of dreck. Shall we begin?"

Kathleen offered a curt nod. "Let's."

After a few welcome-backs from her staff, Taylor kicked off the weekly script meeting in which they'd critique the most recently completed script, in this case, Isabel's. The staff would have already read the script with the goal being to suggest improvements, point out roadblocks, and make sure the storyline advancements fit with what the other writers had been (and would be) writing in the future.

"It's bold," Scruffy said, kicking them off. "It's not something I would expect from Lisette, which is both positive and a shot in the foot." He ran a hand up and down his beard thoughtfully. "We might be showing our footprints."

"So, you think it's heavy-handed," Taylor said. Validation already. This was going well. More of this, please, so she could safely back them away from this pitfall.

"I didn't say that." He glanced at Isabel. "The cub over there has brought us a script that's either brilliant or a disaster. I haven't decided which."

Isabel nodded, but said nothing.

Lyle sat tall with a burst of energy. "I'm just gonna say it. I hated it. I hated it a whole lot, and then I loved it. Finally, the Goody Two-shoes sibling is shaking it up. It's time."

"I had the same reaction when I first heard the direction Isabel wanted to take this episode," Kathleen said. "But it seems to me that she's right. We'd already agreed on the Lisette/Thomas storyline. This episode just speeds us along."

"Right about what?" Taylor asked, feeling flabbergasted by her team's response and more than a little defensive. Maybe more so because having been away for the past few weeks had her feeling like an outsider.

"This is the time to go balls to the wall," Isabel said, finally speaking up. "That's what I told Kathleen, and it's a sentiment I stand by. The show has played it safe for years now, keeping Lisette on some pedestal while her siblings cause all the trouble."

Taylor jumped in. "And will you stand by it if this is our jumping the shark moment and our numbers fall even further?" A pause as she glanced around the room. "Yeah, I didn't think so." She took a seat, frustrated that she didn't see what her team did. Faced with a moment where she had to decide whether to lead or delegate, Taylor took the hard line. She scanned the faces of her staff. "I think we have to reshuffle. Cedric, we'll move your episode, 409, in place of Isabel's. It will require some minor rewriting for continuity, but it's what's going to happen." She saw Isabel out of the corner of her eye fixate on her script, shrinking into herself in either anger or dejection, making notes in the margins of her pages. She offered zero eye contact, which meant she was taking this hard. She'd been sidelined on her first time out, and Taylor knew how much it must burn. Fortunately, she didn't have the time to fixate on the feelings of a fledgling staff member, no matter how much she strangely wanted to and no matter how much Isabel's reaction affected her.

"Let's map it all out." Taylor moved to the whiteboard as details of their upcoming storylines were sequenced and cross-checked. Isabel seemed to perk back up and offered several suggestions on how to make the reshuffle work. She hadn't directed any of her comments to Taylor, however, and that said something. When they finished the restructure, the writers scattered to embark upon their respective assignments. "Isabel, if we could talk in my office?"

It took her a moment to answer, when she did her voice was clipped. "Be right there."

Taylor didn't look back as she exited the room, but after a slight delay heard the sound of footsteps behind her. There would be no value in sitting behind her desk for this particular conversation, so she instead sat in one of the chairs across from it. When Isabel arrived in her doorway, she gestured for her to sit in the other one. "Would you mind closing the door?"

Isabel took a seat and turned to Taylor expectantly.

"I know you're unhappy."

"I'm fine," Isabel said, but there was no hint of a smile, no smart-ass remark that Taylor had come to learn was her signature. Her demeanor was flat and sharp, which said it all.

Taylor's job, however, was to remain calm and in charge. As such, she needed to tamp down her own emotional reaction to letting Isabel down, because why the hell did it matter? She took control of her voice. "You're not fine, and that's to be expected. What I need you to know is that the script itself is excellent. You're just ahead of yourself in the narrative."

Isabel nodded, her eyes still dull. "I defer to your opinion. You know a lot more than I do." She stood and turned to the door, seemingly unaffected and beautiful, but probably pissed off underneath it all. She opened her mouth as if she just had to say something and then closed it again.

"You can say it, you know."

She met Taylor's gaze. "Say what?"

"That it sucks. That I'm wrong."

"Well, you are." Her beautiful blue eyes flared.

Aha, there was the fire Taylor knew was bubbling beneath the surface. Somehow it felt better to have it leveled on her overtly. "It's possible."

Isabel stepped forward, as if with that one sentence, she had unleashed the rest, like a boulder rolling downhill. "It's a good script and we should shoot it. On schedule. Take a chance, Taylor. Maybe I shouldn't be saying all of this, but I wouldn't be able to sleep tonight if I didn't. Fire me, but I have to stand up for myself on this one."

Taylor shook her head. "I know what's best for the show."

"Which is why you're in charge, but maybe you're too close to it. I've been on the outside looking in for a while now, and I feel like I have a perspective that might be unique." It was a bold thing to say, and she saw the recognition flicker in Isabel's eyes just as she started to backpedal. "Maybe I'm naïve and going to regret all of this tomorrow, but I'm asking you to reconsider."

What the hell? Was she actually considering Isabel's request? Taylor sighed. She was splitting her time between shows, barely sleeping, distracted by a new hire, and really, what the damn hell did she have to lose? Her staff was on board and ratings were slipping. Maybe going out on this limb would pay off. She doubted it, but maybe.

"Fine. Let's do it."

Isabel narrowed her gaze as if not quite believing it. "Let's do what?"

"Let's shoot it. Your script."

"No way. You're not serious." Isabel studied her, probably trying to assess the turnaround. Taylor passed her a look. "You mean it?"

"Believe it or not, I do." Taylor sank blissfully into the plush leather of her chair. Now that felt good. So did letting go. She massaged her forehead with one hand. "Would you get everyone back in the writers' room?"

"Uh, sure." Isabel turned on her heel, seemingly mystified and probably afraid Taylor would change her mind.

Five minutes later, Taylor took the floor again. She stared at the faces of her staff as they regarded her curiously, awaiting the announcement that had them gathered once again. "Though it's a reversal, I want to run with Isabel's episode," Taylor told them simply.

Kathleen nodded, a small smile taking shape on her lips. Scruffy laughed sardonically at the new turn of events and closed his laptop. Isabel accepted a high five from Candace, who then turned to Taylor.

"It's the right call, chief."

Taylor smiled at her. "I appreciate the feedback and your flexibility."

Scruffy, ever the pessimist, gestured around the room. "So, we just wasted an hour, then?"

She strolled to him. "We're an artistic mechanism, Scruffy, not a mechanical one. We're looking to tell the best story possible."

He shook his head and sat back in a huff. He'd get over it.

They spent the next two hours, well into the evening, troubleshooting Isabel's script. Certain scenes needed beefing up, while others required scaling back.

"We need a line here," Taylor said, of the action described in the final scene.

Isabel looked up at her and slid a pencil onto her ear. The action sent warmth to Taylor's...everywhere. "Well," Isabel said, "she's staring across the cabin at him wantonly. My hope was that we convey it all with one look."

"One look would be nice, but you're forgetting about the viewer who's multitasking, which is most of them. Knitting as they watch, making dinner, dealing with kids. We need a line."

"She's right," Cedric said.

Isabel nodded and made a note in the margin of her script. "Got it. I hadn't considered that."

Scruffy stared at her. "Why would you? You're a cub."

"Shut up, Scruffy," Isabel said and then tossed him a triumphant smile. It seemed Isabel was finding her footing with the group, and Taylor was happy to see it. Once they were back on track, the writers dispersed. Isabel, however, lingered and met Taylor's gaze.

"Now I'm nervous."

She shook her head curtly. "No way. You don't get to do that. You wrote a killer script. You convinced your EP to run with it even when she said no, and now you have to stand by it, see it through, and nurse this episode into existence."

Isabel nodded. "I just hope that it doesn't completely tank."

"Me too, or you're fired."

"I am?"

"I can joke around, too, you know."

Isabel sighed. "You are not a person I can predict."

"Good," Taylor said with a smile. "I think that makes it more interesting."

"Who? Us? We are interesting." Silence fell, and Isabel tucked a strand of hair behind her ear. "While we have a sec, I just wanted to say thank you. For giving me this shot with the episode."

"Just doing my job." Another pause. "Do you want to grab dinner?"

Isabel tilted her head. "Oh." Taylor's thoughts thoughts sped up as if on a giant hamster wheel and she had trouble settling on any of them. "Really?"

Taylor didn't know where the invitation had come from other than an instinct she apparently hadn't tamed. The problem was, she knew this town backward and forward, and most of the people in it bored her. Isabel didn't. That didn't make it any less stupid of her to acknowledge it…even to herself.

In salvage mode now, Taylor decided to go for off-the-cuff. Casual. "I figure we could talk about the episode and check the dinner box at the same time." A lie that she would turn into the truth if it killed her. "We seem to be good at double duty."

"So, you're asking me to a *working* dinner?"

"A working dinner would be correct," Taylor said. Then she did something idiotic and acted like it just occurred to her how such an invitation might be perceived. "Oh. Oh! I hope you didn't think I was— no. I wouldn't do that. I promise."

Isabel laughed along with her at the abject lunacy, and for the first time she wasn't just beautiful, she was cute. "Taylor, it's fine. You don't have to explain. You desperately want to have dinner with me. I get it. Happens a lot."

"I have no doubt. You know, now that I think about it. It's not the best night for me anyway. I'd just end up paying for it tomorrow if I push aside the pile of work I should be focusing on."

The smile on Isabel's face dimmed, and it was a shame. "Now I'm sad."

They stared at each other. "You are?" she asked quietly.

Isabel nodded. "I vote for the dinner. Working…or non-working."

Taylor forced herself not to swallow as the implication hit home. She'd been down this road earlier in the year with Aspen, who wasn't even a member of her writing staff. Surely the conflict of interest was worse in this case simply due to proximity alone. Call her stupid, or a glutton for punishment, but she didn't seem to be able to resist Isabel, who now wore a very persuasive and sexy smile. "Fine. But we should probably go somewhere close, because I—"

"Have a ton of work to get to," Isabel finished for her. "You say that a lot."

Taylor nodded.

Isabel nodded.

The air around them felt thick and a little bit delicious in the most forbidden way. It was dinner, not her bedroom. She was doing nothing wrong…technically.

"I get to pick the place this time," Isabel said.

"You do?"

"Yes, and I want hot dogs. More specifically hot dogs from Pink's. I read about the place online, and I need to give it a go. Plus, it's only a mile from here, so it fits the prescribed criteria."

"Pink's," Taylor said, not quite buying it. "As in the shack down the road with the crazy line?"

"That would be the one. I'll meet you there in half an hour," Isabel said, as she backed toward the door.

Taylor sighed for effect but had trouble holding back the grin. "Pink's it is."

Alone in the writers' room, it occurred to Taylor that this was likely another one of those stupid decisions that always seemed to surround her personal life. When it came to television, she was golden. When it came to her love life, she crashed and burned miserably every damn time. She decided to make a plan. She'd have dinner, get to know Isabel more, and try really hard not to fall any further into this thing because it already came laced with power.

Wouldn't be hard at all, right?

❖

"Let me have two Lord of the Rings dogs, large fries, and a beer," Isabel told the guy at the counter. They'd waited in line for twenty-five minutes to place their order, and she was anxious to see what all the fuss was about. She turned to Taylor. "For you?"

Taylor eyed the guy. "I don't suppose you have a salad hiding out on that menu somewhere?"

He let out a short laugh and gestured to the menu board above his head. "What you see is what we have."

"Come on. Live a little." Isabel bumped Taylor with her shoulder, secretly hoping it hadn't been a bad call to bring her here. But then something remarkable happened. She watched Taylor steer easily into the skid, the way she so often did at work.

She pointed at the board with confidence. "In that case, I'll need a Martha Stewart dog and some chili fries."

Isabel pulled her face back. "I'm impressed. You're getting bonus points tonight." She gestured to Taylor's starched white dress shirt, the one she paired with jeans and heels—the look that had her preoccupied most of the day. "We're gonna need to be on high alert with those chili fries."

Taylor glanced down at her shirt and waved Isabel off. "I'm a pro."

The confidence sent a shiver across Isabel's skin. What she wouldn't give to see that confidence…in other venues.

They snagged a plastic table around the back of the storefront and let out a collective groan at the killer day they'd just come off. "Does it ever get any easier?" Isabel asked. She loved her new job, but her brain had never felt more taxed in her life.

Taylor offered up an apologetic smile. "It's doesn't. In fact, it gets harder. When you're running your own show, you'll look back on these days with new eyes. I promise."

Isabel nodded, her mouth too full of a Lord of the Rings dog to answer. Didn't matter, she was in hot dog heaven. She grabbed for a napkin and dabbed away a dot of sour cream from the side of her mouth.

Taylor laughed. "You're digging in."

Isabel held her palms up and made grabbing gestures at the air. It was the only way she could properly express her contentment. "Oh my God. Whoever made these is a fucking genius. Sorry, I digress."

"I like when you digress."

"Oh. Well, then I will forever do it." Their chemistry was alive and well and more clearly on display than ever before. "Tell me. Were you at all skeptical about hiring me? I mean, clearly I've blossomed into quite the asset," Isabel joked. "But in the beginning, what was your impression?"

Taylor sat back, and Isabel took note of the fact that she hadn't yet touched her food. "Here's the thing. As a writer, I want to work alongside other writers who I think will enable me to do my best work. That means creative, unique individuals. Not your typical, run-of-the-mill person."

"Did you just call me weird? Pretty sure you did."

Taylor laughed, and Isabel couldn't help but grin at the sound. Taylor didn't put on. In fact, she'd never seen her feign a laugh or any emotion at all, for that matter. What you saw was what you got with her, and it was refreshing. "Weird is a strong word. But, yes, I saw something different in you. You have an edge that doesn't quite match your exterior. Has anyone ever told you that?"

"That I'm a no-bullshit kind of girl who looks, sadly, like a wide-eyed newbie, just off the train from nowhere, USA?"

Taylor nodded. "Yes, that."

"Nope. First time."

Taylor nodded at the obvious lie. "Well, it contributes to your appeal."

Isabel had to take a moment to answer because she was again reveling in her fantastic food. She chewed, and chewed, and eventually pointed at her mouth and shot Taylor the A-OK sign. That's when Taylor reached out and dabbed a spot of chili from Isabel's cheek, a move that had Isabel going still, because the way she did it was affectionate and warm, as if she were enjoying Isabel's happiness. "Thank you," she finally managed. They looked at each other, neither in a hurry to break the eye contact that seemed to wordlessly convey so much. They'd noticed each other. It didn't carry any heavier implication than that.

They'd noticed each other.

"So, you find me intriguing, then," Isabel said quietly.

Taylor lifted her chin from where it had been propped up on her hand. "Did I say that?"

"I think just a moment ago, yes. If it helps, I find you infinitely more intriguing than you find me."

Taylor stared at her. "Is this a contest? I had no idea."

"Yes, it most certainly is. I'm very competitive when it comes to self-deprecation. No one can touch me." Isabel gestured to Taylor's tray. "Speaking of which, you haven't touched your food."

She nodded a few times. "I'm gearing up."

"To slum it."

Taylor balked. "Not at all."

"Admit it. You eat at fancy restaurants like the one I used to work at, and a place like this isn't a part of your weekly rotation."

She leaned in again. "You think you know a lot about me, don't you?"

Isabel blushed. This was Taylor Andrews she was sitting across from, and her own playful, cocky side seemed to have run away with itself tonight. She backpedaled. "No," she said sincerely. "I would not presume."

"That's okay. I know a little bit about you, too. I had dinner with a mutual friend the other night. Stephanie?"

Isabel resisted a face-palm, her worst nightmare come to fruition. "We met once, briefly. She's my neighbor. I wouldn't put too much stock in anything she has to say about me."

"No?"

"I wouldn't."

"Well, that's a shame."

Before Isabel had time to react, to kick herself for discrediting Stephanie, Taylor, wearing that starched white dress shirt, did something highly unexpected. She picked up three of the chiliest cheesiest fries and popped them in her mouth, sans fork. It was sexy, and Isabel held onto her chair to keep herself from visibly swooning. Taylor's big green eyes went wide. "This is good," she said, her mouth still full of fries.

"See? Gotta walk on the regular side of life once in a while. Look at the discoveries one can make. Now try your Martha Stewart before I do." Taylor took that suggestion and fell into silence as she sampled the dog. Isabel waited for the verdict, but instead Taylor took a second bite and looked skyward in surrender. The visual said it all. "You love it, don't you?"

"I haven't had a hot dog in," she thought for a moment, "twelve years."

Isabel's mouth fell open in joint sadness and outrage. "Why have you done this to yourself?"

"About now, I'm wondering that same thing."

"Thank God I'm here, that I found you in time."

Taylor dabbed her mouth with a napkin, though it was in ceremony only. She'd managed to keep herself as neat and tidy as ever. "I'm very much enjoying it." Then she grinned at Isabel, only it wasn't a smile she'd ever seen from Taylor. This one didn't come with the serene confidence she'd grown accustomed to. Instead, Taylor radiated what could only be described as happiness. She seemed relaxed and youthful and content.

"You look..." Isabel was about to say "beautiful," but the word died on her lips once she heard how it might be perceived. "Hungry. Have some more." She slid the remainder of the hot dog closer to Taylor, then reached out and stole a fry.

"Now you're just being cheeky."

It was Isabel's turned to grin. "I own cheeky. I've been called worse." Moments later, Taylor stole one back showing she, too, could be cheeky. Isabel met her eyes. "Touché," she said quietly. Taylor pumped her shoulders in victory and Isabel laughed.

When their messy trays were empty, their table littered with napkins, Taylor, more at ease than Isabel had ever seen her, made one very telling declaration. "We have to come back here."

"Maybe tomorrow."

Taylor met her gaze. "I'm in."

CHAPTER TEN

Taylor drew herself a hot bath later that evening and, because she was feeling extra indulgent, sprinkled lavender bath salts over the running water, filling her bathroom with the most wonderful aroma. She draped herself in one of her favorite oversized bath towels and sat along the tub, watching it fill. She'd had fun at Pink's with Isabel that night, and not just the standard "everything is beautiful" in Hollywood kind of fun, but the genuine kind. She hadn't realized until tonight how much she'd missed that feeling, or even that she'd somehow drifted so far away from it.

This evening had served as a shocking reminder, and she wanted more.

Their conversation had been free of discussions straight out of *Variety* or gossip about one studio head or another. There had been no jockeying for position or assertion of success or the making of deals or the tearing down of others.

No. They'd simply laughed over delicious hot dogs, and it had been the best night Taylor could remember having in years. Dropping the towel, she eased herself into the tub and sighed loudly as the hot water caressed her skin, chasing away the tension she'd spent the day collecting. With her hair in a knot on the top of her head, she leaned back against the small satin pillow she kept behind the tub and ruminated back on a time when she was far from a Hollywood player.

Somewhere between Tubby Taylor and Taylor Andrews the Showrunner, she'd lost a small part of herself. Eating hot dogs and chili fries at Pink's with an outspoken kindred spirit had her reconnecting with it in the most wonderful way. It was good to be back.

❖

Isabel picked up a warm handful of sand and let it trickle through her fingers, enjoying the light translucent quality. For mid-September, they'd lucked out with the weather, the temperature sitting at eighty-three degrees.

"You'd think you'd never seen sand before," Hadley said, watching from her towel next to Isabel's. She wore one of those cute bikinis from the 1950s, sky blue with little white flowers. Isabel's own red two-piece seemed boring in comparison.

"We have sand up north, but it comes with a lot more grit. Like me. This stuff," she said, picking up another handful, "is surprisingly soft."

"Like me," Hadley said, her turquoise eyes sparkling.

After trekking past the Venice boardwalk, Muscle Beach, skateboarders, food vendors, and even a drum circle, Hadley had led them to a much quieter section of the beach, apart from the tourists and much more appropriate for sunbathing and water sports.

"Oh, wait. Okay. Get ready. Here she goes." Hadley sat up straight on her towel and gestured to the water where one surfer emerged from the pack as a large unbroken wave moved in. Isabel shielded her eyes from the sun and sat forward, joining Hadley. Gia caught the wave with ease and Isabel marveled at the fluidity of motion, as if Gia belonged out there in the water with the fish, the dolphins, and whatever else. She looked just as much at home. Gorgeous.

Isabel turned to Hadley. "I've seen people surf plenty of times on television, but this is so much different. Someone I know is killing it out there. I'm on a contact adrenaline high!"

"Isn't it crazy? G's an amazing surfer. And Venice is known for its pretty mellow waves, so imagine her on a bigger beach. She'd blow your mind," Hadley said just as Gia caught another wave. "There you go!" Hadley yelled, her hands cupped around her mouth. "You show that big, bad wave who owns it. You make it your bitch!"

Isabel turned to Hadley, eyes wide.

"Sorry," she said quietly. "About the language. I just get all worked up."

"You do you," Isabel said in amusement.

They watched Gia for over an hour, and she got more impressive each time out. Isabel had no idea how she did what she did on that surfboard. When it came to team sports in school, Isabel was generally picked second to last, only because she schemed behind the scenes, talked to who she needed to talk to in order to ensure she wouldn't be the dead-last pick. She could be wildly persuasive. But the athleticism Gia demonstrated, coupled with a superior instinct, explained her prestigious ranking in the surf world. Isabel sat there in awe.

"Hey," Autumn said, joining them. She quickly threw a towel alongside Isabel and set down a tray of iced coffees. "Anyone need a pick-me-up?"

Isabel looked up at her. "More than air from nature. Thank you, benevolent coffee fairy." Her tone was even, but her heart was full.

"Yay, coffee!" Hadley said, celebrating demonstratively enough for them both.

"Just fulfilling my life's work," Autumn said and took one of the four sweating cups for herself. "Caffeinating the planet." She glanced over at Isabel. "Sorry, I missed you at Pajamas this week. I traded out the early shifts with my assistant manager."

"I tried not to take it personally."

"Atta girl," Autumn said.

Isabel reflected on the bookish little guy she'd chatted up each morning this week. "Your guy is cool, though. Steve. He's from North Carolina originally. Believes if the coffee isn't roasted that day, it's crap. Has a girlfriend who doesn't understand coffee and thereby doesn't fully get Steve." She inclined her drink to Autumn, using her straw to point. "I predict a breakup in the next six months, so you might want to plan for that, scheduling-wise."

"Wow. You might know more about him than I do," Autumn said.

"Just fulfilling my life's work, to understand humankind so I can write them like it's my job. Oh, wait. It is."

Autumn touched her cup to Isabel's in solidarity. "What have I missed?"

"She's killing it," Hadley said, jutting her chin to the water.

Autumn waved her off. "So, nothing new then."

"Not into surfing?" Isabel asked her.

"It's fine, but I come here for the tan and conversation. I leave the rabid cheering to Had." Autumn popped on her shades and lifted her face to the sun. "What's new with you, Iz? You get that No Trespassing sign out of your head yet when it comes to Taylor Andrews? I feel like I'm weeks behind."

Isabel turned to her. "The sign doesn't say that anymore."

Autumn quirked her head. "What's it say now? Take My Clothes Off Quickly?"

The mere idea of taking Taylor's clothes off had Isabel struggling not to choke on her coffee. She shook her head while she composed herself. "My current sign says Proceed with Caution, and I'm doing just that. Proceeding being the operative word. We hung out last week and it was…one of my favorite nights in LA so far. No—scratch that. My favorite."

Hadley must have tuned in somewhere along the way. "So, it's happening? The Hollywood romance I've been hoping for? Newcomer to LA and television goddess fall madly in love and live happily ever after, snapping wedding photos in front of the Hollywood sign at dusk."

Isabel held up a finger. "Didn't say that."

"Damn," Hadley looked crestfallen.

"But it's a cornucopia. It really is," Isabel continued.

Autumn tilted her head to the side in confusion. "That's some sort of personification, isn't it? You're about to enlighten us."

"Taylor. She's the cornucopia—so many things at once that it's like my mind can't keep up. To begin with, she's someone I look up to. I respect her, and that goes a long way. Are you with me?" Two heads nodded. "She also frustrates me, and turns me on, and challenges me, and makes me laugh, because I always forget she can be funny."

Autumn nodded more aggressively. "A fucking cornucopia."

Isabel nodded. "Right?"

Hadley rubbed her hands together. "I'm ready to meet her. Go pick her up, please. Is she free tonight? Let's do a beach fire and invite her. It's perfect."

Autumn nodded. "I'd be down for a beach fire. Would G?"

Hadley nodded happily "She mentioned it last week, which is why it was in my head. It's been too long."

Isabel raised her hand. "Confused New Englander here. Is a beach fire what it sounds like?" Isabel asked. "A fire on the beach?"

"With chill music and beer," Autumn said.

"And my famous steaks on the hibachi."

"You do steaks out here?" Isabel asked, her stomach growling from lack of lunch.

"I do the best steaks out here," Hadley said in ultra-serious mode. "I even bring my own homemade chimichurri sauce because I do not mess around when the hibachi is out."

"Isn't all of that illegal?" She was sure she'd seen signs posted.

Hadley dropped her voice as if the world were listening. "I don't like the idea of breaking the rules, and I rarely do. But beach fires are different. Plus, most of the patrol guys out here know Gia and leave us alone. She signs the occasional autograph for their nieces or daughters, and everyone's happy and full of steak."

Isabel held up her hands. "I can't argue with that. Illegal fires and steaks on a tiny grill it is."

"Great. So, you'll call her?" Hadley asked.

Isabel looked from Hadley to Autumn. "You don't seriously want me to call Taylor Andrews and invite her for hibachi steaks on Venice Beach?"

Hadley grinned. "Oh, but we do."

"When was the last time you were on Venice Beach?" Taylor asked Scarlett, who sat with her MacBook in her lap and her feet stretched across the couch in Taylor's office. Raisin batted playfully at her shoe in between rawhide chewing sessions. While they were working on the upcoming week's schedule for *Sister Dale*, Taylor opted to do so in her own office. Something about the familiar territory kept her focus laser sharp. They'd been working most of that Saturday, and only the buzzing of Taylor's phone had pulled her from the haze.

Scarlett squinted. "Well, that would have been back when I had a life, which means before I met you, so maybe 1986?"

"You're only twenty-five, Scar."

Scarlett turned to her, glazed over. "Why do I feel thirty years older than that?"

"Studio time is like dog years," Taylor said, nodding. She thought about the beach. "I can't even remember the last time I was on Venice Beach. Any beach really." She closed her eyes and imagined the feel of the cool breeze off the water, the sand between her toes. Now, that would be something.

"What makes you bring up Venice?" Scarlett asked.

Taylor held up her phone. "Oh, it was just…Isabel. Not a big deal. She texted about it. The beach." Why was she being so vague? And jittery? The feeling was new and concerning.

It was clear that Scarlett's attention had been snagged as the typing had ceased. Damn it. They spent too much time together. "Did Isabel invite you to the beach?" She sat up on the sofa and pushed her glasses up on her nose as if the soap opera in her head had just taken a juicy turn.

Taylor pointed at her. "Not like that she didn't. Not like that."

"What's funny is that I didn't insinuate anything specific."

"Oh." This had Taylor momentarily stymied, because Scarlett hadn't.

"But the fact that you leapt there says a lot." Scarlett studied her as if working an intriguing puzzle. "You *like* her. You like Isabel Chase."

Taylor looked around at the items on her desk and set about picking them up and setting them down again. Why? She had no clue. "I do like her. What's not to like?"

"What are you doing right now?"

Taylor followed Scarlett's gaze to the handful of paper clips in her hand. "Nothing. Just…making sure we have paper clips."

Scarlett took off her glasses. "You're being weird with office supplies. Do we need to call it a day?"

Taylor glanced at her watch, thankful to see that it was approaching four o'clock, safely within the call-it-a-day range for a Saturday. "Yeah. You know, why don't we do that?"

"Great." Scarlett flipped her laptop closed. "Because I have a date. Not a Venice Beach date, but a date."

"You do?"

"I do." Scarlett walked from the office to her cubicle with Taylor hot on her heels. Scarlett hadn't mentioned that she was seeing someone. Taylor felt her ultra-protective chip click on.

"This isn't someone you met on match.com, is it? Because I heard a girl got murdered when she met up with—"

"No need to worry. My guy is a friend of a friend, and vetted in advance. He's pretty great so far." She smiled and it was heartwarming.

Taylor shook her head, enjoying the playout. "You seem, I don't know, really excited. How did I not know about this guy?"

"It's all very new." Scarlett nodded several times, the wattage of her smile increasing exponentially, almost like a flower blossoming before Taylor's eyes. "It's one of those things. I'm not quite sure how to describe it. When I think about him," she paused to consider her word choice, "I get this jittery thing in my stomach. My day seems brighter and I wonder about the next time we'll talk. I wait for it."

"That sounds fantastic." She didn't identify at all. Not even a tiny bit.

Scarlett picked up her bag. "I hope so. See you Monday?"

"Yeah, I'll be here."

"Oh, and Taylor. If you're headed to the beach tonight, take a six-pack of beer. People love it when you bring beer to a gathering."

"So, not wine then, because I was thinking a bottle of—"

"Beer. And dress casually." She pointed at her feet. "No heels." She paused and squinted. "Do you want me to write this down?"

Taylor grabbed a stress ball from her desk and lobbed it at Scarlett. "Get out of here before I kill you."

Scarlett grinned. "Yes, ma'am."

Alone in the office, Taylor contemplated her evening. What she hadn't mentioned to Scarlett was that she also had a text message from Aspen. She glanced down at her phone.

We should get together tonight. There are things to say. Let me buy dinner for you, Gorgeous.

There were, in fact, things to say. The text didn't lie. But she was now of the opinion that Aspen was never going to hear her, no matter how many ways she told her it was over. If anything, this was just another ploy to get Taylor within arm's length so she could work her magic, try to lure Taylor back into the never-ending cycle of anger and crazy—or more accurately, if anger and crazy were dancing a tango together upside down on the ceiling.

That's what life with Aspen was like.

Only she found herself in the unique position of not being able to properly extract herself from her crazy ex-girlfriend because she was forced to see her every day of her damn life. At the same time, she had to work extra hard to stop Aspen from having a meltdown and halting production—something her budget couldn't afford. Why her, God? Why?

Then there was Isabel and the pretty dark hair and the dry delivery and the ease their interactions always came with…and the working together. The brakes squealed. The same damn issue all over again. She needed someone to smack her across the face—and hard.

She made a hasty decision, stole three pretzels from the bag on her desk, fired off two text messages, grabbed her bag, her dog, and what was left of her sanity, and headed out the door into the wider world.

CHAPTER ELEVEN

Death by speeding train or speeding car?" Gia asked Isabel as they stood at the water's edge. The question stuck out in sharp contrast to their tranquil surroundings. With water caressing their bare feet, the sun dipped low in the California sky, somehow looking lonesome and poetic. Isabel was far from a sap, but even she couldn't deny its beauty. Dusk came with a fleeting glory that she never got used to.

"Train," she said quietly. "Way more memorable."

Gia turned to her. "See? I had you pegged as a car kind of girl. Blend into the crowd."

"You don't know me as well as you think you do. Snake or rat for a pet?" she asked, turning the tables. She could hear music drift their way from their campfire up on the shore.

"I don't want either," Gia said adamantly, turning to her. "No, no, no. New question, please."

Isabel shook her head apologetically. "Sorry, pal. It's the game. You have to choose. Pet snake or rat."

"I just think if you really wanted to, you could let me off the hook on this one. I don't really want to consider either."

"Well, I can't do that," Isabel said matter-of-factly.

She watched the color drain from Gia's face at the thought. The killer athlete and surfing star who'd showed zero fear earlier today was now squirming at the thought of an undesirable, albeit fictional, pet. Isabel smiled as she watched the struggle take place across Gia's face. "Rat, I guess," she said finally. "But it better not try and touch me or I'm moving."

"No guarantees. It'll probably just wave from the cage."

Gia shuddered and pressed forward. "Sex on broken seashells or on hot coals?"

"Ouch." Isabel considered the equally painful choices. "Going with seashells, because I hear sex on the beach can be awesome."

"It's overrated," Gia said, feigning an innocent smile. "I mean, I've *heard*."

"Oh, I'll bet." Isabel imagined Gia wouldn't struggle in the romance department, but from what Isabel had seen, she didn't really seem to date.

Tonight, Gia wore denim cutoffs and a bikini top, an ensemble she seemed to frequent. Her body alone should have women handing out their numbers. Isabel, on the other hand, had changed into jeans, a white T-shirt, and her old faded University of New Hampshire hoodie, the red almost pink from washing.

"Steaks are up!" Hadley yelled from the small grill. "Fantastic steaks over here!"

Isabel and Gia walked back to the fire, and she smiled at the lightness in her step. Every now and then in life, a truly serene moment hits where you're infinitely content with where you are, and the magic is hard to ignore. This was one of those moments for Isabel. The ocean air filled her lungs, the music from the compact radio lifted her, and her new friends made her feel welcome and included. The brilliant sunset over the water didn't hurt much either.

She was beginning to like her new life.

But in that moment, it got infinitely better.

"Is this the place to drop off beer?" They turned, and Isabel blinked to be sure it wasn't some sort of mirage.

Nope.

Taylor Andrews, who'd sent a noncommittal text earlier, still stood there holding a six-pack, her hair swept into a messy ponytail. She looked more relaxed and down-to-earth than Isabel had ever seen her, wearing flip-flops, jeans, and a soft blue T-shirt. She wondered what that T-shirt would feel like against her cheek.

"This is the place," Hadley said, leaping to her feet and taking the beer from Taylor. "Hadley Cooper. So nice to meet you. We've heard amazing things."

"Oh, wow. Thank you for having me. I'm Taylor," she said, accepting Hadley's hand.

"I know." Hadley grinned and didn't look like she'd be letting go of that hand anytime within the century, so Isabel leapt to action.

"Taylor, let me introduce you to Gia and Autumn." Hadley reluctantly dropped Taylor's hand and passed Isabel a look of apology.

No harm, no foul. She understood the infatuation implicitly. "These guys are my neighbors."

"A pleasure," she said, stepping away from Hadley toward Gia and Autumn, who luckily behaved like normal people do when saying hello.

"Grab a plate and load up," Hadley told the group, snapping out of hero-worship mode. She gestured to the fire. "We brought down some extra beach chairs."

Isabel and Taylor allowed the others to fix plates first, the delay buying Isabel a moment with Taylor to herself. "I wasn't sure you'd come," she said quietly. "Glad you did, though."

Taylor smiled, what seemed to be shyly, but surely that wasn't the case. "I think I needed to get out of the office. My eyes were crossing. Your invitation arrived right on time. I was happy to get it."

Isabel's heart soared at those words. "You were at work today? I feel like a slacker now."

"No need," Taylor said, walking them farther toward the fire. The chill increased with the departing sun, and the fire offered a nice compensation. Plus, it was really pretty. Autumn knew how to get her fire on. "You'll have your own show one day and can put in the time then. Enjoy having a life while you can. Not that you don't already work some pretty long hours."

"Delivery service," Hadley said, and handed them each a plastic plate with a steak and leafy green salad.

"Oh, you didn't have to deliver," Taylor said.

"Next time, you're on your own," Autumn joked. "You're only a newcomer once."

They took a seat in front of the fire just as Gia carried over a couple of beers. She touched her can to each of theirs. "Cheers, guys. To making new friends."

"Cheers," Isabel said.

Taylor held up her can. "I can certainly drink to that."

"So, Taylor," Autumn said. "Izzy tells us that you're pulling double duty. Two TV shows at once. That's gotta be insane for you, no?"

"It's certainly not ideal."

"How are things on *Sister Dale* anyway?" Isabel asked.

Taylor sighed. "As well as can be expected. They would be much easier if Lyric wasn't behaving like a human roadblock to the show's progress. Did you guys make the steak out here? It's so tender." The compliment resonated, and Hadley beamed like the sun on steroids.

"Had's pretty great with a hibachi," Gia said. "She should have her own YouTube channel."

Hadley grinned. "I've never considered that before." She jumped up, pulled her phone from her pocket, and began typing quickly. When she finished, she held up the phone by way of explanation. "My list of prospects. One of them is going to pay off one day."

"It will if you keep writing them down like that," Taylor said in appreciation. The salt in the air had inspired a slight curl in Taylor's hair, and Isabel's stomach flip-flopped in lovely appreciation. "I'm awful at remembering the ideas I think I'll never forget."

"Is Lyric Larkin as much of a handful as everyone says?" Isabel asked, pulling herself back into the flow of conversation. Anything to inspire a hiatus from the lust.

"If you promise not to repeat this, she's more." Taylor sighed and took a pull from her beer. "We have a sordid history, though, and I'm sure that doesn't help."

Isabel turned to face Taylor. "You guys have worked on a show together in the past? I didn't know that."

"Not at all. We went to high school together."

"Huh," Isabel said, trying on this new tidbit. "Small world. Who would have guessed?"

"Me. She made my life miserable and seems to think I'm paying back the favor."

"Did she steal your boyfriend?" Gia asked, and then backpedaled. "Or girlfriend?" Gia glanced at Isabel as if in need of help, guidance, a vowel, anything.

Taylor laughed sardonically, saving her. "Neither of those were in the realm of possibility back then. Lyric did steal my ability to exist peacefully, though. I was not popular in high school."

"That can't be true," Hadley said, looking crestfallen. Isabel loved her big heart.

"It was. Lyric Larkin, on the other hand, ruled the world back then, always one of the two captains in gym class. You know the ones who get to pick their team one kid at a time?"

"That practice is proof that gym teachers hate the world," Gia said, shaking her head.

"Yeah, well, Lyric refused to pick me for her team even if I was last. It was that bad."

Isabel's heart tugged. "I'm sorry." Taylor rested her forearms on her knees and glanced up at Isabel just as the waning sun caught the vibrant green of her eyes. Stunning. "I can't imagine anyone not picking you," Isabel said quietly and covered Taylor's hand with hers.

"You're sweet," Taylor said, "but you're going to have to trust me on this one."

Their gazes held. Maybe the half a beer she'd consumed helped give her the courage to not look away. She didn't dwell on the why but simply enjoyed the brief contact before pulling her hand back into her lap with a smile. Hadley and Autumn exchanged an amused eyebrow raise, and Isabel felt the blush heat her cheeks.

Taylor went on to recount the details of her time in high school, the weight, the teasing, the writing. "Which brings me to now, trying to rescue the same girl who made targeting me an extracurricular activity."

"Here's what you do," Autumn said and sat a little taller. "You tell her to clear the hell out of your way because you know what you're doing and she peaked in high school and how sad that must be."

Taylor laughed loudly. "That's good advice. I wish I could say those very words."

Autumn pointed at her. "Well, just tuck that away in case you ever need it. Or call me and I'll come say it for you." She winked.

"I might do that just for fun," Taylor said.

Isabel smiled at the image of Autumn and her beautiful, fiery hair storming the Paramount lot, and her spirits lifted. The evening shifted into a very chill atmosphere, with everyone enjoying the beer, the music, and the company. Gia ran down the beach to talk with a few friends she spotted, and Autumn went for a second beer. Dusk had shifted to night during their conversation, and Isabel pulled her hoodie tighter around her as the breeze nuzzled and lifted her hair.

Hadley leaned in from her spot across the fire and caught Taylor's eye. "I don't know if Isabel's told you, but I'm a big fan of the show."

Taylor beamed at her. "You are?" You would have thought she'd never heard those words before.

Hadley nodded. "I wait each week for the new episode, like my long-lost friends are about to visit me. That may sound cheesy or corny, but it's true and I thought you should know."

"You don't know how happy that makes me. We work really hard, and when you send the show out there, you hope it finds an audience that enjoys the little world you've put together with your team."

Hadley seemed to love that answer, which made Isabel happy. Most people she'd met at the studio, while talented and smart, were also remarkably jaded. They seemed to gloss over the fact that they were participating in something unique and wonderful and uncommon. Taylor got it, though, and it was refreshing. And attractive. Refreshingly attractive. Everything about Taylor was—God, why was she a teenager gawking? *Get it together, Chase.*

"Well, the show is better than good," Hadley said enthusiastically. "Lisette is obviously my favorite. I just keep waiting for her to find the love of her life and make beautiful babies. She deserves something wonderful to happen to her after all her setbacks."

"Right? Especially since her younger sister seems to have found someone," Isabel said innocently and shot Taylor a glance.

Hadley nodded enthusiastically in agreement. "Yes! Thomas. Who's a dreamboat. I'm guessing you guys will be writing a wedding soon, probably with poor Lisette looking on without a date."

"It's possible," Taylor said, giving nothing away. She tossed a look back to Isabel.

Hadley glanced between them. "You guys aren't going to tell me anything, are you?"

Taylor shook her head. "And ruin access to an uninfluenced reaction when the show does air? No way. I'm holding on to you. You'll be a great litmus test." In actuality, there were plenty of test audiences. But what was one more?

"Hey, Izzy?" Gia appeared next to Isabel and rested her chin on her shoulder. "A few of us are going to pack up and adjourn to Dally's on the corner. Cool little bar. Are you guys up for it?"

She turned to Taylor, who opened her mouth to speak and then hesitated.

Isabel squinted. "I'm guessing you're tired."

"Yeah, but I'd love to do it another time," Taylor said enthusiastically. "You guys are great."

"Holding you to it," Autumn said. The group packed up and walked to the street together before saying their good-byes. Isabel's friends headed one way in a haze of fun chatter and she and Taylor stayed where they were.

Isabel turned to her. "Should I walk you to your car?"

The hesitation spoke volumes and Isabel silently prayed the answer would be no. After all, it really wasn't *that* late…

❖

Taylor weighed her options as she stood there on that street corner, remembering acutely, painfully, the tricky situation she'd landed herself in with Aspen. The dramatic scenes, the tantrums, the topless surprises in her office. All of it could have been avoided if she'd just done her damn job and ignored the rest. Why open another can of worms? She was so much smarter than that. But what she had going with Isabel felt like something new, something noteworthy, but also something very dangerous. To her heart, at any rate. "I'm not ready to call it a night."

What?

Who had uttered those words?

Isabel grinned. "We could pop popcorn, pour wine, and watch a movie. I live just over there."

Taylor hesitated, feeling the weight of what that new frontier might mean.

"Hey," Isabel said quietly. "Just a movie. I wasn't suggesting—"

"No, I understand. It's—"

"I thought it might be nice to just relax. Not think."

Taylor nodded and held on to Isabel's gaze. She really, really liked the way that gaze seemed to steady her. No games, no pretenses. Isabel was simply Isabel. "A movie, I can do."

Isabel smiled. "Good."

They walked the three blocks back to Seven Shores in comfortable quiet. "So, the writing thing," Isabel said, "it was your adolescent escape?"

Taylor nodded. "Not the brightest spot in my history, but I wouldn't change anything. It was the catalyst to who I am today."

"And television viewers in the millions thank you for that." Isabel looked over at her as they walked. "I wasn't bullied in high school, luckily, but I can certainly identify with needing an escape." She paused. "I'm about to tell you something big here."

"Oh yeah?"

"Yep. Not something you can ever divulge by penalty of a fiery, graphic death at the hands of fate, which will seek retribution for the betrayal."

Taylor was amused. "Quite an awful consequence."

"Isn't it, though? So here it is. Ready? I had an imaginary friend."

"Me too!" Taylor laughed. "I was six years old and—"

"I was thirteen."

Silence. "Oh." Taylor nodded several times before the laughter broke through. She covered her mouth. "I'm sorry. It's not funny at all. I don't even know why I'm laughing. A teenager with an imaginary friend is one hundred percent normal."

"I see no reason for an age limit on imagination."

"No, of course not," Taylor said, still trying to contain herself. "What was your friend's name?"

"Henrietta. She sold real estate."

"Oh my goodness, an imaginary friend with a job. How'd you manage that?"

"Nope. It's too late to make up for the ridicule from earlier. You're dead to me." There was ice in her voice, but Taylor knew better. God, she was cute.

"Oh, come on," Taylor implored. "The laughter was a knee-jerk reaction, and as you can see, I'm past it now. Tell me more."

"No."

"So, you and Henrietta, the real estate broker, sidled up to all the popular spots in New Hampshire? Did you close deals together or—?"

"Are you jealous?" Isabel asked. "You sound jealous."

"Aflame with jealousy."

"And sarcastic, too. Okay then, who was your imaginary friend?" Isabel challenged. She brushed a strand of hair from her forehead and Taylor was struck. The simple gesture had been one of necessity. That was all. Her hair had been obscuring her vision and she'd moved it, so different from Aspen's sex kitten moves, yet it had her all atingle.

"Alfonso," Taylor said finally. "He got me into all sorts of trouble. It was awful and awesome. We slathered the television with peanut butter while my mom got dressed in the other room."

"Alfonso?" Isabel said blandly, as if not liking a taste in her mouth.

"Yes, what's wrong with his name? It's a great name."

Isabel paused and regarded Taylor with pity. "Oh, Taylor, it's not. I'm concerned that you think so."

"It is, too, a great name. What are you talking about?" she asked, in full defensive mode. "Alfonso happens to be—" That's when she caught the grin on Isabel's face. "Oh, you're awful. You're just giving me shit for fun."

"It's actually not that difficult, which contributes to my amusement," Isabel said, leading the way to her door. "I'm over here."

Taylor glanced around the courtyard, taking in the two-story white building, the wrought iron, the conglomeration of couches. The result was quaint and inviting. "This place is adorable. I love it! The others live here, too?"

"Gia and Hadley live up there in the corner. They're next-door neighbors. Autumn doesn't live here, but she owns the coffee shop next door, so I guess she's an honorary neighbor."

"The Cat's Pajamas. Yeah, she told me about it earlier. I plan to give it a try at some point."

"I wouldn't," Isabel said, unlocking the door to her apartment. "That coffee is like crack, and Venice is a drive. Think of all the time you'll spend on the road once you're hooked."

"That good, huh?"

"Coffee crack. Tell you what. I'll bring you a cup to work next week."

Taylor paused and smiled, resisting the urge to touch Isabel in some way. It was like she craved that contact. What was this pull between them? "You would do that?"

Isabel's smile was so sudden and sincere that Taylor felt like she'd been wrapped in the warmest blanket. "I would and will."

"Thank you."

Isabel turned on a lamp, illuminating the modest apartment, reminiscent of an Arizona desert complete with an actual tumbleweed wall hanging. "Welcome to my place," Isabel said. "Or Celeste's place, if we're being specific. I'm subletting."

It suddenly all made sense. Taylor looked around, strolling from the living room to the adjoining dining room and kitchen. "It's very… Celeste, now that you mention it." She laughed. "Very. I don't see a ton of *you* just yet."

"I'm impressed that you noticed." She shrugged. "I'll get around to decorating once this boss lady at work cuts me some slack in the free time department."

Taylor laughed and strolled back. "I don't know why you put up with her."

"First of all, it's the best job I've ever had."

"Well played."

"And she's smart and successful."

"I see." Taylor nodded thoughtfully. "Go on."

Isabel laughed. "Surprisingly down-to-earth. And very pretty."

That one snuck up on her, and Taylor felt the tingling on the back of her neck. Isabel's tone shifted as she looked at Taylor with an undeniable heat. "So, as you can see, my life is hard."

She felt the sparks from across the room, hot and potent. Instead of embracing that tension, she forced a smile. "Shall we watch that movie?"

Isabel blinked. "Yes. Yes. We should get to that." She grabbed the remote and scrolled for the pay-per-view channel. "I vote for dark and action packed. What about *Blade Runner*?"

Taylor chuckled. "You would. I, on the other hand, was thinking more along the lines of Kate Hudson or Julia Roberts. Garry Marshall is my drug of choice these days."

Isabel passed her a flat stare. "Interesting."

"Oh, that's a judgment-based look if I've ever seen one."

"Compromise?"

Taylor inclined her head. "I'm listening."

"*Breakfast Club*."

"You're on."

Isabel popped popcorn and joined Taylor on the couch. They spent the evening quoting the film and losing themselves in the ease of classic dialogue. "This would never work today," Isabel said midway through the film. "You leave those kids alone in a library and they're going to be glued to their cell phones the whole time."

She glanced back at Isabel and couldn't help but notice the smooth column of her neck. She swallowed the visceral reaction and focused on the words Isabel had just spoken. "It'd be a much quieter film. That's for sure. You know Hughes wrote the draft, tossed it in a drawer, and left it there for a very long time?"

Isabel leaned back. "I can't imagine having written something so profound and then throwing it aside and going on with my life."

Taylor nodded. "Yeah, well, that just shows that we're not always the best judge of our own—" Her cell phone buzzed loudly from its spot on the coffee table. "Sorry," she said, embarrassed. She glanced at the readout, cringed at yet another flirtatious invite from Aspen, and slid the phone into her pocket. But not before Isabel had a chance to see it.

"She texts you a lot, doesn't she? That makes four or five times tonight."

"She's still not out of the transition phase. She'll get there."

"Is that what you want, too?" Isabel asked. "To be out of the phase?"

Taylor sighed, feeling the need to be up front with Isabel but not wanting to get into Aspen and all of the issues that came with her. "It is. And I think she means well, she's just locked in a pattern."

"The pattern of wanting you with her twenty-four seven?"

Isabel wasn't wrong, and sooner or later something was going to have to give. Taylor turned to her. "If it's okay, I'd rather not dwell on Aspen. I'm having too good a time."

Isabel grinned. "Then we won't." They readjusted, closer now on the couch, and focused on the film, a bowl of popcorn between them. Twenty minutes later, Taylor glanced down and noticed that her left hand lay in front of the bowl in very close proximity to Isabel's right. She wondered how long they'd been sitting like that and if Isabel had noticed. Should she slide her hand away, or would that just make it weird? She raised her gaze to find Isabel watching her, a flicker of amusement in her eyes. With her pinkie, Isabel lightly touched Taylor's, just for a moment. When she pulled her pinkie away with raised eyebrows, Taylor laughed. A burst of warmth blossomed in her chest and spread. With a shake of her head, they turned back to the film and, for its duration, relaxed further and further against each other, enjoying the movie, each other's company, and the night. Well, as much as one could relax with Isabel Chase next to them, smelling like cucumber body wash and looking like a model for moisturizer.

Somehow, she managed.

❖

It was after midnight by the time the credits rolled, and Isabel found herself wishing the night could go on. "Another one?" she asked with a sly smile.

Taylor turned to her, sleepy and sexy. "Tempting, but no. Thank you for hosting, and for the invitation tonight. It was nice to just… escape for a short while." Isabel understood the sentiment entirely.

"You're welcome to escape here anytime you like," she said quietly. They stared at each other for a moment, and Isabel enjoyed the light flecks of turquoise that swam in the green of Taylor's luminous eyes. She wondered what the name for that color combination was. She was tempted to look it up. Eyes like those didn't come around too often.

"Whoa!" Taylor said, shattering Isabel's daydream and jerking upright on the couch. "What was that?"

She knew exactly what it was. "Did it feel like the swipe of a furry paw on a mission?" Taylor nodded, her feet suspended in midair. "That would be Fat Tony, who is most likely stalking us quietly from beneath the couch. He's my cat. He's probably been asleep. I should have mentioned him."

"A cat? You have a cat."

"I do. He's a total jerk, so I like him."

Taylor chuckled nervously as Isabel ducked down in search of him.

"Tony, come out and say hello, you adorable ball of fur." His answer was a roundhouse swipe of epic proportions.

"Wow. He doesn't mess around," Taylor said. "Why *Fat* Tony?"

Isabel met her eyes. "If he'd show himself, you'd get it."

"Oh no!" Taylor said, lifting her feet at lightning speed. "Another one. He's bound and determined. I don't think he likes me."

"He doesn't like anyone." The sound of hacking floated their way next. "Hairball," Isabel informed her quite seriously, as Taylor fell into laughter. "Come on. He's a cat with a lot going on."

"I'm gathering that," Taylor said, sucking in a breath as the laughter faded. "I can identify." Just as she lowered one foot to the ground, Tony swiped again mid-hack, which only made Taylor laugh harder. "I'm sorry," she said, wiping her eyes. "It's just the hacking in combination with the attack. It's…unexpected."

"You have a great laugh," Isabel told her, enjoying the fullness of the sound. Maybe she shouldn't have said so, but in that moment, she couldn't make herself care about studio protocol.

"It's not my most delicate attribute. My father said I sound like a drunken sailor when I get going."

Isabel nodded. "That's a unique descriptor. I can't say I disagree."

"Hey!" Taylor said, but she seemed to be okay with the declaration.

"If there's one thing you should know about me, it's that I call 'em like I see 'em."

"Trust me, I'm well aware." Taylor glanced at her bag that sat near the door. "So, do you think it's safe to…?"

"I'll run interference. Follow me." Isabel stood, crouched low, and reached behind her. Taylor placed her hand in Isabel's and was led the short distance to the doorway, unscathed by her stalker of a cat. "Delivered safe and sound," Isabel said, turning back to Taylor. The two inches Taylor had on Isabel in the height department were especially noticeable as they stood in such proximity. She had to say that she didn't mind those two inches at all. Not one bit.

"I appreciate the escort," Taylor said quietly, releasing her hand. It still buzzed with warmth from the contact.

"Tony's all talk. He really is a good boy underneath all his bullshit. He's my guy and he also happens to be the best cat in the world. You don't have to worry about him."

"Good to know I'll live to see another day." She slid her bag onto her shoulder. "Where'd you get him?"

"I found him when he was a kitten, mewing between two trash cans outside a restaurant I worked at on a brutally cold Christmas Eve. Brought him home, fed him, took his photo inside a stocking, and he never left."

"Aww, you're a kind soul."

Isabel made a point of darkening her stare. "Swear to me you won't tell anyone."

Taylor turned the lock on her lips and smiled. "Take care, Isabel Chase. I'll see you at the studio."

"Do we have to say good-bye?" Isabel asked, the air between them popping with all kinds of electricity.

"I think we do." They stared at each other until Taylor pulled Isabel into a tight hug. The kind of hug where she could smell her wonderful hair and feel each and every curve as it pressed against hers. She experienced Taylor all over and didn't want to let go. It seemed Taylor didn't either, as her hands moved slowly down Isabel's back, stopping at her waist. The result was a staggering shot of arousal, and Isabel was about to embark on a mission to satisfy it.

"Good night," Taylor said, releasing Isabel with a final squeeze.

Isabel smiled back. "Good night, Taylor." She opened her door and Taylor walked through it. "Will you do me a favor?"

"And what is that?"

"Just send me a quick text when you get home, so I know you made it safe."

Taylor seemed to take a minute with that one. Finally, she nodded. "I can do that."

"Is that an annoying request? I'm sorry. It just puts me on edge to think of you out so late on your own and—"

"No. The opposite," Taylor said, running her hand through her hair, looking thoughtful. "It's been a while since anyone's..." She waved her hand as if to move past it and adjusted. "Thank you. Let's just leave it there. I'll be sure to text you. Good night, Isabel."

"Good night, Taylor. Tonight was…" Isabel grappled, not sure what word would do it justice.

"Yeah, it *was*." Taylor smiled and headed off across the courtyard and Isabel watched, filled with so many conflicting feelings she wasn't sure which end was up.

Thirty-five minutes later as she pulled back the blankets to climb into bed, Isabel's phone buzzed.

Safe and sound, the text message read. *Thank you for caring.*

Isabel smiled and typed back, *Fat Tony will be glad to hear it. I am, too*. As she clicked off the light and slid between the cool sheets, she ran a hand under her shirt, across her stomach, landing on one of her breasts. She gasped at the little pulses of pleasure that hit and radiated outward. While her brain relaxed and craved respite, her body felt alive, awake, and anything but sleepy. Taylor had done that. Her nipples ached with sensitivity and her skin tingled almost uncomfortably.

If only she'd made a move. She hadn't been alone in that moment at the door. Taylor had felt it, too.

She shifted beneath the weight of the covers and couldn't help but wish it was Taylor pressed up against her. She blew out a slow breath, closed her eyes, and let herself imagine. Was her ridiculous heart beating way too fast, all inspired by a hint of pinkie action on a couch and a long hug good night? Why, yes, it was.

It was going to be a long night.

Chapter Twelve

When Taylor arrived at the *Water* offices on Monday morning, she found a sixteen-ounce cup of some of the best coffee she'd ever experienced waiting for her on her desk. The dark blue to-go cup came with the logo of a cartoon cat wearing some very loud pajamas. She smiled at just how quickly it brightened her day.

"Courtesy of the newest staff writer," Scarlett told her from the doorway. She held up a cup of her own. "Why is it so good? Why?"

Taylor took a moment to bask in the amazing sip she'd just taken. "Something to do with the roasting technique. I'll need to investigate further."

Scarlett sighed. "We needed this today."

"Don't remind me." She powered up her laptop, ready to tackle all the email that had slipped past her over the weekend.

"Are you ready for it? The table read?" Scarlett asked. It was a big day. The cast and crew would gather for a table read of one of the more controversial scripts they'd put out, and Taylor, for one, wasn't sure how the new storyline reveal would go over. With Aspen in particular.

"Ready as I'll ever be, I guess. Would you let Lyric know that I'll head to the *Sister Dale* set later this afternoon? Remind her that we have a story meeting so she doesn't book a manicure or something." It sounded snarky, but she'd already been stood up for a variety of spa appointments in the middle of the workday and wasn't about to let it happen again. But first, she anticipated fires on her own set and needed to be present to put them out.

Her fears were not misplaced.

"Wait. What?" Aspen said loudly, glancing up from her script in horror. The cast and creatives dotted the long table, assembled for the read-through. Isabel sat across the table from Taylor, looking on with a steady gaze. She was bound to be nervous. This was her baby. But Taylor had anticipated Aspen's reaction and had prepped her staff well in advance with a "leave her to me."

"Lisette is stealing her sister's fiancé?" Aspen spat out. "Do I have that right? The very couple that you guys have been writing as endgame since last season? She would *never* do that. She would never break them up. She loves her little sister."

"So much for America's Sweetheart," a male cast member said, with a smile.

Taylor shot him a look. Not helping. Not helping at all.

"I think that's why it works, honestly," Isabel said. "We're exploring a new side to Lisette, one the audience, and maybe even Lisette herself, hasn't seen. She's only human."

Taylor had to give her credit. Not too many fledgling writers would publicly push back against the star of the show.

"You wrote this?" Aspen asked, holding up the script.

Isabel nodded, steady as ever. "I did."

Aspen turned her focus to Taylor. "And you greenlit her script?"

"Why don't we finish the read before we move into discussion?" Taylor said professionally. She needed to steer them back on course and avoid a tantrum in front of the very cast Aspen was supposed to lead.

"Because I'm not sure I want to finish." Aspen looked Taylor straight in the eye and sat back in her chair, arms crossed like a petulant child. The challenge was clear. This wasn't about the storyline as much as it was Aspen's need to be universally loved and revered, even via her character, which was unreasonable. It probably didn't help that Taylor hadn't answered her texts Saturday night.

Taylor stood and addressed the room. "Let's take ten, everyone, and meet back here for the rest of the read then." She watched as the cast and production team exchanged nervous, knowing, and in some cases, amused looks across the table. Aspen, however, stormed immediately to her trailer.

Isabel turned to her, eyes wide. "What do we do?"

"Let me handle it." She rose from her chair calmly, grabbed a bottle of water from the craft services table, and walked the row of trailers outside until she found Aspen's. No big deal. No need to draw attention to an already unfortunate situation. People would look to her for cues, and she would be the picture of serenity if it killed her. She knocked softly and smiled at the second AD as she walked past.

"Come in," Aspen called, sounding as if someone had died. Taylor didn't let the dramatics faze her. She let herself in and found Aspen sitting on the couch, perusing a magazine, her eyes never leaving the pages. "I'm not okay with this," she said without looking up.

"I'm gathering." Taylor took a seat across from her. "Tell me why."

"Because Lisette is an icon, damn it. She struggles. She has her flaws, but she's not a man-stealing whore without any loyalty. She has to be the glue at the center of all their lives, or the whole thing doesn't work."

"She's been the morality police for four seasons. Don't you think it's time to shake things up?"

"Not at the expense of Lisette," she said with an aggressive flip of the page. Totally unreasonable.

"We haven't written the rest of the arc yet, but the goal is a Lisette and Thomas relationship at the expense of her relationship to her family. Think of what a compelling playout that would be for you. You'd slay those scenes."

"Maybe." But she could see the spark of interest shoot to life behind Aspen's stare. She was also fluffing her hair, which meant she was feeling energized.

"Do you trust me?"

Aspen set the magazine down, and her expression dropped to sincere. She had always been good at trading one emotion for another on a dime, especially when there was something to gain. "You know I do. I've always trusted you. You're my Taylor."

"Then don't stop now, okay?"

Their eyes met, and those feelings from the past floated to the surface just enough for Taylor to remember how things used to be. They'd laughed together a lot, stolen moments for themselves during downtime on the set. Aspen liked high-risk situations and got off on the adrenaline. Kissing just around the corner from where people were working was a favorite of hers, and she sometimes pushed for more. Yes, life with Aspen had been exciting and unplanned, like a drug you couldn't get enough of. But that kind of high only lasts for so long, and on the flip side, Aspen was also manipulative, working things out so that she always got her way, playing the victim if necessary. She went out of her way to do nice things for Taylor. Aspen was known to surprise her with elaborate dinners or romantic evenings away, complete with expensive lingerie, Champagne, and a choreographed seduction. It had been nice at first, but then the fact that everything had to be over-the-top and orchestrated started to wear thin. Aspen never went small, or simple, or everyday, which proved exhausting. Sometimes it would have been nice to just sit on the couch and talk or read books together. With Aspen, those things weren't really an option.

She also learned that for every nice thing Aspen planned for them, Taylor was expected to reciprocate quadruple-fold or never be forgiven. The relationship had taken its toll on Taylor, to say the least, and that hadn't even touched on Aspen's fiery temper tantrums. No dish was safe when Aspen's ire rose to the surface, another example of her overly theatrical tendencies. In the end, Taylor had to ask herself what kind of life she wanted and whether she'd be okay replacing her dishes for many years to come. The answer had come easily. Aspen's acceptance had not.

"You really think this is good for the show?" Aspen asked.

Taylor nodded. "I do. Can we get back to the table read?"

"One question first. Where were you Saturday?" She fluttered her eyelashes and set the magazine down. "You avoided me all day, and you know how much that hurts my feelings. I waited to hear from you. Canceled any and all plans, just in case I did, because that's how much I care."

Taylor closed her eyes. "We're not together anymore, Aspen."

"I know that," she said, placing a hand on Taylor's knee and giving it a tiny shake. "We're not together right now."

"Not just right now, though. At all. We're colleagues."

Aspen shook her head, but a slight smile still played. "If you say so."

"Do you think we can get back to work?"

"We can just as soon as you tell me where you were Saturday night. I'm just curious as to what had you so preoccupied." It was a bargaining chip, which was often how Aspen worked: everything accounted for on a scorecard that always added up to a win for her and loss for whoever else had the misfortune of playing. In this case, there were hundreds of people held up from doing their jobs until Taylor played the silly game.

"I hung out on Venice Beach with friends."

Aspen eyed her. "You don't go to the beach. Especially all the way out in Venice."

"I did Saturday. What's the big deal? Let's just finish the read-through. That's all I'm asking. If you're still unhappy with the direction of the episode, we can set up a meeting."

Aspen played with a strand of her own hair and lowered her voice, purring the way she did when she was trying for sexy. "Did you wear a swimsuit? The white two-piece is my absolute favorite." A year ago, it would have worked like a charm. Today, not so much. "Remember that time in the pool when it had to come off?"

"Aspen."

"It was begging to." They locked eyes and Aspen straightened, offering a sigh. "Fair enough. You don't have to tell me the color."

"You'll read?"

She smiled warily. "I'll read."

Ten minutes later they were back around the table. The episode read even better out loud than it had on the page. Isabel jotted notes, glancing up occasionally with a whisper of a smile on her lips. Taylor watched the faces of the team as they heard the episode for the first time. Folks were sitting up tall in their seats and turning pages eagerly. That was a positive sign. Whatever fear she still carried dissipated as she watched the journey play out on their faces. By the end of the read-through, the room clapped heartily.

People shook their heads. She heard a few "wows," a few "damns," and even a murmured "that was hot."

"Man," Luke said, and turned to Aspen. "This is news to me. Did you know they were putting us together?"

Aspen smiled demurely, seemingly much happier with the script after the reaction it had just pulled. "I had a sneaking suspicion."

Lies.

All great big lies.

But if Aspen needed to seem in control, Taylor was more than happy to let her. She chatted briefly with the line producer and the director of the episode before glancing around the room for Isabel, who had mysteriously disappeared. She found her sitting at her desk surrounded by a virtual barricade of snack food. The rest of the writers were either not back from the read-through or they'd headed off to lunch, which would not have been uncommon.

"What are you doing?" Taylor asked lightly.

"Chili Cheese Fritos. Mainlining them. Desperate times. Have to," she said, between bites. Her crisp blue eyes were wide as she crunched. Too wide. Beneath the desk, her foot bounced like a panicked little basketball.

"You're freaking out about the episode, aren't you?"

Isabel nodded about eight times. "No."

"It's the first time you've had a script make it to air. It makes sense that you'd be on edge."

Isabel reached for an Oreo and bit into it heartily. "I'm fine. Not on edge. Just eating lots of junk food. Oreo?" She chomped another one.

"Don't mind if I do." Taylor took an Oreo and slid the lid off with ease.

"Oh, perfect. You even eat Oreos gracefully. I bet you've never been freaked out a day in your life. And why would you be? You're fucking Taylor Andrews. I'm fucking Isabel from nowhere. And I'm swearing at my boss."

Taylor had to laugh. "First of all, you're not Isabel from nowhere. You're from Keene, and that's definitely somewhere. And you should have seen me on my first job. It was that preteen kids' show, *Out of Touch*. I threw up three times the week we shot my first script, which happened to deal, quite dramatically, with one of the characters getting the flu and missing his big basketball game."

Isabel smiled.

"So, as you can imagine, it was too important to screw up. I didn't sleep that week at all. I walked around a pale shade of green, trying desperately to look like I knew what I was doing."

Isabel slowly lowered a Twizzler en route to her mouth. "Did not." Then a pause and a long stare. "You did? *You?*"

"Yep. Let me show you something." She took Isabel by the shoulders and led her to a mirror on the far wall. "What do you see?"

"An amateur with Frito crumbs on her face."

Taylor closed her eyes and smiled at the candor. "Let me tell you what I see. A very capable, very sharp, very intelligent writer who has blown everyone away in the two months she's been on staff."

Isabel scoffed. "Strong language."

Pessimism was her go-to, Taylor was finding. "Well, I didn't say 'fucking,' but it does the trick." That earned her a smile through the mirror. She gave Isabel's shoulders a squeeze and was surprised when Isabel turned in her arms and hugged her. She blinked several times at her body's response to the unexpected contact, as little pinpricks of pleasure moved through her. She returned the embrace, and for just a second or two, allowed herself the luxury of getting lost in it without question, doubt, or overanalysis. The warmth from Isabel's body comforted her, the round swells of her breasts excited her, and the solidity of her arms grounded her. So many things all at once. And then, just like that, it was over.

Who was this girl?

This was the second time she'd slayed Taylor with just an embrace. She imagined the effect of more and nearly had to sit down. How did Isabel come with this kind of power?

"Thank you," Isabel said, and smiled. "For what you said. I needed that boost."

Taylor nodded, now feeling like the off-kilter one. "I better head back to *Sister Dale*. Make sure Lyric hasn't burned the place down. Entirely possible."

"Taylor?" The room was quiet except for the slightest buzz from the fluorescents overhead. Isabel's voice echoed delicately.

She turned back. "Yep?"

"Will I see you soon?" God, the vulnerability in Isabel's voice hit her right in the stomach.

"Do you want to?"

Isabel nodded, her eyes uncharacteristically soft. Her guard was down.

"Then you will."

Three days later, Isabel sat in a director's chair off to the side of set, watching as Greg Beckett directed her episode. As in, the actual episode *she* wrote, the one that would appear on network television. Not the made-up-land in her head where things like this usually happened. Trippy was an understatement.

"All right, and we're going again," he called to the set after a brief conference with the actors. In this case, Aspen and Luke, who took their beginning positions on the set of the cabin.

And they were off!

Isabel sat forward, taking in the fact that the characters she'd known for years were now speaking her words. She stayed out of the way as Taylor had instructed but was on hand to consult and advocate for her script as needed. It was hard not to jump in each step of the way and offer her opinion; she had so many. But it wasn't her place, and she gave Greg room to work. Luckily, they seemed to be on the same page creatively, and Greg's vision only enhanced her dialogue.

"Cut," Greg yelled, after a particularly saucy take, where Lisette and Thomas were practically breathing the same air, yet not actually touching. She had to hand it to Aspen—the woman was on fire and bringing the scene to life with more quiet passion than even Isabel had first imagined. And then there was the fact that Aspen was stunning— wide-eyed, with gorgeous thick dark hair and a sexy voice, and that didn't even touch the way she moved—full of grace and confidence, all the things Isabel lacked. But Aspen's past with Taylor was never far from Isabel's mind. In fact, given the incessant text messaging the other night, a small part of her couldn't help but wonder if maybe it wasn't as *over* as Taylor seemed to think.

Once they called a five, Isabel made a grab for a bottle of water, finding herself standing alongside Aspen at the craft services table. She wore a silk white robe, her wardrobe for the scene, and began making herself what looked to be a lettuce sandwich.

"You should be quite proud of yourself," Aspen said, eying her.

Isabel glanced behind her. "Oh, sorry. Me?"

"You." Aspen relaxed into a dazzling grin. "For the episode. I will admit to being a skeptic at first. You saw my reaction at the table read. How awful of me! But honestly, Isabel, it's pulling in some big reactions." She glanced around at the various members of the crew.

"I hope so. Just trying to tell a good story." She looked up tentatively at Aspen, who was a good four inches taller than she was, and, wow, this woman was pretty, even more so when she flashed that catlike smile.

"You're talented. You should know that," Aspen said. And then there was that charm. Even with all she knew about Aspen from Taylor, she still felt somehow honored that Aspen was paying attention to her. What the hell was that about? When Aspen focused on her, it felt like bathing in a warm light. An impressive skill.

"Thank you," Isabel said, feeling the blush arrive, right on cue. "That's really nice of you to say."

Aspen reached across Isabel for a spoon to stir her tea. "So, what's your story, Ms. Chase?"

Oh, okay. She hadn't expected more questions, but that was all right. "My story? Oh. Well, um, I don't really have a good one. From the northeast. New Hampshire, specifically. A recent transfer. I came to LA for the job."

"How long have you been writing?"

"For as long as I can remember. Shorts, features, spec scripts for television, anything really. Been trying to get my foot in the door for quite a while now."

"So this is your very first show?" Aspen asked as if it were the most adorable thing in the world.

Isabel nodded, unsure if admitting that was to her benefit. Aspen was a hard one to predict, she was finding.

"That is so exciting," Aspen enthused. "How did we get so lucky?"

"Good timing. That's all. I think I might be the lucky one. Taylor was nice enough to give me a shot."

"She's our rock, Taylor," Aspen said reverently. "We're all so thrilled to be working for a brilliant visionary like her. I know I am. And you're all settled?"

"Yep, subletting a place in Venice Beach and learning the crazy tricks to maneuver LA traffic."

Aspen stopped stirring her tea and instead stared at Isabel as if she'd said the most remarkable thing. "Venice Beach, did you say?"

"Right. Yeah, a small apartment complex not far from the water. I'm subletting from another writer."

"How exciting!" she exclaimed, once again breaking into animation. "And do you make it to the beach much?" She could apparently get all glowy and radiant in the span of five seconds.

"Yeah, in fact, a few of us hung out there this weekend. It's a really cool place. Lots to do."

"My goodness, that sounds like a blast. Taylor mentioned how much fun she had."

"Did she?" Isabel asked, happy to hear it. She was surprised to learn that Taylor had gotten around to returning those messages from Aspen, but then she didn't have their relationship all that figured out. "I'm glad. I had fun, too."

"If you'll excuse me, I think we're about to go again." She moved past Isabel to the set, where she stepped into Luke's space, ready to pick up from the spot they'd left off. As Isabel watched them shoot the scene, she couldn't quite shake the odd exchange with Aspen. It did, however, serve as a reminder that Aspen was a force.

One she didn't want to go up against if she could help it.

Note to self.

CHAPTER THIRTEEN

"Y ou're sleeping with the staff writer?" Aspen practically bellowed.
"Excuse me?" Taylor looked up warily from her desk to find
Aspen leaning against the doorjamb of her office, her expression dialed
to hurt and betrayal. It was close to midnight, and Taylor thought she'd
steal a few quiet hours now that everyone had gone home. Apparently,
shooting had run late. At the sound of Aspen's voice, Raisin leapt into
her lap and pressed his cheek against her arm. He'd never been a huge
fan of Aspen's, and, honestly, he'd had the right idea all along.

After twelve hours on the *Sister Dale* set, she'd snuck back to her
office to figure out a way to afford rain for an upcoming *Water* episode
in which Lyle's script depended on it. And now this? She needed a
complaint card directed at the Fates, because she had some serious
concerns about fairness.

Aspen pushed herself into an upright position and walked slowly
into the office, returning to a semblance of calm. "You two have a thing
going on. There's no reason you should hide that from me. I can be
supportive if this is what you truly want. God knows why. It's not who
I would have picked out for you, because let's be honest, we both know
you can do better." Ice cascaded from that sentence.

"Isabel and I write for the same show. And yes, we've become
friends."

Aspen nodded and trailed a finger along Taylor's desk. "Who
spend time together on the beach."

"How do you even—? You know what?" She paused and waved
her hand. Someone had been doing some detective work. "Doesn't
matter. Yes, we hung out on the beach this weekend."

"That's very cute. She is, too. Her episode's coming along nicely,
thanks to Luke and me."

She ignored that last part. The feedback from set had all been quite positive, and Taylor was proud of Isabel and the risk they'd decided to take with the storyline. "Yeah, well, let's hope the rest of the world thinks so."

"They will after they see my scenes." She smiled triumphantly. "But that's not why I'm here."

"It's not?"

"Your party next week."

"That's next week?" God, where had the time gone. While Taylor loved to entertain, was known for it in fact, she preferred to do it with finesse and flourish and would be pushed to make that happen now. She immediately scribbled a note to get the lights on the pool replaced and finalize that catering order.

"Don't worry. I'll be there to help you." Before she could protest, Aspen pressed on. "Patrick McMartin is coming. I know because I saw him at Nobu last night, and we hit it off."

"That's great, Aspen," she said distractedly. Too much to do. No time for small talk with Aspen.

"I want him to consider me for the Sally Ride biopic." She took a seat across from Taylor. "Don't you think I'd be fabulous?"

"As the astronaut?" Taylor asked. Aspen was all wrong for that. Soft and sultry was more her wheelhouse. "I'm not sure it's a fit."

"Which is perfect. I need to branch out, and you know him well. You could surely, you know, put in a good word for little ol' me." She batted her eyelashes.

Taylor hadn't known that was an actual real-life thing people did until Aspen. "I will do what I can with Patrick." It was a half-hearted promise, but the best she could offer. The sound of the door snagged Aspen's attention. Taylor was thrilled for the out.

"Oh, hey. Didn't know anyone was still here," Isabel said, waving from the hallway outside Taylor's door. "Just gonna grab my stuff and head out." Right on cue, Raisin jumped from Taylor's arms and ran into the hallway to greet Isabel.

"Hi, Hotdog," she said, looking down from a standing position, hands on her hips. It was clear that things had gone well on set, and Isabel was on a high. A good sign. "You're trying to lick my face but you're all the way down there. Too short to make it."

Taylor smiled at Raisin's attempt to close the distance with a series of ineffective leaps.

"I guess I could come down to you. That might be one way to solve it, or whatever." He whined softly as Isabel lowered herself to the carpet on all fours, prompting Raisin to bathe her face in kisses. Isabel leapt into doggy voice. "Who's a goofy hot dog? Who is? You're the goofiest one ever." Once the lovefest recessed, she pushed herself off the floor and grinned.

"Someone missed you," Taylor said.

"Raisin's a nice guy is all."

Aspen grimaced at Isabel. "Here," she said, grabbing a tissue from Taylor's desk. "You might want to take care of your face."

Taylor watched as Isabel's grin slid away. She accepted the tissue and her cheeks reddened. She glanced from Taylor to Aspen and quickly dabbed at her face. "My bad. Guess we got carried away."

"There's nothing better than doggy kisses," Taylor said by way of support.

Aspen passed her a heated stare. "I can think of a few things."

"Right, well," Isabel said, noticeably bothered by the exchange. "I think I'm in the way here. Better head out. You were great today," she said to Aspen.

"Just doing my job for this one." Aspen hooked a thumb at Taylor. "Walk me to my car, T-Bear?" she asked Taylor.

Isabel quietly retreated and Taylor stared after her. "Can't. Not ready to leave yet. And please don't call me that."

"Force of habit. Is that a no?"

Taylor stared at her in confusion. "I thought you were using a car service?"

"Oh, that's right."

Convenient slip, Taylor thought.

"Don't forget about the party and Patrick. Night night." And she was gone.

Five minutes later Taylor heard footsteps in the hall. "Iz?"

"Yeah. What's up?" Isabel asked, appearing in her doorway. The blush was gone. So was the embarrassment. She was fresh-faced and very much herself again, and for whatever reason, it made the stress of Taylor's day fall away. "You've never called me Iz before," she said with a small smile.

Taylor thought on it. "I suppose I haven't. Just came out of my mouth."

"I like it."

"Me too. You leaving?"

Isabel nodded.

"Let's walk together. We can take the extra lap."

"There's an extra lap I don't know about? Is that studio-speak?"

"Yep. Don't tell anyone." Taylor gathered her belongings and leashed up Raisin, who raised a sleepy gaze to her and snuggled back into the couch. "Okay, maybe a lap first, then I come back for you." She placed a kiss on his head and set the leash on her desk.

The night was a nice one but came with a September chill. Taylor rubbed her arms as they exited the building. Instead of taking a right, which would have led them to the parking lot, Taylor took a left. She walked them past Stages 20 and 21, telling Isabel little bits of history about each one. At least, as much as she knew. "And this"—she pointed to a little courtyard they happened upon—"is my favorite place on the lot. During the day, you can hear children playing from the daycare center behind us."

Isabel glanced around and moved farther into the space. "I've heard them playing when I've walked through here on the way to the Coffee Bean, but wasn't quite sure where the sound was coming from."

Taylor pointed at the series of doors across the courtyard, illuminated now by a quaint street lamp. "These were the original DesiLu Productions offices. That one belonged to Lucille Ball, and over there, that was Desi's office."

Isabel stared in awe. "Wow, that's...I don't even...I have no words right now."

"I suspected you might appreciate the history, being that you're a fellow TV buff."

Isabel walked over to a handsome little tree. "You have no idea how awe inspiring this is. Working on such a historic lot has to be the coolest part of this job. I've been meaning to take the official tour on a day off."

"In that case, let's walk around a little more. I like this place at night."

Isabel turned around and faced her. "You don't mind? You've got to be exhausted."

"Maybe I want to."

She smiled. "Then, who am I to say no?"

They walked on. She showed Isabel the spot where several drunk cast members from *Cheers* had written their names in what had been wet cement. She walked her through the New York City backlot, complete with stairs resembling a subway entrance that descended to nowhere.

"Movie magic makes my head explode," Isabel said, pretending to jet down the steps in a hurry. "I will never grow tired of it."

Taylor laughed. "Then you're in the right business."

Tonight felt different, Taylor noted, as they walked the streets of the lot. The energy between them was lighter, and the electricity that much more on display. They looked at each other a lot. Glances turned to stares. Quick touches extended into longer ones. They were being downright flirtatious. For whatever reason, the magic of the mostly empty studio seemed to have granted them a sort of permission to just be...them.

"And here we are at Stage 5. You may or may not know this, but this was where they shot—"

"Holy hell. *The Brady Bunch*, right?" Isabel moved to the building as if hypnotized. She touched its exterior. "It all happened behind these walls. Do you understand that? Hallowed ground. Marcia got hit with a football just feet away."

Taylor laughed. "She did."

"Alice made dinner right through there," Isabel said, pointing at the now locked door, and dipped her head to the side. "Right there. Just through that little door."

"Quite true."

She righted herself and smiled. "I'm geeking out and not really sorry about it."

"I was hoping to meet your inner geek at one point, so mission accomplished."

Isabel chattered away blissfully. "Thank you for bringing me here. I mean, if we're being honest, it was on my list to seek out, but you've hit me with the element of surprise, and that's got me a little gaga. Ignore me. I'm a lost cause. But if loving the Brady Bunch is wrong, then I don't wanna be right!"

"Your cause is noble. But I can't ignore you, you're my entire tour. Shall we walk on or do you need a moment of silence?"

Isabel took a last glance up at the building and nodded. "I'm ready. But don't think I won't be back," she said more to the building than to Taylor.

"I'll alert security later. Follow me."

As they walked, they ran into a working set and watched from afar at the shooting of an exterior scene. Isabel looked like a kid at Disneyland, and that only made Taylor want to show her more.

"Evening, Ms. Andrews," said a security guard on a golf cart. "Late night for you?"

"It's turning into one, Clint. We're decompressing with a walk."

He nodded. "Not too bad a night for one."

"I couldn't agree more."

They ended their walk at the Forrest Gump bench and took a seat. Isabel ran her hand across the commemorative plaque, beaming. She was, simply put, luminous. Her dark hair was halfway pulled back tonight and the rest fell down her back, her eyes danced, and her mouth was full and formed into an exuberant smile. Taylor could sit right there and watch her forever.

"I've seen this movie upward of a hundred times," Isabel said.

"Well, I have you beat at well over two hundred."

"You're competitive."

"The most. I do a really good Forrest."

Isabel straightened, preparing. "I'm so ready."

Taylor nodded and ran a hand across her face to wipe away any emotion that wasn't straight from Forrest himself. She turned to Isabel in character. "Life is like a box of chocolates. You never know what you're going to ge-at."

Isabel studied her. "Mmm-hmm. Okay. I see."

"Come on. That was killer."

She reached over and covered Taylor's hand. "You should be proud of the effort you put in."

That pulled a gasp from Taylor because she'd always been told her impression was flawless. Dammit, and it was. She was type A. She did things right. "I don't care what you say. People love my Forrest."

"Do they?" Isabel asked knowingly.

"I'm keeping it."

"Yes. You should keep it. Tucked away."

Another horrified gasp, and Taylor shoulder-checked Isabel, who didn't budge. In surprise, she turned, which left them face-to-face, only a whisper apart. Neither looked away. Neither pulled back, stunned by their proximity. Instead, they gazed at each other on that lonely studio block.

"Taylor." Isabel had whispered the word, and it sent a wonderful chill through Taylor. "Am I crazy, or is there maybe something at play here?" Isabel gestured between them. And there it was, a blatant question, an out-loud acknowledgment of whatever had them following after each other, stealing moments or opportunities just to have a conversation or squeeze the other's hand. Taylor could dodge the question, but she knew it would only come back around again later.

Taylor shook her head. "You're not crazy." She stared at the sky as she tried to find the right way to phrase it. "I haven't had a great run of luck when getting involved with people at work."

"No, I guess not."

Taylor dropped her gaze to her lap. "And there is the fact that, even though it's Hollywood, I'm still your boss."

"Another hard-to-ignore point." A pause. Isabel dropped her gaze to the ground and then back up. "I guess that takes us into conflict-of-interest territory. What do we do about that? About us?"

Taylor sighed, not liking the answer. For once, she needed to do the smart thing when it came to her love life. "As much as I hate to say this, I've found that when you're not sure what to do, it's usually best to do nothing at all." She waited for several long moments for Isabel to respond.

"Wise words," she said quietly, but they were still sitting so very close on that bench. It would be so easy to just close the distance and put an end to the whole thing, and what a delicious ending it would be. "Doesn't mean I don't have fun with you."

"I have fun with you, too. A lot."

Isabel met her gaze. "Even if it's fleeting, it's nice to be close to you without having to pretend I'm not trying to be close to you."

"Do you know how hard it's going to be now, knowing that you want to be?"

Isabel lifted a shoulder. "Consolation prize for me. It would be worse if I were the crazy new staff writer, taken with her boss in a one-sided crush both embarrassing and desperate."

"That version has the word 'pilot' written all over it," Taylor said and looked up. It seemed the sky had spared not a single star, and they all twinkled down on a moment that could have been so very different. She turned her chin to Isabel and smiled ruefully. "You make this really difficult, you know that?"

Isabel chuckled. "Well, at least there's that." Her smile faded, causing something in Taylor to dim as well. "Maybe we should head back. It's pretty late."

She nodded as a wave of regret for what would never be washed over her.

They walked quietly back through the faux version of Manhattan that shifted from modern to historical as they went. Gone was the flirtation. A pallor had settled over the evening, and Taylor hated it.

As they traveled the darkened streets of 1930s Brooklyn, Isabel turned to her. "Something else you don't know about me is that I can be reckless. I once stole the keys to my dad's car and ran it into a ditch."

"Your teenage rebellious years?"

"Something like that. But it never fully went away, that rebellious streak. When I know I should pump the brakes, I tend to floor the gas."

"So, when you're feelin—" But she didn't get to finish that sentence because Isabel kissed her. Wrapped her damn arm around Taylor's waist, held her in place, and kissed her expertly, authoritatively, and had Taylor's pulse surging hard and fast.

What in the world kind of kiss is this?

Her head swam and her libido raced. And then there was Isabel's mouth, which, dear God, was doing wonderful things to hers. She slid a hand behind Isabel's neck, into her thick, soft hair and held on until the amazing experience was over, leaving her reeling on that sidewalk.

"See what I mean?" Isabel said through shallow breaths. "Reckless. It's always been a problem."

Taylor nodded, still searching for air. "I think I get it now."

"For what it's worth, I'm sorry."

Taylor nodded again, touching her swollen lips and trying to keep up. "Me too. Deeply." She glanced around, because, where were they exactly? Had that kiss transported them back in time? Cognizant thought floated back to her and she realized that no, they were simply making out on the studio backlot in the dark of night. No need to be alarmed, except that her body was. In fact, it was on *five*-alarm status and in desperate need of a continuation of that decadent encounter. Except that they'd agreed to circumvent whatever it was between them in the name of workplace integrity. Whose *stupid* idea was that? Who cared about workplace integrity at a time like this? All she really wanted to do was take Isabel home right now and take her sweet time.

"What do we do now?" Isabel asked.

"I think I pick up my dog and we walk back to our cars. And tomorrow, we come back here and do our jobs." She hated those words. Hated them.

"Right. I can do that. And the other part? What should we do about that?" She had the sexiest look in her eyes, and if Taylor didn't watch herself, there'd be some fireworks on one of these fake fire escapes.

"Let's table that for now."

"As in, *on* a table or…?" Isabel grinned like the smart-ass that she was, and the tension melted away.

"I like you," Taylor said, with a great deal of confidence. That kiss had given her the courage to say so. "I really like you, Ms. Chase."

"I like you, too."

"Shall we return to the world?"

"The one in which you're my boss?"

"Unfortunately, yes."

Isabel nodded her acquiescence. "Back to the harshness of reality we go."

Only, when Taylor drove home that night, it felt nothing like the reality she'd known. She was altered after that stolen moment and carried it with her as she snaked her way up the hillside to her home. Raisin, fully awake now, rode with his paws on the passenger door, watching the world go by. "She's so different, Raze. She makes *me* feel so different. What's one to do about that, huh?" Raisin glanced over at her, wagging his tail, but left her to solve the problem that was Isabel Chase on her own.

CHAPTER FOURTEEN

The morning traffic that came through the Cat's Pajamas on this particular Tuesday seemed to have hit a lull as Isabel slid into what was now her customary chair.

"I have news," Autumn said with a sigh. She came around the counter and placed a carafe of coffee on the table inhabited by herself, Hadley, and Gia. Meeting for a cup of joe and pastry before heading to work was turning into a regular occurrence, and one she looked forward to each day.

"Well, hit us with it already," Gia said. "I don't do well with suspense. It's like a jack-in-the-box, but with words."

Hadley turned to her slowly. "You're a competitive surfer, weirdo. You have nerves of steel. Is this Colombian?" Autumn nodded proudly and brought over a tray of warm pastries that left Isabel drooling.

Gia waved off the comment. "Nope. Totally different. That's something I have control over. If Autumn has news, what if it's bad news?" She motioned to her stomach. "See? My muscles are already tight."

Isabel pointed at her. "You're an empathetic person who is worried for her friend."

Autumn patted Gia's head. "A softy with killer abs. I appreciate you, Gia-Pet."

Isabel smiled at the nickname. "So, what's the news?" She took a sip of the divine coffee and sat back in her chair as goodness rushed over her.

Autumn threw a glance to the counter to make sure Steve, the barista, had it covered and then took a seat with her friends. "My ex is engaged. It was all over Facebook last night. Ring shots, posed kissing. A total punch in the gut."

Hadley sat up. "Someone's agreed to marry Olivia?"

Autumn smiled at the comment, but it was the tiniest of smiles, and that said something.

"What's this Olivia like?" Isabel asked. She seemed to be the only one who didn't know her.

"She sucks," Gia said.

Hadley jumped on and tried to explain in gentler terms. "If Cruella de Vil was from Calabasas and blond, you'd be somewhere in the right neighborhood. She was amazing to Autumn in the beginning, until she wasn't anymore. Then she turned just plain awful when she started working out at this elite gym, which we sort of realized was more of a cult than a gym. Olivia quickly rose in their ranks and became awful and vapid. We don't miss her."

Gia shook her head emphatically. "We don't. Because she sucks."

"I miss the nice Olivia from the good part of our relationship," Autumn said sadly, staring into her mug. "She wasn't always awful."

Isabel felt for her as the new vulnerability on display was so unlike the badass, outspoken Autumn she'd come to know. It was clear this Olivia had done quite a number on her.

Gia slid Autumn a croissant from the center of the table.

"No, thanks. I don't have much of an appetite. Besides, I put those out for Had. She loves bread."

Hadley held up a hand. "While I appreciate the looking-out, get thee back, Satan. I've been killing myself to fit into a dress designed to fit no reasonable living female, but it's beautiful, so I have no choice."

"I'm not sure I could do that for any dress ever," Isabel said, reflecting. "No," she added, snagging a croissant. "I'm sure. There would be no way. I'm obsessed with food."

"What's the dress for?" Gia asked.

"The store's having a gala for our designers. It's all very upper crust and Beverly Hills. Thereby, I need to fit into a memorable dress I can work like Tina Turner on a Proud Mary tour. I'd show you my legs, but as I said, they're a work in progress."

Isabel made a show of taking a big bite of a flaky croissant. "I don't know, Had. I'm not sure any dress, designer or not, is worth missing out on one of these warm bad boys. It melts in your mouth. How do you get it to do that?" she asked Autumn.

Autumn shook her head. "Pajamas secret. Can't tell you that."

Isabel nodded in overly interested mode. "See, Had? They're *secret* recipe pastries. Better get on it."

Hadley blinked at her and then at the tray. Back to Isabel enjoying the croissant and then again to the tray. It was a *Sophie's Choice* moment for the pastry books. "Hand me *half* of one."

Autumn smiled and tore a croissant for Hadley. "You're gorgeous already, by the way, dress or no dress."

"Aww, you're a very sweet enabler." Hadley made a gesture as if to push it all aside. "Back to Olivia, queen of the solo orgasm." She turned in happy greeting to her half croissant.

"Does that mean what I think it means?" Isabel asked. "The solo orgasm?"

"She could be selfish in bed," Autumn said. "Or just overly sleepy. It was hard to tell."

Gia leaned in. "She accepted what was given to her and moved the hell on, adding to her suckage."

Isabel's jaw fell. "I see why you broke up with her."

The look on Autumn's face dimmed. "I didn't. She dumped me for the woman who owns the gym. And now they're getting married, something I will never do," she said with very little inflection in her voice. "I'll probably die old and alone, standing behind that counter right there, begging people to buy coffee from the old coffee lady."

They all followed Autumn's gaze to the spot in question, prompting Steve, who stood there, to wave happily. Of course, they all waved back at him.

Isabel shook her head. "You're too awesome to die alone, Old Coffee Lady. I'll die with you. Fuck it. We can be spinsters united in dreary."

Gia shook her head. "I don't really think you're gonna be alone either, Iz. Not the way your pal Taylor was cruising you the other night on the beach. I needed a fire extinguisher."

Autumn nodded. "We looked for one."

Isabel released a breath. "Yeah, I don't think that's going to work out. We kissed. It was epic. And now we move around each other at work, pretending it didn't happen."

Hadley stood up in anger. "Hold it. You guys kissed, and you said nothing?" She sat down again and leaned forward, her voice returning to soft and tender as she attempted to tamp down her outrage. "I don't know what friends are like in New Hampshire, but here we tell each other that kind of thing. It's an unbendable rule."

Isabel smiled, as she'd never seen Hadley's eyes get so big. But then it was also cute in a feisty puppy kind of way. "Got it. I would like to formally apologize for breaking this unperceived rule. But there really wasn't much to tell."

"You were kissed…or kissed someone—we don't actually know which, because you haven't told us. Either way, you failed. Failed," Hadley said sadly. The feisty puppy was now a wounded puppy.

Isabel nodded slowly. "I'm sensing your melancholy and acknowledging it."

Gia folded her arms. "Had's right."

Autumn picked up her mug and shrugged. "She just expresses herself with a little more heart. So why are we still sitting here waiting? Dish."

"Fine. Okay," Isabel said. "A few nights back, we had a great time walking the studio lot after work. And I mean late-night after work. We passed all the cool spots and ended up on the Forrest Gump bench, where we talked about what was happening between us."

"And then she laid one on you?" Autumn asked. "Hopefully with a few more moves than Forrest Gump."

Isabel shook her head. "The opposite. We were in 1930s Manhattan and I grabbed *her* and went for it. I had to."

"Yes!" With two hands in the air, Gia grinned. "My new hero."

Hadley grabbed her heart and leaned back in blissful surrender like something out of a Charlie Brown special. "My heart is swelling. I am incredibly happy right now. Press on. I'll rejoin your already-in-progress conversation soon."

Isabel closed one eye. "Slow that swell. It's been tumbleweeds between us ever since. Desolate." Isabel thought back over the last few days. Taylor had been at *Sister Dale* quite a bit, but she'd checked in on Isabel once her episode had wrapped.

"And?" Taylor had asked, standing next to her cubicle in anticipation.

"I think it went really well," Isabel said, admiring Taylor's look. She had her hair fastened in a knot. Translation: The gorgeous and elegant column of her neck was on display. She looked professional and hot and just downright beautiful. Isabel tried hard to not think about that flood of pleasure that came with kissing Taylor. At least, not right now when she was expected to produce words that sounded somewhat professional.

"It did go well. I've seen the footage. And here it goes." Taylor took a deep breath. "You were right. I have no problem admitting that. The storyline was the right way to go, and it's gonna be a killer episode."

"Thank you. That means a lot." A long pause, and not the comfortable kind. Isabel cringed and forced a smile. "I look forward to its air date."

"Not long now." It was Taylor's turn to smile as proverbial crickets filled the large gap of silence. Kissing had apparently stripped them of their ability to construct sentences in easy succession, which was unfun and disastrous for their day-to-day. "Right, well, I'll let you get back to work on..."

"Story notes," Isabel said, pointing at her screen. "For Lyle's script."

"Right, well. Enjoy your day."

"Back atcha. Have a good one." Yep, she'd actually said *have a good one*, probably the stupidest phrase in the English vernacular. Isabel had clicked her pen a few dozen times in frustration. And then a few dozen more for good measure. That kiss, she understood, was beginning to cost them...well, *them*.

Gia shrugged. "Maybe she's just gathering enough courage to turn the tables."

"Yeah, I don't think so," Isabel said. "Though she is having a party this weekend at her house and invited me. You know, in addition to the whole staff. I'm told everyone important in Hollywood should be there. No pressure or anything."

That perked Hadley right up, her first stop always fashion. "What are you wearing?"

"I have my go-to dress," Isabel said. "An old standby. Simple, black."

Hadley nodded. "Sounds serviceable enough, but I have other options. Alluring ones. Let me run with this one, okay?"

"Yeah?" Isabel asked. "You would do that?" Having someone with actual fashion sense help her get ready for a party that already had her out of her comfort zone was a fabulous idea. She'd owe Hadley.

Hadley passed Isabel her phone. "Type the date and time of this party. Taylor Andrews is not gonna know what hit her when I'm finished."

"I'm in." Isabel sat back to enjoy her coffee, feeling better about the looming party, and reaffirmed for herself that she would, in fact, attend. It might even be fun.

CHAPTER FIFTEEN

Taylor loved a good party. In fact, it was one of her favorite things about Hollywood, hobnobbing with fancy food and drinks in a beautiful setting. What could be better? Sure, she rolled her eyes at the starlets who tried to outshine each other and impress the powerful producers present, but beyond the petty, major deals were made around lavishly lit pools. She surveyed the expanse of her own outdoor living space, the wait staff, the entertainment, and the abundance of twinkling lights (intricately placed for maximum aesthetic). Her gaze moved across the happy faces of her guests, sipping cocktails and enjoying themselves. She spotted a group of cast members from *Water*, and just as she was about to head their way, the world tilted. She froze for a moment, not knowing what hit her.

Isabel Chase had just walked into her backyard looking like she'd stepped out of the Golden Age of Hollywood and, in one quick moment, changed the stasis of her night entirely.

Taylor blinked to clear her head, but the effect hadn't worn off. Isabel was Audrey Hepburn and Grace Kelly combined. She wore a simple but elegant blue dress that hugged her curves. The neckline was modest and the sleeves short. Tiny diamonds dotted the bodice and elevated her elegance even further. Her hair was curled and her lipstick red, making her lips pouty and perfect. The outfit was finished off with a pair of killer black heels. It was Isabel, but in a way Taylor'd never seen her before. But then, why would she have? And how was she supposed to carry on her hostess duties with this kind of distraction hovering? Good God.

Taylor stood with an old producer friend who was chatting her ear off near the bar, and she nodded and laughed in what she thought were all the appropriate places. Meanwhile, her heart beat way too fast and her stomach was in perpetual somersaults at the exquisite woman across the pool. She stole glances at Isabel, who was speaking to Richie Lords, the dashing actor known for all those superhero movies. He gestured to the waiter carrying a tray of Champagne and snagged a couple for the two of them. Of course he'd noticed her. Who wouldn't?

"If you'll excuse me," she said to the gabby producer. "I see someone I must say hello to." She moved across the outdoor space, smiling and greeting her guests on the way to Isabel, pulled along by some sort of invisible magnet. Her guests didn't make it easy.

"It's beautiful out here, Taylor."

"I adore this house. Did you remodel?"

"Who is the caterer? This crab is heaven sent."

"Is that actually Kevin Cohen on guitar? Didn't he win a Grammy? How did you score him?"

She answered their questions and turned to where she'd last seen Isabel, only to come face-to-face with Aspen. If Isabel was the picture of old-school glamour, Aspen could best be described as modern overindulgence. Her boobs were pushed up, her hair had been swept to the side, and she had a pretty aggressive spray tan going. The contrast between the two continued to startle her.

"You, T-Bear, look radiant," Aspen said, kissing her cheek and lingering a few seconds too long. "And this party is bustling with everyone who is anyone. I don't know how you managed to get them all in one spot."

"Not as easy as it looks." Taylor studied the guests and had to admit that Aspen was right. Producers, actors, directors, and even a handful of politicians had all come out to her not-so-little gathering. She'd started throwing the occasional cocktail party years ago, once she had a good handful of industry friends. Hollywood was all about who you knew.

As her career took off, so had her parties. Although now they were some of the most talked about in the business—not for being wild or crazy, but designed for drinks and discussion in what she hoped was a scenically pleasing backdrop. She glanced at the glorious hillside view and knew she didn't have to hope too hard. Toss in a fantastic caterer, attentive wait staff, and few A-list musicians crooning from beside the pool, and the evening was complete. Well, almost. Where was Isabel?

"Come with me," Aspen said, taking her hand with a gleam in her eye. "Patrick McMartin is in your living room as we speak. We can chat him up together about Sally Ride. Tag-team him." Before she could protest, Aspen pulled her toward the house, a route that would take her right past—would you look at that—Isabel.

"Can I join you in a minute?" she asked Aspen, attempting to free her hand.

"This won't take long. I promise." Aspen held on to Taylor tightly. "And then I'll be happy to help you play hostess. I'm great at it." Taylor could argue and break away or put in the ten minutes to make her night easier in the long run. As they approached Isabel, who was talking to, bless her poor heart, Lyric Larkin, they locked eyes. Isabel broke into a smile, the warmth of which smacked Taylor squarely in the chest.

"Hi," Taylor said. "I've been trying to talk to you all night. We're just going to say hello inside—and then I'll be right back. Don't go anywhere." Isabel nodded, and Aspen tugged, ignoring Isabel altogether.

"Come on, Tay. You can get me a drink first. You know what I like more than I do."

Isabel's smile faltered and Lyric seemed to launch back into some sort of story. Damn it. Taylor did her best to send Isabel an "I'm sorry" stare as she was whisked away, but she wasn't sure it was received. She'd fulfill her obligation to Aspen, circle back to Isabel, and make up for what may have felt like a slight. While she didn't have the Isabel puzzle all figured out, she wanted to try and assemble as many pieces as possible.

Twenty minutes later, and Aspen was still talking Patrick McMartin's ear off. She was also touching him a lot, which was typical Aspen. Her sex appeal was her go-to weapon of choice, and she didn't discriminate. "You have impressed so many people with your bare-bones aesthetic," Aspen purred, rubbing his arms. "You're a fantastic director. I can't get enough of your work."

"I have to give credit to my cinematographers." Patrick adjusted his tie. "They make me look better than I am."

"Oh, I don't know about that." An eyelash bat.

Classic. Predictable. Boring.

Patrick was young and seemed to enjoy the attention, however. Once it seemed that the two of them had a good give-and-take happening, Taylor managed to excuse herself without causing much distraction. She'd fulfilled her obligation to Aspen and had delivered her right into the hands of a director who would be crazy to want her for this particular part. Not her problem.

Now, on to her own enjoyment of this party.

❖

Isabel was intrigued. Lyric Larkin was one of the more interesting characters she'd come across in a while, and Hollywood had a lot. In the midst of their exchange, she would have given anything for a notepad to jot a few of her observations. She'd be yet another fantastic character for a future script. Well, as long as it called for a vapid and entitled Hollywood wannabe.

"Did I tell you that my husband is an energy drink mobile?" she asked.

Isabel took a sec with that one. "You mean mogul?"

"Energy drink mobile," Lyric said, emphasizing each word as if Isabel were hard of hearing.

That was Isabel's cue to give up. "Oh, an energy drink mobile! Got it. Super cool. You're so lucky. I bet you're never thirsty."

"Right? And I have my own TV show that's killing it right now. Not sure if you've seen it."

Isabel nodded. "*Sister Dale*. I have. It's hard to look away."

"Right?" Lyric favored that word. "Wait till you see the upcoming episodes. You're going to die. I don't mean to toot my own horn, but it's some of my best work."

Isabel swallowed the words that threatened to fly from her mouth. The ones that said Lyric was a fucking liar and hadn't written a single word of the soon-to-air episodes. But she also wasn't stupid and knew who Lyric's father was. She smiled sweetly instead, as soul-sucking as it was. "I can't wait."

"I like your dress," Lyric said, sipping a margarita through a tiny straw. "It reminds me of Rita Hayworth. I mean, if you're into that kind of thing. It's pretty, I guess."

"Thank you," Isabel said of the underwhelming compliment. It certainly didn't compare to Lyric's ensemble, which had her huge breasts exploding from her itty-bitty waist. Isabel worried about the stress to her rib cage and felt compelled to find Lyric a cheeseburger for reinforcement. Her overblown lips, however, would make the cheeseburger hard to eat, so she shelved the idea altogether.

"The television business is hard," Lyric went on to say. "But I think I've finally conquered it."

Isabel opened her mouth to combat the declaration because, God of Gods, someone had to. But she paused at the sensation of a hand on the small of her back. Right on cue, her skin heated. She didn't even have to turn to know who had done that to her—only one person could.

"Sorry about earlier," Taylor said with a sincere smile. That, coupled with the killer silver dress with a slit up the side, had her mouth dry. Taylor's hair had been pulled up and back. Small strands fell delicately alongside her face, each with a slight twist. "I was upholding an agreement or I would have, of course, stopped to talk. Please know that."

"It's okay," Isabel said simply. Aspen was there, and Aspen commanded a lot of attention, she was learning. Attention Taylor seemed willing to dole out whenever Aspen asked. She pushed the thought aside, choosing to not think ill of Taylor. It was a nice night, and she should enjoy herself and Taylor's company, now that she was free.

"I love you in this dress," Taylor said. And then quietly in Isabel's ear, "You're gorgeous, and it's driving me a little crazy."

Isabel willed herself not to blush. "You're kind, and looking beautiful yourself." She dropped her voice. "And I'm not just saying that."

"Taylor's come a long way from high school," Lyric chimed in. Isabel had completely forgotten she was standing there. How unfortunate to learn she still was. "Did she tell you we used to call her Tubs?"

Isabel turned a sharp eye to Lyric. "Not specifically. No."

Lyric giggled, high pitched and piercing. "She looks night and day from the way she did back then. She's taken off the pounds, man. You'll have to tell me how you did it at some point, Taylor. Personally, I'm all about the wheatgrass, but you might have your own method."

"I've never tried wheatgrass," Taylor said politely.

But Lyric's mouth ran full steam ahead. "Oh! And it took you forever to get picked in gym class! Remember that? It was a running joke. No one picked her." Lyric laughed merrily, and Isabel watched as the light dimmed in Taylor's eyes. She wanted to throttle Lyric. Vivid fantasies of doing just that quickly took shape. "Those were the days, I tell you."

"They were days, all right," Taylor said, with classy reserve.

Lyric turned to Isabel. "So, as you can tell, Taylor and I go way back. We're old friends."

"Doesn't sound like it," Isabel said flatly. "In fact, it sounds like you were mean in high school and not much has changed since."

Lyric waved her off. "It's all in good fun, right, Taylor? Is that Bruno Mars by the shrimp dip?" She didn't wait for an answer and dashed off to find out.

When they were alone, Taylor turned to her. "You didn't have to go to bat for me. I'm used to girls like Lyric Larkin. Well, women now. That's the sad part."

Isabel looked her right in the eye. "There is not a world in which I won't go toe-to-toe for you with a witch like that."

"And there's the feisty side I love. Remind me not to get on your bad side."

Isabel nodded. "Don't get me started on lane changes without a signal. I give those people the downcast eyebrows." She demonstrated with the deepest furrow possible.

Taylor laughed, which meant she was feeling lighter again. Goal achieved. "Well, it seems Miss Larkin got off easy, then. She should count herself lucky."

"Very." Isabel turned so she faced Taylor dead-on. "We haven't talked about your wildly impressive home."

"Oh, that's right!" Taylor glanced around. "You haven't been here before. What do you think?"

"Is it odd to say that it's exactly what I imagined for you, only even more impressive? My imagination, wild as it is, didn't quite do it justice." She shook her head and walked a few steps in the backyard living space. "I don't know how you leave for work every day with this kind of view waiting for you at home."

"Only because I know I'll be back to enjoy it." A pause. "Iz," Taylor said quietly.

The casual nickname, when it came from Taylor, continued to give her goose bumps. She rubbed her exposed arms and hoped Taylor hadn't noticed. "Yes?"

She took a step closer so not to be overheard. "I wasn't kidding. The dress is…amazing, and I'm having a really difficult time. I don't mean to behave poorly, so perhaps I shouldn't confess that, but…it's the truth."

"Thank you." She glanced down at the dress, nervous because Taylor's eyes were on her, but also invigorated, because *Taylor's eyes were on her*. "Hadley helped. When it comes to this stuff, I'm out of my depth. But hearing that you like it makes it all worthwhile." Apparently, it was Taylor's turn to blush as they stood there, staring at each other. The world around them had gone still, making Isabel feel like she and Taylor were the only two people there. The conversation around them dimmed and the people faded away. Was that weird? She decided it wasn't. In fact, she relished the effect. With the kind of crackle and pop that was passing between them now, if someone lit a match, the whole place would most certainly go. "I have to confess I was nervous."

"For what?" Taylor asked, looking somewhat dazed.

"First Hollywood party and all."

Taylor lit up, pulling them back on track. "That's right. It is! I should introduce you around. Show you who the important people are, the ones to get to know."

She grinned. "I would love that."

"Tay, I need you." Taylor paused and dropped her head at the desperate sound of Aspen's voice from not too far away. Isabel cringed when she saw her. Why did Aspen have to look so fantastic? Why? Moments later, she appeared, glamorous and perfect, at Taylor's elbow. Isabel felt herself shrink in her spot, because who was she kidding? She was out of her league with these people. With Taylor. All of it.

Aspen gave her a once-over. "Oh, hi, Isabel. Don't you look adorable in that getup. I didn't realize some people would attend in costume. I love the tenacity."

Ohh, war had been *declared*. But the comment packed a punch whether she wanted it to or not. Maybe Hadley's retro idea had been too ambitious for someone like Isabel to pull off. She felt meek and silly under Aspen's gaze, and she hated that she allowed her the satisfaction.

Aspen didn't miss a beat and turned to Taylor. "I got out that old cutting board, the one your mom sent from your grandma's house and wound up with a giant splinter right in the middle of my poor index finger." She held up the finger in punctuation, her sad little face executed flawlessly. "It's just killing me, Tay. Do you think you can give me a hand?" She inclined her head in the direction of the house.

"I'm actually in the middle of a conversation," Taylor said and then brightened, her tone shifting to one of encouragement. "I'm sure you can handle it. There are tweezers—"

"On the top shelf of your medicine cabinet in the master bathroom. I know." She looked to Taylor, with big helpless eyes. "I'm just not sure I can stomach this, and my finger is really starting to throb. Would you mind?"

"It's fine. Go ahead," Isabel said. Her voice sounded normal. She was almost sure.

"Sorry," Taylor mouthed before rolling her eyes and following Aspen, who waved all five fingers in victorious farewell.

Isabel hated herself for the jealousy that crept in and circulated. She squared her shoulders, deciding then and there not to let Aspen Wakefield under her skin. If Taylor wasn't free to make introductions, she'd set out on her own. She snagged a glass of something pink and bubbly from a passing waiter and took a lap around the yard. She made eye contact with a few of the guests and smiled, but never did find the right moment to strike up a conversation with the people Taylor had pointed out. Everyone was good-looking and intimidating. Another lap and another glass. These glasses were really so very pretty. Shiny and light, and how crazy that she could see the moon through hers. Okay, maybe no more of the pink bubbly wonderfulness. She focused on the music and bopped her head as if having the most fantastic time beneath the gazebo. Still no sign of Taylor, but she probably had hostess duties to attend to…or, you know, some intimate Aspen ones. It was fine, really. It was *fine.* Taylor owed her nothing. A third lap and oh, look! There was Kathleen, a friendly face, at long last.

"Well, hello, there!" she said to her friend and producer, feeling more at ease from the alcohol. "I didn't know you were here."

Kathleen smiled. She wore a dignified green dress with a pair of sassy yellow heels. Her gray hair was spiked, making her look extra fun tonight. "Isabel Chase, look at you!" Isabel did a simple twirl for Kathleen and kissed her cheek. "This is my husband, Bruce. He knows all about the new wonder kid at work, so your reputation precedes you."

"Bruce, so nice to meet you!" She extended her hand, which he accepted and kissed.

"Likewise," he said. "You have a fan in Kathleen."

"She's being generous."

"She is not," Kathleen remarked.

Isabel and Kathleen had developed a sort of alliance since she'd submitted her episode. It became increasingly clear that they collaborated well together, which was necessary given Taylor's absence. Kathleen was patient, smart, if not slightly soft when it came to laying down the hammer. She'd hit a few speed bumps in getting the higher-ups to listen to her the way they would have Taylor. She'd also confided in Isabel that maybe the showrunner gig wasn't for her. She didn't have the disposition or temperament. Isabel couldn't imagine anyone feeling that way, but she liked Kathleen and would go out of her way to support her.

Isabel leaned in and whispered, "This party is too important for me. Any second they're going to escort me out of here. Mark my words."

"All of us together," Kathleen whispered back. "But it's very Taylor Andrews. That woman knows what she's doing and the right people to assemble."

Isabel whistled low. "She certainly does. How am I going to make it in this town?"

"Oh, I suspect you're going to do just fine." A thought seemed to occur to her. "You know, while you're here, let me introduce you to Gerald Hagerman, he's a very important man at the network. Vice president of programming. You'll want him to know your name."

"Who's this lady?" Gerald Hagerman asked jovially between puffs of his cigar. So that's where the syrupy sweet aroma emanated from. In the other hand, he clutched a bourbon, neat. He was a portly guy with a mustache. Didn't fit the LA exec profile in the slightest, but then again, neither did she.

Kathleen gestured to her. "Gerald, you need to meet Isabel Chase. She's new to the writing staff on *Water* and has an episode airing next week that's going to knock your socks off. Lots of positive word of mouth already. You'll be hearing her name more in the future, I assure you."

She extended her hand. "Pleasure to meet you."

"Isabel Chase, you say?"

"Yes, sir. That's me."

"I look forward to your work. I read the episode and was heartily impressed. I'll take any little ratings bump you can give me, too. You deliver me numbers, and I'll do more than remember your name."

Oh, okay. So this was what parties like this were for. It was all coming together.

"Gerald, I see you've met Isabel." They turned to see Taylor, looking tired but still smiling up a storm. The bubbly seemed to have given Isabel's eyes a mind of their own as her gaze swept across Taylor's dress, lingering on the dip of cleavage. She swallowed and looked away. And then back. She preferred looking back.

"I like her already," Gerald said. "I'm giving this woman her own show if next week goes well."

Taylor held up a hand. "Not so fast. I'm keeping her."

Isabel impulsively threw her body between Taylor and Gerald. "Pay no attention to the crazy woman." It gave them all a good laugh.

"Taylor," Kathleen said, once Gerald moved on to a conversation with a nearby starlet. "I've adored your gathering tonight, but I promised my doting husband an In-n-Out burger if he was patient enough."

Isabel sidled up next to her. "A burger, you say? Can I stow away in your trunk?"

Taylor smiled. "You're not going anywhere just yet, I hope." She and Taylor locked eyes, and the radiant green did things to her. No, she would definitely not be walking away from those eyes.

"Only joking," she said quietly.

Kathleen eyed them for a moment and, with an amused smile, kissed both of their cheeks. "Thank you for a memorable evening. Don't have too much fun without me."

"Never," Isabel said with a smile. "Eat a burger for me!"

"Done." Kathleen winked at them and headed off.

Isabel spent the next two hours chitchatting with various guests, Taylor staying firmly by her side. Except for that time Aspen couldn't find the extra glasses or needed Taylor to come tell her friend that joke she'd once told Aspen at a fancy restaurant ("Remember that really romantic one?") She truly had perfected the art of commanding Taylor's attention, and Isabel felt her resolve slipping with each passing moment.

She should have gone out for that burger after all.

On her own again, Isabel wondered if she'd ever get used to a gathering like this one, packed with celebrities at every turn. The kid in her had been freaking the hell out all night in awe of just about everyone she encountered, while the adult was doing her best to appear calm, cool, and not at all a crazy, wide-eyed newbie. This was the world she'd always longed to work in, write for, and here she was, doing just that. But Isabel's ambition didn't stop there. She wanted to learn, absorb, and understand what it took to run her own show. Being here and seeing it all up close had only stoked that fire higher. As long as she worked hard and played her cards right, she might actually have that shot at running her own show someday. She'd put in the time, kill herself to do good work, and play nice with those around her. Whatever it took.

When the final guests began to trickle out just after one a.m., Isabel waited off to the side as Taylor said her farewells. She'd also looked on as she put an inebriated Aspen into her sober friend's car.

"You don't want to take me home yourself?" Aspen had purred and run her hand down Taylor's shoulder. She was about as subtle as Liberace under a strobe light.

"No, I've got stuff to tend to here." Taylor turned to the friend. "Do me a favor. If there are paparazzi outside her place, take her around the back drive."

The girl nodded and offered Taylor the thumbs-up sign. "You got it."

Isabel and Taylor stood in the circular drive and watched the car pull away. The image of Aspen waving at Taylor with sultry eyes served as a gentle reminder of what the situation actually was. The reality hit her in the face like a bucket of ice water.

"I better head out, too," Isabel said.

"Wait. Not yet. There's something I wanted to show you."

"Okay." Intrigued, Isabel followed Taylor to her laptop. She quickly pulled up an email string from several studio execs who had viewed the rough cut of Isabel's episode.

"Take a look at these," Taylor said, and folded her arms.

One exec had written, *You guys hit this one out of the park. Kudos to you and your new writer. Keep that one around.*

Another chimed in, *My jaw dropped. Well done, Taylor. Things are heating up. Excited for the rest of the season.* There were several more of similar sentiment, and by the end Isabel was beaming.

"I wanted to congratulate you personally," Taylor said.

Isabel scoffed. "I didn't do much."

"You did. You had a great idea and you fought for it. One of the many ways you've impressed me."

"I don't know what to say." The way Taylor was looking at her had Isabel's toes curling and her mouth dry. She flashed to their kiss on the studio lot. The visual was interrupted when out of nowhere she imagined Aspen running up and tapping Taylor on the shoulder. A total buzzkill. What the hell? She tried to shrug it off, only it wasn't that easy. "And now I should get out of your hair and let you relax. You must be tired after tonight." The caterers had long since packed up and restored the place to status quo. It was only the two of them left, and the hour was late.

"Not really." Taylor stepped out of her heels and lost a good three inches. She seemed more accessible now. Sexier, too, if that was possible. Isabel wanted nothing more than to reach out and touch her.

She shrugged and decided to level with Taylor. "Just seemed like you had your hands full with Aspen tonight."

"Ah." Taylor's head dropped and she rubbed the back of her neck. Isabel wanted to do that for her, but something held her back. Taylor raised her gaze. "So, this is about Aspen. It's hard to relax with her in the room. That's true. It's different with you, though. With us."

"She seems to really need you. A lot."

Taylor nodded and walked back into her living room. "It's what she does."

"Yeah, but to what end? Can I ask that? Because when will it be enough?"

That's when silence hit.

Taylor closed her eyes briefly. "You know I didn't *want* to cater to her tonight. It's a delicate situation. I thought I explained that already."

Isabel couldn't stop herself. "But you *did* cater to her, and whether you explained it or not, your giving in only goes to show her that her tactics work."

Taylor nodded. "It's tricky. I just didn't want her making a scene."

"Or maybe things with you two aren't as squared away as you tell yourself." Her pathetic side was beginning to show, but she couldn't seem to hide it.

"What does that mean? No. Isabel." They stared at one another for another uncomfortable moment, the kind that felt way longer than it actually was. "She's my ex, and our relationship was a train wreck on top of a ten-car pile-up of awful, and now it's over. I'm thrilled about that part."

"Are you?" Isabel regretted the veiled accusation. It wasn't her place to stick her nose into Taylor's business. She had no claim. She was no one. "This time I really am going. It's late and getting… awkward. And if there's one thing I don't want, it's anything that's going to overtake us. Whatever we are, I happen to like it. So, thank you for having me to your party tonight. I had fun."

"Iz, don't go." The words reverberated in the air all around them. Taylor grabbed her wrist and with a slight tug, pulled her in until their bodies pressed. Taylor's arms moved to Isabel's waist and around, holding her there. Isabel's lips parted at the unexpected contact, and her temperature rose.

"I don't want you to go," Taylor said simply. She searched Isabel's eyes for some sort of permission, which was silly because Isabel had no willpower where Taylor was concerned. It was a good thing Taylor had hold of her, as she felt her knees wobble.

"What are we doing?" Isabel whispered, her gaze dipping from Taylor's eyes to her mouth.

"I think we both know," Taylor said simply.

This time Isabel waited. The move had to be Taylor's.

"You are so beautiful," Taylor said, and traced the neckline of Isabel's dress with her finger. The air left the room. All sound vanished. She closed her eyes at the surge of need, of desperate want. She swallowed against the acute assault on her body only to have her desire ignite exponentially with each second that ticked by, with each trace of that finger across her heated skin. Her center throbbed and her breasts ached to be touched. Taylor's hands were so very close. She watched with rapt interest as they inched closer. With the back of her hand, Taylor brushed against the fabric at the front of Isabel's dress, causing it to rub uncomfortably across her nipples. She did it again more purposefully, meeting Isabel's gaze, watching her reaction with intense focus. What Isabel wouldn't give to be done with that fabric, with the dress entirely. Explicit images rained down as she ached for more.

She knew in that moment that Taylor wasn't finished. Taylor was going to have her, and Isabel was done trying to resist the pull.

Oh, this was happening.

This was *definitely* going to happen.

Isabel's breathing turned shallow as Taylor's finger traced the dip in her cleavage. She heard herself hiss in a breath. Their eyes held steady, and the lust in Taylor's was like nothing she'd ever seen. Combusting, right then and there, beneath her fingertips was a definite possibility. Taylor ran her hands down the length of Isabel's arms and intertwined their fingers. She crossed their hands behind Isabel's back and studied her lips as she leaned in, on a mission. The kiss would go down as one of the most memorable Isabel had experienced. There was no buildup, no preamble. Taylor caught her mouth, and instantly she knew she better buckle up, because she was about to be owned. Her knees shook pleasantly at the thought. Their lips moved together in a delicious tangle and Isabel gave back every bit that she was given, pushing her tongue into Taylor's mouth, tasting her.

It felt as if everything had been leading up to this moment.

If the kiss on the studio lot had been sexy, this one brought a promise of torrid things to come. It forced the air from her lungs in a hot rush, and a low sound came from her throat. She'd been dreaming of touching that gorgeous blond hair from the very first day, and she didn't hold back now. She slid her fingers into thick tresses, pulling Taylor in that much further. Her center throbbed uncomfortably as she grasped that silky hair.

Isabel was acutely aware that they didn't have long, and once they arrived at a bed, at a couch, anything sturdy, she would have seconds before Taylor rendered her powerless. Therefore, she needed Taylor wearing significantly less than she wore now.

A preemptive measure. She was nothing if not a planner.

Isabel's fingers searched for the zipper tucked slyly on the side of Taylor's dress and tugged aggressively. Taylor broke the kiss and watched with careful attention as Isabel slid the dress off her shoulders and let it fall to the floor. The matching yellow lingerie halted her action. She had no choice but to feast on the sensual image. "I've never seen anything like you," Isabel said reverently and took a step into Taylor, taking in her skin, the generous curves of her breasts, her absolute beauty.

Music, still left over from the party, played from a sound system in the corner of the living room as Taylor took her hand and led her to the stairs. Taylor only made it to the first step before Isabel turned her around, unable to wait another second. With her hands on Taylor's waist, she kissed just above the yellow lace waistband and higher across her stomach. Taylor's hands slid into Isabel's hair, freeing it from the pins that held it back. At the metallic sounds of them falling, Taylor leaned down and crushed her mouth to Isabel's once again.

"Upstairs," she breathed. "Now."

"Lead the way." Isabel nodded against her mouth. "I'm yours."

She couldn't tell you what Taylor's bedroom looked like, as all she could see, hear, or touch was Taylor herself. Taylor made quick work of Isabel's dress, leaving her body on display. A potent shiver hit in response to her gaze as it moved across Isabel's skin. She didn't have the matching lingerie and probably never would, but the look on Taylor's face told her that she didn't care. "Iz," she breathed, kissing her shoulder. "God, Isabel, come here. I've been dreaming of you." Her hands moved down Isabel's back as they kissed, then lower to her ass and dipped inside the back of her bikinis, cupping her tightly. She lay down on the bed and pulled Isabel with her, never breaking contact.

Isabel slid between Taylor's legs and rocked her hips, slowly, purposefully, and watched as Taylor's face changed. She reached up and palmed Isabel's breasts through her bra, prompting Isabel to toss her head back, surrendering to the pleasure that ensued. She pushed herself up and straddled Taylor, ready to grant her more access. She slid one bra strap off her shoulder, then the other, before unclasping and discarding the bra onto the floor.

"Look at you," Taylor murmured. "God. Just look at you." Taylor's lips parted and she licked the bottom one. She tried to sit up, but Isabel placed a hand on her shoulder, holding her right where she was. She lowered a breast to just above Taylor's mouth and braced herself on her forearms above. Taylor greedily pulled the nipple in and sucked. She sucked hard. Isabel's eyes slammed shut and she swore quietly. Taylor lavished the same attention on her other breast as Isabel dropped her hips and pushed against her.

"I'm going to hell for this," Taylor breathed, slipping a thigh between Isabel's. "Totally worth it."

Isabel smiled and slid down to capture that mouth she couldn't get enough of. "We can go together."

With Taylor's tongue caressing hers, she was so distracted she didn't even notice she'd been flipped easily onto her back until she stared up into green depths. "I love your eyes," she whispered.

"My eyes?" Taylor asked, with a quiet laugh. "That's what you're focusing on?"

"Mmm-hmm. They undo me every time."

Taylor smiled and slipped her hand down the front of Isabel's bikinis. The long-awaited touch pulled a quick gasp from Isabel, who turned her head against the pillow, bucking her hips. She'd never responded to anyone this quickly. The sensation startled her. Taylor's fingers fluttered and grazed her lightly. Isabel had never been more aroused in her life, almost to the point of pain. The quick touches continued, sending her into a tailspin. She was coming undone beneath the featherlight attention. One graze, then another. She almost came right then, but Taylor pulled her hand away, moving to a new spot.

"You're unreal," Taylor breathed and watched Isabel's face for approval as she explored, stroked, and played. Isabel needed release badly and thrashed her hips in desperate search of it. Finally, she reached down and attempted to free herself from the constraints of her underwear. Anything to help this along. She was dying, absolutely drowning in a sea of overpowering want, and something had to change.

"You want these off?" Taylor asked, breathless. "Good. Me too."

She slid down the bed in that matching lingerie and with her teeth pulled down one side of Isabel's bikinis and then the other.

Was this actually happening?

Isabel moaned, knowing acutely that she would relive that moment for years to come. Taylor bent her head and began to take Isabel places she'd only imagined. With just a touch of Taylor's tongue, she nearly levitated off the bed altogether.

"Don't you go anywhere just yet," Taylor breathed against her. She gripped Isabel's hips and angled her so that she was completely vulnerable to all the things Taylor wanted to do to her, which was more than fine with her. Isabel shivered as she waited, the anticipation just another form of welcome torture. A second swipe of her tongue. Oh, dear God. But not yet quite where Isabel needed her. A third swipe. A fourth.

"You're a tease," Isabel managed. "You're teasing me."

Taylor lifted her beautiful face. "Isn't it fun?"

Another swipe that sent shock waves on a tour through her every inch. Taylor's hair tickled her stomach, only amplifying the barrage of sensations. Her hands found their new home, nestled snugly in Taylor's hair, and how wonderful that felt. Taylor devoted her attention to everywhere but where she'd be most effective, finding a rhythm all her own that Isabel had no choice but to match, making it clear whose show this was. Taylor built her up and then brought her back down in a mind-blowing performance that left Isabel intoxicated, if not maddened. Finally, Taylor entered her with a firm push of her fingers, and that was all it took. Isabel clenched down around her, the feel of Taylor inside her almost more than she could stand. Taylor filled her, twisting and searching, and good heavens, there it was. Taylor had found it and sent Isabel tumbling, capped off with a direct stroke of her tongue.

Isabel said Taylor's name as she came, turning her body against the sheets beneath her, as points of light danced behind her eyes in blissful display. Her body accepted wave after wave of glorious pleasure. She lost track of time, space, and reason.

The next thing she was aware of, Taylor moved up the bed and gathered her in, holding her close. She kissed Isabel's temple and ran a hand softly across the expanse of her back as Isabel recovered from the mind-numbing orgasm that had topped all others. She felt limp and limbless, like a really happy rag doll lying next to the gorgeous and smart woman who'd just taken her expertly. Yes, that's right. She'd been *taken*. She raised her gaze and met Taylor's eyes. She didn't have words just yet, but Taylor seemed to know what they would have been. She dipped her head and kissed Isabel tenderly.

"Do you excel at everything?" Isabel finally asked.

That pulled a laugh. "No. I think you've just proven you're funnier than I am."

"But *you* have matching underwear. Really pretty ones." She traced the underside of the bra Taylor unfortunately still wore. Not for long.

Taylor nodded. "I might have a vast collection."

"Dear God." Isabel covered her eyes as her body came to life in one big tingle. "How are you able to turn me on again so quickly?" But she couldn't wipe the grin off her face. Taylor caressed her breast softly, circling Isabel's nipple with her index finger, not helping the cause.

Taylor blinked in innocence. "I can take care of that. Pretty quickly, too."

"Oh no, you won't," Isabel said, easing herself on top. She slid her hips between Taylor's legs and closed her eyes. Even through the fancy lingerie she could feel how wet Taylor was, and it did things to her. Lustful things that motivated her exponentially to explore.

Taylor's eyes went wide and her lips parted as Isabel slid against her firmly. Once. Twice. "I figured you'd need some recovery time first."

"No way." Isabel shook her head as she looked down at Taylor, circling her hips, pressing them to Taylor's center, pulling quick little sounds from Taylor. This was heaven. "I've waited long enough. Wouldn't you say?" She winked and dove in, pulling down the cups of Taylor's bra, staring in awe at the perfectly round, full breasts that were revealed to her. Taylor's blessings seemed never ending. Isabel swirled a nipple with her tongue, and she palmed the other breast with determination.

"You don't mess around," Taylor breathed, bucking beneath her. Taylor, she was learning, was a talker, and Isabel liked it. It projected confidence, her favorite trait of Taylor's. She pushed the bra over Taylor's head and made quick work of the lace underwear. She could still hear music playing faintly from the living room. How far away that earlier party now seemed. As she lowered herself and their bodies came together, skin on skin, it felt like she and Taylor were the only ones on Earth. Taylor's eyes went hazy as she watched Isabel above her, rocking softly and then harder against her. That wonderful friction hit and Isabel knew she was on her way again, too. The pressure rose steadily and she wondered if she'd beat Taylor there.

"Oh, wow. Iz," Taylor groaned. "More of that, please. Yes, that. Good good good." Her eyes slammed shut and she sucked in a sharp breath, her hips bucking as Isabel struggled to hold her still. She loved the feel of Isabel's hands on her, of her hands on Isabel. "I'm not going to be able to—oh, God."

Isabel rocked her hips from above, increasing the friction. Taylor growled, grabbed her ass, and pulled her in, searching desperately for the purchase Isabel withheld. Isabel let her hand take over, shifting her hips to the side. She began to circle Taylor intimately, paying careful attention to Taylor's signals. As her cries turned wordless, Isabel plunged two fingers deep, causing Taylor to arch her back. Her hips moved wildly, urgently. Isabel memorized the moment, the sensation unlike anything she had ever known. She plunged again and again and again until Taylor thrust wildly in a frenzy against her hand, uncontrollable and gorgeous. Finally, Taylor arched her back, her body rigid as she cried out long and hard. Her eyes burned into Isabel's, and the power of their connection stunned her. *This* was what she'd needed, what she'd craved. That unmistakable link, something she'd been chasing for months. She didn't know Taylor that well, except that she did. And she wanted more. Lots more.

Isabel stretched out next to Taylor, unable to focus on anything but the sight of her. Naked, sated, and beautiful. Taylor reached out for Isabel, who obliged, wrapping Taylor up in her arms tightly, their limbs intertwining as if designed to fit that way. Isabel ran her fingers through the softness of Taylor's hair as they lay there quietly for several long minutes.

"You said my name," Taylor said quietly in the dark. "Just before you came."

Isabel reflected languidly on that earth-shattering moment. She didn't remember too many of the details, which was understandable. Her mind and body had been happily occupied in other ways. She lifted her head and looked down at Taylor. "Did I?"

"You did." A long pause. "I really, really liked it. I can still hear you."

Isabel wrapped her arms tighter around Taylor and smiled. "Good."

And then Taylor did something remarkable. She kissed Isabel's chin softly, and then her nose, and each eyelid, followed by her mouth. There was no lingering question of whether Isabel would stay. It was simply understood in the way they looked at each other. There was no prying them apart. Not a chance.

As she drifted off to sleep with Taylor in her arms, Isabel knew unequivocally that after an experience like this one, she would never be the same again. Nothing would.

And that was just fine with her.

CHAPTER SIXTEEN

Taylor's eyes flew open at the sound of very loud music. No, not just loud, blaring. Sunday morning had come with a roar, which was fitting after the fireworks of Saturday night. She sat up straight in bed and blinked, gathering her faculties. The music stopped. Then started again.

"Sorry!" she heard a voice call. Isabel. Sexy Isabel who she wanted back in bed with her. Now. She smiled. "Just trying to turn off the sound system down here, and I'm bad at it!"

Taylor laughed, blinked against the burst of sunshine streaming in, and brought her hand to her still-swollen lips. In fact, everything felt swollen in the most welcome way. She remembered waking sometime before dawn, turning and finding Isabel Chase right there in her bed, naked and tucked snugly beneath the covers. Her dark hair was splayed out across the pillow behind her, a fist tucked under her chin, and the most peaceful look on her face as she dozed.

Taylor needed to see that face.

She quickly brushed her teeth, found her white fluffy robe, and descended the stairs into her living room. She found Isabel staring at the sound system tower in the corner with three remotes in her hand. She wore a pair of shorts and an old USC T-shirt—in other words, Taylor's clothes. She could easily get used to that image.

Isabel held up all three remotes, her brow furrowed. "I'm great with a laptop, I swear. Not so much these things." Music that seemed to be in French filled the room.

Taylor smiled. "So, you've broken my sound system."

She nodded sadly. "I'm afraid you're relegated to learning French now."

"That, or fix it all with one little click of a button." Taylor took the remotes from Isabel and reset the system with one touch.

Isabel shook her head. "You know how to do all the things."

Taylor turned back to her. "In fairness, I have some experience to draw from." A pause as they stared at each other. The newness of what had happened between them manifested in a jolt of nervous energy shooting through Taylor. She steadied herself. She didn't regret their night of passion. If anything, she relished every memory. She felt alive this morning, happy, and wouldn't trade this wonderful drug for anything. Taylor was an astute person, and maybe if she went into this thing with her eyes wide open this time, she could avoid some of the relationship pitfalls of the past. Honestly, why hadn't she decided on that course of action from the beginning? What had she been so afraid of?

Isabel glanced down and grabbed a handful of her shirt. "I stole from you."

"I caught that." She reached for Isabel's hand and pulled her close. "I like you in my clothes. You're welcome to them anytime you like."

"Good. They smell like you, lavender and success all mixed together." Isabel's smile faltered momentarily. "We're okay, right? *You're* okay? I mean, you didn't say you're not, but I thought I should check in. I am, by the way."

Taylor nodded, enjoying the Isabel neurosis that crept in. "I'm definitely okay." Very slowly, she leaned down and hovered just shy of Isabel's mouth, and her heart clenched happily when Isabel closed the gap for her. There was something so easy about their dynamic, so comfortable.

"Well, that felt more than okay. In that case, good morning," Isabel murmured, sliding her one hand inside the robe and circling Taylor's breast.

"It is that." She moaned, wanting to march them right back to bed, yet remembering her manners. "Let me make you peanut butter pancakes. You're my guest." She stalked with purpose to the kitchen with Isabel hot on her heels.

"I didn't know there was food service, too."

"For you, definitely. But enjoy this. It's all I can make. I'm awful in the kitchen. Took me years to perfect this one dish, and I gave up there."

"Then I'm honored. But are you sure? If you have things to do, work or plans, I can get outta here." There was that little hint of nervous energy again. She was learning that Isabel projected a lot of confidence she didn't always feel. She wanted to assuage that any way she could.

Taylor picked up a spatula and pointed it at Isabel. "Don't you dare. Who will tell everyone how great my pancakes are?"

"No one would. I'm forced to stay."

"Good." Taylor dropped her tone to sincerity. "Besides, I'm very happy that you're here."

"Even despite our circumstances?" Isabel traced a pattern on the countertop. "We kind of threw all of our best laid plans out the window last night."

Taylor nodded, ruminating on the topic. "Yeah, well, maybe making plans isn't the best way to go."

"No plans, it is." Isabel slid onto one of the tall chairs that lined the counter. "For the record, I would never want to screw up anything for you at work. I wouldn't do that."

"I know you wouldn't." She paused. "I don't think either of us know what this is, but for whatever reason, I'm feeling less afraid of it today."

"Me too."

Taylor went back to cooking six thick and fluffy pancakes, enjoying Isabel's company from nearby.

"If you lost the robe as you worked, I honestly wouldn't complain. Not a peep," Isabel said, blinking back at Taylor, her cheek resting on her hand.

Taylor turned around and raised an eyebrow.

Isabel held up both hands in defense. "I'm incredibly honest."

"I can't distract my customers, even if they're really cute." Taylor set down three of the pancakes drizzled with peanut butter sauce on a plate in front of Isabel.

"Yeah, well, I think it's a surefire way to get them to come back," Isabel said dryly, pulling a laugh from Taylor.

"I see your point. Plans today?"

"I was supposed to meet my friends at Pajamas this morning, but I had a better offer. Peanut butter pancakes and you in a robe trumps gossip and lattes."

"I'm so happy you think so." Taylor took a seat next to Isabel at the counter and turned inward. "The friends being the neighbors I met?"

Isabel nodded. "Right. Hadley, Gia, Autumn."

"Do you guys do this a lot?"

"Lately. We've developed what I would call a breakfast club at the coffee shop each morning. Like Lesbian Steel Magnolias, but with coffee."

"That could be your mission statement."

Isabel nodded. "Right?"

"I like that you already have a group of friends."

"Forgive me for prefacing," Isabel set down her fork, "but I think it's important you realize that this friends thing is not normal. For me, I mean. I'm not a social butterfly. In fact, I've been known to be an awkward loner, not necessarily by choice."

"Okay," Taylor said gently. "I don't know about awkward, though."

"Yes, you do. I spilled coffee on you day one."

Taylor had to laugh. "Right. That did happen."

"I've had friends here or there, acquaintances, but my life in LA is already so much bigger than it was back home. I'm...grateful. For the new friends, for my job. For...you."

"You're sweet when you want to be," Taylor said, watching her.

"Don't tell people that. I have a rep."

"Your rep is safe with me. Honestly though, Iz, you should be proud of yourself. You've only been here a handful of months and you've already accomplished a lot."

"Including falling into bed with my idol, who also happens to be an amazing person, lo and behold."

Taylor paused. "I'm your idol?" That was new information.

"Pshhh." Isabel dug into her pancakes, her cheeks flashing pink. "You know you are. You've already accomplished everything I've been dreaming about for years."

Taylor was aware of the fast-track career she'd led. In fact, she prided herself on it. Yet hearing Isabel compliment her hit from a whole new angle. She felt herself inflate. "I didn't know you felt that way. Thank you. But if you keep working, churning out those ideas and executing the way you have, you could easily do the same. It's only a matter of time."

Isabel sat back in her chair and shook her head. "There's nothing I want more. Except maybe to eat tons of these pancakes in the future."

"You like them? It's my one culinary gift handed down from my Grandpa Joe."

"Well, Grandpa Joe was no slouch."

"He'd be happy to know you think so. Grabbed life by the horns kind of a guy. And I don't mean to get off topic, but you have peanut butter sauce on the side of your mouth right now." Taylor smiled at the look of horror that crisscrossed Isabel's face mid-bite.

"See?" Isabel said, sinking. She set down her fork and grabbed her napkin. "Again, beyond awkward, even when I think I'm being suave." She took several quick passes at her cheek, which only smeared the sauce.

Taylor smiled because Isabel really was endearing, and funny, and captivating.

"No? I didn't get it?"

"No."

"What a disaster. Of course I didn't." A sigh. "I'll be right back."

Taylor held up a hand. "No, no, no. I can help." She leaned into Isabel's space and very lightly licked the sauce from Isabel's cheek. Without missing a beat, Isabel picked up a glob from her plate and wiped it on the other side of her face.

"Oh, you're bad," Taylor said, leaning in happily to repeat the action. Just as she pulled away, however, Isabel caught her mouth with a kiss, and an incredibly sensual one, too. She sank into it automatically, all parts of her vibrating. She had things to do that day. Calls to make, scripts to read, and budgets to review, but that kiss had her willing to postpone every part of her life for more time with Isabel. She smiled against Isabel's mouth as she felt a firm tug on the belt of her robe. Apparently, she wasn't alone in that sentiment.

Thank God, she thought as the robe parted.

❖

It turned out that Taylor's bedroom was grayish blue in its color scheme, spacious, with a vaulted ceiling and skylight. Isabel knew this because she stared up at it from flat on her back on Taylor's bed. She'd just been led, once again, on a field trip to Orgasm Nation and wasn't sure she ever wanted to leave this place.

"We're good together in bed," Taylor mused, coming down from her own little excursion. "Or maybe it's just you."

"It's *us*," Isabel said, blinking to clear her head from all the powerful sensations that still accosted her body. She tickled Taylor's shoulder as she took in her surroundings. "You have huge windows," she said, still breathless. Taylor followed her gaze from her spot alongside Isabel.

"The views are what sold me on this house."

Isabel pushed herself up on her elbow and stared. "You're looking down on all of Los Angeles. As in, all of it. I'm pretty sure you own Hollywood from this spot."

Taylor smiled lazily and slid her thigh between Isabel's. "The way you just owned me?"

Isabel liked the sound of that. "Exactly. Yes. That's what I'm known for, owning exceptionally good-looking women on the daily." She paused, reflecting on the lunacy of that statement. "I'm out of my league here, you know that?"

"You're ridiculous."

"*You* are. I'm just a girl from small-town New Hampshire." She kissed Taylor. "But for fuck's sake, I really like you."

Taylor chuckled. "Well, for fuck's sake, I really like you back."

"And right now," Isabel said, "I don't care about your league. I'll punch your league in the face and run away with you forever."

"Do you know what I want?" Taylor asked. "I want to know more about you. Everything. I'm glad there's time for that." She trailed several fingers across Isabel's skin, tickling her stomach. "How is anyone's skin this soft?"

"No sun up north. We hibernate like bears to escape the snow, leaving our skin white and untouched." She placed their arms next to each other. "Notice the difference. I've been here months and I still don't have anything close to a tan." Taylor, however, glowed healthily. "It's that forever pool you have out there."

Taylor quirked an eyebrow. "Do you mean the *infinity* pool?"

"That one."

"I like to read alongside it for work."

"See right there? That's really glamorous. I don't know what you're doing with me. You should kick me out. Right away. Call your doorman."

"I don't have one."

"Well, that's an outrage," Isabel said, getting louder. "Every infinity pool should come with a damn doorman."

"I'll make a note." Taylor kissed her deeply and murmured one word. "Shower."

"Fine. Okay," Isabel said grumpily. "I guess I could join you in the detailed marble shower. But then I gotta jet. I have important scripts to write."

Another kiss. "Because you're going to be a famous screenwriter."

"And get my own doorman-pool guy. You can come over."

"Deal." Taylor pulled herself away and in glorious naked form walked to the bathroom with the kind of confidence Isabel would kill for. Well, if she had a body like that, she wouldn't have to. Taylor turned around and crooked her finger in a come-hither that had Isabel's blood running hot once again.

Two memorable hours later, and Isabel really did have to go. Not only did she not want to overstay her welcome, but things between her and Taylor were still new and uncharted, and as such, required a delicate hand. In other words, she was careful to give Taylor space just in case she had any second thoughts or doubts.

"Will I see you tomorrow?" Isabel asked from the entryway. Post-sex good-byes had always been awkward in Isabel's experience, but this time felt entirely different. She and Taylor grinned easily at each other and the mood was light. Dare she say, hopeful? They'd packed her clothes from the night before in a small backpack, and she borrowed shorts and a shirt to wear home.

"You will see me tomorrow. I should be around in the afternoon after a production meeting over at *Sister Dale*. Maybe we can steal a late lunch?"

"You're on. But don't expect me to eat any wimpy salad."

"I wouldn't dream of offending your respect for greasy diner food."

Isabel stared at her serious-faced. "We're gonna get along just fine."

"What's this?" a voice asked from down the walk. They turned to see Aspen making her way toward them, her blue Porsche parked low on the driveway. She pulled her sunglasses from her face and glanced from Taylor to Isabel, her eyes hard and her lips pursed tight.

"Isabel was heading home," Taylor said calmly. "What can I do for you? I thought we talked about calling first."

"I would have if I hadn't left my handbag here last night. The one containing *my phone*. But I see I've interrupted your sad little morning after. Your standards aren't what they used to be, Tay. But then again, people change."

Isabel felt about two feet tall but held her composure. "I'll see you soon," she said evenly to Taylor, who squeezed her hand.

"Don't let me stop you," Aspen said innocently and made a sweeping gesture with her hand to the sidewalk. "Walk of shame is that way."

Okay, so that's how it was going to be. Isabel swallowed, her defenses flaring. Yet no good would come of a confrontation with this woman. She could squash Isabel like a bug at any given point. No. Best to maneuver this as gracefully as possible. "I'll call you," she told Taylor, who nodded solemnly back. Oh, that was not an encouraging sign.

"Of course you will," she heard Aspen say, in a patronizing tone, behind her. So, the friendly pretense was effectively gone. She could handle that. Wouldn't make work at all weird or difficult. She deflated in the realization that this thing with Taylor came with more angles than even she realized. Didn't matter, she decided as she slid into her boring and basic Honda. She wouldn't let Aspen ruin her high from the past twenty-four hours. Everything would be all right. She glanced up the drive to the two beautiful and successful women who seemed involved in a deep and important conversation. Her stomach turned uncomfortably.

As she drove back to Venice, Isabel tried not to imagine all the ways Aspen would slam her to Taylor, make her look like a child who'd stumbled into the big kids' playground. She refused to believe that she was a rebound or a subplot to the larger relationship in Taylor's life: Aspen. But then again, she'd seen this story play out a hundred times in popular narratives. The main couple fought like cats and dogs, proclaimed the relationship unhealthy and over, only to fall madly back in love with each other, the tumultuous ride a big part of their dynamic. Some couples longed for drama and conflict. It's what got them going. Maybe that was Taylor and Aspen.

Nope. She wouldn't let herself go there. She would not be the cliché. Isabel placed a hand briefly over her heart and allowed herself to wonder just how long it would be until it was broken in two over Taylor Andrews.

Chapter Seventeen

Isabel and Hadley sat in the courtyard two evenings later, enjoying the last of the warm temperatures before winter would creep in. The night sky overhead looked cobalt and calm, which juxtaposed nicely with the swirling complications of Isabel's heart and mind. She utilized the serenity of the evening as a much-needed decompression from a week riddled with debilitating panic attacks. She did her best to understand their source and what, exactly, had her crouched in closets, restrooms, and her car waiting for the terror to pass. The best she could come up with was the night she'd spent with Taylor and how fantastic it had been. For the first time in as long as she could remember, there was someone in her life who she could truly see herself falling for.

It was exciting and scary and wonderful and awful at the exact same time because she wasn't quite sure how to manage the risk. If the new job had brought the first wave of attacks, she'd say her relationship with Taylor had taken them to a whole new level.

It had her concerned, to say the least.

In addition to her own problems, her work week hadn't been so hot either. Scruffy had argued against every suggestion anyone had for him, making the process a lengthy one. While Isabel adored her, Kathleen didn't have the courage to go head-to-head with Scruffy, leaving them sorely lacking in the leadership department.

Hadley, similarly, had worked a full day at Silhouette doing inventory, a task she apparently hated more than rain on weekends. She had her foot resting flat on the edge of the couch and did her toenails in a striking bright blue while they chatted.

"Your outfit the other night, was it a hit?" Hadley asked. "Since I couldn't be there, you owe me at least a few details in payback."

Isabel smiled as she realized once again how very important fashion was to Hadley Cooper. "The dress. The look. It was all well received. It turns out, your sense of style was not oversold."

"What did they say? Tell me what they said."

"Well, the nod to old-school Hollywood was lost on no one." She chose to omit the snarky comment from Aspen and spare Had's feelings, as it had more to do with taking a cheap shot at Isabel than the dress itself.

"What did Taylor think? I think our target audience carries the most weight."

Isabel looked skyward and concentrated on hiding the blush she felt threatening. Damn it, she was losing that battle handily. "I believe the word 'beautiful' was used more than once."

Hadley placed a hand over her heart. "Well, of course it was. She's so into you, Iz. I could tell on the beach, and this is just further confirmation."

Maybe it was because Hadley had already become such a great friend in a short amount of time, but the words fell from her lips before she'd even decided to say them. "I stayed over."

Hadley stared at her for several long moments and slowly placed the bottle of nail polish on the table. "I'm sorry. Did you just say that you stayed at Taylor's house that night? With her? You slept with Taylor? Had," she glanced around and then whispered, "sex?"

"Aww, you're cute. You can't say the word."

Hadley balked. "Can too. Sex." Only she whispered it again. "Damn it."

Isabel laughed. "I've never met anyone who couldn't say 'sex.' I have to write this into a character somewhere." She typed a quick note into her phone.

"That's fine," Hadley said. "But it won't be based on me because sex happens to be one of my favorite things next to bunnies and salted caramel. There."

Isabel wagged her finger. "No. You whispered it again."

"I didn't!"

"I'm afraid so."

"Man." Hadley wiggled her body into the couch in annoyance as Isabel grinned. "Anyway, we shouldn't be talking about me anyway. I want to get back to you and your forbidden office romance. When's the wedding? I would be thrilled to help design. I'm already envisioning colors. I hear you're a huge fan of the Southwestern motif."

"Funny, very funny. First of all, no wedding. Second of all, I don't even know that you can categorize what's happening between us as a romance. I was hopeful you could. I still am, but…it's complicated."

Hadley sat forward. "I'm good at helping people work through things."

Isabel nodded. "I'm starting to think that I'm the obstacle between the *real* romance, her and her ex."

"Aspen Wakefield."

"Right."

"You realize that sounds more like the TV show you write for than real life?" Hadley asked.

"Where do you think writers draw inspiration from for those kinds of things?"

Hadley studied her. "Good point."

"And how am I supposed to compete with someone like Aspen anyway?" Isabel asked, getting riled up just thinking about it. "The woman is God's gift to lesbians everywhere, provided no one has to actually interact with her for too many days in a row."

"That part's true," Hadley said, nodding too emphatically. "She's dreamy. And sometimes the right brand of crazy can be hot."

"That's the problem. She's dreamy *and* crazy. Don't get me started on her boobs. I'm guessing they're fake but still. You should *see* them."

"What? I'm sorry. You've seen her boobs and this is the first you're mentioning it?" Hadley looked around the courtyard as if to see to whom she could report this injustice. "Why didn't you start with that? Why didn't you knock on my door the moment it happened?"

Isabel shook her head. "The boobs are fabulous, trust me. But the incident in which I encountered them wasn't. Honestly, it was a creepy moment to walk in on. She surprised Taylor in her office, the door wasn't locked, and there I was in the middle of it." She shuddered. "Bottom line, she makes me feel like a dusty Honda in a sea of Porsches, and that's not even a euphemism. It's literally my truth."

"That's lunacy." Hadley's eyes were kind when she said it, her tone soft. "I've met Taylor. She seems down-to-earth and solid. If I had to guess, I'd say Aspen has nothing on you."

"And now I know you're not only one of the nicest people I've ever met but also a liar."

Hadley pushed on. "You honestly don't get how great you are, do you? I've known you for going on three months and I can say that easily. You're a catch, Iz, and you should know it."

The words took root and blossomed as she sat there. Isabel had never been more grateful for a pep talk in her life. While Hadley *was* a very nice person, she also wasn't a ridiculous one and wouldn't fill her head with nonsense just to do so. Knowing that she saw something, well…*worthy* in Isabel had her glowing. She wondered if it showed.

"What's going on down there?" a voice from above asked. They lifted their heads to see Gia leaning over the railing.

"Where have you been?" Hadley asked. "You're missing so much."

Gia shook her head in regret. "I fell asleep. Waves were all over the place today and I got beat to hell. What's the dish?"

"Iz saw Aspen Wakefield's boobs. They're apparently amazing."

Gia's face fell. "Now I'm sore *and* intrigued. I hate missing stuff. Especially celebrity boob sightings."

"We can catch you up at breakfast," Hadley said. "You need anything?"

"Elle Britton's retirement announcement," Gia said dully. "Can you make that happen?"

Isabel looked to Hadley. "And who exactly is Elle Britton?"

"Number one in the world," Hadley told her. "Gia's been chasing her ranking for years and is not a fan."

"No can do, champ," Hadley called back up. "But we can make fun of her perky princess persona together."

"That might be fun," Gia said glumly, thinking this over. "Maybe tomorrow morning at Pajamas when I get the boob story. Gonna jump in an ice bath now."

"If it makes you feel better, Hadley can't say 'sex' without whispering," Isabel said with a grin.

"Ask her to say 'fuck.' You'll be there all night." Gia offered a wink and went back inside.

"I'm happy you all enjoy my wholesome disposition, but it's all a ruse." She leaned forward and met Isabel's eyes. "I've seen porn."

Isabel reached over and patted Hadley on the knee sincerely. "Aww, I'm sure you have, sweetie. And that's awesome."

❖

Taylor was going through Isabel withdrawal in the worst way. She thought about her a lot, her smile, her quick comebacks, their give-and-take conversations. She luxuriated in the memory of their bodies pressed together and daydreamed about future encounters, which meant she had it bad. Since their night together ten days ago, they'd managed to steal a few moments here or there. A lunch. A chat. Due to their conflicting schedules, it was always very brief and only enough to whet her appetite for more.

Tonight would be different. Isabel's episode was set to air at eight p.m., and knowing what a monumental occasion this was for a young writer, she wanted to make it special. After grabbing a bagel for herself and a donut for Isabel from the Water Tower Market, she and Raisin, who trotted happily next to her on his leash, headed over to her office. She knew damn well it would make her late for the long lineup of *Sister Dale* meetings she was slotted to attend, but it didn't matter. Today was too important.

Isabel didn't notice her approach her cubicle and seemed lost in her laptop, probably gone on her own imagination. Taylor loved the look she got on her face when she concentrated, her lips slightly parted, her eyes distant, not noticing the happenings around her.

"Happy first episode day," Taylor said, breaking that concentration reluctantly.

Isabel's gaze flew up to Taylor as she stood next to her desk. She laughed and shook her head. "How long have you been standing there? Embarrassing."

"Long enough to see that you're immersed in something pretty spectacular."

She smiled. "Kathleen is giving me another episode. One that was originally scheduled to be freelanced. The guy backed out."

Taylor beamed. "Kathleen is smart."

"You don't seem surprised. You knew about this?"

"It's possible we colluded. We both feel you're ready for more. You proved it with the first one, which airs tonight, I might add."

"Is it weird that I'm nervous? As if there's something that could go wrong. The episode is done, shot, edited, and completely out of my hands. So why can't I relax and enjoy this?"

Taylor came around Isabel's desk and leaned back against it. "Because you're Isabel and it's what you do."

"I should see someone about that."

"Better yet, you should see me tonight. For a viewing party at my house. Guest list of two."

Isabel took a moment before a smile took shape on her face and grew exponentially. "You mean it? You want to watch it with me?"

"Of course I do. I'll supply the popcorn and wine. Wear comfortable clothes."

Isabel raised a suggestive eyebrow. "Because?"

"Because we'll be lounging as we watch a really cool episode." But the implication, even when it came in a teasing manner, had Taylor envisioning all the other reasons easy-access clothing might be helpful.

"What time?" Isabel asked, her eyes still dancing with flirtation.

"Seven thirty."

"I'll be there."

Isabel arrived right on time that night, and while Taylor popped popcorn and uncorked the wine, she excused herself to freshen up. When she still hadn't returned ten minutes later, Taylor called up to her. "Did you fall asleep up there? Fifteen minutes until go time!"

Isabel didn't answer.

Taylor poured a glass of wine for Isabel and one for herself and took a seat on the couch. "Iz? Everything okay?" she called again. Silence. Interesting. What was the proper protocol here? While it was her instinct to go check on Isabel, maybe she should give her some space. What if she wasn't feeling well? But after another five minutes had passed, Taylor headed up the stairs. She no longer cared about etiquette, only Isabel.

But when she arrived, both the hall and master bathroom stood empty.

"Isabel? Hey, where are you? You're starting to worry me. Did you sneak out when I wasn't looking?" She chuckled quietly to keep the mood light as she glanced from room to room, finally returning to the master. Something caught her attention. Her closet door was closed, and her closet door was never closed. She approached the door curiously and knocked, waiting only a moment before placing her hand on the knob. "Okay, ready or not, I'm coming in."

The light in the closet was off, but enough of the bedroom light spilled over to illuminate Isabel, sitting on the floor with her back against the wall. She had crisscrossed her arms over her chest and gripped her shoulders tightly. The image about tore Taylor's heart in two.

Taylor knelt in front of her. "Iz, are you okay? What is it?"

Isabel's only movement was a slight flick of her gaze to Taylor before looking straight ahead once again. "An attack. Just need time."

"A panic attack?" Taylor asked. "Is that what's happening?"

Isabel offered a slight nod.

"Okay, we can handle that. What can I do?"

Isabel shook her head. "I just need to sit here," she managed through a clenched jaw.

"Then I'll sit with you." And that's exactly what Taylor did, taking a spot on the wall next to Isabel. At first, she didn't say anything, wondering if maybe Isabel needed the silence. But something compelled her to fill it, to try and do something to see Isabel through this. She spent the next ten minutes telling Isabel all about her day, chatting about the mundane details as if it were the most natural conversation in the world. Two friends just hanging out. By the time she got to the very specific description of the chicken noodle soup she'd had for lunch, she noticed that Isabel's hands had relaxed into her lap. When she finished the part about dropping her keys on the concrete next to her car, Isabel allowed her to hold one of her hands. She pressed on, all the way up to the present timeline.

"And that brings me to the popcorn I just popped, which I have to confess, was the second bag. As you may have guessed from the smell in the kitchen, I burned the first."

Isabel smiled and Taylor relaxed in relief.

"How are you feeling?"

"Much better," she said, exhaling slowly. "Thank you."

"I didn't do anything. Just entertaining myself over here."

"More than that," Isabel said, taking another deep inhale. "That helped a lot."

"Does this happen all that often?"

"Comes and goes." She wiggled her shoulders, as if trying to loosen them up. "Sometimes it's two or three times a year. Lately, it's been…more."

Taylor nodded and squeezed Isabel's hand. "Any idea what brings them on?"

"Seems to happen when the stakes are high. When I feel like I have something to lose, which there's been a lot of lately. Might be me worrying about the episode today. It could be anything really." For the first time since Taylor had arrived in the closet, Isabel looked around. "Sorry I hijacked your closet. Small spaces seem to help."

"You're welcome to my closet." They sat in silence for a few moments. "What now?"

"You think we could still watch the show?"

"If you're up for it. We don't have to."

Isabel pushed herself up off the ground and offered Taylor her hand. "I'm not letting my stupid issues ruin tonight for me."

Taylor stood. "If you're sure. We can sit in this closet for as long as you need." And she meant it. She was fully ready to ride this thing out with Isabel if it took all night.

Isabel attempted a wobbly smile. "Take me to the burnt popcorn." And so she did.

With freshly popped buttered popcorn, the third bag of the night, and an open bottle of Cabernet on the coffee table, they watched Isabel's television debut from Taylor's white leather couch. Raisin, to his credit, seemed to know the show was an important one, his little gaze glued to the screen as if he followed the action from his spot, on Isabel's lap.

Isabel pointed at the screen. "See, that part right there is where I kind of imagined he'd grab hold of her and that's what would shut her up."

"Yeah, I gathered that from the script. Looks like your director had other ideas. You can always throw up your hand for a consult, you know."

"You can throw up *your* hand, Madame Executive Producer. I'm low on the totem pole." Isabel was joking again, which was a fantastic sign. With each moment that passed, she seemed to return to herself more and more.

"Doesn't matter," Taylor said. "You have to advocate for yourself, Iz. Just like you did with me on the storyline. You won't always win, but at least you'll have spoken your piece." She gestured to the action on the screen. "Doesn't matter, in actuality. The moment is still killer."

"Is it weird that we're sitting here together watching your ex-girlfriend on television, who also happens to be wearing very little clothing?"

"It probably should be," Taylor said conservatively and then relented. "No, it is."

"She hates me, you know, ever since that morning. Looks past me when we run into each other. Fakes pleasantries when people are around and then drops them the second they're gone."

"That's Aspen for you. I'm sorry. She's not exactly thrilled that we're..." Taylor trailed off, unsure how to finish that sentence.

Isabel turned more fully, shifting Raisin on her lap. "Yeah, what are we doing exactly? I'm not even sure I know myself."

Taylor looked skyward, realizing that this might be a longer conversation than what the commercial break they'd just shifted to would allow. Still, she gave it a shot, putting it all out there. "Dating?" A pause. "Giving what we have a chance?"

Isabel didn't say anything. She stared at Taylor, which made her regret the words. Too soon maybe. Isabel would be running for the hills if they weren't already in them geographically.

"I wasn't expecting that," Isabel said evenly.

"No?" Another pause, as Tide and all its wonders were professed on the screen. "Am I jumping the gun? You can say so. I can back off."

"Jump away." Isabel was smiling now. Good. Smiling was a vast improvement. She took a deep breath. "My only concern is Aspen."

"That she's on a warpath?" Taylor felt confident that she was, given their last interaction.

"No. That you're still captivated by her, which trust me, I get. The whole world is captivated by her."

"But I'm not." Taylor shook her head, as nothing could be further from the truth. Spending time with Isabel had placed her warped and labor-intensive relationship with Aspen in startling perspective. Isabel was a breath of fresh air. Aspen was a full-time job. She chose her words carefully. "There are a myriad of reasons why we shouldn't be sitting here together from a logistics standpoint."

Isabel nodded. "A myriad."

"But we tried ignoring the chemistry and ended up—"

"In bed."

"Yes, that."

A pause. "It just sucks that we're really good in bed."

"It does *suck*," Taylor said, borrowing the word. It was very Isabel. She reached out and touched a strand of Isabel's hair, loving the way it felt between her fingers. "But of all those reasons, Aspen is most definitely not one of them. My heart is available, if a little cautious."

"So maybe we go slow."

"If I could just figure out how to do that with you. I'm not sure it's possible."

Isabel smiled, which left Taylor craving a kiss. As their lips came together, Taylor marveled at how startling it still was, that little shock of desire that came with kissing Isabel. Goose bumps took shape on her arms, and a warmth washed over her. She should have learned to expect it by now, but it got her every time. As their lips danced, Taylor realized distantly that the show was back on and that Raisin had ditched them for the backyard, as evidenced by the sound of the swinging dog door. "Show's on," she managed between kisses.

"I've seen it before." Isabel's hands were under her shirt at the small of her back.

Taylor wanted more. She wanted those hands everywhere. As they kissed, that need only grew. "Tell you what," Taylor said finally, pulling her mouth away against her better judgment. "We finish the show, because it's an important milestone, and then we'll have our own show."

Isabel blinked. "Do you know how hard it's going to be to concentrate now?"

"You can do it. You're really good at your job."

They watched the episode. They did. They also couldn't keep their hands off each other and appeased themselves with little touches. Isabel's hand on Taylor's thigh. Taylor's fingers playing with the hair at the back of Isabel's neck. Isabel's hand on the *inside* of Taylor's thigh. Taylor's fingers dipping into the back of her shirt, to feel her warm skin. It was a progression that left Taylor uncomfortable and counting the moments until the episode ended.

As soon as the credits hit, Isabel's phone blew up. Texts from Hadley, Gia, Autumn, and even her dad had her grinning from ear to ear, which made Taylor glow bright with pride for her. Her friends were going nuts, sending Isabel screen shots of her name on their television. "This is crazy. Even my dad watched," Isabel said, shaking her head, as she typed back.

"Congratulations, Ms. Chase," Taylor said. "You're official now."

Isabel's answer was to set her phone down and slide onto Taylor's lap. "Officially wanting you." They stared at each other for a beat before bursting into laughter at the terrible line. Isabel held up a finger. "While you're embarrassed that I just said that, you should probably know there is a lot more where that came from. Gear up for a parade of cringe-worthy Isabel moments."

"My brain is exploding with all of the awful predictions."

"Meanwhile, I *predict*...kissing." Isabel slowly descended to Taylor's mouth. And they were off, right there on Taylor's couch. The clothes came off quickly, and what started on the couch moved out of necessity to the fluffy rug on the floor. And oh, the wondrous places they took each other on that rug.

A milestone of a day, most assuredly.

❖

November was on track to be a memorable month in the life of Isabel Chase.

After her episode aired, Isabel noticed a remarkable shift in the world as she knew it. Not only was the episode highly reviewed, but the storyline seemed to give the ratings the shot in the arm they needed. As a result, Isabel's stock rose. People on set knew her name, her coworkers listened to her opinion, and her confidence soared.

"Why aren't we writing Jackson into this scene at the hospital? Talk about tension if we do," Isabel said to the room of writers.

Scruffy blew out a breath. "The cub thinks we should write Jackson in." He glanced around the room. "Thoughts? It actually might make sense."

"Agreed. Cub is right," Cedric said. It was his script they were picking apart, and he looked worse for the wear. "I can make the adjustment."

She smiled. People were paying attention to her. Even Gerald Hagerman seemed impressed with her when he visited the *Water* set a couple of weeks later. "Isabel Chase," he crowed when he passed her in the hall. "Bring me more ratings like the one your episode pulled in, would you?"

"Workin' on it." And she was. She spent a lot of time staring at the wall, watching the screeners, and imagining new scenarios for the characters in the *Water* universe. She brought her ideas to the table and found they were becoming more and more well-received.

Gerald had pointed at her. "Got my eye on you."

She smiled and returned the awkward finger gun gesture he'd made but knew that, underneath it all, she didn't want to screw up the pretty powerful momentum she was building.

Things with Taylor had progressed as well. Not only did they have fantastic chemistry, spending hours together in bed, but they learned that they enjoyed regular days together as well. That was the really awesome part, how easy it was to just exist together.

Isabel started spending lazy weekends at Taylor's house. They'd have long talks over dinners on the patio, outdoor heaters ablaze. Sometimes Isabel cooked. Other times, Taylor tried. She was just as she'd proclaimed, however: a disaster in the kitchen, inspiring more than one take-out order to save the day. In the afternoons, they'd work by the pool or Isabel would read books while Taylor threw the tennis ball for Raisin. At night, they'd ravish each other appropriately before falling asleep in each other's arms. The serenity of it all was a godsend in Isabel's life. Taylor was a godsend.

"You two are a pair," she said one Saturday afternoon to Taylor, who lay on the floor with Raisin, rubbing his exposed tummy as he wiggled around because he was ticklish or gleeful—it was unclear which.

"Raisin loves me and I love Raisin. It's a ridiculous love fest. Isn't it?" She manipulated his paws in a series of gestures. "It is." Taylor Andrews was a dignified woman, known as a ballbuster in many circles, and hearing her speak baby talk to a dachshund on the floor said a lot about her feelings for him. Isabel smiled and turned the page of her crime novel. "So," Taylor said, pushing herself into a sitting position. "I have news from my morning chat with Gerald."

"Oh, yeah? What's up?"

"First of all, the network loves your newest script."

"They do?" Isabel perked up at the news, setting her book aside. She could read about that girl riding around on that train anytime. "I don't believe you."

"Because you're predisposed to pessimism. They did, too, like it. Gerald thinks you're the bee's knees. I told him he has good taste."

"He did not," Isabel said, joining Taylor on the floor because she had energy exploding from everywhere and had no outlet. "He did not say I'm the bee's knees." She sat on Taylor's stomach and held her down by her wrists. "What else did he not say? Tell me."

"I've not seen your smile stretch that wide ever. Aww, baby, look at your pretty teeth."

"Taylor."

"Yes?" She blinked up at Isabel with those big green eyes.

"You're stalling, and I will be forced to tickle you."

"Which I *hate*, so don't you dare, or I will turn Raisin on you. He's vicious. You don't know." They were both smiling now. Taylor took a breath. "Gerald mentioned that maybe it wouldn't be such a bad idea to tag you in a little more often."

Isabel sat back, releasing Taylor's wrists. "He did not."

Taylor studied her. "You have a reality acceptance problem that we should work on. Reality check: You're a really talented writer. Second reality: People are noticing. Third: We should go out to dinner tonight. Somewhere nice, so I can stare at you across candlelight."

"I'd be down for dinner. I don't have anything nice with me to wear, though. Can we stop by my place?"

"Of course. Oh, and Gerald has released me from my shackles at *Sister Dale*, due to a much-needed ratings hike. Lyric has been cleared to fly solo. I have no doubt she will fly that show into a cliff, but it's not my problem anymore. I'll be back at *Water* full-time on Monday."

Isabel paused before launching a full-on tickle attack on Taylor. "You buried the lede! You buried the lede, and now you must pay dearly." Beneath her fingertips, Taylor laughed, squirmed, and gasped.

"Uncle!" she yelled. "Truce!" she shouted when "uncle" didn't work.

"Say you're sorry, and that I'm the best tickler ever."

"I'm sorry," Taylor wheezed, as tears leaked from her eyes. "But I'm not saying the other thing." Isabel moved the tickling from her stomach to her ribs, upping the ante. Taylor screamed and laughed. "Fine!" she yelled finally in desperation. "You're the best tickler ever. Now please, God, stop. No more!"

Isabel sat back calmly. "See? Was that really so hard?"

"It was very hard. I can't believe you resorted to tickling. It's fiendish. It's devilish. It's very you."

Isabel grinned proudly as Taylor caught her breath. They stared at each other.

"I have fun with you," Taylor said simply. "Even when you hold me down and tickle me against my will. Why are we so good together?"

"Because you're put together, polished, and successful and I'm a creative mess who sometimes knows where my shoes are. What could be more perfect? We're like Laurel and Hardy, but who have sex." Isabel shook her head. "We're weirdos for waiting as long as we did to hang out."

Taylor sat up and rested on her forearms behind her. "Hanging out, huh? We've been *hanging out* a lot lately."

"Mmm-hmm. It's a multipurpose phrase. I'm good at words—you just said so." Isabel placed a kiss on Taylor's nose. "I like your nose. And I get to see it every day again. I don't have to share custody of this nose with any other show now."

"That's a fascinating way of looking at it."

Isabel took a moment, her tone softening because this mattered. "I don't mean to downplay it. I'm just so happy that I get to see you every day. The best moments are the ones you're in, Tay."

Taylor broke into a grin, and it was like the sun coming out. "I wasn't expecting that. How do I reconcile the fact that with just a few simple words you absolutely slay me?"

Isabel's heart smashed in her chest, hummingbird fast. She pulled

Taylor in. "Just know I mean them, okay? I'm not the most outwardly sentimental person, but I need you to understand how much you matter to me."

Taylor pulled back and looked her in the eyes, her gaze communicating a depth of emotion. "I do now."

"Good." Isabel nodded and ran a nervous hand through her hair. She wasn't great at confessions from the heart, but she planned to get better. "Now, are we ready to go get that dress so we can eat fancy food and celebrate your return?"

"No," Taylor said, wrapping her arms around Isabel's middle. "Have you already forgotten? We're celebrating you and your rising star."

"Let's do both."

"Deal."

"And let's kiss before we go."

Taylor relaxed into a lazy grin. "You're on a roll."

They parked in Isabel's designated space and made their way to the courtyard of Seven Shores. Taylor had never been here in the daylight and realized now how much she'd missed. The small complex was cute, homey, and charming. She glanced to the left and caught a glimpse of a blue sign peeking from just behind the trees. "Is that the cat? *The* cat?" Taylor asked, feeling like she'd spotted a celebrity. She'd been drinking magnificent coffee from cups featuring that very cat for a long time now, and to actually see his face out in the larger world had her beyond excited.

Isabel followed her gaze. "That's him. In pajamas again. That guy never gets ready for the day. Probably collects cat unemployment."

"Do you think we have enough time to pop in so I can see it?"

"Aww, look at the hope and suspense on your face. As if I'm going to say, 'Absolutely not. We are on a strict timeline with very little flexibility. Keep moving, Andrews.'" Isabel shook her head and smiled. "It's a beautiful Saturday, and I'm chillin' with you, and if you tell me you want to skip dinner altogether and just have coffee at the Cat's Pajamas, I will happily buy."

"Let's just pop in and see it. Then dinner."

"Follow me."

Autumn grinned at them from her spot behind the counter as

they entered the coffee shop. It was midday and the place was quiet. A couple of tables had folks focused intently on their laptops, and two blond women played chess in the corner by the couches. She wasn't positive, but that might have been Jimi Hendrix playing over the speakers, which was not your typical coffeehouse fare at all. Then again, this was Venice, and it was nothing if not unique.

"Alert, everyone," Autumn said as they approached. "Writer types on the premises. Look extra smart." The customers glanced up, offering a nod or a smile. The place was entirely laid-back as the clientele seemed to be.

"Don't act smart on my account," Isabel told her. "I don't even know what fennel is." Autumn and Taylor swiveled to her and she waved them off. "Long and bitter story."

"It's an herb," Autumn said gently.

"I know it's an herb. Just a ridiculous one." She looked from Autumn to Taylor. "I have a lot of anger toward fennel."

"I'm sensing that," Taylor said, intrigued. "You're going to have to explain that one later." She smiled at Autumn. "I'm so happy to finally see your shop. I've been telling everyone how amazing the coffee is here. I feel like that cat is my friend."

"He is. PJ's everyone's friend. As for coffee, I don't even ask for an order anymore," Autumn said. "I just have two to-go cups ready for Izzy each morning, once she's ready to hit the road."

One of the things Taylor simply couldn't get used to was how thoughtful Isabel could be. Even on days when Taylor was all the way across the lot at *Sister Dale*, she'd still find a cup of coffee from the Cat's Pajamas sitting on her desk when she emerged from whatever meeting or event had her occupied. It gave her a boost each time, and not just from the caffeine but from the reminder that a woman she was crazy about was thinking about her that morning, too.

She turned in a circle to take in the space fully. "Autumn, this space is amazing." It was more than she'd imagined, decked out with colors and memorabilia in a hodgepodge that somehow really worked. One of those places she didn't feel cool enough to inhabit, traces left over from her high school days. She moved herself right out of that familiar pitfall. "I love it! It's even more unique than I imagined. Is that an astronaut in the corner?"

"Not an actual guy," Autumn said, as she fiddled with the many silver pieces of what looked to be a large espresso machine. "Just the suit. I bought it at auction and painted it that shade of blue myself. Any coffee for you guys or are you just here to keep me company? Which I love, by the way."

Friend or not, Taylor felt like she ought to buy something. Manners were big in her world. "No, we'll take two coffees."

"Two coffees, one black and one sweetened with cream coming up."

Taylor hooked a thumb at Autumn. "She's good."

"It's kind of freaky how good. It's not just me. She knows everyone's order. Watch." Isabel approached the counter to pay. "Hey Autumn, see that guy sitting near the door?"

Autumn followed her gaze. "I do."

"What's his usual?"

"Oh, Blake is an iced coffee with three shots and four pumps of vanilla. The only time he deviates is the holidays when he trades out vanilla for mint."

Taylor stared at her in awe. "You're like Rain Man for coffee."

"Good God. I'm having that engraved," Autumn said seriously.

They laughed and accepted the coffee she handed them.

"No Steve today?" Isabel asked, taking a sip. Taylor winced. Isabel didn't shy away from the hot, burn-your-throat-overtly sip. Taylor, on the other hand, preferred to wait a few minutes, until the coffee had a chance to cool a few degrees. Honestly, it was a metaphor for how they approached life. Taylor erred more on the side of caution, she was finding. Isabel went for it every time. Isabel turned to Taylor. "Steve is one of my favorite baristas. He's one of the friendliest guys I've ever met. Young and wide-eyed, but he's from Ohio, so that probably explains it."

Autumn glanced behind her. "Steve is in the back with my new hire Katrina. Katrina, you should know, is less friendly than Steve. She sort of seems like she's working a very difficult puzzle in her head when she speaks to you. Or an atomic bomb. Six of one, half dozen of the other. Jury is out on how she'll do with the customers."

As if on cue, Katrina appeared. She was a teenager, with extra-long blond hair pulled into a ponytail and meticulous bangs. "Excuse me." She studied Autumn, her brow furrowed, as if in intense concentration. "I'm not finding those boxes of sweeteners you asked me to unpack."

"Top shelf on the right in the storage closet."

Katrina placed a finger on her bottom lip and tapped a few times. Autumn was right. Katrina was solving for x in a parallel conversation. "Riiiight. Thank you. I'll get back to it."

Once they were alone, Autumn whirled back to them. "See? What's that about?"

Isabel shrugged. "Beats me." She dropped her tone. "Here's hoping she doesn't kill you."

Taylor elbowed Isabel. "How awful! I assure you, Autumn, she won't kill you. If it helps, I had the same thoughts when I hired Isabel. Her weapon of choice was coffee."

Autumn reached across the counter and offered Isabel a fist bump. "Truth is, I hire mostly kids, and besides Steve and me, the roster is constantly rotating. You meet some interesting folks."

Taylor exchanged a glance with Isabel. "You just said a writer's dream sentence. Keep us in the loop."

"Of course."

With coffee in hand, they stopped by Isabel's apartment, where Fat Tony attempted to play hockey with Taylor's feet while Isabel changed. When she emerged from the bedroom, Taylor's heart squeezed and her body warmed pleasantly. Isabel looked stunning in a casual red dress with three-quarter sleeves paired with a pair of low black heels.

"That dress is gorgeous. Look at you. God, Iz, you have fantastic taste."

Isabel stared at her, her eyes going wide. She started to say something and then stopped and held up a hand. "No. It's a sham. All of it. I have mediocre taste at best. I messaged Had and told her we were going to a nice place and asked if she had anything. She dropped off the dress because she has a key from checking in on Tony on weekends." Isabel covered her eyes and sat on the couch with a thump.

Taylor laughed and sat next to her. "Why would you characterize that as a sham? And why wouldn't you tell me you weren't sure what to wear?"

Isabel gestured up and down Taylor's body. She'd selected her white dress with a slash of blue down the middle. "Because look at you. How am I supposed to keep up with you? With designers and glamour and...*you*. All you are."

"First of all, this dress was on the clearance rack at the mall. I'm not nearly as sophisticated as you seem to think I am. Second of all, you've made similar comments along the way. Does this have anything to do with the panic attacks? Maybe we should talk about the root cause."

"Maybe."

"Tell me one thing that you're afraid of." Silence filled the room.

Isabel tucked a strand of her dark hair behind her ear and studied the wall carefully. "Iz? Talk to me."

She turned to Taylor, her blue eyes carrying vulnerability. The type Isabel tucked away anytime Taylor glimpsed it. "What if it's ten years from now and I'm still in your shadow? The less attractive sidekick who never amounted to much. And there you are, wishing you were with someone glamorous and exciting like you are. Instead, you're stuck with me."

"Is that how you feel?"

"No." A long pause. "Yes."

Taylor smiled, and not to make Isabel feel better but because what she'd just heard was ludicrous, ridiculous, and she couldn't see her way to dignify it with a serious response. Isabel was beautiful and smart and creative and the fact that she didn't see it was baffling. "That doesn't make any sense to me."

"I just need for you to know that I'm never going to be an Aspen. You're never going to wake up and find that's happened." She looked so crestfallen as she said the words, as if she truly thought she had failed some sort of important test.

"Thank God," Taylor said, slipping her hand into Isabel's and pulling it into her lap. "I would never want you to be anyone but you." Isabel didn't say anything but she also wasn't looking at Taylor anymore, which both hurt and pulled at her heart at the same time. "Isabel, you have to believe me when I tell you this, okay?" That had her attention. Isabel faced her, and that's when Taylor saw that there were tears pooled in her eyes. "I've never had anything like this with someone. Ever. Normally, I wouldn't say these things, because it's only been three months since we've been...hanging out." The use of her term had the corners of Isabel's mouth turning up ever so slightly. "But it happens to be very true. I was married to an amazing person, and we really clicked. But not in the ways we needed to. I've had fast and furious affairs, but they've always burned out. Aspen would fall into that category. But with you, Isabel Chase, it's so very different. We click in *all the ways* and I can't seem to stop myself from hoping that this is something bigger than the both of us, because what if it is? What if this is it?"

Isabel was up and walking across her living room, shaking her arms as she walked. She turned back to Taylor with the expression of an investigative journalist on a mission. "So, you're saying you think there's potential for a future? With us. Potentially. I know I already said the potential part. Ignore it. It's whatever. But do you?"

Taylor grinned and waded through the neurosis. "I do."

Isabel's hand went to her hips and she blew out a breath looking gorgeous in that dress. "Good. Okay. That's helpful to hear." The smile crept in slowly, but once it took shape on Isabel's face there was no better visual. "I'm a mess when it comes to you. You should know that."

Taylor nodded. "I'm filing it away."

"I've just…never been happy like this before." The sentence hit Taylor square in the center of the chest and blossomed.

"I make you happy?"

"Yes." Isabel nodded several times. "And it feels like a precarious height to fall from, you know?"

Taylor stood and walked to Isabel, understanding that she needed reassurance and the knowledge that they were in this together. She slipped her hands around Isabel's waist and met her gaze squarely. "I have a suggestion." She brushed the hair from Isabel's forehead. "No one falls from any kind of height, and no one gets hurt." She kissed her softly. "And we take this one day at a time." Another kiss. "And continue to have important conversations like this one." This time Isabel kissed her in what felt like a promise. Taylor's eyes fluttered closed and she accepted the unspoken words, tucking them close to her heart.

Isabel pulled her mouth away and rested her forehead against Taylor's. "I like the proposed plan."

"Good."

"Is it wrong that I don't want to go to a fancy dinner tonight?"

Taylor smiled. "No. Where would you like to go instead?"

"The beach."

"Take me there."

❖

It was still daylight when they arrived on the beach, but Isabel knew it wouldn't be long before the glorious sun, already sporting all sorts of fantastic colors, would descend further from its spot in the sky, leaving night and the chill that came with it to creep in around them. She'd swapped her dress for jeans, and luckily, Taylor fit as well in her clothes as she fit in Taylor's. It amused her, the visual of Taylor in her knock-arounds. Another way to describe it was hot, which had her stealing glances as they walked the length of this bustling section of the beach, stopping at each of the retail stands.

"Could you see me wearing this?" Taylor asked, picking up a vintage Alice Cooper T-shirt and holding it against her chest.

"I could," Isabel said confidently. "Taylor the Rocker Chick has possibilities. I could write that story. An executive in the prime of her career abandons all to go on the road as the best groupie to ever group."

Taylor pointed at her. "And I just made you a millionaire. You're welcome." She set the T-shirt down and they walked on. "We'll need food, don't you think?"

"Oh! I know a spot."

Isabel walked them past Muscle Beach, the outdoor weightlifting platform where some sort of raucous competition was taking place. Oiled-up shirtless men flexed one at a time for a cheering audience. In other words, it was a Saturday. They rounded a corner and came to a nondescript window with a menu card taped to it.

"I'm not having a salad tonight, am I?"

Isabel laughed. "Would you prefer a salad? I will find you one on this beach if it's the last thing I do."

"I was kidding. Let's eat beach food. It's the weekend."

"Perfect, because Gia brought me to this place, and she knows all the good beach spots. They have killer wraps. My favorite is the Santa Fe. Messy as hell and big and awesome."

Taylor nodded thoughtfully. "You really know how to sell a girl. Make it two."

Isabel grinned and appreciated how Taylor was willing to step outside of her comfort zone and do the things Isabel enjoyed. Because she was a sport, she'd joined Taylor many times in the past for a large salad and even endured the lecture on the wonder that a large salad is. Especially one with chicken and oranges, apparently. Who knew?

"So, I've had an idea percolating for a show," Taylor said as they walked, eating their wraps and people-watching. "Is that woman over there topless? And is that a giant snake around her neck?" Taylor glanced around as if to be sure she wasn't hallucinating.

"It is. She should rethink that combo, because ouch."

Taylor rolled her shoulders in empathy. "Yeah, ouch."

"But back to your idea," Isabel urged. "I didn't know you were still generating new show premises."

"Always. However, working on another show got the wheels churning more than usual. So, I'm thinking a former CIA agent, the trained lethal kind, who goes into social work, vowing to leave her darker days behind her."

"Only the losers who beat their wives or the parents who hurt their kids might challenge that sensibility."

"Exactly. I'm imagining an internal struggle between her new and old lives."

Isabel nodded. "Maybe she adopts a child of her own along the way. She could be the Girl Scout troop leader. Attending PTA meetings by day."

Taylor's eyes went bright. "Vigilante assassin by night."

"Right? I love this. You have to write this show one day."

"Could be a little dark," Taylor said hesitantly.

Isabel stopped walking and turned to Taylor, who ended up a few steps ahead before turning back in question. "Are you kidding? That's what makes it awesome."

Taylor laughed. "I forgot who I was talking to." She took a bite of her wrap, and Isabel grinned as Southwestern dressing dribbled down her cheek. She handed Taylor a napkin.

"Told you it was good and messy."

"You left out fabulous. How are they not lined up around the block?"

"Apparently, a local secret. Back to our girl. She needs to be gay. Would you agree? Or better yet, bisexual. And hot."

"Definitely hot. Maybe she'll look like you."

While it was a silly suggestion, it did give Isabel an extra boost, warming her cheeks. "I'm too short and not nearly ripped enough for assassin status."

"If you want her taller, she can be taller. And ripped. I'm flexible on the topic. Definitely brunette, though. At least in my head she is."

"I like the idea."

"Just something for someday. Maybe we could work on it together."

Isabel smiled. "I would love that. For someday." A pause as they nodded to the clown on Rollerblades as he passed. "Have I ever told you how much of a turn-on your brain is?"

Taylor took a minute to finish chewing. "No, but that's good, because bathed in salad dressing like this, the rest of me is pushing it."

"Please," Isabel said, glancing at her up and down. "You've never been more attractive to me than when you're eating and wearing street food at the same time. In fact, I'm so into you right now that we should probably get away from all of this. Find our own spot." The boardwalk was a lot of fun, but the crowds, the noise, and the spectacle generally ran its course quickly. Isabel craved one-on-one time with Taylor.

"We can drive up the shore some," Taylor suggested. "Find a spot to park and watch the waves."

"Yes," Isabel said. "Absolutely yes."

They quickly learned that the closer they got to the water, the less they could bear the cold. After a short walk along the shoreline, they made a mad dash back to Taylor's car, where they snuggled up in the backseat, laughing, and watched the last sliver of sunlight disappear on the horizon. With Taylor on her back, Isabel lay in the crook of her arm. They listened to the sound of the waves crashing, their feet propped just outside the rolled-down window.

"Who knew I'd be such a beach person? We had one close to where I lived up north, but I never went."

"Northern beaches are different," Taylor said. "More mysterious, at least in my opinion."

"I can see how you'd come to that. California is more, 'Here's some glorious sand and relentless sunshine. Just play around in it for a while.'"

"Exactly," Taylor said with a chuckle. "You're starting to understand our little corner of the world more and more each day." She slipped her hand under Isabel's shirt and ran her fingertips back and forth across her stomach. Isabel loved it, almost as much as she loved the woman who had taken over her heart completely.

Back that truck up.

The word "love" was a lofty one and not something she took lightly. She amended the traitorous thought. She loved it almost as much as she *adored* the woman who had taken over her heart so completely. Much better. Oh wow, the fingertips fluttering against her skin were really starting to do things to her. Isabel wondered what the rules were for fooling around in public. Technically, there was no one around this section of the beach. The colder temperatures had left it desolate. They were entirely on their own.

Isabel looked down, startled by the green eyes burning back at her. Aha, Taylor was as much affected by the contact as she was.

"Are we allowed to fool around?" Isabel whispered. "On a beach?"

"I don't see anyone, do you?" Taylor popped her head up and looked around. It was all the encouragement Isabel needed.

"I only see you."

Taylor smiled, and the corners of her eyes crinkled. "Hi."

"Hi back."

Isabel slid down in the seat until she and Taylor were face-to-face. She unbuttoned the jeans Taylor had borrowed and slipped a hand inside and watched as Taylor's face transformed. "That's unreal," Taylor murmured, her eyes fluttering closed, her skin flushing as her hips moved. "Iz." It never failed to amaze Isabel how much she enjoyed bringing Taylor pleasure, studying her as the pressure built slowly to a full-on explosion. She stroked Taylor's perimeter, getting closer, brushing across her and then pulling away. Several times over. She listened to Taylor breathing, the only sound in the quiet car except for the tide rolling in yards away. This moment was everything. Taylor's eyes crashed into hers, and in them she saw the need, the lust, the want looking back at her. Isabel knew Taylor's body well enough to understand that she could give her what she wanted in a matter of moments. She stroked her more firmly and they found a rhythm. She pushed her fingers into Taylor and curled them, searching for the spot she knew would undo her.

"Don't stop," Taylor breathed, her mouth centimeters from Isabel's as they sucked in the same air. It was perhaps one of the most sexually charged moments of her life. With a final shiver, Taylor went still in her arms, her lips parted as she rode out the release that Isabel had just given her in public, thank you very much. She smiled. Now, *this* was an interaction she would relive for weeks.

"You shock me every time at how quickly you can make that happen," Taylor whispered.

"I was inspired. I've never had sex in a car before," Isabel said, wrapping both arms around Taylor's waist. "There's probably some sort of form I need to fill out. You know, declaring it."

"I think California might be corrupting you," Taylor said with a smile. "I'm not going to complain."

"You've already filled out the form, haven't you?" Isabel eyed her.

"Maybe."

She shook her head. "I have so much catching up to do. We should do more of this. Are you free tomorrow?"

Taylor laughed and kissed her. "Happy to assist in any way I can."

And with a tenderness Isabel had never experienced, Taylor reached up and gently traced the lines of Isabel's face, outlining each feature as if it were precious to her. "I could lie like this forever, you know. Stare at you."

Isabel stared back, understanding the sentiment entirely. Her heart soared, because maybe she wasn't just a fling for Taylor, or a human shield against Aspen. What they had just might be the real deal. But the thought terrified her just as much as it made her happy, and she knew she'd be dealing with the repercussions soon, likely on the floor of her closet. In the meantime, she chose to shelve that depressing reminder and enjoy what was right in front of her.

She snuggled closer to Taylor. "Can I just say that I love the beach?"

Chapter Eighteen

As Isabel drove home from Taylor's that Sunday night, her hands shook. She felt the tightening of her jaw and her thoughts raced. She thought back to the day before and their conversation. She'd downplayed her answers about the attacks. She couldn't bring herself to tell Taylor what a large part she played in their manifestations. Was *still* playing, Isabel realized as she gripped the steering wheel with all her might. It seemed like the more time they spent together, the stronger their relationship grew, and the more out of control Isabel's anxiety ran.

She didn't get out of her car when she arrived in the Seven Shores lot. She couldn't seem to leave the safety of its interior. Half an hour passed. An hour. She swallowed and held on to the steering wheel. It was cold enough that she could see her breath, and she shivered slightly.

"You're doing fine," she whispered.

"Isabel? That you?" A knock. "Hey, you okay in there?" She glanced sideways to see Autumn staring at her through the window. She managed a slight nod. Autumn wasn't satisfied. "Open up, okay?"

It took a great deal of mental fortitude, but Isabel managed to let go of the steering wheel to crack the car door.

Autumn opened it the rest of the way. Her voice softened when she got a look at Isabel. "Hey, there. You don't look so good."

Isabel couldn't disagree. "Long day," she managed to say. She attempted a smile but didn't quite succeed.

"Let me walk you in."

Isabel nodded and accepted Autumn's hand. She appreciated the warmth it brought along with her supportive gaze. She didn't look at Isabel with pity or shock or horror, just kindness. They took it slow up the walk, one step at a time. Autumn seeming to get it was what she needed.

"Thanks," Isabel said, once Autumn helped her into her apartment. "I just need sleep."

"You sure?"

"Yeah. Starved for it." She heard her own voice, clipped and unusual sounding, but there wasn't much she could do to change it.

Autumn nodded. "Call me if you need anything, okay?"

Isabel rolled her shoulders, begging the tension to leave them. "Will do." With a final concerned glance, Autumn left the apartment.

Embarrassed and alone, Isabel took a seat on the floor until the world came back into focus. She couldn't live this way. She had to find a way to rid herself of this hell once and for all. The question was how.

For Taylor, Monday morning hit like a breath of fresh air. Birds chirped, people waved at one another, and the world felt full and boisterous. After a fantastic weekend, Taylor was back on her own show, and it felt good.

There would be no running back and forth between shows. No hearing about decisions on *Water* secondhand because she'd handed over the reins to someone else. Nope. She was back in control and ready to go.

When she arrived at her desk and saw her Pajamas coffee front and center, she smiled and took a healthy sip, letting the fantastic brew work its magic as she thought about the beautiful woman who'd left it for her. Raisin had hopped up on her couch and quickly took his favorite spot on the cushion to the left where he could prop his chin up on the armrest and watch the door. He was a people watcher. Taylor was pretty sure it was a trait she'd passed on to him.

"Hey, Scar," she called. "Did we ever get final notes on episode 519 from Tim Rossi? He's directing this week." Good thing, too. Tim was one of their regulars, a consummate pro who knew the show inside and out. He would make the week an easy one for everyone.

"I forwarded them your way moments ago."

"Awesome. I'm on it." She opened the email and scanned Tim's notes, which would help her understand how their creative visions overlapped or in some cases, perhaps, didn't. This was the confrontation episode in which Lisette's younger sister stumbles upon evidence of the affair. The episode belonged to Kathleen, though she'd be in and out—her husband was undergoing a minor heart procedure that week—so they'd all be pitching in to usher the episode along in her absence.

Scarlett's head swiveled around her door, and Taylor smiled gleefully at the prairie dog imagery she'd missed so very much. "Hey, Taylor?"

"Yep?"

"If I haven't said it enough, I'm really glad you're back."

Taylor took a fortifying breath and grinned. She'd missed Scarlett desperately herself. "Me too. Let's shoot a killer episode this week to commemorate."

Scarlett winked. "Deal."

Only the week didn't go as smoothly as she'd planned.

After a table read the next day panicked the art department, concerned wardrobe, and set off a neurotic actor, Taylor found herself putting out fires rather than making any forward motion on the week. What was worse, apparently, Tim Rossi had run into a handful of problems on set with, wouldn't you know it, Aspen Wakefield, lead actress and drama queen extraordinaire. It was a situation she'd need to keep an eye on.

That Wednesday afternoon, Taylor sat with her line producer, trying to figure out how they could afford the tiniest bit of rain for a pivotal scene to shoot two weeks from now. "I know I outlawed rain," she told Emily Tanner, who crunched numbers and made things happen for Taylor on a weekly basis, "but if there's any way we can undo that directive and drum up the funds for the tiniest bit, I will owe you big time. I will happily accept a drizzle."

Emily sighed. "You realize I'm not a miracle worker?"

"I do. But I also know that you're the best in the business."

She narrowed her eyes. "You're doing that flattery thing you always do."

Taylor grinned. "Is it working?" Her phone buzzed in her jacket pocket, and she checked the readout. *You need to get to set*, the text from Scarlett read. *Tim is threatening to walk and Aspen is demanding your presence.*

Well, well, well. When it rained, it poured.

"Emily, I have to run, but I will leave this matter in your capable, and let me just remind you, *genius* hands."

"Yeah, yeah," Emily said wearily and went back to her laptop with the weight of the weather on her shoulders.

When Taylor arrived at Stage 9, the first thing she noticed was that the working set, Lisette's home, was eerily quiet, and not because they were rolling. Aspen's script lay on the kitchen counter and she stood over it studying lines. Claudia, the actress who played Lisette's younger sister, sat at a kitchen table and shot Taylor a "don't blame me" look as she approached. Tim, the director, spoke quietly to a camera operator, and a gaggle of production assistants stood around looking shell-shocked and nervous, only attempting to look busy when they noticed her presence. The tension hung thick and imposing.

"What's going on?" Taylor asked Tim. "I heard there was a disagreement."

He nodded and walked her outside of the soundstage and onto the sidewalk, where she squinted up at him, shielding her eyes from the insistent sunlight. "I asked Aspen to take it down on the next take so that I had options in editing. This is an important argument we're shooting between the sisters, but we have a lot left in the episode and she's got nowhere to go with those kind of levels, and honestly it was reading like a melodramatic soap opera. It's my job to rein that the fuck in."

Taylor nodded. "Right. Okay. Makes sense."

"And she told me that she knew the character inside and out and that she was playing the scene the way it needed to be played or some other such nonsense." Taylor had heard that line from Aspen before. It was her go-to excuse to get in front of any creative decision she didn't agree with.

"And then what happened?"

"I told her to just do it once for me. We'd get the take and move on."

"And she didn't like that?"

"She folded her arms like a princess and said no. I called her that, a princess, and she told me to go fuck myself. I told her she could go to hell, she demanded to see you on set, and here you are. That's what's happening."

Taylor sighed deeply and forced a smile, knowing she was about to go to battle and it wasn't going to be pretty. The most important thing was to not lose time, as that meant money. "I'll talk to her. Thank you, Tim."

"Yep. I'm gonna grab a smoke."

Taylor took a breath and headed back to set in search of Aspen. She found her chatting with Claudia at craft services as if nothing had happened, serene, innocent smile firmly in place.

"Aspen, hey," Taylor said, as if approaching a bear that could claw her eyes out at any moment. Aspen had been distant since she'd started seeing Isabel officially. They spoke in regard to the show, but the last personal conversation they'd had was on Taylor's porch the morning she'd encountered Isabel there. She'd said very little to Taylor that morning after Isabel drove away, but the piercing glare had told her everything she needed to know on the subject. Aspen was angry, and the likelihood of her lashing out at Taylor the way she had Tim was high. Her goal was to defuse any and all hostilities right off the bat.

"Taylor," she said as if surprised to see her there, when she was the one who, in fact, had summoned her. "To what do we owe the pleasure?"

Taylor sent her a knowing look because she honestly couldn't help herself. She forced herself to brighten. "Can I steal you for a moment?"

"Back in a few," Aspen said to Claudia and then waved her fingers over her shoulder as she walked. Once they were alone in a darkened corner of the soundstage, behind the set, Taylor turned to her.

"Sounds like there was some trouble on set. Want to tell me about it?" She was aiming for caring friend and concerned boss all in one. That generally scored well with Aspen.

"Yes," she said, her eyes now ice cold. "I want him removed from the episode."

Taylor hooked a thumb behind her. "Tim? Who's won six Emmys and is one of the best directors we have working on the show?"

"He's an overrated asshole, too big for his britches." She ran a hand through her luxurious hair, that somehow always magically fell back into place perfectly. Taylor used to love the effect. Now it just creeped her out. "He goes or I do."

Taylor hated ultimatums. They made the person making them seem threatened and childish, not that she could tell Aspen that. "You have a contract, Aspen. That's not an option." Taylor took a moment to regroup, find her Aspen skills, which had dulled since she'd been off set for so many weeks. "You and I both know that you value your professionalism as an actor immensely."

"No, you and I don't," Aspen said, her eyes blazing. "Don't say *you and I* in the same sentence ever again." She leaned in close, her face red and determined. "Get Rossi out of here or find a way to shoot around me this episode, because I won't work with him."

In a huff, she turned to go. Instinctively, Taylor reached for her arm. "Aspen, wait. I promise, we can solve this."

Aspen's gaze flew to Taylor's hand on her arm. "Did you just grab me?"

"What?" Taylor instantly pulled her hand back. "No, I was just—"

"I can't believe you did that!" Aspen rubbed the spot where Taylor had barely touched her. "Ow! That's going to leave a mark. You just viciously grabbed me on my own set. I knew you were passionate about the show, but you just crossed a line. I won't put up with physical violence."

The insinuation was ludicrous, but it was like Taylor's mind couldn't keep up with the pace Aspen was setting.

"Did you see her grab me?" Aspen asked a nearby grip, wrapping cable. He glanced away, but Aspen was on him instantly. "What's your name? You saw the whole assault."

"Kip. But I don't want to—"

"Aspen, stop it," Taylor whispered, trying to keep the escalating scene under control. Interested faces were starting to turn their way. "Can we not do this? I'm sorry I reached for you."

"You lunged and grabbed me, holding me against my will." She again rubbed the arm that now hung limp and lifeless at her side as if broken in several places. Her face was pouty and there were tears gathering bountiful and thick in her eyes. She'd sailed from outraged to victimized over the course of twenty seconds in a move that had Taylor stunned and afraid. Where Aspen was concerned, anything was possible. Taylor stepped toward her in attempt to calm her down, get her to come back to reality. "Let's just talk about this for a minute before—"

"Don't come near me!" Aspen yelled, taking a large step away from Taylor and holding her "good arm" in front of her in defense. There were now people gathered on either side of them with more walking around the perimeter of the set to see what all the commotion was about.

Luke, who'd just arrived to shoot an upcoming scene, stepped forward and said something quietly in Aspen's ear. She nodded and he led her away, probably to her trailer. "Everyone saw that, right?"

Aspen yelled over her shoulder. She pointed at Taylor. "She grabbed me violently and wouldn't let go! Everyone saw."

Taylor held her ground, her brain not quite sure what to do. She glanced around at the myriad of shocked faces all trained on her. She couldn't react, and it would seem lame to defend herself to the people who worked for her, yet she had to say something. "I apologize for that misunderstanding. We'll get everything under control shortly." She turned to the first AD. "In the meantime, can we powwow privately and maybe see what we can reschedule, so as not to lose the day?"

He nodded, but it was clear the incident had him flustered. "Of course, Ms. Andrews. Let me grab my—sure."

But it felt like a fire alarm had been pulled and Taylor wasn't sure how to unpull it. Aspen left for the day, shutting down most of their shooting options, and was rumored to still be muttering about the unprofessional director and the abuse she suffered at the hands of a maniacal showrunner. Perfect. Taylor remained on set for the rest of the day, just to smooth things over and let everyone see that it was business as usual. Underneath it all though, she wondered about the larger implication of the run-in. For the show. For her. For everything they'd worked for over the past five years.

❖

"She thinks you assaulted her?" Isabel asked in horror. It was dark as they walked a lap around the studio lot, a relaxing practice they'd taken up every few nights.

"It was wild," Taylor said. "She lost her temper and pointed and accused. I barely touched her, Iz. But you'd have thought I maimed her for life."

"I believe you. Do you think this happened because of us?"

Taylor seemed pensive and took a moment before answering. "I can't think of any other reason. She pulled back all her attention that morning after my party. I thought it was a good thing, that she'd moved on. But maybe she's just been seething and letting her anger build. I don't have a good gauge of her state of mind. The problem is, she holds too many cards. The show is entirely dependent on her, and she knows it. Now she's playing her hand."

"Sounds like she has a chip on that perfect shoulder of hers and is hell-bent on making you pay the price." They looped around the Coffee

Bean, now closed for the evening, and headed over to Lucy's park. They nodded at a security guard who whizzed by in a golf cart, but the conversation trailed off and they walked in heavy silence. Isabel could tell that Taylor had taken the events of the day hard. People thought the world of her on set, and she wouldn't want that reputation tarnished. "I wish I had the magic words to make today better. What can I do?"

Taylor glanced over at her, then away. "You just being here with me right now, supporting me, makes a big difference." She followed up the statement by taking Isabel's hand and offering it a squeeze.

"Yeah, well. I will always support you."

"That means a lot." She met Isabel's eyes. "I'm sorry I'm not better company tonight."

"I don't need you to be," Isabel said. "We can just walk together." Taylor nodded and they did just that. Walked. Maybe the exercise would help, the fresh air and the studio lot that Taylor loved so much. But the sides of Taylor's mouth were turned down in a way Isabel had never seen, and it sat uncomfortably on her heart. They walked south down Avenue A, and before long, they were at their cars.

"Tomorrow will be better," Isabel said. Taylor nodded but didn't say anything. "Want me to come home with you?"

Taylor forced a smile. "Thank you, but I think I need to decompress on my own for a bit."

For whatever reason, the rejection hit her harder than it should have. Taylor had a bad day and needed some alone time. Totally normal. Except that Isabel was once again experiencing that ever-present vulnerability that said she wasn't good enough, which was stupid but real. Sometimes she hated herself and the way her brain worked to sabotage her. She shook it off.

"Okay, well, call me if you change your mind or just want to talk."

"I will."

"Taylor Andrews," said a man exiting the car next to Taylor's.

"Yes."

He handed her an envelope. "Ma'am, you have thirty days to answer the complaint with the summons. Please understand that these are official court documents. You've been served. Have a good day." He nodded his head and returned to his car as Taylor, looking about as stunned as Isabel felt, stared down at the envelope.

"What the hell?" she asked.

"Is he a process server?" Isabel whirled on the car and knocked on his window. "Are you a process server?"

He nodded. Once she stepped back, he pulled away, leaving them alone under the night's sky with the sound of his engine revving in the distance.

Taylor fumbled with the seal and managed to extract the documents inside. She glanced over them, then raised her gaze. Her eyes carried an anger Isabel hadn't witnessed from the levelheaded, generally serene Taylor.

"What does it say?" Isabel finally asked, unable to stand it a moment longer.

"I'm being sued. By Aspen Wakefield."

"For what?"

"Sexual harassment."

Oh, hell no. "You've got to be kidding me."

Taylor folded the envelope sadly. "Except I'm not."

CHAPTER NINETEEN

Taylor didn't sleep that night. She didn't even try. Instead, she sat at her kitchen table poring over every memory she could summon that related to her and Aspen. Was there something, anything, she could have done or said that could have been misconstrued?

No.

There absolutely wasn't. Aspen had first pursued the relationship, and Taylor had resisted for quite a while. They'd fallen into a sexual relationship first that had blossomed into more. And it *had* been a relationship. They'd met each other's families, talked about the future, and made appearances together in public. The relationship had been two sided and anything but forced on Aspen's part.

Taylor was being set up.

The next morning, she met with her attorney. Brooks Horton was well into his fifties and had always reminded Taylor of the quintessential silver fox. He was at the height of his career and had been Taylor's attorney from her early years in Hollywood. He fought hard for his clients and went the extra mile. If she was going up against Aspen in a court of law, she wanted Brooks on her side.

He spent the first part of their meeting going over the paperwork, murmuring indecipherably to himself as he read. Finally, he glanced up and took off his reading glasses. "She's alleging unwelcome sexual advances and a quid pro quo environment in which she was expected to sleep with you if she wanted any kind of airtime on the show."

"That's insane," Taylor told her lawyer. "We had a relationship, a legitimate one that she initiated. Hell, she seduced me, and it was elaborate."

He flipped through the documents. "She asserts it was the other way around and that your behavior was aggressive. She professes to have dates, times, and descriptions, the last of which was apparently yesterday when she alleges you grabbed her forcefully when she refused your most recent advances."

"There were no advances yesterday."

"That's not what the other side will argue. She's claiming there were a variety of witnesses who will support her story." He closed the file folder on his desk.

Taylor couldn't believe this was happening. "So, what do we do?"

He held up a hand. "I'm not sure if you're aware, but she's also named the network, WCN, as a defendant in the lawsuit."

"She's suing the network?" That one really threw Taylor.

He nodded. "For failure to prevent discrimination and a hostile work environment. I spoke with their representation earlier this morning. Ms. Wakefield never filed a complaint with them or voiced any concern, which is good for both parties. However, because of her high-profile status, they are understandably concerned and moving into damage control mode."

"What does that mean?"

"They don't want you to return to work at this time."

The words hit her squarely in the chest, stealing her breath.

"You'll be hearing from them shortly."

She shook her head as the information settled and blared like an alarm. "They're firing me?"

"Not at this point. But I've worked in entertainment law for too many years not to prepare you." He ran a hand through his thick gray hair. "You'll likely be compensated handsomely but removed as EP to keep the matter from escalating in the press. They'll use another reason, of course, a ratings dip. Or they'll say something generic and safe like 'it wasn't working creatively.'"

She nodded. "So, I'm out."

"We'll know for sure soon, but my guess is, that's likely."

Taylor tried to take a deep breath, but the air wouldn't fit, which made sense because the world now felt as if it were closing in on her. How could this have happened? That television show was her life, her creation, something she'd built upon from the tiniest kernel of an idea, and now it would go on without her? That didn't seem fair.

"Thank you, Brooks. You'll keep me updated?"

"I will." She turned to go. "Taylor?"

"Yeah."

"We can go to war with Aspen Wakefield, but I want you to at least consider a settlement, only because it can save you the heartache, the public scrutiny."

"So, someone can make up lies about you and just because they're a hot commodity, they get away with it."

He frowned like a father trying to explain the ways of the world to a brokenhearted child. "In Hollywood, you know as well as I do that what's reported in the press is unfortunately more relevant than the actual facts."

She did know that. She just never expected it to slice so close to home. "Thanks, Brooks." She nodded numbly and headed home, as there was nowhere else she was needed any longer. What she wanted was to wipe the makeup from her face, don her rattiest sweatshirt, and drink wine straight from the bottle.

The Friday morning after Taylor had been sidelined, the writing and production staff of *Thicker Than Water* were led into the large conference room across the street from the writing offices. A representative from the studio, a buttoned-up fortysomething Isabel had never seen before, was waiting to meet with them.

"I know you all have a number of questions regarding the on-set incident earlier this week. While I can't go into detail, I can express to you that a decision has been made." Isabel glanced around and saw several people nodding. Others looked confused. Isabel felt nauseous. Taylor had prepared her for the probability that she'd be let go permanently, but she couldn't imagine that happening. *Water* was one hundred percent Taylor's baby. They wouldn't do that. "Ms. Andrews will not be returning as showrunner. The cast is being notified in a separate meeting as we speak."

The faces of the people in the room mirrored what Isabel felt. She saw shock, outrage, and downright disgust. "Well, that's bullshit," Scruffy said, sitting back in his chair heavily, his arms crossed. "Who do you expect to pilot this ship?"

"It's a mistake, is what it is," Kathleen said loudly. "I think we deserve to know why."

"Like I said," suit guy replied, "the details are sensitive. Overall, it was not the best fit for the success of the show moving forward, and that's what we must focus on, what's right for the show."

"How is there a show without Taylor?" the head of the art department asked. "I'm with Scruffy. This blows."

"Fucking Aspen," Scarlett muttered, exchanging a disgusted stare with Isabel, who sat next to her. The others nodded. Gossip had wings. The network could negate mentioning Aspen's role in Taylor's departure when it made an official statement, but those who worked on the show knew full well why she was dismissed, and who was behind it. What it came down to, as Taylor had explained to her the night before, was that the show could go on without Taylor. It would be a lot harder without Aspen, the reason people tuned in each week.

The meeting had been short and to the point, and the shell-shocked group scattered once it concluded. Instead of returning to her cubicle and staring at a blinking cursor, she took a walk and called Taylor.

"I'm sorry you didn't hear it from me directly," Taylor said. Her voice was flat and lifeless, almost as if she didn't quite have the energy. "I think we were told at the same time."

"Who called you?" Isabel asked.

"Gerald. He probably volunteered because of our history. He was apologetic, said all the right things. The network is interested in working with me again in the future. If there's anything he can do for me personally, just let him know. Blah, blah, blah. It's exactly what my attorney predicted."

Isabel sighed into the phone. "I hate this. It's awful. I'm coming over tonight. I'll bring dinner and we can hate the world together. Make WCN voodoo dolls."

Silence. "I would like that. Well, maybe not the voodoo dolls, but seeing you would be nice. It's been an awful week."

"Good, because a perpetually awkward and slightly outspoken woman will be on your doorstep with Chinese food close to seven thirty. Keep the porch light on."

"I hope she's into the emotionally unpredictable types." Taylor's voice cracked on that last sentence. She sounded raw, and on the edge. Damn it.

Hoping to redirect the sadness, Isabel went for playful. "She is! She's all about the emotional types. The more tears, the more anger, the better, she always says."

A pause. She could hear the sound of quiet sniffling. "Isabel?"

"I'm here."

"Thank you."

When she returned to the office, she found Scruffy and Lyle packing up their belongings in cardboard boxes as loud music played from Lyle's laptop. "What's going on?" she asked, though she already had a feeling.

"Outta here," Scruffy said, not even pausing to talk. "We're a team, and they just took down our leader. I got connections on at least a dozen different shows and don't need to sit around this show while it tanks."

"There are plenty of jobs out there, Iz," Lyle said. "I'm not going to write for this one after Taylor's been kicked to the curb because a too-big-for-her-britches actress is making demands. I passed her outside earlier. She was laughing with a makeup artist like it's any other day." He straightened and addressed the room. "Taylor is the reason I'm here. So if she's out, I am, too."

"Okay, I'm out as well," Candace said, nodding. "I don't really think I could write for Wakefield anymore anyway. Lisette would wind up in jail or a ditch in under three episodes."

Isabel took it all in, everyone rallying behind Taylor. Of course they should stand by Taylor and walk the hell out of there. Of course. Why hadn't it occurred to her initially?

"What about you?" she asked Kathleen, who looked on as she thumbed the fabric on her sleeve absently.

Conflict crossed her features. She turned in apology to Isabel. "I need the work too badly. My husband is out of commission for the short term. I'd like nothing more than to walk. I wish I could." Isabel nodded and squeezed her friend's hand. Full of energy now, she took a seat at her cubicle, not really sure what to do with herself as a hundred thoughts crashed down on her, including the ones tied closely to reality.

She needed the money, and how exactly would it look if she walked off her first real writing gig? She cringed at her own ambition.

Although the season was winding down and there were only a couple of episodes left to shoot before they went on a short hiatus, the show was in production on and off throughout the year on a less traditional calendar. If she walked with Scruffy and Lyle and Candace, what would she do for work? Would she go back to waiting tables until something came along? The thought turned her stomach. Still, it didn't feel right to not stand up for Taylor the way some of the others were.

Isabel had some major soul-searching to do.

CHAPTER TWENTY

That night, as they unpacked dinner from the take-out bag in Taylor's kitchen, Isabel turned to her. "Scruffy, and Lyle, Candace, and Scarlett are leaving *Water*."

Taylor's eyes were red, and though she hadn't cried in front of Isabel, it still gutted her to know that the tears had come. "I talked to Scruffy. I told him he didn't owe me his job."

"Yeah, well, he doesn't want to be there if you're not. Turns out the angry little guy has a loyal heart."

"I always suspected he might."

"I'm leaving, too."

Taylor paused midway through opening the lid on a container of wonton soup and set it down. "You are? Iz, you don't have to—" Another long pause as she seemed to melt. "You are?"

"It doesn't feel right without you there. I stayed late to talk with Scruffy, and he's going to see what he can do about putting me in touch with some of his contacts."

Taylor held up one hand silently as she walked from the kitchen to the living room. She was crying, Isabel realized, and she quickly followed her. "Tay, are you all right?"

"I'm fine," she said, fanning her face as tears fell. "I didn't expect everyone to…care so much. The fact that you're willing to leave your job for me…I don't even have the words."

"Then don't say anything." Isabel squeezed her hand. "I'll need to find a way to make money in the meantime, but staying on just didn't feel right."

"Hey," Taylor said, "I don't want you to worry about any of that. If you need help financially, I'm here. Plus, I have contacts of my own all over town. In fact," she turned and headed back to the kitchen for her phone, "I have a friend over at ABC who needs a staff writer for that new show *Postman*. It's getting a lot of attention. You'd be great actually."

"That postapocalyptic show? I caught an episode once. That would be awesome."

"Cindy is going to love you." Taylor seemed happy, almost in project mode, and Isabel knew she'd made the right decision.

"And what about you?" Isabel asked and watched as Taylor's exuberance dimmed. "What's next in line for you?"

"I'm going to take some time out, I think. The Hollywood rat race is a little too much for me to deal with right now." She eased a strand of hair behind her ear. "There's still the lawsuit to handle. Brooks wants me to settle. Offer her half a million to drop the suit, though I'm thinking she's already gotten what she wanted. She may just drop it herself. This was never about money. She has more than God."

"I think that sounds like a solid plan."

The night was a quiet one, and for Taylor, it helped immensely having Isabel there, to sit with her and talk or not talk. The silences between them were the easy kind. They sat on the terrace with the outdoor heater going and stared out at the countless lights of Hollywood. All those people out there, living their lives, gearing up for the holidays.

"Have you ever thought of living anywhere other than California?" Isabel asked. "You've never really known anything else."

"That's true," Taylor said, and then tapped into a pocket dream she sometimes carried around with her. "Occasionally, I imagine myself making pies in the country and going for nature walks. Not exactly practical for my type-A personality, but maybe that can be my retirement, you know?"

Isabel nodded and stared into the night. Her silhouette was every bit as beautiful as the rest of her. There were crickets chirping in the distance. Apparently, the impending California winter couldn't keep them down.

"You might burn the pies," Isabel said resolutely.

"What?" Taylor turned to her, jaw hanging open.

Isabel shrugged. "I'm just saying, maybe stick with pancakes. Remember when you burned the cookies you just slice from the tube?"

If there had been something close by to throw at Isabel, Taylor would have gladly scooped it up. "I just confessed to you a long-term dream of mine and you insult me? On the very day I was fired?" But she felt the corners of her mouth turn upward and understood how important that was. "I could turn out to be fantastic at baking pies. You don't know."

"Sadly, I do." Isabel walked to Taylor's chair and sat across her sideways, looping an arm around her neck. "I'm just looking out for you, boss lady. You have so many fantastic talents, despite the pie baking predisposition for failure."

With Isabel so close and warm like a much-needed life preserver, Taylor drifted further away from the rest of the world and the awful circumstances she faced. She focused instead on the smiling face in front of hers and made sure to count Isabel as one of her biggest blessings.

"Why are you looking at me like that? You're giving me the 'soft eyes' look. Not that I'm complaining. The 'you left the cap off the toothpaste' look is way worse, and trust me, I will not be repeating that little misstep in the future."

Taylor rested a hand on Isabel's thigh and looked into her eyes. "You're my friend, you know that?"

"Okay." Isabel paused. "I hope I'm more than that." Her smile faltered as she glanced at the ground. It's what she did when she was feeling less than sure.

"No. Of course you are. I just mean that in addition to being sexy and smart and funny and the woman whose clothes I constantly fantasize about removing, you're also my honest-to-goodness friend. You've beyond proven that today."

"I am your friend. For always." Isabel touched her cheek gently and they stared at each other for a quiet moment before Isabel leaned down and kissed her, gently at first and then with purpose. "Remember when we used to fight this?" she asked.

Taylor nodded sincerely. "We never stood a chance. Can you stay tonight?"

"Oh, my God. I thought you'd never ask."

❖

"I'm on my third croissant. You guys need to call the cops," Hadley said, as if her little heart had been smashed in. Isabel decided that when Hadley pouted, it was universally gut-wrenching. A rare talent.

"Not illegal," Autumn pointed with her mug from her spot across the table. It was Monday morning and the breakfast club was in full session.

"I'm going to be run out of Beverly Hills fashion if I can't make the boutique's clothes look good. 'You had one job this morning, Hadley,'" she said, in a terrifying voice Isabel didn't even know she was capable of. "'Avoid the flaky pastry.'"

"What the hell was that?" Isabel asked. "You sounded like Cookie Monster on steroids."

"It's how she talks to herself," Gia said, resting her chin on her folded arms. "It's the freakiest thing. I'd explain it, but, you know, there's no explaining it."

Hadley waved them off and turned to Autumn. "It's your fault. You've enabled me, and now look who I'm turning into." She held up half a croissant as evidence.

"I've done no such thing," Autumn said, with nonchalance. "I'm a smart businesswoman and know how to hook a client when I need to."

"So do the crack dealers on the corner," Isabel offered and accepted Hadley's fist bump. She turned to Autumn. "But your coffee's better than crack."

"Put that on the sign out front," Gia said. "Do it."

"Done. The Cat's Pajamas: Better Than Crack." Autumn and Gia exchanged a fist bump of their own.

"Any updates to Taylor's situation?" Hadley asked Isabel. "It's like something out of a soap opera, which is, well, ironic."

Isabel sat back in her chair, cradling her warm mug between both hands. "On Friday, they fired her. Full-on."

"No fucking way," Gia said. "Because of that actress's lawsuit?"

Isabel nodded. "I'm guessing they didn't see any way for them to work together after all this, and Aspen is the center of the *Water* universe, so…"

Autumn shook her head. "Taylor pays the price. Unbelievable."

"Well, that does it. I'm taking down my life-size cutout," Hadley said emphatically.

Isabel covered Hadley's hand. "I'm sorry, Had. I wish she were a nicer person. Also, I'm resigning today."

Three mouths fell open and began talking at once.

"What?"

"Wow."

"For Taylor?"

Isabel nodded. "Yes, for Taylor. I'm not going to lie, it was terrifying to imagine myself quitting the best job I've ever had, but Taylor has a lead on another writing gig for me, as does another coworker of mine, and it just feels that standing solidly with her when her dismissal was so unfair is the right thing to do. I'll be okay."

"Noble of you," Gia said. "It's definitely the right move."

Hadley and Autumn nodded.

"You'll land on your feet," Autumn said, and without looking, pointed to the cat logo on the wall behind her.

Isabel grinned. "I see what you did there." She stood and downed the last of her coffee. "I'm off. Thanks, you guys. It helps to know you're in my corner, or whatever." She felt the blush that hit out of embarrassment. She'd never had friends like these before, and the well of emotion was foreign to her.

"We love you, Iz," Hadley said squeezing her hand. "Come over later and let me know how it goes."

"You're on."

An hour later, when Isabel arrived at the studio, she hadn't been at her desk five minutes before Gerald Hagerman rounded the corner and headed straight for her on some sort of mission. She stared up at him nervously.

"Morning, Isabel. I was hoping we could, uh, have a conversation."

She closed her eyes briefly. So, he'd heard about her intentions to follow the others out the door and was probably not thrilled about it. She geared up to explain herself and let him know how unfair the whole thing was. "I'd be happy to chat."

"Why don't we head into the office?"

She followed him around the corner and down the short hallway to the office, Taylor's office. Her belongings had been packed up and the place had been virtually gutted, leaving just the desk and a bookshelf in the corner. The lifeless room made Isabel feel sick, as she flashed to the day she'd spilled coffee on that very desk.

Gerald closed the door and took a seat in Taylor's chair. "I know you're unhappy. I can see it all over your face." He rested his big hands on his stomach.

"I don't like the way all of this has played out. Taylor is the one who brought me on."

"She's a dynamo at spotting talent, which is why I'm here. We're taking a look at options for *Water* moving forward."

"Speaking of the future, I need to let you know—"

"Hang on." He raised his hand to hold her off. "Hear me out first. I want you to take the show."

She stared at him. "Take it where?" He wasn't making sense.

"I realize you're green and that you've never so much as produced before, but that's why we bring in someone who can guide you through those processes until you're fully ready to fly solo. In the meantime, these folks around here need a familiar face at the helm, and I need your creative storytelling in that writers' room. So whaddaya say?"

"You want to make me showrunner?" She glanced around the room to try and make sense of what was happening.

"That's exactly what I'm saying."

She opened her mouth to answer but then closed it again, shocked at this new turn of events. "Just like that?"

"Ms. Chase, I'm a man who enjoys betting on the ponies, and I do well out there. I do. I could hand this show to Kathleen, but I'm not convinced she's the most dynamic choice. Are you following me?"

"I think you just said I'm the pony you're laying your money on."

He smiled and regarded her like he was about to collect from the house.

Taylor had spent most of the day watching *Judge Judy* with Raisin in her lap. She'd shelved the sweatpants and put on real people clothes, which was a step in the right direction. She missed work. She missed her staff and had all but turned off her phone, as *Variety* wouldn't stop calling for a comment regarding her dismissal. November was turning into a cold and rainy month, which was the perfect backdrop for her present situation: pathetic.

"She should never have lent her boyfriend the car," she told Raisin and pointed at the screen. "He owes her that three hundred fifty outright. Judy'll put him in his place."

At the sound of the doorbell she smiled, still not quite sure why she hadn't given Isabel a key. Weren't they getting close to that phase of their relationship? She scooped up the Champagne she'd had chilling and carried it with her to the door. She swung it open and presented the bottle. "For you. Welcome to the world of unemployment. We're so glad you're here." She leaned in for a kiss but Isabel walked past her, head down.

"It was a weird day," she said finally.

"Transitions usually are. I'm sorry. Let's have a glass of Champagne and try to look forward and not back."

"You're not going to like what I have to say," Isabel said slowly, "and I've spent the last few hours preparing myself for that." Isabel moved rapidly around the room and didn't quite seem to know what to do with her hands. "In fact, you may just kick me out of your house."

Taylor went still. "What is it? Just say it, Iz. It can't be *that* bad."

"They picked a new showrunner for *Water*."

Taylor took a seat, sobering. "Well, I'm not going to blame you for that." But she didn't like the idea of someone stepping into her shoes, taking over what was hers. In fact, the concept made her stomach fill with ice. To lose control of that world, her characters, was devastating. "Who'd they get?" She'd made a list of probable candidates days ago.

"That's the interesting part. They offered it to me."

Taylor's head swiveled and she played the sentence back. "They did? Wow."

"I know. I was just as floored."

"I can only imagine. It's a huge compliment, though, when you think about it."

"I guess so."

"What did they say when you told them you were leaving? I bet that threw them." Taylor shook her head, just imagining the whiplash of that conversation.

"Right. That's the thing." She met Taylor's gaze. "I took the job."

The walls seemed to inch in on Taylor. "I'm not following you."

Isabel met her gaze evenly. "I'm the new showrunner on *Water*."

Taylor felt like she'd been punched in the gut. Hard. "Oh. You are?"

Isabel's eyes flashed apologetic, like poor little Taylor might break in half at any moment. She didn't want Isabel's pity. In fact, she couldn't stand it.

"The opportunity was too huge to pass up," Isabel explained. "It's the reason I came to LA, only I thought it would take years, but then this morning, there it was, handed to me."

"There it was," Taylor said blankly. Her mind splintered and she struggled to keep up with the emotions that came in ever-shifting waves. Just as she settled on one, a new one took over. Shock first. Then a slash of pain. Betrayal descended. Understanding. Betrayal again. Understanding. Too many things at once. She closed her eyes.

"The network sees something worthy in what I've done so far, and they want to work with me and develop my skills on the producing end. They're going to pair me with—"

"Emma Wade," they both said in unison.

"Right. Emma. To work with me as a mentor. You know Emma?"

"I know Emma." They stared at each other, Taylor doing her best not to react until she was sure what that reaction should be. The tension hovered thick and uncomfortable. It was awful enough imagining the series moving on without her, but to see Isabel so easily discard her plans to stand with Taylor and to take the reins herself was…a bitter pill to swallow. Scruffy, Lyle, Scarlett, and Candace had all walked from the show *for her*. Yet Isabel had done the proverbial opposite and taken the network's hand. At the same time, she understood Isabel's perspective. She was new to all this. Hungry. Ambitious. And this was the opportunity of all opportunities.

Isabel stepped forward, but there was a chasm between them now that had nothing to do with their proximity. "I had to weigh it all, Tay: my hopes and dreams coming to fruition in one moment against the fact that you would hate me, probably never speak to me again."

"You thought I would hate you?" Something clicked and the knife twisted. "You thought that taking the job meant you and I would be through."

Isabel blinked back at her.

"Yet you did it anyway."

"Trust me when I say that it was the most difficult decision I've ever made."

"Nobody was asking you to choose, Isabel. I would *never* have made you choose. Don't you get that?" Taylor stood there, letting the implication sink in fully. She shook her head. "But it's apparent what your choice would have been. God. I get it now. As awful as it is, I understand who I'm dealing with."

Panic flared in Isabel's eyes. "Don't get me wrong. I was hoping more than anything that you *would* understand, that we'd be okay."

"But that was just a side note, right? An afterthought to your larger goal." Taylor nodded a few times as she worked through the larger implication. To Isabel, she was disposable, and that realization leveled her like a two-by-four to the chest. She hadn't imagined it. She couldn't have predicted it. And she certainly couldn't continue with that knowledge. How could she possibly?

Silence enveloped them as those unspoken words reverberated loudly. Raisin, realizing for the first time that Isabel had arrived, ran in from the laundry room and leapt up at her repeatedly.

Isabel's voice was quiet and thin when she finally spoke. "What if I had turned it down and we didn't work out? I couldn't erase that thought from my head. What if we woke up tomorrow and you were bored, or you met someone more beautiful, more alluring, more *everything* than I am, because I would fully expect that to eventually happen." She held her arms out and let them drop. "I'm just me, Taylor. Boring, unexciting me. There had to be a time limit."

And the hits kept coming.

"If that's the kind of person you think I am, then you were right. This probably wouldn't have worked out. My need for exciting, glamorous, vapid women is never-ending! How could someone like me possibly maintain a healthy, normal relationship? Impossible! Do you understand how that sounds? How that makes me feel?" She was yelling now, and she never yelled.

"That's not what I'm saying," Isabel bit out, her own frustration apparent as she gestured wildly. "But I feel like I'm constantly waiting for the other shoe to drop with you. Sitting in my closet, anxiety ridden, because I can't quite imagine that any of this is real. That you're mine."

"*Was* yours," Taylor amended with distinction. "You chose the job, remember? Since I'm so shallow in my ways and would never have understood."

Isabel's eyes flashed. "You would have done the same."

"No. I wouldn't have. But that part doesn't matter."

"Taylor." Isabel held out her hand, her eyes pleading. "Don't hate me for this."

"You should go now."

"Wait. We're not done here."

"I think we have to be. Besides, it was your call. Not mine."

Taylor walked slowly to the stairs, and once she was safely in her bedroom, she covered her eyes and let it all come. Distantly, she heard the front door click closed downstairs and covered her mouth, only to

Chapter Twenty-one

For Isabel, December moved at an excruciatingly slow pace. Work was insane, keeping her busy much of the time, which was helpful. Every moment that her brain wasn't occupied was a struggle for air, and she was failing miserably.

Her heart ached and she wondered if she'd ever feel whole again.

She thought about Taylor when she woke up in the morning. When she took a moment between meetings to catch her breath. When she sat in the chair that used to be hers and felt like a total imposter. When she drove home at night and wondered what Taylor was doing and fought the urge to drive straight to her house and find out. Perhaps, the worst of all were the very vivid dreams of the two of them together that descended when she slept. With each morning came the harsh slap of reality once she remembered they were done.

But it had been the right decision. The attacks had recessed and that meant she'd find her footing soon, right? She'd return to a boring, mundane personal life, but one that would allow her to relax and exist without the fear of losing.

As the days crept by, she held out hope that things would get easier with time.

They didn't.

She'd steered clear of the closet but missed her mentor, the woman so proud of her own pancakes that her smile reached from ear to ear, and who tickled Isabel behind her ear when she was interested in morning sex, and who could speak intelligently on just about any subject Isabel cared to name.

None of it mattered. She'd made her decision and would have to live with it.

"So, he just refused to say the line?" Autumn asked, taking off her Pajamas apron. "Actors can do that?"

Isabel nodded. "He wasn't a fan of the word 'pucker.' I had a real close replacement for him once he held up production for over an hour." It was close to nine p.m., and Autumn was in cleanup mode at the shop. Isabel followed her around the place like a puppy, needing someone to just…be around, keep her busy.

Autumn handed Isabel the dispenser for plastic stirrers and the box to refill it from. She set to work. "So, work's awful. How's the rest of you? Any better?"

She offered Autumn a wan smile, but the tears that seemed ever-present beneath the surface once again pooled. She pointed at her face and took a moment to get some air in her lungs. "Apparently not. Sorry."

"Oh, sweetie. Come here." Autumn held open her arms and Isabel moved into them, needing the contact, the comfort.

"I miss her," Isabel managed to say.

"Of course you do."

"It was the right thing, though," Isabel said, for probably the hundredth time. Maybe if she heard it enough, it would somehow make her feel better. Autumn gave her a squeeze but didn't say anything. Isabel pulled away. "It was. I know it was. It just sucks, the getting through this part."

"Why are we crying?" Gia asked, blowing through the front door. "Is it too late for a cappuccino?"

"Iz still misses Taylor, and not too late. Give me two minutes and I'm your caffeine angel."

"You're my everything angel," Gia said appreciatively.

"Flattery will not get you free coffee."

Gia snapped her fingers. "Damn."

Autumn finished refilling the dispenser herself, as Isabel had proven incompetent given the meltdown. "G, why don't you tell Isabel *your* feelings about her ending things with Taylor."

Isabel held up a finger. "I didn't end anything."

"Kinda did," Autumn said, and headed behind the counter. "It sounds like you went over there and announced, without prompting, that you preferred your career to a future with her."

Isabel shook her head. "It wasn't *exactly* like that."

"The fact that you had to emphasize the word 'exactly' is telling. Gia?"

"I'd rather not," Gia said conservatively.

"Why not?" Isabel asked, pointing at Autumn. "This one doesn't seem to have any problem laying it all out there."

"Because you and I are cool."

Isabel balked, tears still in her eyes. "So? Is your opinion really that inflammatory?"

Gia sighed. "I just think when you love someone, you love them, you know. So, I was surprised to see you—"

"I never said I was in love with Taylor." True. She hadn't *said* it. She'd refused to even *think* it, because the spot that would leave her in would be too precarious to fathom.

"You didn't have to," Gia said. "Whenever you said her name, you practically levitated. It was nice."

"And then you wussed out," Autumn said, with her back to them at the espresso machine.

Isabel whirled on her. "What did you just say?" But the steam from the machine drowned out her question by design. These two could tag-team her all they wanted, but no one seemed to understand that this had been about self-preservation and risk management.

Gia pointed at Isabel. "You know what? I'm gonna text Had. She's better at this kind of thing. Softer touch."

"Does she think I'm a wuss, too?" Isabel asked, incredulous. She only had to wait about thirty seconds to find out, as Hadley entered the coffee shop straight from work, decked out in a designer navy skirt and jacket combo.

"Well, hey there, everyone." She flashed her phone at Gia. "Got your text. What's up?"

That was Isabel's cue to promptly burst into tears again. Something about Hadley's presence, nurturing and kind and nonjudgmental, gave her permission to let loose. Kind of like when her dad picked her up from school after a particularly rotten day.

"Uh-oh." Hadley's arm was instantly around Isabel's shoulders as she led her to a nearby table. "Is this what I think it's about?" she asked soothingly.

Autumn and Gia nodded in unison.

Isabel continued blubbering. "I guess I'm a basket case, and no one knows what to do with me. Myself included."

"Well, I do," Hadley said, and handed Isabel a packet of Kleenex from her purse. "Because I think it's important for you to know one very important thing."

"Okay," Isabel said and blew her nose loudly. "What's the one thing?"

Hadley looked her right in the eye. "You're going to be okay. No matter what has happened or will happen. *You* are going to be okay."

Isabel took comfort in those words. "I will. And underneath all of this, I probably know that, but thanks, Had…it helps to hear it."

"Now, you may not be over-the-moon happy, but you'll get by."

Okay, well, that sounded worse.

"Don't get me wrong," Hadley said, with a wave of her hand, "there's a lot to be said for a mediocre existence."

"Ouch." Wasn't Hadley supposed to be the nice one? Interestingly enough, she'd yet to lose her comforting, calm delivery. "What is that supposed to mean?"

"It means you're going to be just fine, but if it's happiness you're after, Iz, you're going to have to learn to get out of your own way."

"Hear, hear," Autumn said, and then held up her hands in innocence when Isabel sent her a look.

"How am I in my own way?"

Hadley continued. "Instead of focusing on what matters, the fact that Taylor wanted to be with you and you wanted to be with Taylor, you let your own insecurities take over and call all the shots. You trusted that hateful voice inside your head that was sabotaging you more than you trusted the woman you love."

Isabel stared at Hadley. "It's not that I don't trust Taylor."

"It kind of is like that," Gia said. "But I get that I'm not Had and don't have the finesse she has."

"Who does?" Hadley said, with a serene smile. Gia popped her lightly on the head as she passed. She pulled up a chair on the other side of Isabel. "That woman wanted you, not someone else, but *you*, and you decided for her that she didn't. Or wouldn't. Same thing."

"There's something I haven't mentioned." All eyes were on Isabel. She focused on the table as she spoke. "I've been dealing with these attacks. Panic attacks, most people call them. When they hit, I seize up and feel like the world is about to end as I sit there." Hadley squeezed her hand. "They stem from insecurity, and being with Taylor brought on a whole lot of that."

Autumn's hand flew to her mouth. "That night in the car."

Isabel nodded. "Yep."

"I can't believe you didn't say anything," Gia said. "I dealt with those when I was a kid. If you ever want to talk about it, I'm here."

"Thanks," Isabel said and flashed a smile. "Maybe someday."

Hadley took it from there. "The problem is that you doubt yourself and you shouldn't. We haven't known you very long and we already know you're awesome. In fact, we're hanging on to you, in spite of your insecurities and enabling of Gia's gaming habits."

Gia shrugged.

"I think you guys are great, too," Isabel said, with a small smile.

Autumn placed Gia's cappuccino on the table. "Isn't that your cue to break up with us, then?"

"Oh, man." Isabel clutched her heart. "You're awful, you know that?"

"I don't mind being awful, if it means you'll hear me."

Isabel threw up her hands in frustration because it wasn't like there was any going back now. She had the job and Taylor was gone. "What is it you want me to do?"

"Fix it," Hadley said.

Gia nodded. "Fix it."

"That's three for fix it," Autumn said, authoring a checkmark in the air.

"And what if all the insecurities, the anxiety attacks, what if they all come back?"

"Let me ask you this," Autumn said, with a hand on her hip. "Is it better to work on losing the insecurities or lose Taylor forever? Because I know which I'd be trying to rid myself of."

Isabel sighed, wondering which way was up. She ruminated on her friends' advice as she stared up at the beveled ceiling above her bed that night. Though, as always, her thoughts shifted quickly to that time in her life when she was happier than she'd ever been.

It felt so very far away.

Maybe Hadley was right. Maybe this whole thing was more about working on herself, and not about running from what scared her. The question was, where in the world should she start?

❖

"Did you hear?" Kathleen asked, leaning her shoulder against the doorjamb of Isabel's office.

"Hear what?" she asked, half listening, half glued to the email asking if she thought the leaves in the upcoming episode had to be green. She did. The episode took place in April. Apparently, that would cost another few thousand dollars. Really? For green leaves? She'd have to ask Emma about that one.

"That Taylor's discreetly shopping around a new show."

"She is?" Isabel asked, her attention fully snagged. "What show?"

"From what my friend at the network could tell, something about a former CIA woman." Kathleen sighed. "Sounds intriguing. I'm wildly jealous."

Isabel smiled and flashed to that perfect night on the beach, the night they'd fleshed out Taylor's idea together as they walked along the boardwalk, and then again in the car after…well, *after*. She could almost smell salt in the air and feel the sea breeze against her face, the memory was that potent. Her smile wilted when she remembered that there would be no more nights like that one, as she wasn't a part of Taylor's world anymore. She would only hear these kinds of details from secondhand sources. "Good for her," she said sincerely. She turned back to her monitor, fighting off the wave of emotion that threatened.

"Right? She's gonna show all of 'em," Kathleen said. "That's what I think. I don't know if you caught the ratings for *Sister Dale*, but now that Taylor's episodes are airing, they're up by a wide margin."

"I did catch that. There's no one like her."

Kathleen glanced behind her and dropped her voice. "They were stupid to let her go. Just plain *stupid*." For the rest of the afternoon, that sentence played on repeat in the back of Isabel's mind. She daydreamed through most of the table read and found herself blindsided when Aspen pulled her aside. Up until this point, she'd kept their one-on-one contact to a minimum. She couldn't stand the woman but had done her best to remain professional. Today, she felt like she might lose that battle.

"You're doing a great job, Isabel. Have I told you that?" She batted her eyes, and Isabel cringed. The falsities hung off this woman like branches on a willow.

"No, I'm not, and everyone knows it." As far as her job went, Isabel was making it up as she went along, doing whatever Emma told her to do, because her heart wasn't in it. Her heart was elsewhere, and that became more and more apparent as the seconds ticked by and the larger world faded to the background.

"Well, I think you are, and I was hoping we could have lunch. Clear the air. Not sure if you saw the quote from me in the trades."

Isabel had seen it. Aspen had told the press that the show had never been more exciting to work on and was running smoother than ever now that Isabel had taken over. At first, she'd allowed herself to feel flattered and rode the high of being a big fish. Then she remembered the duplicitous source and came crashing right back to reality. Aspen was not to be trusted.

Isabel shook her head. "There won't be any lunches, no matter what you told the papers. Nothing even close to a lunch. Is there anything else? If not, I'm going to go stare at my wall and figure out how else I can be ineffective at this job."

"Don't sell yourself short," Aspen called after her, because of course it was in her best interest to turn this thing around so she could return to star status in the eyes of anyone who'd been paying attention. "It'll be great."

Isabel couldn't tolerate another minute of it. She turned. "No, it won't be great. But you know what? You had great and you torpedoed it in the most malicious fashion. Every step of the way you took advantage of your position here." Aspen's eyes went wide, but Isabel wasn't deterred. "You're an awful person, Aspen. *Awful.* You should know that."

Aspen's expression turned to ice. There she was. There was the real Aspen. "I don't know what's come over you Isabel, but—"

"The only thing that's worse than how awful you are is how awful I am, because I tossed her away, too. We're both idiots. You're just also a manipulative bitch, which must suck in the worst way. I mean, you have to wake up to yourself every morning."

Aspen took a step forward. "You're going to regret speaking to me this way."

Isabel smiled calmly. "Trust me when I say I'm not."

As she walked back to her office, the implication of what she'd just done hit her fully. Her throat constricted, the first sign of an attack. She braced herself until she was safely behind the closed door of her office and took a seat and waited.

Any minute now…

Only nothing happened. In fact, as time ticked by, she felt freer than she ever had in her entire life, liberated and ready to take on the world. She wanted to be a television writer, yes, but not under these circumstances. Not even close. Taking control of her situation had helped her avoid a colossal attack. If she could continue to plug away at the source of her anxiety, she could continue to conquer it one day at a time. This was a sign. There was hope for her.

She also knew that more than anything else, she wanted Taylor, needed her, and if it meant she had to serve up a hundred plates of fennel to a throng of angry diners, she was more than willing to do it. Bring on the fennel! How was that for taking control?

She was fired up now, on a roll. She threw a Rocky-style punch and cringed at how lame it would have looked to anyone watching. Uh-uh. No! She had to stop that. That kind of thinking was the opposite of what she needed right now. She threw another punch, harder this time, and smiled.

There were a few loose ends she needed to tie up on *Water* and then she'd be free to figure out just how she was going to undo the damage, wondering at the same time if that was even possible, then pointedly correcting herself, because anything was.

Chapter Twenty-two

God, Taylor had needed a day like today.

After weeks locked away from the world in her bedroom, eating Twizzlers with the drapes closed and trying to figure out how to feel like a person again, she'd come up empty. Nothing had worked. The television reminded her of the job she missed, and everything else reminded her in some way of Isabel, right down to the T-shirt of Taylor's she'd slept in the last night she'd stayed over. It still smelled like her. She couldn't even bring herself to make pancakes anymore without her mind taking her to happier times…the two of them laughing in the kitchen, kissing in the kitchen, or just existing quietly.

As a last resort, with tears streaming down her face, she'd sat in front of her laptop. For several hours, she'd stared at the blinking cursor. Finally, something eased into place and she'd started to type, using those potent emotions to force words on the page, much the way she had in high school, an escape from the details of her reality. She'd emerged a few days ago with an actual script in her hand. While still very much in draft form, the pilot glimmered with potential.

Her meeting with WCN that afternoon had gone better than she'd thought possible, and she'd been informed that Aspen had dropped the lawsuit after a closed-door meeting with the network. While she'd ridden that high for a short while, it had already started to drift away, leaving her once again feeling empty and alone. So, she would curl up with Raisin and a good book and hunker down from the cold temperatures that had crept in from the north. She hadn't been able to bring herself to put up a Christmas tree. Maybe she'd gather the motivation later.

Only Raisin hadn't come running as he always did when she

arrived home and, upon further investigation, wasn't in any of his usual spots.

"Raisin! You sleeping?"

She checked the laundry room, her bedroom, even under the couch.

She cupped her hands to her face. "Raiiiiisin!" she called in a loud and singsongy voice. That one got him every time. Only it didn't.

Fear crept up her spine as she checked the backyard, and quadrupled when she found the gate unlatched.

"No, no, no," she murmured, cursing the lawn guy who had been scheduled to remove dead foliage. She didn't have time to dwell, however, and hopped in her car, hoping against hope the little adventurer hadn't had time to go too far. She drove the neighborhood, peering at the space between houses for any tiny sign of him. Nothing. She pulled over and asked anyone she passed if they'd seen him. They hadn't. Another lap through the neighborhood, then another. Night was falling. A group of Christmas carolers thought they'd seen him two streets over but then decided that the dog they saw had been too big. Taylor thanked them and checked anyway. No Raisin. She was beginning to panic.

She headed home just in case he'd returned, though she wasn't sure if he knew the way. She was crying now and feeling desperate. Where could he be? She pulled into her driveway, caught off guard by the Honda Civic. She exited her car to see Isabel walk back down the driveway toward her. When their eyes collided, Isabel paused abruptly and then moved to her.

"What's wrong? Taylor, are you okay?"

"What are you doing here?" Taylor asked, walking past Isabel and brushing the tears from her cheeks. She hated that the sight of Isabel was as comforting as it was. What she wouldn't give to fall into Isabel's arms until it all went away.

"I came to talk."

"Can't right now. Raisin is missing."

Isabel followed her up the walk to the house. "What? Oh, no. Well, let's look for him. I'll help."

"I've combed the neighborhood. He's nowhere. I thought maybe he came home." She ran a desperate hand through her hair.

"You check the backyard. I'll start calling shelters."

This time, Taylor didn't argue. She needed help, and Isabel was there. It was almost dark, and the weather was changing rapidly. There were storms forecast for tonight, and she couldn't bear the thought of him out in the elements, huddled under a tree somewhere. He was an indoor dog for the most part and wasn't equipped.

"Iz, it's going to be cold tonight," she said, as fear whipped through her.

Isabel squeezed her hand. "Doesn't matter. We're going to find him."

Only, two hours later, there was still no indication, no clue to where he might have gone. Isabel had called all the shelters. They hadn't had any dachshunds brought in. They'd circled the surrounding neighborhoods and came up empty-handed.

So they moved into a rotation. Drive around, check back at home. Drive around, check back again. Taylor closed her eyes against the beep, beep, beep of the weather report that crawled across her screen as she stood in her living room, a short break from the cold. This wasn't happening. Not only were the temperatures dropping rapidly, but the newscaster was now predicting freezing rain.

"This is a nightmare," Taylor said. She eased herself onto the couch like a crumpled little doll as the wind whistled loudly against the window. Isabel took a seat next to her.

"He's not outside. Trust me. He's the smartest dog I know. He's curled up in someone's house with them, waiting it out, probably in front of a fire."

"Thank you for helping me," Taylor managed to whisper. She didn't look at Isabel. She couldn't, but she didn't pull away when Isabel took her hand. The warm strength of it brought comfort.

"You were there for me once in a very dark moment," Isabel said. "I can do the same for you."

Taylor nodded. "I'm not sure I can just sit here anymore. It's after midnight. I need to do something. I need to be proactive." She was up and moving.

"It's too dark to see much out there," Isabel said. "I think we need to be here in case he finds his way home."

"One more drive," Taylor said, taking charge. "One more." But they still didn't find him, and hope was beginning to seem out of reach. She should call Todd and let him know in the morning. There was nothing he could do from Denver.

When they got back to Taylor's house, Isabel made them some cocoa. For the rest of the night, they sat together, watching the dog door, listening for any sound. They must have fallen asleep somewhere after three a.m., slumped side by side. When the rain pelted the windows,

Isabel put her arm around Taylor and held her close, which really did make her think that maybe, just maybe, it would be all right.

Isabel was here. She wasn't alone. They were going to find him.

❖

In the morning, the sunlight cut through Taylor's living room crisp and bright. Small icicles hung from the eaves outside. Isabel had only slept for an hour or two tops, and her body felt heavy and tired. Taylor stirred in her arms then, her face pressed into Isabel's neck. She took a deep inhale of the familiar shampoo and shook off the startling nostalgia, reminding herself of the circumstances.

"He didn't come home," Taylor said flatly, pushing herself up into a seated position. She rubbed her red eyes and glanced at the back door, which just about broke Isabel's heart.

Isabel shook her head. "Not yet."

"I'm going to make some coffee and get online. See if anyone in the neighborhood posted anything."

"That's a great idea."

Taylor headed to her laptop. "You were more than gracious to stay with me last night, but I can take it from here. You need to get to work. You're in charge now." She glanced away as she said it, the reality still apparently hard to swallow. Isabel decided that this wasn't the time to tell Taylor that she'd stepped down, even if that had been her whole point in coming over. Taylor needed to focus on Raisin and bringing him home. Today should not be about her.

"Right. Work. I'll get going. I'll check in on you later."

"You don't have to do that," Taylor said, finally meeting Isabel's eyes. "You've gone out of your way already."

A long silence hit. "And I will again. Every time, for you."

Taylor didn't say anything as Isabel picked up her bag, nodded to her, and left.

But she didn't head home.

Instead, she hit every animal shelter within twenty miles. While each attendant showed her what dachshunds they had, they also pointed out that none had been brought in in the past twenty-four hours. She thanked the attendant at the final shelter and walked the aisles of the dog wing, wincing against the overwhelming volume of their barks while she planned her next move. Flyers would be a good way to start. She could certainly pitch in her skills on—

Two paws flew to the gate in front of her and between them a brown wiggly nose. She knew that nose! And that crazy dappled black, white, and brown fur. "Raisin!" she practically shouted, sinking to her knees as relief flooded her senses. "What in the world are you doing here, Hotdog?" Happy tears sprang into her eyes. He wiggled his rear and leapt up and down as if to celebrate someone finding him at long last. She plopped down in front of the wire mesh, allowing him to lick her hand through its squares. She seized the paperwork from where it hung on his gate and saw the problem. "You're not a toy fox terrier," she said. "You're not even close, other than a little black and white." He whined softly, clearly ready to bust out of that place. There was a scratch under his eye and he seemed to be holding up his front left leg when on all fours.

"You've had a scary adventure, haven't you? Let me go talk to them so we can get you the hell out of here."

"You're the owner?" the female attendant asked skeptically. "Of this dog?" She turned the paperwork around to face Isabel, Raisin's mug shot visible.

"Yes. I'm the owner of this *non–fox terrier*," she lied. "This *dachshund* is mine, and I'd like to take him home with me now."

"Must have been a clerical error." She shrugged. "Happens. Well, we're happy to have reunited the two of you. He was running around loose, so you'll want to keep a closer eye on him in the future. And there's a fee, you know."

"Of course there is." Isabel took out her wallet, happy to pay whatever fee necessary to spring Raisin from the big house and get him back where he belonged.

When she pulled up the long drive to Taylor's house in the hills, Raisin seemed to start vibrating right there in his seat next to her. He knew he was home, and when she put the car in park, he leapt into her lap, waiting in anticipation for her to open the door. "You want to see your mommy, don't you? You miss her. Just one more minute."

She typed a quick text to Taylor. *Stopping by. Can you meet me outside? Important.*

They only had to wait a moment or two until Taylor exited the house, still wearing yesterday's clothes and with a haggard look on her face. But her hands flew to cover her mouth when she saw Isabel standing there with Raisin. Isabel walked him up the sidewalk before finally dropping the leash and letting him run the rest of the way. She watched as Raisin raced to Taylor, who snatched him into her arms.

"Where were you?" she asked him before peppering his face with a million kisses as he whined loudly in celebration. "I was so worried. You can't ever leave again, okay?" Now it was Raisin's turn to lick Taylor's face in a never-ending stream while Taylor cried happy tears. Finally, she stood with Raisin in her arms and walked to Isabel. "How did you do this?"

"He was mislabeled at one of the shelters."

"You kept looking, even after you left?"

Isabel nodded. "I knew he was out there. I had to try. And now things are back as they should be. Well, almost."

Taylor met her gaze and held it for moment. "Thank you." She gave Isabel's hand a squeeze. "I don't know what I would have done if I'd lost him."

"Now you don't have to think about it." She ruffled the fur on top of Raisin's head. "I'll get out of here. Let you two spend some time together, have some beers as he recounts his adventures." She walked to her car, hands in the pocket of her jacket. She could see her breath and realized the temperatures were continuing to drop.

"Iz?"

She glanced back over her shoulder. "Yeah?"

"You saved the day." Taylor shook her head. "Regardless of us, everything that's happened, you saved me. I want you to know that."

Isabel nodded. "I'm glad. Maybe we can sit down at some point soon. Have…I don't know…a conversation. An important one."

She saw the hesitation in Taylor's eyes. "Maybe."

It was all she could ask for. She would keep a tight hold of that maybe, and wouldn't let it go, her last little shred of hope.

Because just *maybe*…

Scarlett studied Taylor as if working through a difficult math problem, all the while slowly stirring her Old Fashioned from across the table. "Let me see if I have all this straight."

Taylor nodded. "Go for it." Scarlett had insisted Taylor come out with her that night, citing the fact that she'd barely left the house in weeks, and only then out of necessity. Once they'd arrived at the quiet little night spot, Taylor had proceeded to pour her heart out to her friend, much to her own shock. But there it all was, thrown at Scarlett in one giant run-on sentence, an emotional all-you-can-eat buffet.

"Let me see if I have it all." Scarlett held out her hand and began to list things on her fingers. "You think about her constantly. It was the most rewarding romantic relationship of your life. She's smart and sarcastic and awesome. You're over-the-top attracted to her. In spite of your fallout, she stayed by your side all night when you were in crisis and eventually found your dog for you, but you still can't get past the fact that she stole your job." Scarlett sat back and resumed the slow stirring of her cocktail, regarding Taylor with skepticism.

Taylor moved her head from side to side. "Technically, she didn't *steal* my job."

"Exactly," Scarlett said, palm out. "She merely accepted what was offered to her."

Taylor sat back in defeat. "And in the process, made the decision to throw me over if need be. I don't know if that's something I can just get over. She broke my heart, ya know? And it's not even close to healing."

Scarlett covered Taylor's hand. "I'm sorry, Taylor. I wish you'd have called me. Do you think she regrets it? She might."

She sighed. "She wants to talk, so maybe. I'm not sure I'm up for it."

"Well, she did quit the job. Gave her notice and walked. So give her *some* credit."

The sentence didn't make sense. "She didn't."

"She *did*. From what I hear, they're forcing Kathleen into that spot, but we all know she's not comfortable there. I bet she walks, too. And have you seen *Variety*?"

Taylor was still struggling to keep up, everything a foggy haze. "Isabel quit? What's in *Variety*?"

Scarlett slid her phone across the table, and Taylor read the headline on the screen. "A Second Showrunner Out at 'Thicker Than Water.' Insider Says Aspen Wakefield Hard to Work With."

"Whoa," Taylor said, mystified.

"I have a hunch who the insider is," Scarlett said, taking the phone back. "And that's one hell of a parting shot, wouldn't you say?"

Taylor stared at the table, imagining Isabel placing that call. A small smile crept onto her face. "Isabel pushes back when someone behaves badly. It definitely could have been her."

"Trust me, it was. Aspen's probably having a conniption. She hates bad press."

"She does."

"Though I'm sure her new girlfriend will help her through."

"Aspen has a girlfriend?" How had so much happened?

Scarlett grinned. "I saw her making out with Lyric Larkin at the Viper Room two nights ago."

Taylor's head almost exploded. "I can't think of anything more perfect."

"Except maybe you and Isabel." Scarlett pushed her glasses up on her nose. She wasn't going to let this drop. "She deserves a second chance. It's only fair."

"Is it?"

"My God, Taylor, do you hear yourself right now?" Realizing that she was loud and worked up, Scarlett reined it in, tossing an apologetic glance at the table next to theirs. She dropped her tone. "Sorry for that, but I watched for months in horror as you gave Aspen fucking Wakefield chance after shocking chance. And she behaved really badly, Taylor. Isabel, conversely, made one wrong move." She held up her hands. "Okay, I can admit it was a pretty big one, but it sounds like it stemmed from issues of self-worth. So come on!" She winced and turned to the other table. "Sorry, again."

"So, what you're saying is—"

"Doesn't Isabel deserve that same clean slate? Why doesn't Isabel get a second chance?"

"I wish it were that simple."

"Why isn't it?" Scarlett asked, confused.

If Taylor could see past the glaring pain she still carried, Scarlett had a valid point. But at the core, she knew exactly why she hadn't afforded Isabel the same forgiveness, and it was because she was in love with her. She met Scarlett's eyes. "Because the ones you love always have the power to hurt you more."

Scarlett's eyes instantly softened and she took Taylor's hands in hers. "All the more reason to hold on to this one," she said softly. Scarlett sat back and took a sip of her drink as Taylor looked on, struck.

"I thought I was supposed to be the wise one in this duo."

"How about we rotate?"

Taylor laughed. "Deal." A pause. "Hey, Scarlett. You want a job?"

Scarlett eyed her, and it looked like she was trying to tamp down a burst of excitement, her eyes wide and her mouth open. "What are you trying to say?"

"WCN greenlit my pilot. We're a go for spring, and we need to get to work ASAP." She lifted her drink, and an elated Scarlett mimicked her. "To the next chapter." They touched glasses, and Scarlett couldn't stop smiling.

"This is amazing. Do you understand how amazing? I need to call my grandmother. She's going to freak." And then an idea seemed to percolate. "Hey, know anyone else we could add to the team? Someone who might be newly on the job market?"

Taylor sighed. "I'm thinking over my options."

As she lay in bed that night listening to Raisin's soft breaths from his bed on the floor, Taylor stared up at the winter night's stars while "Have Yourself a Merry Little Christmas" played quietly on her radio. Sleep wouldn't come easily. She couldn't shake the feeling that she stood at a very important crossroads. She could take a dangerous leap that would forever affect her life for the good or awful, or play it safe and be content with who she was and where she was headed. There was something to be said for an uncomplicated life in which she relished the little joys that came her way and avoided the messy interactions that came with matters of the heart. Matters of *love*. She had a new creative project to lose herself in, a fresh start. Why open herself up to the potential for more devastation when she was just beginning to rebuild her life?

It seemed so easy when she thought about it that way, so staggeringly clear.

But when she woke the next morning alone, her first thoughts were, as always, of Isabel. She ran her hand across the pillow next to hers and acknowledged the way her heavy wistful heart clenched uncomfortably. She sat up and ran a hand through her tousled hair. If she could manage to make it a few more weeks, surely all of this would get easier. Wasn't that what they said? Time heals all wounds?

That's all she needed. More time.

Dressed and ready for her work session with Scarlett, Taylor leashed up Raisin and headed to her car. She stopped short, however, when sitting on her front step was a hot cup of coffee from none other than the Cat's Pajamas. She glanced up and down her street but saw no sign of anyone. Didn't matter. She knew exactly who had left it there. She knelt with the beginnings of a smile on her face to see *I'm sorry* scrawled in black marker across the side of the cardboard cup. The words slammed her in the throat as she imagined Isabel's earnest eyes looking back at her.

She looked down at Raisin and sighed. "C'mon, buddy. We can't get distracted right now. We have work to do."

Chapter Twenty-three

Are we ready to order?" Isabel asked what had to be her fiftieth table of the night.

"We are. We've just been waiting on you," the older gentleman said, and pointed at his menu. "I'll take the filet, medium rare, with the whipped potatoes, but make sure there's not too much salt on those. A side of asparagus, but only if it's crispy and not drenched in butter." He handed her the menu.

"Got it," she said with a smile, all the while dying inside. "And for you?" she asked his twentysomething dinner companion. The four-star restaurant seemed to attract the older man, younger woman pairing like none other she'd ever seen.

"I'll take the pasta special. Can you tell me what's in the sauce?"

Isabel took a moment. "As in, a list of ingredients?"

"Exactly," the gentleman said for his date.

She took a deep breath. "Salt, pepper, garlic, butter, cheese, parsley, and a little white wine."

"Perfect!" her young customer crowed. "I'll take that and a Caesar salad, dressing on the side."

She plastered her smile back in place. "I'll have it all out for you shortly." Isabel walked to the computer to input her order, wondering if her legs could make it for the additional hour she had left on her shift. Everything hurt, and that didn't even include her soul. What she wouldn't give for a hot bath and a cocktail.

"Hey, Isabel," the bartender said.

"What's up, Jay?"

"Someone left a tip for you over here. Wanna come pick it up?"

"Yeah, just a sec," she said, finishing the order. She looped around the bar, as it was also on the way to her next table, just sat, only to have him slide a to-go cup of Pajama coffee her way.

"Where did this come from?" she asked, glancing around for Autumn.

"A woman dropped it off for you."

"Awesome red hair?" she asked, using her hands to insinuate curls.

"More like pretty blond hair," he said and went back to mixing his martini.

Isabel wrapped her hands around the cup, allowing the warmth to seep through. That's when she saw it, on the side of the cardboard. *I miss you.* She lost her next breath and quickly turned around. Her eyes scanned the restaurant.

"Nah, she headed out after leaving that," Jay said. Well, how in the hell was she supposed to work now? Her mind went white, because the little *maybe* she'd carried around in her back pocket all week was now a medium-sized maybe, and that was everything. She used the extra shot in the arm to move her around that freakin' dining room like a rock star. Hell, she practically floated, taking orders, laughing at bad jokes, and making purposeful trips to the bar to steal a sip of the coffee that had brightened her night. Her holiday season. Her life.

She emerged from her shift exhausted but hopeful, spilling out onto the parking lot with an extra spring in her step, but came to an abrupt halt at the sight of Taylor, sitting on the trunk of her Honda Civic. Holy hell. She slowed her walk once she saw her, tilting her head curiously but beaming because she couldn't help herself. Taylor wore jeans and one of her white dress shirts capped off with a blue leather jacket. She didn't say anything when Isabel arrived in front of her, but the look in her eyes told Isabel everything she needed to know.

"We miss each other?" Isabel asked quietly.

Taylor nodded, and from on top of that car, laced a hand behind Isabel's head and pulled her in slowly for a toe-curling kiss to end all kisses. She heard herself gasp at the contact before she sank into it, like water to the thirsty. Her soul soared. Her heart did flip-flops in wonderful celebration. Her hands slid up Taylor's jeans because she just had to reach out and touch her, to understand she was real.

"Is this okay?" Taylor whispered, cupping Isabel's face. "I didn't want to just show up at your job, but I had to—"

Isabel placed a finger in front of Taylor's lips. "Best tip I've ever had."

Taylor searched her eyes. "You left the show. Gave up your big chance. Why?"

"Wasn't worth what I lost," Isabel said matter-of-factly. "Nothing is."

Taylor traced circles with her thumb on the top of Isabel's hand. "Do you honestly mean that?" She knew the look she saw on Taylor's face, because it mirrored the vulnerability Isabel had carried with her for the past few months. Taylor had been hurt, and she wouldn't let that happen again.

"I've never meant anything more. I'm sorry. I let my own issues get in the way. The anxiety, the self-doubt, those are all my problems, and they're what got us here. But I want you to know that I'm dealing with them, or trying to. Taking walks has helped me relax, and I'm going to start a yoga class on Tuesday nights." She sighed. "I also made an appointment to see someone. Maybe I can pick up some relaxation techniques, you know? For when that doubt hits. Anyway, I feel really good about all of it."

"Good for you. I think that sounds like a fabulous idea, and maybe I can come to yoga sometime."

"Okay," Isabel said, loving that idea.

"Just know that I'm here and willing to help in whatever way you need me."

"Let's hope for less closet time in our future." Isabel smiled.

"Besides the first half of my life when I lived in there, I happen to like the closet."

A pause as they looked at one another, getting used to the fact that they got to do that again. "Taylor, I need you to know that there is literally nothing I would choose over you."

"I do know now." Taylor nodded and kissed her again, this time more aggressively, with authority, and Isabel thought her clothes might just magically fall off her body right there in that public parking lot. Thank God the restaurant was closed, but then again, who really cared?

"I do come with other issues, though," she said coming up for air. "I swear too much."

"You do." Another kiss.

"My cat's a pain."

Taylor mulled this over. "He's spirited."

More kissing. "I'm just a regular person."

"I don't see anyone regular in front of me. Not even close."

Isabel beamed. "What's awesome? I'm starting to believe you."

A pause. "So, we're trying this thing again?"

Isabel nodded. "Say yes. I can't imagine my life if we don't."

"In that case, we have to." A final heat-inducing lip-lock made the parking lot feel way too constricting. "Take me home?" Taylor whispered in her ear.

Isabel pulled the keys from her back pocket. "Way ahead of you."

Everything slowed down when they made it back to Taylor's house. They kissed their way into her living room. Slowly. Her hands moved generously over Taylor's curves. Slowly. The unhurried attention created the most epic slow-burn situation Isabel had ever experienced. Every part of her had missed Taylor and wanted her desperately. But she planned to relish every moment, cherish every bit of her.

She gently bit Taylor's lip, gave it a tug, and let it go, all the while worshiping Taylor's thighs with her hands.

"More," Taylor breathed, arching her back as she leaned against the side of the couch. The living room lights were off, but Isabel could see Taylor by the light of the entryway as it drifted in. It was enough illumination to take in the beauty of her body as she slowly undressed her, piece by piece. She hungrily drank in the sight, the image of Taylor standing naked there in front of her. Not a memory. Not a mirage. But the real thing.

"Iz?" Taylor said, stepping into her and placing her arms around her neck.

"Yeah?"

"I wouldn't have come there tonight, come back to you, if I weren't in love."

"What? With who?" Isabel asked, thrown. They'd never discussed love. It had been a word they'd only danced around, but she knew. Hadn't she known all along?

She stroked Isabel's cheek softly. "I love you, Isabel."

The jolt of happiness was instantaneous and awesome, and with those words she knew without a doubt that she could give herself over to Taylor fully. She could trust Taylor with her heart for now and for always. In fact, she'd never wanted anything more.

"What do you need for this to work?" Taylor asked, her eyes searching Isabel's.

"Only you," she said quietly. "You're my only requirement, because I'm so in love with you that I can't concentrate on anything else." Her heart was hammering so loudly, she could barely hear herself speak.

"So now that you're mine and I'm yours, can I be honest with you?"

Isabel nodded.

"You're wearing too many damn clothes."

Isabel smiled and felt about ten feet tall. Taylor did that to her, and she would never get used to it.

Taylor led Isabel silently to her room, and just as Isabel had done to her, she undressed Isabel piece by piece, stopping along the way to touch her, kiss her, and murmur wonderful words against her skin. Finally, she lowered Isabel onto the bed. Taylor went still at the sight of her, and an erotic thrill moved through Isabel as she bathed in the richness of Taylor's stare.

When they came together that night, it shook her. The wealth of feeling that brimmed with each touch, each whisper, catapulted her to somewhere new she didn't recognize, where she didn't underestimate what they meant to each other but embraced everything that they were and what they would become.

Taylor parted her legs and went to work until Isabel's body shuddered and she cried out, and until there was no more thinking, only the feel of Taylor in her arms.

For now. For always.

"I love you," Isabel sighed, submerging herself in happiness. "I need an app to keep track of all the ways."

Taylor beamed. "I can think of a better use of your time."

"Like what?"

Taylor pulled Isabel on top of her. "Have you ever considered writing for television? I have a job on my kick-ass new show that you might be perfect for. I'll need to see your résumé, of course."

Isabel grinned and slid a thigh between Taylor's. "I can supply one. How do you feel about coffee spills? More specifically, all over your desk."

"Oh, they're a must."

"I think this might work," Isabel said and kissed the woman that she loved.

EPILOGUE

Six Months Later

"I love Saturdays," Isabel said, when she woke up in Taylor's fluffy bed. "Especially the ones where we don't have to work."

Taylor turned from where she stood at the window wearing the cutest little pink nightgown that Isabel distinctly remembered taking off her the night before. Pesky little thing. "Hey, baby. I didn't know you were up," Taylor said, breaking into a smile and returning to the bed. She sat on the edge and ran a hand through Isabel's hair. "You were so peaceful. I thought I'd let you sleep a bit, rest up for today."

"Did we buy sunscreen?"

"We did, and I will make sure that it's applied amply to your gorgeous skin." She ran her hands down Isabel's bare shoulders, inspiring a shiver.

Isabel pulled Taylor back into bed. "Speaking of ample..." Her hands moved immediately under the nightgown to Taylor's breasts, causing Taylor to make the most wonderfully sexy sounds.

"Do we have time? I'm not sure we do," Taylor said, glancing at the clock. "We honestly don't."

"I'll make time," Isabel said, rolling over and taking Taylor with her. "Buy some on Craigslist." She nibbled on Taylor's ear. "Whip some up on the stove. Conjure it with my book of spells."

"You have spells? You're so resourceful," Taylor breathed. "And right about the weekends. Do you realize I count the days?"

They'd been back together now for almost six months. In an effort to do this thing right, Isabel hadn't moved in with Taylor, knowing she'd need time. They'd taken things slow, and that had paid off in spades in terms of her anxiety. She was now a part of the most healthy, exciting, and passionate relationship she'd ever witnessed. They were more in love than ever and grew closer each day. In fact, Isabel couldn't imagine her life without Taylor. She refused to.

"You'd get sick of me if we worked together all day and came home together at night."

"Never," Taylor said, tossing the nightgown over her head. "We have six minutes."

"Then I should get to work."

"We both will." Taylor grinned and kissed her as Isabel drifted into the blissful oblivion.

Three hours later, they arrived at Huntington Beach and found themselves among wall-to-wall people, all decked out in bathing suits and sunglasses for a day of surfing, food, and fun. It was the last day of the US Open of Surfing, and they were there to cheer for Gia in her final heats. The day couldn't have been nicer. Blue skies, white fluffy clouds, and an even seventy-nine degrees to usher out June. Holding hands, they located Hadley and Autumn in the seats Gia had reserved for them.

"Well, well, well," Autumn said, turning to Hadley. "If it isn't the writers of that hit new show!"

"Do you mean *The Sub-division*? The one about that kick-ass CIA agent turned regular woman? Why, I love that show!" Hadley turned to the man next to her. "Have you seen it, sir? You should really tune in, Wednesdays at nine."

He nodded politely.

Taylor leaned across and hugged Hadley, then Autumn. "You guys are the best street team ever. Did we miss it?"

Autumn grinned. "Nope. Her heat's next."

Isabel turned to Taylor and dropped her tone. "Told you we had time."

Taylor squeezed her hand, popped on giant sunglasses, and chuckled. "And what a time it was."

Isabel stole a kiss. She had to.

The heat began a few minutes later, and they watched as their friend went to battle against the other surfers. While Isabel didn't totally follow the scoring system, she could tell from the crowd's reactions that Gia was in top form. "Whoa. She's literally riding a wall of water. They're going nuts for her."

"You don't understand," Hadley said, excitedly. "She's pulling in scores she hasn't seen in over two years. She's rebounding. Say goodbye to number eight."

"She'll be seventh in the world?" Taylor asked.

"If she wins this, higher," Autumn said, hooking her thumb at the sky.

The announcer's voice came over the microphone. "And Gia Malone forces a late heat lead change, ousting Elle Britton from the top spot in a stunning switcheroo."

They joined the roaring crowd, screaming for Gia. Autumn shook her head. "This is crazy. She's going to be stoked. We need to celebrate with her tonight. You guys in?"

"Of course we're in!" Isabel said, over the crowd. The adrenaline hit she received from watching her friend do magnificent things was amazing. They stuck around until the end, when Gia was announced as the Open's winner in an upset that had everyone talking.

"I'm so glad we got to be here for this," Taylor murmured to Isabel. "We should come to more of these."

"The more events where I get to see you in a swimsuit, the better."

They celebrated that night with Gia and the other surfers at an outdoor luau on a private section of the beach. Isabel and Taylor raised excited eyebrows at each other as they presented their VIP tickets to the party and were each awarded a lei upon entry.

"You don't know what it means to me that you guys were there," Gia said, approaching their group with an ear-to-ear grin. She'd taken her hair down and traded her bathing suit for white pants and a crop top. She radiated.

Isabel grabbed her. "Do you know how crazy that was? How exciting? How proud of you we are?"

Gia laughed. "I agree about the crazy and exciting, and I'll take the proud. I needed this."

A striking woman with a headset appeared and tapped Gia on the shoulder. "Hey, Gia, can we get a shot of you by the water? The sun is setting and it could be a nice way to cap off the day of the tournament."

"Sure thing, Jordan." She turned back to her friends. "Be right back. Part of a documentary they're shooting on the surf tour. I'm one of the surfers they're featuring."

"Go," Hadley said. "Be important. We'll be right here drinking piña coladas and swaying to the music."

And that's exactly what they did. Gia returned a short time later and they spent the evening dancing on the beach, and laughing, and talking about their plans for next week.

"Who's the hot producer?" Autumn asked, as she swirled her hips to Jimmy Buffett.

"Totally taken," Gia said, twirling Autumn easily. "I asked. Married."

"Lame. My life is boring." Autumn pouted. "I need some action, some excitement, someone like that!"

Isabel laughed. "Give it time. Eventually, the right one will surprise you." She looked deeply into Taylor's eyes as they danced, and she found herself undone once again.

Taylor nodded, never taking her eyes from Isabel's. "The love of your life could arrive at any damn moment."

Hadley sighed. "I love it when you two get all dreamy-eyed. Don't you guys love it?" Hadley asked Autumn and Gia.

"Yep," Autumn said. "And since I'm jealous and alone, the next round is on me."

"They think we're cute," Taylor said quietly with a gleam in her eye.

"Objectively, we are. Have you seen us?"

She relaxed into a radiant smile. "A stunning couple, I'm told."

Isabel stared at her, lost in the onslaught of emotion that hit. "I love you," she whispered in Taylor's ear. "I really, really love you."

"Good," she said, leaning in close to Isabel. "Because you're all mine, and I'm all yours, and that is never going to change." It was a common phrase from Taylor, and Isabel couldn't hear it enough.

"You know what?" Isabel said, inclining her head to the side. "You have a way with words."

Taylor laughed. "I've never heard that before. Not once."

As Isabel danced with Taylor in her arms, her heart swelled and she realized just how ridiculously lucky she was. With amazing new friends, a job she was thrilled with, and a woman she loved, she'd never felt more fulfilled. While there might be more shaking in the closet, the attacks were now few and far between. She kept her monthly appointments with Jim, a therapist who helped her learn better ways to cope. When those dark times came, however, she now had her friends to see her through. More importantly, she had Taylor. Though she still had work to do on herself, Isabel wasn't alone, and she never would be again.

"Here you go, buddy," Autumn said, presenting her with a fancy-looking fruity drink and then handing one to Taylor.

"Would you look at that?" Isabel said. "Now, that's a pretty drink."

Autumn nodded. "Not as pretty as that married producer over there, but it's all I've got."

"Hey-o!" Gia said, dancing with her drink over her head.

But the best part of all of this? Isabel knew inherently that there were a million more moments like this one to come—with the people she loved around her. There would be more dancing on the beach, more Pajamas coffee, and more stolen mornings with the love of her life. She smiled at Taylor, who danced, carefree and beautiful. God, with eyes like those looking back at her every day, how could she go wrong?

Isabel Chase was right where she was supposed to be.

About the Author

Melissa Brayden (www.melissabrayden.com) is a multi-award-winning romance author embracing the full-time writer's life in San Antonio, Texas, and enjoying every minute of it.

Melissa is married and working really hard at remembering to do the dishes. For personal enjoyment, she spends time with her Jack Russell terriers and checks out the NYC theater scene as often as possible. She considers herself a reluctant patron of spin class, but would much rather be sipping merlot and staring off into space. Coffee, wine, and donuts make her world go round.

Books Available From Bold Strokes Books

A Date to Die by Anne Laughlin. Someone is killing people close to Detective Kay Adler, who must look to her own troubled past for a suspect. There she finds more than one person seeking revenge against her. (978-163555-023-8)

Captured Soul by Laydin Michaels. Can Kadence Munroe save the woman she loves from a twisted killer, or will she lose her to a collector of souls? (978-162639-915-0)

Dawn's New Day by TJ Thomas. Can Dawn Oliver and Cam Cooper, two women who have loved and lost, open their hearts to love again? (978-163555-072-6)

Definite Possibility by Maggie Cummings. Sam Miller is just out for good times, but Lucy Weston makes her realize happily ever after is a definite possibility. (978-162639-909-9)

Eyes Like Those by Melissa Brayden. Isabel Chase and Taylor Andrews struggle between love and ambition from the writers' room on one of Hollywood's hottest TV shows. (978-163555-012-2)

Heart's Orders by Jaycie Morrison. Helen Tucker and Tee Owens escape hardscrabble lives to careers in the Women's Army Corps, but more than their hearts are at risk as friendship blossoms into love. (978-163555-073-3)

Hiding Out by Kay Bigelow. Treat Dandridge is unaware that her life is in danger from the murderer who is hunting the woman she's falling in love with, Mickey Heiden. (978-162639-983-9)

Omnipotence Enough by Sophia Kell Hagin. Can the tiny tool that abducted war veteran Jamie Gwynmorgan accidentally acquires help her escape an unknown enemy to reclaim her stolen life and the woman she deeply loves? (978-163555-037-5)

Summer's Cove by Aurora Rey. Emerson Lange moved to Provincetown to live in the moment, but when she meets Darcy Belo and her son Liam, her quest for summer romance becomes a family affair. (978-162639-971-6)

The Road to Wings by Julie Tizard. Lieutenant Casey Tompkins, Air Force student pilot, has to fly with the toughest instructor, Captain Kathryn "Hard Ass" Hardesty, fly a supersonic jet, and deal with a growing forbidden attraction. (978-162639-988-4)

Beauty and the Boss by Ali Vali. Ellis Renois is at the top of the fashion world, but she never expects her summer assistant Charlotte Hamner to tear her heart and her business apart like sharp scissors through cheap material. (978-162639-919-8)

Fury's Choice by Brey Willows. When gods walk amongst humans, can two women find a balance between love and faith? (978-162639-869-6)

Lessons in Desire by MJ Williamz. Can a summer love stand a four-month hiatus and still burn hot? (978-163555-019-1)

Lightning Chasers by Cass Sellars. For Sydney and Parker, being a couple was never what they had planned. Now they have to fight corruption, murder, and enemies hiding in plain sight just to hold on to each other. Lightning Series, Book Two. (978-162639-965-5)

Summer Fling by Jean Copeland. Still jaded from a breakup years earlier, Kate struggles to trust falling in love again when a summer fling with sexy young singer Jordan rocks her off her feet. (978-162639-981-5)

Take Me There by Julie Cannon. Adrienne and Sloan know it would be career suicide to mix business with pleasure, however tempting it is. But what's the harm? They're both consenting adults. Who would know? (978-162639-917-4)

Unchained Memories by Dena Blake. Can a woman give herself completely when she's left a piece of herself behind? (978-162639-993-8)

Walking Through Shadows by Sheri Lewis Wohl. All Molly wanted to do was go backpacking…in her own century. (978-162639-968-6)

Freedom to Love by Ronica Black. What happens when the woman who spent her life worrying about caring for her family finally finds the freedom to love without borders? (978-1-63555-001-6)

A Lamentation of Swans by Valerie Bronwen. Ariel Montgomery returns to Sea Oats to try to save her broken marriage but soon finds herself also fighting to save her own life and catch a murderer. (978-1-62639-828-3)

House of Fate by Barbara Ann Wright. Two women must throw off the lives they've known as a guardian and an assassin and save two rival houses before their secrets tear the galaxy apart. (978-1-62639-780-4)

Planning for Love by Erin Dutton. Could true love be the one thing that wedding coordinator Faith McKenna didn't plan for? (978-1-62639-954-9)

Sidebar by Carsen Taite. Judge Camille Avery and her clerk, attorney West Fallon, agree on little except their mutual attraction, but can their relationship and their careers survive a headline-grabbing case? (978-1-62639-752-1)

Sweet Boy and Wild One by T. L. Hayes. When Rachel Cole meets soulful singer Bobby Layton at an open mic, she is immediately in thrall. What she soon discovers will rock her world in ways she never imagined. (978-1-62639-963-1)

To Be Determined by Mardi Alexander and Laurie Eichler. Charlie Dickerson escapes her life in the US to rescue Australian wildlife with Pip Atkins, but can they save each other? (978-1-62639-946-4)

True Colors by Yolanda Wallace. Blogger Robby Rawlins plans to use First Daughter Taylor Crenshaw to get ahead, but she never planned on falling in love with her in the process. (978-1-62639-927-3)

Heart Stop by Radclyffe. Two women, one with a damaged body, the other a damaged spirit, challenge each other to dare to live again. (978-1-62639-899-3)

Undercover Affairs by Julie Blair. Searching for stolen documents crucial to U.S. security, CIA agent Rett Spenser confronts lies, deceit, and unexpected romance as she investigates art gallery owner Shannon Kent. (978-1-62639-905-1)

Taking Sides by Kathleen Knowles. When passion and politics collide, can love survive? (978-1-62639-876-4)

Unexpected by Jenny Frame. When Dale McGuire falls for Rebecca Harper, the mother of the son she never knew she had, will Rebecca's troubled past stop them from making the family they both truly crave? (978-1-62639-942-6)

Canvas for Love by Charlotte Greene. When ghosts from Amelia's past threaten to undermine their relationship, Chloé must navigate the greatest romance of her life without losing sight of who she is. (978-1-62639-944-0)

Repercussions by Jessica L. Webb. Someone planted information in Edie Black's brain and now they want it back, but with the protection of shy former soldier Skye Kenny, Edie has a chance at life and love. (978-1-62639-925-9)

Spark by Catherine Friend. Jamie's life is turned upside down when her consciousness travels back to 1560 and lands in the body of one of Queen Elizabeth I's ladies-in-waiting…or has she totally lost her grip on reality? (978-1-62639-930-3)

Thorns of the Past by Gun Brooke. Former cop Darcy Flynn's heart broke when her career on the force ended in disgrace, but perhaps saving Sabrina Hawk's life will mend it in more ways than one. (978-1-62639-857-3)

You Make Me Tremble by Karis Walsh. Seismologist Casey Radnor comes to the San Juan Islands to study an earthquake but finds her heart shaken by passion when she meets animal rescuer Iris Mallery. (978-1-62639-901-3)

Girls Next Door, edited by Sandy Lowe and Stacia Seaman. Best-selling romance authors tell it from the heart—sexy, romantic stories of falling for the girls next door. (978-1-62639-916-7)

Complications by MJ Williamz. Two women battle for the heart of one. (978-1-62639-769-9)

Crossing the Wide Forever by Missouri Vaun. As Cody Walsh and Lillie Ellis face the perils of the untamed West, they discover that love's uncharted frontier isn't for the weak in spirit or the faint of heart. (978-1-62639-851-1)

boldstrokesbooks.com

Bold Strokes Books

Quality and Diversity in LGBTQ Literature

victory
EDITIONS

Drama

MATINEE BOOKS

E-BOOKS

SCI-FI

SOLILOQUY

MYSTERY

HE
erotica

BOLD
STROKES
BOOKS

EROTICA

YOUNG
ADULT

LIBERTY
EDITION

Romance

W·E·B·S·T·O·R·E

PRINT AND EBOOKS

Printed in the USA
CPSIA information can be obtained
at www.ICGtesting.com
JSHW082157140824
68134JS00014B/277

9 781635 550122